BODY OF LIES

When he looked at her again, he gestured toward her attire. "I take it you haven't packed anything yet."

"No."

"You know you can't stay here, Alex."

She did. She didn't want to stay, either. She'd found sleep only because she was exhausted, but since waking, every creak and groan of the old house had put her on edge.

More than she feared anything this killer might do, she didn't want to feel so isolated any longer. At least in her home, things were familiar. Even if the memories haunted her, they were hers.

Obviously he took her silence as protest. "This man is dangerous, Alex. If he's set his sights on you, there's no telling to what lengths he'll go in order to get to you."

She heard the concern in his voice and wondered if it was the cop in him that engendered it or the man who had once meant a great deal to her. "I know," she said. "But don't waste your time trying to scare me. I'm already scared."

"Then maybe I can persuade you to get ready to leave. It's getting late."

True, it was. She needed to stop stalling. "Do you suppose I can just show up at the Sheraton or should I call for a reservation?"

He shook his head as if he couldn't believe she'd made that comment. "Alex, you're staying with me."

BODY OF LIES

Deirdre Savoy

Kensington Publishing Corp.

http://www.kensingtonbooks.com

Acknowledgments

Thanks to fellow author Sandra Kitt, for helping me to acclimate myself to her part of town.

Thanks to my editor Karen Thomas for having faith in this series and the dynamite cover. I couldn't have asked for better.

Thanks to my agent Manie Barron for his humor and insight, and his willingness to fight the good fight.

Most of all, thanks to my family, most of all my husband and children, who put up with my moods, my late nights, and other inconveinences in sevice of my writing. I love you guys.

Prologue

"What's a nice girl like you doing in a place like this?"

It was a corny remark designed to be humorous, as no one in their right mind in this day and age would say such a thing in sincerity. Still, he got the reaction he'd wanted. Even though he was in the crappy station wagon he'd boosted from in front of some apartment building on 233rd and she was a safe distance away on the sidewalk, she darted a glance at him, more annoyance than wariness in her gaze.

He smiled to himself in a way that didn't show on his face. She wasn't his usual type, but she would do for tonight. She was too old, for one thing, and too skinny. He could tell despite the short black coat she wore. He liked them thick, with big legs, big asses, big tits, sloppy. More like *her*. Her mouth held promise, though—wide, loose, painted a dark shade of crimson, like blood. He would enjoy that mouth.

He leaned farther toward the passenger door, while keeping the car at a crawl. This time he smiled for real. She had no idea of the favor he planned to do for her. He was about to make her famous. "You may not have noticed, but this isn't the best neighborhood at night."

She cast him a look that would have translated to "no

shit" if she'd spoken. This stretch of the service road of the New England Thruway was deserted from Connor Street on down to the new rows of two- and three-family houses on Baychester Avenue. Four blocks of near desolation, save for overflow from the highway, which could be heavy, but not at this hour, the couple of motels, the patrons of which were more interested in shielding their anonymity than anything going out on the street, and a couple of blocks of unfinished houses, empty and dark, their facades looking like enormous gaping faces. Some places, like the bit of road she stepped onto now, had no sidewalk to speak of.

"I'll be fine," she said finally.

He heard it in her voice, the fear that maybe she'd stumbled into the wrong place at the wrong time. He'd seen her get off the highway at Connor Street. He was at the BP station filling up the piece-of-shit station wagon when her car hobbled in with a flat right front tire.

He'd listened to her asking the attendant if she could leave it there until she came back with help in a few minutes. At this time of night all the nearby shops extolling Flat Fixed had pulled in their signs for the night.

She hadn't seen him, or at least he hadn't registered on her radar. He'd given her a five-minute head start, then followed.

Now he smiled in a self-deprecating way and held the expression until he was sure she'd noticed. "I'm not trying to be a nuisance. In truth, I'm lost. There weren't so many houses or new houses around the last time I was here."

"What street are you looking for?"

"Givan."

She gestured with her hand. "It's that way. Keep going and you'll hit it."

"Thanks. You sure I can't drop you anywhere?"

As if on cue, an Explorer rolled up on them, seemingly

out of nowhere, like a huge dark specter, its stereo blazing, its headlamps casting garish light as it passed. The yahoo on the passenger side threw a beer bottle out the window. The projectile hit the ground with a dull crack, spewing liquid and glass onto the already filthy street.

For one sweet moment he watched the car pass. Sometimes the universe was just with you. He knew he had her now. "Sure you don't need that ride?" he asked, but it was a tease. He knew what she'd do. She'd get in thinking she was safer with him than she was on her own.

"Maybe I will take you up on your offer." In one move she stepped toward the car, pulled the door open, and slid inside.

He pressed the button on the driver's-side door panel to depress all the locks. "Relax," he said, pulling away from the curb. "You're safe now. Where do you want to go?"

"Just two blocks down, near the corner. Givan is the one after."

He nodded, as if it made any difference to him. He concentrated on accelerating the car and the choice he had to make.

"Hey, slow down," she said. "It's right there."

He glanced at her sideways, grinning a little, just enough to let her know she'd miscalculated.

"Let me out," she demanded, pulling futilely on the door handle. "Let me go. If you hurt me my father will kill you."

Fear or pain. Pain or fear. The choice was always the same. He was close enough to the highway now to make the choice necessary. Traffic was light enough to ensure him an easy entrance if he timed it right.

Just as the girl started to launch herself at him, he reached his left hand between his legs where he kept both a .38 and a stun gun concealed beneath his T-shirt.

He settled for the .38 and aimed it at her chest. "Keep still and I won't shoot you."

The girl froze. She was crying now, her threats forgotten.

He grinned again. He'd chosen fear. The pain would wait for later.

One

Alexandra Waters pulled her Volkswagen Passat into her usual parking spot in the small lot behind the building on East Tremont Avenue housing Astor Health and cut the engine. She got out of the car and stared up at the two-story, redbrick structure. The first floor boasted a dentist's office, a chiropractor, and some sort of business that did both tax returns in season and realty all year round. The second floor was all hers, or hers and her partners'.

She was the lone psychologist in this practice designed to meet the health needs of the Eastchester section of the Bronx. Roberta, the social worker, concentrated on domestic issues of parenting, marriage, and abuse. Nancy, the nurse practitioner, was primarily a midwife and out on maternity leave herself. Alex took whoever walked in the door. All three were affiliated with nearby Einstein Hospital.

The partnership had been Roberta's idea. All of them had been tired of what they were doing, though Alex herself had been the only one whose career was sliding into the tail end of nonexistent.

Even Alice had tired of her well-paid position as the assistant to a prominent attorney, knowing her effort was

wasted on keeping society's undesirables on the street. It
hadn't taken much to convince any of them to strike out
on their own.

The office was laid out with a large anteroom that included Alice's reception area. Farther down the hall
were the practitioners' offices, a conference room, and
several treatment rooms that varied in size and differed
in purpose—from examination rooms for Nancy to
single and group therapy rooms for her and Roberta. As
usual, Alex was the first one in.

She dropped her purse, jacket, and briefcase in her
office, then went to the small communal kitchen to start
coffee brewing. That accomplished she returned to the
front door to retrieve the daily newspapers. She hadn't
bothered with the TV news that morning. She'd have to
settle for getting her morning ration of gloom and
doom from the *Daily News.*

She pulled the confining rubber band off and slid it
on her wrist like a bracelet. She'd add it to her stash
later. Thanks to the local paperboy they'd never need to
buy another one. She shook out the paper as she walked
back toward the kitchen. AMAZON KILLER STRIKES AGAIN.
Below the unoriginal headline was a gritty photograph
that took her a moment to recognize as an extreme
close-up of a woman's battered face.

Alex's heartbeat picked up as she flipped the page to
reveal the story on page 3. Until then, she hadn't been
aware there was an Amazon Killer, but apparently, he'd
struck seven times since last summer. His appellation
came from the fact that the right breast of each of his victims had been excised, reminiscent of the Greek Amazons said to have originated the practice. Apparently the
killer had been on a two-month hiatus, but now he was
back again. She felt confident in speculating that the
killer was male. Not only had he brutally raped each of
his victims, but it fit the percentages. Serial killers were

predominantly male, predominantly white, and they predominantly preyed on the most vulnerable segments of
the population—kids, old people, or in this case young
prostitutes.

But hookers didn't usually make headlines.

She scanned the article until her gaze snagged on a
name: Ingrid Beltran. Daughter of Mount Vernon City
councilwoman Ilona Beltran. No wonder it had made
the front page. Prostitutes might not make the front
page but politicians' daughters did.

"I see you heard."

Alex gasped and turned to face Alice, who'd spoken.
Alex had been so engrossed in the newspaper she hadn't
heard anyone come in. "I read."

Alice shook her head. "What a shame. Her car broke
down coming off the Connor Street exit of the Thruway.
She figured she'd walk the rest of the way to her friend's
house. She was only seventeen years old."

Mmm. Alex dropped the paper to the table. Ingrid Beltran might have been young, but three of the killer's five
victims had been younger—girls whose desperation had
led them to sell their bodies to feed either themselves or
their drug habits. As Alex saw it, the whole situation was
a shame, not only the death of the one girl whose life
showed promise. But no one was asking her, were they?

A lifetime ago, it might have been different. She'd
been an up and comer in the forensic psychiatry department at Bellevue Hospital in Manhattan. A lifetime ago,
it wouldn't have been unusual to be called on to evalu-
ate a patient for competency or treatment of the convicted. But it had been a long time since anyone came
calling for her opinion. A large part of her preferred it
that way.

Alice sighed, a gesture that said she wouldn't waste any
more time dwelling on something she couldn't change.
Alex had learned that lesson long ago, the hard way.

Alex filled her cup, added milk and sugar. "Do we have any messages?" Although the office officially closed at eight o'clock, the answering machine picked up all night, listing emergency contacts for each of the women and urging all nonemergency callers to call back during business hours. The machine didn't block anyone from leaving messages; however, they had to be logged in and funneled to the right person by Alice each morning.

"Haven't checked yet, but the light was on."

"Let me know if I've got anything," Alex said, taking her coffee and her paper back to her office. She hoped not. She had a full day ahead, and for some reason sleep had proved elusive the previous night. It had been a long time since insomnia had dogged her, and she hoped this was not a signal of its return, especially without provocation.

She'd barely made it behind her desk when the intercom buzzed. Alex made a face at it, but pressed the necessary button. "Who is it?" she asked, before Alice had a chance to speak. "Please tell me Frieda Underwood hasn't started seeing her husband's ghost again."

"No ghosts, just cops, if that's any better. A Sergeant John McKay called you. He wants you to call him back but doesn't say about what."

And Alex hadn't a clue what he could be calling her about. "What's the number?" She wrote it down on the top slip of a pad of Post-it notes. "Thanks." She checked her watch: 7:47. If McKay worked the day shift he'd be on at eight o'clock. She waited fifteen minutes and dialed the number.

"McKay," he answered when he came to the phone.

"Sergeant McKay," Alex said. "I received a message this morning that you called. This is Alex Waters."

"Dr. Waters, thanks for returning my call. I'm working on a case I hope you'll be able to help me with."

Alex's first thought was that a mistake in identity had

occurred. "Are you sure you have the right Dr. Waters? I don't work in forensics anymore."

"I know that, Doctor."

There was a certain smugness in his voice that annoyed her. No doubt he'd had her checked out before calling. Five minutes on the Internet would have been all he needed to find out about the debacle that ended her former career. So if he knew all that, why was he calling? "What can I do for you, Sergeant?"

"I'm interested in your opinion of a case."

Alex sighed. Although most of her was glad to have left her former life behind, there was a small part of her flattered by the prospect of someone seeking out her expertise. A little bit of ego that resisted being crushed. "What sort of case?"

"Why don't I explain that to you when you get here? Suffice it to say I'll be disappointed if I have to look elsewhere for someone else."

Jeez. From superciliousness to sycophancy in one easy minute. Although she was tempted by the offer, his attempt at flattery fell flat. Moreover, she sensed deviousness in McKay's desire to keep her in the dark. "I'm afraid I'd have to know more than you're giving me to know if it's worth shuffling my day."

She let her words hang there. If he wanted her badly enough, he'd tell her. If not, she'd just lost five minutes of her life she'd never recover. Either way, she didn't give a damn.

"It involves Walter Thorpe."

Alex squeezed her eyes shut. That was the last name she expected to hear. The last name she ever wanted to hear again. Her misdiagnosis of him had been the catalyst for the destruction of her career. Thorpe had come to her at the outpatient clinic at Bellevue as a condition of his parole after being arrested on a misdemeanor sex offense. Three months later he'd been arrested again.

This time as the Gentleman Rapist that had been preying on Upper East Side women. Considering the furor
the city had been in to apprehend the man, no one, especially the police, had been amused to find she'd been
treating him. Part of any psychologist's job was to predict
a client's future behavior. Alex had never seen that
coming.

And now, Thorpe was back again. She'd heard he'd
been released from prison less than a year ago. Although
he had been accused of raping seven women, he'd only
been convicted on one count, the only one in which his
semen had been found in the victim's body.

Damn. If Walter was at it again, it looked liked six
years' reprieve was all she was going to get.

"Dr. Waters?"

"Yes." Alex squeezed the bridge of her nose with her
thumb and index finger. A migraine was building
behind her eyes. She could feel the blood vessels con-
tracting one by one, or at least she imagined she could.
If she didn't put an end to this she'd need to lie down in
half an hour.

"You know Thorpe was my patient." There was no
point in denying that, considering that the fact had been
plastered across the face of the *Daily News* in a slightly
more catchy headline than it sported that morning.
DOCTOR DUPED. Beneath it a picture of her, openmouthed and wide eyed, taken as a reporter out for a
scoop had tripped her. She hadn't fallen, at least not literally, anyway. Either way, there were plenty of photogra-
phers around to capture her at that unflattering
moment.

Alex squeezed her nose harder. "You know I can't tell
you anything."

"Your diagnosis is a matter of public record, Doctor. All
I'm asking you to do is come in and tell me if you think
Thorpe is capable of the crime we're looking at him for."

Was this man insane? If he knew the case he had to know her judgment wasn't the most reliable one they could go on. Her mind flashed to that morning's paper. They couldn't be trying to pin that on Walter. She might have been wrong about him once, but that she couldn't believe. "I'll think about it."

"Don't think too long. Can we say one o'clock, Forty-first Precinct?" He rattled off an address she didn't bother to take down. If she decided to go, she could always have Alice call and find out the details.

McKay rang off with one additional plea, "We really need you, Doctor."

And she needed this like she needed another migraine. Why now, when her life was finally smooth and boring like she wanted it? She hung up the phone, then searched in her bag for a couple of ibuprofen and a Claritin. She downed them with a swig of the tepid coffee in her cup. Luckily, her first client wouldn't be in until eight thirty. She'd have a few minutes to lie down in a dark room before the migraine's full effect claimed her.

She crossed to the doorway, flicked off the light and lay down, on the brown leather couch along one wall of the small room. A cold compress would have been nice, but having lots of options wasn't her strong suit now.

She knew she'd go to see McKay, if only to find out what was going on, what she was being dragged into. She didn't have to tell him anything and she wouldn't, regardless of what she'd gone on record about before.

She closed her eyes, inhaling deeply. If she read things right, here it went all over again: another high-profile case, another media frenzy, another opportunity to be made a fool of.

No wonder she hadn't gotten much sleep last night. The second worst nightmare of her life was, in all likelihood, about to begin all over again.

Two

Alex paused at the door to the interrogation room she'd been escorted to by a uniformed officer she'd picked up at the front desk. After seeing her first few patients, Alex had gone home, changed into a power outfit from the old days, and driven here to the Forty-first Precinct servicing a section of the northeast Bronx. Her wardrobe selection, a winter-white wool suit, was intended to send McKay a subliminal message—she was one of the good guys. It wasn't exactly a white hat, but it would have to do.

Alex's first sign that things were not as she suspected came when the young officer tapped on the door. "They're waiting for you."

"*They?*" she wanted to ask, but before the question made it to her lips he pushed the door open revealing exactly who "they" were.

The room was slightly bigger than the average interrogation room, but it was painted the same institutional green as every other wall she'd seen. The room was dominated by a long wood table surrounded by a host of chairs, most of which were occupied by grim-faced men in dark suits. Most of them stood as they were alerted to her presence, but only one stepped forward to greet her.

Nearly six feet tall with short sandy hair and a fair complexion explained by his Irish heritage, John McKay extended a hand to her. "I'm glad to see you changed your mind, Doctor. I'm Sergeant McKay."

She'd already figured as much. Annoyance tightened her jaw. He'd led her to believe that they'd be meeting alone. Why he hadn't mentioned that others would be present she couldn't begin to guess. "I didn't expect the whole cavalry to be here."

He shrugged, as if it made no difference. "Why don't we get started?"

He spent the next few minutes introducing her to the rest of the men, most of whom apparently worked out of the Forty-first, but there were others, representatives of special units like homicide and vice. For the most part, they greeted her with the enthusiasm with which one welcomes a cold germ into the room. To some degree she couldn't blame them. There wasn't a cop she knew who had much use for shrinks. But more than that, she surmised that if McKay knew her history these men did, too. She suspected there wasn't a man here who didn't blame her, at least in part, for those murders.

McKay led her to one of the seats before taking his place at the head of the table. McKay puffed out his narrow chest as if he were a bird in search of a mate. "As you all know, we've been assembled to find the so-called Amazon Killer that has been working one end of the New England Thruway since June twelfth of last year. His victims, except the last one, have all been young working girls unfortunate enough to venture into his hunting area. This was the killer's first victim, Shashana Bright, age fourteen."

McKay nodded to someone at the back of the room and the lights grew dim. A gruesome picture showed itself on the wall to Alex's left—a head and torso shot of a young woman with nut-brown skin and short, dyed blond hair. Her face had been brutalized and among other indignities her right breast was missing, not excised, but appeared to have been hacked off in several motions, leaving open, jagged flesh.

Alex swallowed reflexively, as McKay went on, cataloguing her injuries as if he were discussing cutting up a side of beef. The picture itself wasn't as disturbing as McKay's dispassionate droning. She didn't expect the police to weep over every victim; they'd never get their job done that way. But if investigators were supposed to serve as the victim's silenced voice, what sort of champion would McKay make?

As McKay went on, flashing photos of the victims, citing other dates and names and circumstances, she wondered if he had another agenda besides finding out who'd killed all those girls. She doubted it was the thrill of the hunt with McKay, since he showed so little emotion. Perhaps he hoped being lead on this case would advance his career. That seemed a more likely assumption. Or maybe he was just a coldhearted son of a bitch.

Alex tuned in again, hearing Ingrid Beltran's name. Her photo was almost identical to every other.

"Beltran was in the area, dressed for a night clubbing after she picked up her friends. We speculate the killer assumed she was a pro." The photo on the wall remained, though dulled by the fluorescence of the overhead lights. "So, what do you think, Doctor? Could your guy have done this?"

Alex blinked, trying to adjust her vision. She scanned the faces of the men staring back at her from around the conference table, before answering. She'd noticed that not one of them had made a sound during McKay's presentation. No expressions of surprise or disgust or even any speculations or questions. This was either the most incurious bunch of cops she'd ever seen or they'd all seen this before. She'd wondered why McKay had bothered to drag her over here in the midst of his briefing, and she thought she knew why now. More than likely, this session had been designed as a public embarrassment, a graphic reminder of what her perceived incompetence had led to. Too bad for him she didn't cower that easily. Not anymore.

Perversely, a small smile formed at the corner of her mouth, as she focused on McKay. "So far you haven't shown me anything to suggest Walter Thorpe had anything to do with these murders."

MacKay's expression hardened. "Perhaps you weren't paying attention, *Dr.* Waters," he said.

She recognized the man's attempt to dress her down, but she wasn't fazed by it. "Perhaps you weren't, Detective." She shifted in her seat to straighten her back and cast an icy glance around the room. Most of the men, the most experienced in their fields, looked away when her gaze settled on them. Only one man, an older grizzly cop she'd been told came from homicide, looked back at her with something close to admiration in his eyes.

She sighed and fastened a glare on McKay. "Walter Thorpe was convicted of committing a series of push-in rapes in the Wakefield section of the Bronx. He didn't murder anybody. His victims were all women in their early thirties, young mothers, not teenagers, and certainly not underage prostitutes. Thorpe didn't even use a weapon."

She paused, inhaling. This was preposterous. Thorpe was so mild-mannered none of his victims had required medical attention for as much as an abrasion. The one woman who'd fended off one of his attacks had done so by merely screaming. How did such a man, without any apparent provocation, morph into a killer so vicious as to mutilate his victims while they were still alive?

Then again, she hadn't seen Walter since before his

conviction. Prison changed a man, most often for the worse. Maybe she was only seeing what she wanted to see, but she suspected that these men around her hid something from her, making vision into this case more difficult.

Whatever bombshell they possessed, she wished they'd hurry up and drop it already instead of playing head games designed to make her look bad. "What do you know that I don't?"

McKay smiled, a feral expression that didn't surprise her, but unnerved her, as she supposed he intended. "Would you change your mind knowing that both the rear and side view mirrors were smashed on each of the vehicles in which the bodies were discovered?"

She lifted one eyebrow. That was all the reaction she'd allow them to see. Thorpe had smashed the bedroom mirrors in each of his victim's homes. When questioned why he committed the rapes, he answered that the mirror, not he, had committed the crimes. She supposed that beat out having little dogs or demons or pygmy statues telling you what to do. But it had been his semen found in one the women's bodies, so that was that.

A dislike of mirrors was hardly a unique phobia among criminals. A mirror could be another pair of eyes, watching, recording, judging. It could stand for truth or self-reflection. If the police had gone looking for a rapist with a similar m.o. they wouldn't have had to go far. When Thorpe had been apprehended, the *Daily News* ran his picture on the front page under a misquoted caption: THE MIRROR MADE HIM DO IT.

Still, she was certain McKay had something else. He didn't wait long to prove he wouldn't disappoint.

"Your boy's getting sloppy. We found his fingerprint on the seat-release button—a six-point match for his right middle finger."

Alex sat back, saying nothing. McKay's admission

confirmed a host of things, primarily that they had been looking at Thorpe before they ever found the fingerprint. But a six-point match wasn't enough to conclusively prove anything. They needed more, which she supposed was where she came in. Given the fact that she hadn't seen the man in more than six years, she doubted she could offer up much information.

"If that's true, what do you want from me?"

"According to the super in his building, Walter Thorpe disappeared a week before the first girl turned up. He called your office three times in the month before he went missing. Each of the calls was less than a minute in duration."

Alex shook her head. She'd received no such calls that she was aware of. All calls were logged in by the secretary in the office where she worked. She didn't miss McKay's implication either. Calls of such a short duration implied that Thorpe had been leaving messages for her to call him. She wasn't sure whether McKay believed she'd spoken to Thorpe or blown off his calls, but she suspected neither answer would suit him. In any event, he hadn't called her, so she really couldn't tell McKay anything.

She opened her mouth to speak at the same time the door opened. The room's focus shifted to the tall man who strode in. He wore a charcoal-gray suit molded to a muscular body. His sandy brown hair was cut close to his scalp. Alex drank in this information, but his eyes were what captivated her—a deep chocolate brown. Bedroom eyes, her mother would have called them. Though she hadn't seen him in thirteen years, she immediately knew who he was. One word formed in her mind and took up residence: *Zach*.

While the other men welcomed him into the room in a way that denoted both familiarity and respect, Alex sat back and tried to breathe. It hadn't occurred to her before that moment that the one area of expertise missing from this little confab was someone from sex crimes, or what they now euphemistically called special victims.

Despite what was wise, she'd followed his career. She knew he'd made a name for himself, solving some of the most notorious cases in the Bronx, the most infamous of which was Nigel Brooks, a man wanted in three states for molesting children. She should have known he'd turn up in this somehow, but she hadn't expected it. Nor had she expected the flood of emotions that swept through her on seeing him. Anger, betrayal, shattered trust collided with the remnants of a humiliating case of puppy love she'd mistaken for the real thing. She'd been a week shy of her eighteenth birthday the day he walked out of her life. Emotionally, time might as well have stood still.

Neither he nor the men in this room needed to know that, however. She was glad for the moment's diversion for the opportunity to school her features back into some sort of normal expression. Neither McKay nor any of the other men saw fit to offer him an introduction to her, which suited her fine. He slid into one of the chairs, his eyes on her, but they bore no sign that he knew who she was. She almost wanted to laugh. He didn't recognize her. In all her imaginings of what it might be like to see him again, she'd never figured on him not knowing her.

"Getting back to what we were discussing—"

Alex cut McKay off before he could ask the question. "To my knowledge Thorpe never called me. I can check the incoming logs if you like, but Alice, the receptionist, is very conscientious. If Thorpe had called, I would have known about it."

"You can't think of any reason why Thorpe might have tried to contact you?"

Alex ground her teeth together. Either this man was obtuse or he didn't believe her. More than likely it was the latter. More than likely McKay believed that Thorpe had reached out to her for help before he did something tragic. If that were the case, she might have been able to stop him or at least notify the authorities that he was dangerous. But that hadn't happened. At least she thought she had an explanation for some of McKay's animus. He blamed her for not acting and allowing a killer to roam the streets free.

She fastened a hard look on the detective. "You may not believe this, but if Thorpe had called, I would have spoken to him. I'm not in the habit of turning away clients, even those I'm no longer treating."

The homicide detective broke in again before McKay had a chance for a comeback. "Right now, we're looking to pick up Thorpe. As you know he disappeared from his apartment. We know he's got a sister living somewhere upstate. Is there any other information you can give us? Old haunts? Old habits?"

Any information she had was more than six years old, but she nodded. Besides, any information she had, the police must have collected back before he was convicted. Why did they need it again now? She scrutinized the old cop's face. He seemed to be offering her a way out and she was going to take it.

She stood and slung her purse over her shoulder. "I've got an address on the sister. I can look through his file for what else I might have. If you gentlemen will excuse me, I have clients to get back to. If you need anything else, you know where to reach me."

For one brief second her gaze settled on Zach. He'd stood when she did, a testament to his upbringing. For the last few minutes, she'd felt his gaze on her. His face now bore the expression of a man who knew he knew someone but couldn't figure out exactly who they were or how he knew them. Fine. Let him figure it out at his

leisure. She was out of there. She strode to the door and
let herself out.

Once outside with the door shut behind her, she
leaned her back against the wall and dragged in several
long breaths. She did not need this, not any of it. Not
now when she'd just gotten her life back on track. Not
when she'd finally gotten rid of all the old hurt, the old
guilt, the old self-doubt and self-recrimination. Finally,
she was herself again after being part of the walking
wounded for half her life. She didn't need to see him
again, nor did she deserve to have the men in the room
believing she'd had the opportunity to influence a killer
and passed it up. Even if she'd seen Thorpe, there was
no guarantee she'd have been able to stop him. No therapist held that much power.

She would check the logs as soon as she got back to
her office, but she doubted Alice would have neglected
to inform her Thorpe called. But the question that
nagged at her was, if Thorpe hadn't called her, who had?

Three

As the door closed, Zach settled back into his seat, dismissing from his mind the woman who'd just walked out. It had been a hell of a day already and it was only one o'clock in the afternoon. He'd been in court that morning, doing his damnedest to get some son of a bitch named Brady Anders locked up for trying to molest a kid, while the defense attorney tried with some success to prove that Zach had it in for his client.

To some extent it was true. Anders had been picked up three times for preying on children in the area where he lived. Each time he'd been arrested, his lawyer had found a way to get him off—either he found some technicality to negate the evidence, or the kids were too scared to testify. Zach hadn't intended for that to happen another time.

As Zach saw it, Anders had made two mistakes in his life. The first was being a pedophile. The second had been moving into the Bronx neighborhood where Zach lived.

One of Zach's neighbors told him one of the kids in Haffen Park had been approached by some Rastadude looking for a lost puppy. The kid had been smart enough

not to fall for the ruse. He'd run off to tell his mother, but
before she could find him, Anders had run off.

Given the boy's description, it wasn't hard to pick out
Anders as the culprit. Anders was over six feet tall, had a
jagged scar on his left cheek and sported waist-length
dirty and matted dreadlocks. Anyone looking at him
could tell his elevator stopped short of the top floor.
That's probably what earned him representation from
some Let's Feel Sorry for Sickos society in the first place,
rather than some overworked soul out of the public de-
fender's office.

Zack had alerted the local precinct, but considered
Anders his own personal mission, spending every free
moment tracking his whereabouts. He'd become a fix-
ture in the park, either playing basketball with the older
kids or as a spectator at the Little League games. When
he noticed Anders trailing one of the kids into the bathroom, Zach had followed, too. In that short space of
time, Anders had made his move.

Had he gone too far in surveilling Anders as his lawyer
asserted? Maybe, but no one made his client try to
fondle that kid. Okay, Anders had made three mistakes.
He hadn't noticed that in his haste to get to the bathroom the kid had forgotten to drop his bat.

Zach's phone had rung almost the instant he'd walked
out of the court building. His captain was on the other
line, informing him that he'd been "volunteered" for a
task force set up to hunt this killer no one knew about
until he picked on the wrong victim. Or at least the
public at large knew nothing. Even the papers hadn't covered the story much, figuring their readership wouldn't
be all that interested in a bunch of dead hookers.

"They want the best minds in the business on this
one," his captain had said, probably to mollify him more
than anything else. Zach knew how these task forces
went. Those who signed on early got to sort through all

the shit, running down every lead, dealing with the crazies and the press. Then when it looked like someone might actually get pulled in for the crime, everybody wanted to be in it for the takedown.

So now the pursuit was on full tilt. It wasn't the first time politics motivated police work, but it always irritated him when it did. Nine times out of ten, interference from higher-ups meant some case that deserved more attention got shunted for one that carried less urgency to anyone except the people involved.

Truthfully Zach looked forward to bringing in this particular scumbag, so it was all the same to him. Although the party line said different, nobody got too upset over someone having at it with a few hookers—not cops and definitely not citizens. They didn't belong where they were, anyway. They annoyed the neighbors by emptying their bowels and bladders on their property, brought unsavory types looking for action. They shot or snorted their poison of choice and left their garbage wherever it pleased them. No one cared how they left, as long as they were gone.

Damn, he sounded cynical, even in his own mind. When had his thoughts taken on such an edge? Maybe it was just the damn trial this morning, but he doubted it. In truth, he'd been at this a long time, maybe too long. Maybe he was starting to be one of those cops counting down their twenty, measuring their time not in years served but in how many left before they could retire.

McKay's words snapped Zach out of his reverie. "By a show of hands, how many think the Ice Princess is hiding something?"

Zach focused his attention on the other man. Zach wasn't exactly sure what he'd missed, but from what little he saw of the woman he couldn't agree with McKay's assessment of her character. She'd seemed cool

and professional with her stark-white business suit and
hair swept up in some kind of bun. If anything, he'd describe her as self-possessed.

That is, until she'd given him that parting look. For all
he knew, she was some woman he'd bedded and she was
pissed at him for forgetting who she was. It wouldn't be
the first time.

From the grumbles of dissent around the table, obviously the others didn't agree with him either. Zach
didn't know what kind of tear McKay was on, but apparently he was the only one on it. That wasn't too surprising. Although Zach hadn't had much contact with the
man, he disliked McKay, who always looked like he'd
had prunes for dinner. The look was exaggerated now as
McKay leaned back in his chair and crossed his arms, as
if to defend himself from the others.

"Lighten up, John-boy," Denton Smith, known as
Smitty, said. Smitty was rumored to be older than dirt
and to have worked homicide since God was in short
pants. "You got her down here on false pretenses,
treated her to chiller theater for no purpose I can
gather, then accused her of at the least aiding a criminal.
Were you really expecting her to tell you anything?'

"I wanted her to know exactly what that bastard's
done. You know how these shrinks are, more concerned
with their patients' rights than—"

Smitty cut him off before he had a chance to finish.
"Don't you even know who you're talking about?"

McKay sputtered and his complexion mottled red.
"Why don't you enlighten me? Us?"

Zach wouldn't mind being enlightened himself, since
no one had bothered with an introduction. He knew her
from somewhere, though he couldn't say how or why. So
it didn't completely surprise him that Smitty looked directly at him before speaking.

"She's Sammy the Bull's daughter."

For an instant, everything inside Zach seemed to freeze over. The woman who had been here, in this room with him, was Alex? His Alex? He had no right to think of her in that way, but he did. Unconsciously, he turned his head toward the door, the way she'd left, as if he expected to still find her standing there. Part of him wanted to go after her, but there would be time for that later. He'd wondered about that look she cast him before she left, part expectation, part condemnation. He had more to answer for than not recognizing her after all these years.

Then again, the Alex he'd known had been a shy, sensitive girl whom on his better days he credited himself as having helped coax out of her shell. She'd exhibited none of the confidence or command that the woman who'd sat at this table had. He'd seen little of the beauty or grace he'd seen today. The years had been good to her, much better than he had been.

Now he understood why Smitty had looked at him and why now he was the focus of all of them. Sammy "the Bull" Yates had been his training officer years ago when he'd first come on the force, green as a blade of grass and eager to prove himself. Sammy had been a legend long before any mobster coopted his nickname. There wasn't a man in the room who wouldn't know Sammy by reputation or that the man had died in Zach's arms felled by the only gunshot he'd ever taken.

"Shit," he heard one of the men say, voicing his own sentiments as well.

"You know her then?" McKay asked.

Zach didn't like his tone, or the avidity in his gaze when he asked the question. Had he not been in a roomful of men, who were probably equally curious as to why he hadn't mentioned knowing her, he would have asked exactly what McKay was implying. Maybe Alex's last unguarded look hadn't gone as unnoticed as he'd thought.

"In a manner of speaking," he said finally.

"She's your problem, then," McKay said flippantly. "Find out what the doctor knows and maybe we can get some place."

Zach sat back in his chair, disgruntled. Maybe they'd get some place if McKay employed some actual police work instead of innuendo. Whoever claimed they needed the best minds had picked from the wrong end of the barrel for that one.

Still, McKay's words echoed in his head. *She's your problem.* McKay couldn't know how right he was.

Four

The first thing Alex did when she got to her tiny office at the corner of the building was to strip out of the power suit she'd worn to her encounter with New York's finest. She never wore such formal attire here.

Unfortunately, McKay and maybe some of the others had decided against her before she'd gotten one butt cheek on a seat. Who knew? Maybe they were right about her. Maybe if she'd seen Walter Thorpe's true character she could have saved a few dozen women their misery. Maybe she was misjudging him again. She couldn't have a clue without interviewing him and even then she couldn't know for sure. She could only render an opinion.

She changed into a pair of beige wool pants and a cream-colored sweater before taking a seat behind her desk to examine Thorpe's file for the second time that day. Before she got the cover to the file open she heard a cough from her open doorway. Roberta stood at her doorway, her hands braced on either side of the jamb. Roberta was the youngest of the three of them and also the most cynical, for what reason she had never made plain. She usually wore her black hair in a single long braid that hung nearly to her waist. Today her hair was

unbound and she actually had on mascara and blush
applied in a way that flattered her Mediterranean features.

"How'd you make out in cop land?" Roberta asked.
"You don't look much worse for wear."

If Roberta expected her appearance to go unnoticed,
she was mistaken. Besides, Alex needed a distraction. She
didn't relish reliving that meeting. "Are we expecting a
visit from the mayor or has hell frozen over already?"

Roberta rolled her eyes. "So, I'm trying to impress a
certain young lawyer. What's it to ya?"

Alex shrugged, chuckling. "Nothing. It suits you. Let
me know when you want to venture into lipstick. I've got
a color that would suit you."

Roberta came forward, plunked herself in one of
Alex's visitor chairs, and crossed her legs so that one
ankle rested against the opposite knee. "I'll have to remember that. But don't think you're going to duck out
of my question. What did the boys in blue want?"

"Nothing. It was the men in black, detectives. They
seem to think one of my patients is the Amazon Killer.
Walter Thorpe."

"The flasher turned rapist?"

"One and the same." Thorpe had first come to her
under court-ordered counseling after he'd received pro-
bation for flashing a group of schoolgirls on their way to
St. Catherine's Academy, a Catholic high school off
Pelham Parkway, from the confines of his car. The girls
had gone inside the Catholic school and returned with
two nuns and a lay teacher in tow. The women stood
guard until the police showed up.

When arrested, Thorpe claimed he'd been living out
of his car and was in the process of taking a leak into an
empty gallon milk container. He hadn't known the girls
were there until they'd started shrieking. Nobody, not
even his own court-appointed lawyer, had believed him.

In session, his story never varied, but his explanation

of why he was picked up swung from self-blame to the fact that others were out to get him. Either he was a good guy wronged or he was a bad man who deserved to be punished. His affect swung from an odd sort of euphoria to bursts of anger directed at her, the girls who'd accused him, and society in general to bouts of anxiety about his future all in the span of minutes. Her initial diagnosis was BPD, borderline personality disorder, even though the disorder was more common by far in women than in men. He'd come for three of the mandated sessions before the police arrested him for the series of rapes on the other side of the Bronx.

"If that's true, that's one hell of a slippery slope that boy is sliding down."

"Mmm," Alex agreed. It wasn't uncommon for sex offenders to start out small, either peeping at the neighbors or flashing, then graduating to other, more damaging crimes. Like an addict they needed a bigger fix, or a more lasting one. But often this occurred over a longer span, sometimes a lifetime. If Thorpe was the Amazon Killer, that would mean he'd gone from flashing to raping young women almost simultaneously, and if she had the timeline right, he'd morphed into a killer within a month of being released from prison.

It wasn't impossible, but she knew she didn't want to believe it, either. Thorpe's guilt would be an additional defeat when she could little afford one. Life was supposed to be on the good side now. She'd earned that, hadn't she? Maybe not, but for now she wanted to think of something else, anything else.

To Roberta, she said, "I've got to get ready for a session in fifteen minutes."

Roberta didn't miss her cue. She stood, brushing her pants legs back into place. "Anything I can do?"

Alex read the sympathy in her friend's face but didn't

want it. "Let me know if someone tall, dark, and dangerous shows up."

Roberta's eyebrows lifted. Before she could ask the obvious question, Alex forestalled her with the lift of her
hand. "I'm figuring one of those detectives will show up
here looking for information."

Roberta's hopeful expression deflated comically.

"Sorry to disappoint you."

"You're worse than I am when it comes to men,"
Roberta said, shaking her head.

"Well, we do see so many fine specimens of masculin-
ity in a day. No wonder our heads are so easily turned."

"Amen to that," Roberta said, her usual cynicism
showing.

After she left, Alex copied the phone number and ad-
dress for Thorpe's sister she had on file, intending to call
Detective McKay with the information she'd promised.
She buzzed Alice to ask her to check the logs for last
May, a month before the Amazon Killer became active,
to see if any calls came in from Thorpe. None had.

Alex grabbed her notes for the next session, a group
of sex addicts in various stages of recovery, locked her
office, and headed for the appropriate treatment room.
By the end of the day, Zach hadn't shown up. An odd
jumble of emotions accompanied that knowledge, the
foremost of which was self-doubt at having miscalculated
again. She put on her coat and headed home.

Zach sat in one of the leather chairs in his older
brother Adam's study, nursing a scotch while wondering
when Adam would get around to telling him why he'd
been invited here in the first place. Dinner, as had been
the case since nearly a year ago, had been a somber
event; this conversational dessert wasn't much better.
Adam stared out the window, lost in whatever thoughts

he possessed. Adam had always been a man of few words, but this was ridiculous.

"So, how's work?" Zach asked finally, hoping any question might spur his brother to talk.

Adam didn't answer, but his gaze swung around to settle on him. Adam's expression gave away nothing, but then it never did. "Stevie wants to stay with you a while."

Zach's eyebrows lifted. His niece rarely paid him much attention except on occasions on which a present was required. "What brought that on?"

"She and my wife aren't getting along."

When had Adam started referring to the woman in question not as Barbara, but as my wife—impersonal? Zach couldn't remember. Maybe it was tonight. He thought back over the course of dinner. He hadn't noticed any particular strain between his brother and his sister-in-law, not that either of them was the most demonstrative person on the planet. Barbara was the most resolute woman he'd ever met; Adam was just Adam.

In an odd way, none of them had been the same—not him, not Adam or Barbara, not their younger brother, Jonathan, and certainly not their sister, Joanna, since the death of Joanna's husband eight months ago. Ray Haynes had been killed by one of his childhood cronies in an effort to keep secret their part in the death of a priest twenty-five years ago. That same man had tried to kill Jonathan's fiancé, Dana, who had stumbled on damning evidence. Ray had died defending her.

They had always thought they were a strong family. Their parents' premature deaths had made them so. But lately it seemed that everything was falling apart, as if someone had pulled a thread and unwittingly unraveled the whole garment.

Joanna walked around like the living dead. Jonathan, who'd never been around much, was around much less, since both he and Dana served only to remind Joanna of what she'd lost. Now the wondercouple Adam and Barbara were seemingly having trouble.

Not that anybody confided any of this to him. It was simply evident. Not that anybody ever came to him seeking advice or counsel or even invited him for the occasional beer unless they wanted something. He didn't mind having his niece stay with him, but he resented the cursory explanation given him, as if his understanding was unimportant as long as he did as asked.

Just to be perverse, he asked, "What sixteen-year-old girl *does* get along with her mother?"

Adam's lips compressed, about the only sign of irritation Adam ever showed. "If you're going to say no, say it already."

"Of course she can stay with me. What kind of a man do you think I am?" He regretted the question even before he'd finished asking it. He already knew what kind of man his brother thought he was, and Adam didn't approve. Neither did Jonathan, for that matter. The two of them were like bookends, each vying for the honor of Mr. Stoic for whatever the current year happened to be. Or Jonathan had been part of that competition until he'd met Dana. Zach hadn't seen enough of Jonathan since then to gauge if his opinion had changed toward his middle brother. Adam's obviously hadn't.

Zach sighed. "I just figured World War Three had to be going on here if you were willing to entrust your oldest child to me."

"Things have been a bit strained, lately."

Even that little bit of an admission surprised Zach. As far as he knew, Adam didn't confide anything to anyone except God. "I'm sorry to hear that," Zach said and meant it.

Adam shook his head, as if to clear Zach's words from it. "It's only for a couple of weeks."

"As long as we understand I'm probably not going to be around much. I'm working a new case and—"

Adam held up a hand to forestall him. "As long as we understand none of your women are to come anywhere near my child."

Zach almost laughed. Adam made it sound as if he were keeping some sort of harem in his apartment. He didn't. There hadn't been a female in his apartment aside from the cleaning lady since before his divorce became final last year. Hell, he hadn't even bothered to tell Adam that Sherry had finally gotten around to divorcing him after all these years. Good God, he was just as bad as the rest of them.

Disgusted with himself and the conversation, he stood. "I have something to take care of tonight. I'll pick Stevie up tomorrow after work, if that's okay with you."

"That's fine." Adam rose to his feet and extended his hand. "Thanks."

Rather than shake his hand, Zach deposited his empty glass in it. "See you tomorrow."

For one bare moment, he contemplated telling his brother where he was heading. Like him, both of his brothers were cops. Both of them knew of Sammy; both of them had heard him speak of Alex. But this was his burden. He left with the weight of it fully on his shoulders.

Five

She had known he would seek her out, so it didn't surprise her to find him on the other side of her front door. But why did he have to choose here instead of her office, impersonal territory that held no memories for either of them? She could have handled it there, much more easily.

Once he hadn't appeared at her office, she'd assumed he'd show up the next day. Otherwise she would have prepared herself both mentally and physically for his arrival. She'd have put on something slightly less revealing and vulnerability-inducing than a pale peach robe with nothing but a pair of fuzzy slippers underneath it. Part of her wanted to escape to her bedroom to put on something more appropriate before she opened the door to him. She had no idea if he'd wait that long, and she wanted this over.

She took one last look through the peephole, steeling herself for the encounter that was to come. She might not have changed much, but he had. Thirteen years ago, he'd been a young man just coming into his own—thinner, more wiry than he was today. Back then, he'd been clear-eyed and avid—hungry for the job. Today she'd seen something in his eyes, a world-weariness and fatigue she would never have expected to see in the eyes of the young man she knew. She suspected that, more than the sensual quality of his eyes, had been what captivated her that afternoon. For the first time she'd seen depth in his eyes and couldn't help wondering how they'd gotten so deep.

The doorbell buzzed again, spurring her to action. She pulled the door open and saw him, the real him, not distorted by the glass in the door. He stood inside the glass storm door, one hand braced on the jamb.

He offered her a faint smile, a sardonic bend of his lips that reminded her of the first time she'd opened that door for him. It had been a Saturday night, a day her father hadn't worked. He'd spent all day cleaning the house, or rather overseeing her clean it, since men didn't stoop to doing anything so unmanly as wielding a dust cloth. He spent the latter part of the evening readying himself as if he were preparing himself for a date.

He'd made her dress, too, for what reason she couldn't fathom since no one was coming there to see her. Besides, the only person they were expecting was his new partner, some rookie he was training, a kid barely five years older than her own fifteen years. What was the big deal about that?

When the doorbell rang, he'd literally pushed her toward the door. "Go answer the door, girl. He's liable to think you don't have any manners."

A year ago, she might have been excited to meet the man who worked with her father, but nothing excited her now. Not since her life ended and all that remained was the existence she had left. She trudged toward the door. With wooden movements she pulled it open. On the other side stood the most beautiful man she had ever seen. He smiled at her, just a hint of a thing, like he had some secret he might whisper in your ear if you let him.

She didn't smile back, simply stared into his eyes colored a warm chocolate brown shaded by long sooty lashes. It wasn't a look of interest, though she knew half of her friends would have swooned already just from looking at him. Her gaze was an assessing one, one that sought to gauge his character. He appeared not to notice.

"You must be Alex," he said. "Your father's told me a lot about you."

I bet, she thought without rancor. *But certainly not everything.* "Please come in," she'd said, stepping aside for him to enter.

She hadn't admitted to herself then, but that smile of his got to her. It still did. It spoke of a charm he didn't turn on or off but simply possessed, like the color of his eyes or the cleft in his chin.

But she wasn't any more ready to make a fool of herself over him now than she had been then. She stood silent, waiting for him to speak. This was his show. If he wanted something from her, he'd have to ask for it.

"Hello, Alex," he said finally, as if to confirm he'd figured out who she was. "It's been a long time."

For a moment, Alex simply stared at him, his words echoing in her ears. *It's been a long time.* Part of her wanted to hit him with her fists and rail, "Whose fault is that?" She wasn't the one to disappear. She was the one whose phone calls went unanswered or even acknowledged.

She'd told herself that if he wanted something from her he'd have to ask for it. But she saw in his continuing silence that he wouldn't even give her that.

With a sigh of capitulation, she said. "I suppose you want to come in."

"That was the plan."

"Then don't let me stop you." She moved aside and gestured for him to enter.

He did as she suggested, stepping over the threshold, crowding her in the small foyer. The lion hadn't quite finished with its end of March, making a coat necessary.

Zack wore a khaki duster that he didn't bother to remove. He still had on the gray suit he'd worn that afternoon, suggesting that he'd come here straight from work, although it was already past nine o'clock. Both his failure to relieve himself of his coat and the fact he hadn't changed suggested he intended to keep this visit brief. She could hope, couldn't she?

She turned and headed for the living room that opened out from the foyer to claim one edge of the sofa, tucking her feet beneath her. "Then what can I do for you, Zach? Despite what McKay thinks, Thorpe did not call me. I checked the logs. Maybe he called and hung up or didn't give his name. Even if he had, I couldn't tell you what he said. You know that. If it hadn't been plastered all over the papers that I'd been treating Thorpe I couldn't have told you that much. I can't help you."

She'd hoped to put him off with her comments, to make him see he was wasting his time. He appeared not to notice, his attention taken up by examining the room from where he stood by her father's favorite chair.

When he finally settled his gaze on her again it was with a look of nostalgia. "I take it you're not much on redecorating."

No, in the past thirteen years, she'd left things pretty much where they'd been. Right now, she couldn't remember having even painted the place. The house was frozen in time, much like she'd allowed herself to freeze, until recently. This place, this home, no longer suited her and she'd contemplated selling.

"I'm sure you didn't come here to discuss my décor. What do you want, Zach?"

"If I wanted to talk to you about Walter Thorpe I would have come to your office."

He spoke with a quiet intensity and in his eyes she saw the only hint of uncertainty she'd ever witnessed there.

He brushed a hand over his hair. "Look, Alex, now that I'm here, I don't know what to say."

"There isn't anything for you to say." The past was the past, a history neither of them could go back and change. What she needed from him she'd needed thirteen years ago. Any apology, any explanation came too many years too late. She didn't need anything from him anymore.

His expression darkened. "I don't blame you for hating me."

"I don't hate you," she said. She never had. She crediting him with leaving her to the wolves, much the way her mother had by dying when she was twelve years old. That seemed to be the way of things in her life, the ones she loved the most never stayed. But, in truth, he'd never been responsible for her. She'd only wanted it that way.

She stood, crossing her arms, a posture she recognized as defensive. "Go home, Zach. There's nothing for you here. If you want a trip down memory lane, I can't travel it with you. If you want absolution, call your priest. If you need some counseling, make an appointment like everyone else. I have an early morning tomorrow and need to get some sleep."

He shoved his hands in his trouser pockets, rocking backward, considering her. "You didn't used to be so hard, Alex."

Annoyed at his implication, she snapped, "I didn't used to be a lot of things." She sighed, letting her pique abate. "I'm sure you can find your way out."

He didn't say anything for a long moment, but she could sense the capitulation in him. He withdrew his hands from his pockets to let them hang by his sides. "For what it's worth, I am sorry."

He shrugged and turned toward the door. She waited, her breath held, listening for the sound of the door opening and shutting, leaving him on the outside. Hearing them both, she released her breath, got up from her perch on the sofa, and went to the door to lock it.

For a moment, she leaned her back against the wooden surface, breathing deeply. He was gone. That's what she'd wanted from the moment he'd shown up at her door. The only thing marring her relief was the notion that she'd hurt him by dismissing him so abruptly. That wasn't her plan, but she knew that's what she'd accomplished. Oh well, she'd have to live with that, since as much as he felt he had to answer for, if she let him in, he'd want answers as well. They weren't kids anymore. He'd expect the truth from her, and that she couldn't give him. She wouldn't go back, wouldn't revisit the past, not for anyone, not even him. She'd barely survived it the first time.

Better to let him think she blamed him than to risk opening the past to scrutiny. That's what she told herself, anyway, as she pushed off the door, ascended the stairs, and got into bed. But she lay in bed a long time, watching the patterns cast by the headlights of passing cars dance on her bedroom walls.

Zach sat in his car, still staring up at the house long after the light in Alex's bedroom window had flickered on and off. Or, rather, the bedroom that had been hers a lifetime ago. It surprised him that she still used it. Why hadn't she moved into the larger bedroom at the back of the house? Sammy was long dead and the house was hers to do with what she liked.

Mentally, Zach shrugged. Wondering about Alex's sleep arrangements was only a distraction from what really bothered him. He'd known she wouldn't welcome him into her home, but he hadn't expected her to throw him out so roundly, at least not before he got out any of the things he wanted to tell her—words that now tum-

bled through his mind but none of which had made it
out of his mouth. At least he'd gotten to give her some
sort of apology even if it wasn't what she deserved.

The expression "too little, too late" came to his mind.
That's what anything he could say to her now would be.
He accepted that, just as he accepted that coming here
had served one purpose only, that of making himself feel
better. So far, even that was a bust.

His gaze shifted to the entrance to the house. A five-
foot wire and post fence guarded the perimeter of the
property that had once belonged to Samuel Yates. As
realty spaces went, it wasn't a large plot; big enough for a
patch of lawn out front, a barbecue pit and an inground
pool out back, but not much else. The house itself wasn't
large either, but big enough to feel like a real home.

He'd once asked Sammy why he'd bought this house,
in the shade of million-dollar homes in Riverdale, when
elsewhere in the Bronx he could have gotten more for
his money. He'd said, "I bought the best house I could
afford in the best neighborhood. You can't do any better
than that." That was Sammy; everything he owned or
liked or respected was the best, including Sammy himself. His way was the right way; his ideas were the best
ideas. No one was a better cop than he was.

Rumors abounded that Sammy's bullheadedness had
earned him his nickname, but there were other stories,
flattering in a way that only other cops appreciate:
Sammy was built like the proverbial bull with beefy
shoulders, a broad muscular back, and a thick midsec-
tion. By the time Zach met him, his hair had thinned in
such a way that the tufts remaining at the top of his head
stood up like horns when not slicked down.

Some said that Sammy could fell any door he put one
of his massive shoulders to. According to Sammy, that
one had started when he burst through a steel-plated
door to get to the victim of a child snatching that had

been traced to that location. Sammy attributed his feat to being hopped up on adrenaline, too much caffeine, and too little sleep to think before he acted. The little girl on the other side of the door had been too over-whelmed with relief to care.

Some said committing a crime was like waving a red flag in Sammy's face; he'd keep coming after you until he got you. Then there was the time Sammy was in foot pur-suit of a man who'd robbed a woman's pocketbook at gunpoint. Legend had it the suspect turned and fired on Sammy, hitting him three times. But Sammy still kept coming, until he tackled the perp and took his weapon. In truth, Sammy'd been hit once, a flesh wound that barely nipped his shoulder, but like any other myth, its ve-racity wasn't based on anything so mundane as the facts.

If you asked Sammy, he'd earned the name on his first post, walking a beat in Spanish Harlem. Sammy was old school, a relic from before the police department went PC, one of the first black cops the department deigned to admit. To hear Sammy tell it, it wasn't uncommon in those days to draw the worst assignments or be cast as the screwup when things went sour or, worst of all, to call in for backup that never showed. He got used to going it alone, charging in and defusing a situation before it got out of control. And, Sammy had once told him with a grin, he'd been young and stupid and willing to fight anyone that swung on him. He wasn't quick enough to use his hands or handy enough with a stick. He'd put his shoulder in the perp's gut and take him down that way. Worked every damn time.

Zach had been assigned to the Forty-second Precinct in the Morissania Section of the Bronx straight out of the academy. That first day, Sammy had come up to him. "I hear you're a good cop."

Zach couldn't imagine who'd said that or what anyone had to go on to make that type of statement. He hadn't had a chance to prove much of anything to anyone yet. But he knew who Sammy was. A smile sneaked across Zach's face at the compliment. "Yeah?"

Sammy gave him a once-over that suggested whoever had given him the good word had lied. "If you want to stay alive, you'll ride with me."

Zach laughed to himself in the confines of his car, remembering. That was Sammy, as much as he gave, he could often taketh away. But Sammy had taken him in hand, as if it were his personal mission to school Zach in the way of all things. For a kid whose father had died and whose siblings ignored him for the most part, that was a big thing.

They'd been partnered about six months when Sammy made the pronouncement that Zach should come to his house for dinner the following night. Had he been asked, Zach would have turned him down. It was his day off, time to think of something more fragrant than the smell in the sector car and softer than its upholstery. But nobody argued with Sammy; at least nobody won.

Given Sammy's over-the-top personality, Zach had assumed his daughter would be more of the same. He hadn't expected the girl who opened the door to him. Tall and skinny, dressed in a navy shirtwaist dress with a white collar, her hair styled into two braids that hung past her shoulders, she struck him as an older, darker yet equally morose version of Wednesday Addams. She'd stared up at him with huge, dark eyes that assessed him, and worse, found him, in some way, wanting. Or maybe she'd simply been dismissing him as a nine-second curiosity and nothing more.

During the ensuing meal of roast beef, mashed potatoes and gravy, and string beans, she hadn't spoken one word and fled the table as soon as the last morsel of her food passed her lips.

After she'd left, Sammy had turned to him, his face split with a grin of fatherly pride. "So what do you think?"

Zach shrugged. What was he supposed to make of an unsmiling, utterly silent girl who looked at him like he was as welcome as a case of chickenpox? "She always so talkative?" he asked finally.

Sammy lifted one shoulder as he shoveled another forkful into his mouth. "She'll come around."

Zach shrugged again and focused on his own food. Even if she did, what difference would it make? He didn't plan to make a habit of dining here.

He didn't see her again, until after he bid Sammy good night later that evening. He'd walked out to his car and looked back at the house. She was standing at the window on the second floor. Without thinking, he lifted a hand and waved to her. In reaction she lifted her hand and gave him the finger before retreating. He shook his head and laughed. Maybe there was a bit of Sammy in her after all.

She hadn't wanted anything to do with him then, and it looked like they were back where they started. Part of him wished he could do what she wanted and leave her alone, but he knew he wouldn't do that. He had a case to solve, and more than that, an opportunity to make right what he'd messed up so long ago.

Sammy had taught him well. He wouldn't give up until he got what he wanted, both personally and professionally.

He smiled to himself as a plan formed in his mind. He'd worn her down once and he could do it again. "This isn't over, Alex," he whispered to the night air, started his car, and pulled away.

Six

The following morning, Zach was waiting for McKay when he came in to the station. Zach leaned back in McKay's chair, with his feet propped up on the desk, his eyes closed. He was tired and testy, having fought a losing battle in the bid for sleep the previous night, but neither his lack of sleep nor his mood was responsible for his posture. He hoped to annoy McKay, put him on edge.

He knew he'd succeeded when McKay stomped to a stop next to the desk. "You got something for me already?"

Zach opened his eyes and focused on the other man. He did have something for him, but not the way McKay meant. After the meeting broke up yesterday, Smitty had told him about the way the rest of the meeting had gone. He said Alex had held her own, but she shouldn't have had to. McKay had been hoping to rattle her with his little slide show and had gotten exactly what he deserved for that: nothing.

On top of that, word had it that McKay had been assigned the case right after the first body was found. He hadn't done much with it until the councilwoman's daughter turned up. Apparently some vics were worth the effort in McKay's book and some weren't.

Zach adjusted his position, but didn't move off, as McKay obviously wanted him to. "I heard about how you sandbagged Alex Waters to get her here yesterday."

McKay scowled. "What's it to you? Just because you used to partner with her old man—"

Zach cut him off. "She's not a suspect and you can't believe she knows where Thorpe is."

"Why can't I? For all I know he's camped out in her basement. We all know none of those cars was the primary crime scene. Thorpe has no known address. He'd need somewhere secure, where he wouldn't be disturbed, and someone he knew who wouldn't turn him in. At the very least, he called her. If she's keeping his whereabouts a secret, that's obstruction of justice."

Zach did stand then, topping McKay's height by a couple of inches and his weight by a good fifty pounds. "Are you ready to charge her with that?" Zach asked, though he knew the answer.

McKay seemed to shrink even more. "No."

"Then leave her alone." Zach had said all he came to say. He'd enjoyed putting McKay in his place, but he had better things to do. He turned to walk away.

But apparently McKay wasn't finished yet. "You might want to warn your girlfriend we're releasing Thorpe's name in a press conference this afternoon."

Zach turned back to face McKay slowly and purposefully. What idiot okayed that? He wouldn't bother to address that girlfriend comment, since McKay wouldn't believe him no matter what he said. But now he thought he knew the man's game.

Zach advanced until the men were only inches apart, forcing McKay to look up. "Enjoy the spotlight while you can. We both know you don't have the juice for the boys upstairs to let you keep running this thing. Your new boss will be remembered as the one who cracked the case and you'll be the complainer that never wanted it in the first place."

Seeing color rise in McKay's cheeks, Zach knew he'd hit his mark. He winked at the man. "You have a nice day now." Without waiting for a response, he turned on his heel and left.

Alex stood at the window to her office staring down at the goings-on on Tremont Avenue, but seeing nothing. Despite what she'd told Zach about not revisiting the past, she couldn't seem to focus on much else. One memory in particular seemed to haunt her, the reason for which she couldn't fathom. It was a nothing memory, nothing important, but still it pulled at her.

It was maybe the fourth or fifth time Zach had been over. Her father had taken to dragging him home like some stray puppy in need of a meal. As usual, she'd escaped from the dinner table as soon as possible. She was as interested in all their cop talk as she was in ice fishing in Siberia. All that macho posturing, and for what? She knew her father liked the adrenaline rush of being on the streets. They'd tried to give him a detective's shield a few times, but he always turned them down. She didn't know what Zach's problem was.

She'd been in the living room, reading, her refuge. She didn't have to be poor old Alex Yates anymore; she could be anyone she wanted, travel anywhere she chose. So she was not happy to sense someone's presence in the doorway or to look up to find Zach standing there.

He leaned against the door frame, lazy. His face bore the sort of curious, smiling expression adults reserve for children they don't know how to handle. "Whatcha reading?"

She'd been lying on her stomach. She immediately rose to a sitting position. "A book."

"No kidding." He took a step into the room, walking

toward the fireplace they never used. "I thought all girls your age liked to read was *Seventeen* magazine."

If that was supposed to be an attempt at humor, he ought to have his funny bone checked. Couldn't he tell she didn't want him here, not only in this room but in her house? She didn't trust him, couldn't remember trusting anyone absolutely aside from her mother. She watched him closely as he stopped at the mantel, picking up one of the pictures that rested there.

"Is this your mother?" he asked after a moment. He gazed over his shoulder at her. "You look like her."

"That's what they tell me."

He sighed, and she acknowledged his frustration with her. He was trying to be nice. She was sure his comment was meant as a compliment. But she didn't need him to tell her whom she resembled. And if her surliness bothered him, good. Maybe then he'd leave.

He settled the picture back where it belonged. "My mom died when I was twelve, too."

He wasn't facing her then. His attention was still on the photograph. She narrowed her eyes, studying him, wondering if he'd said that merely to capture her sympathy or if it was true. But even seeing only his profile she saw the melancholia in his expression. "I'm sorry." The words escaped her mouth before she had a chance to stop them.

He turned to face her. "Me too."

She knew he was referring to her loss, but she couldn't bring herself to say the obligatory "Thank you." Instead she frowned, letting her shoulders droop. "Anything else?"

He actually laughed, which surprised her. "Your father asked me to tell you we got called back in. He's upstairs changing."

She shrugged. She didn't mind the prospect of having the house to herself, but something major must be happening for them to be called in so soon after signing out. "Have fun."

Shaking his head, as if in defeat, he turned to leave, but almost immediately turned back. "If my being here bothers you . . ."

She lifted her book and pretended to read it. "I don't care what you do."

"Then why do you disappear every time I come around?"

She lowered her book and rolled her eyes. "All that cop talk. Do any of you guys ever tell any stories that are true?"

He laughed again. She bit her lip to disguise the fact that she liked the sound of it. "I remember thinking the same thing about my dad," he said.

"He was a cop, too?"

"A c.o., a corrections officer."

She didn't need him to explain what a c.o. was. She shrugged. "Same crap, different uniform."

The words were barely out of her mouth when she heard her father's heavy tread on the stairs. And then they were both out the door. She'd risen to her knees and turned to look out the window to watch Zach climb into her father's car.

Now, in the present, Alex sighed. She wondered what it was about that memory that haunted her. Perhaps, because it was the first time she'd felt herself softening toward him, felt even the most tenuous of connections. He'd been through some of what she had. But unlike her, he'd gotten along with his dad. She heard that in the few simple words he'd spoken about him. She'd envied that.

But any peace between them hadn't lasted long. The next time he'd come, he ventured into the living room where she was watching TV. She would have preferred to lock herself in her bedroom, but that far away and with the door closed it would have been impossible to gauge how much her father had been drinking.

Without preamble, Zach said, "I bought you something."

She'd looked up, wariness in her gaze. He held a book in his hand that he extended toward her, *Sense and Sensibility* by Jane Austen.

She bit her lip, not knowing what to make of this unexpected offering. He was giving her a gift? She didn't want it. She'd never received a gift that didn't eventually cost her something. "What do you want?"

The smile didn't fade from his face, but she sensed his exasperation as he tossed the book onto the table. "I noticed you were reading *Pride and Prejudice* before. I thought you'd like it." He turned and walked from the room.

She leaned forward and picked up the book and hugged it to her chest. She did want it. Every book she read came either from school, from the library, or from the meager allowance her father gave her. Most times she got them from the used bookstore on Fordham Road to make the most of her money. A brand-new book was a treasure.

Still, she went to her room, to the secret compartment in the base of her bare jewelry box where she kept her money and everything else she didn't want her father to find. She took out two dollars, enough to cover the cost of the book. Later that night she sneaked it into his jacket pocket along with a note that said *Now we're even*.

The intercom on Alex's desk buzzed, startling her. "Tall, dark, and dangerous just showed up," Alice said.

That's all the warning Alex got before a knock sounded at her door. An instant later, the door pushed open. "Alex?"

Alex took a deep breath, swallowing down the emotion the memories had dredged up. Her gaze traveled over him. Damn, he looked good. She didn't know why that thought had to pop up in her head. Probably all the damn reminiscing.

She crossed her arms. "What can I do for you, Zach? I thought we said all there was to say last night."

He stepped farther into the room, closing the door behind him. "I told you if I wanted to talk to you about Thorpe I'd come here."

So he had, but she'd thought he meant that he'd come to her home on personal matters, not that he intended to show up here with more questions. "And you know I can't tell you anything."

He reached into his breast pocket and pulled out a sheaf of blue-backed folded papers. "I thought this might help."

She crossed the room and took the papers from his fingers. She unfolded them, but she knew what they were—a subpoena for her files. She'd expected they'd get around to it eventually, but not this soon. They didn't have anything on which to base a warrant, at least she didn't think they did. She scanned to the bottom of the page to see who'd signed off on it. Judge Franklin Roberts. No wonder. Roberts treated the Fourth Amendment as if it were a guideline instead of the law.

She refolded the papers and dropped them onto her desk. "I'll see that my secretary gets them to your office." She expected him to say that wasn't good enough, but he surprised her.

"In the meantime, why don't you tell me why you don't think Thorpe is the guy?"

She leaned her left butt cheek against her desk and refolded her arms. For a moment she thought of refusing him, but nothing she was about to say wasn't already part of the public record.

"You and I both know what kind of man you're hunting for—a Ted Bundy, a John Wayne Gacy. Men with no conscience, no fear, a lust killer, excited by his own violence. Thorpe wasn't violent. He coerced women into submitting to him with the threat of discovery by their children in the next room. None of the women wanted to risk having their children walk in on that scene, or worse, having him select another target. He even apologized when he was through. In my opinion, they're trying to make Walter Mitty into Hannibal Lecter and it just doesn't fly."

"You never saw that degree of pathology in him?"

"Frankly, no. He never even admitted to committing the crimes. If you'll recall, he said the mirror did it."

"Wouldn't that point toward a diagnosis of schizophrenia?"

She knew what he was getting at. Many serial killers faked hearing voices or alternate personalities, anything to try to convince their shrink or their friendly neighborhood jury that they weren't responsible for their actions. It might mean the difference in sentencing between a maximum-security prison and a mental hospital. The latter was more desirable, since there was a chance of faking a miracle "cure" and tricking some fool doctor into releasing them.

"If you believed him, it might. I didn't."

Honestly, if it hadn't been for his semen in the girl's body, she would have had a hard time believing he committed the crimes at all, a fact the prosecution used to their advantage. Thorpe's major life problem was his impulsivity. He'd go into a rage over something minor, a fact that had cost him more than one job, even though he'd go docile and apologetic the moment his pique faded. He'd swing from mania to depression with no apparent provocation for either, which made interpersonal relationships impossible. He swung from ideation of and contempt for the one constant in his life, his sister.

But the rapes the prosecution had pinned on him had to have been planned. Each of the victims was a single mother with two children, an older girl and a younger boy. In each case, the perpetrator had broken into the woman's apartment and hidden in her closet or waited until she ventured into the bedroom alone. Then he'd pushed the women down on their bed and raped them. His parting shot had been to smash any mirrors visible.

Thorpe didn't have the wherewithal for all that. With the smashed mirrors linking all the cases and his semen in one of the women, no defense attorney in the world was going to keep him from getting convicted of something. With the help of her subpoenaed testimony, Thorpe's attorney had painted him as a hapless copycat, too inept to get it right, and the jury bought it. So instead of being convicted on eight counts of rape he was only convicted of one. The difference allowed him to be out on the streets instead of being locked up. No wonder the cops hated her.

"You didn't have any clue what Thorpe was up to? No hints of violence? No rape fantasies?"

She exhaled, wondering if he thought her incompetent, too. Did it not occur to anyone that she hadn't been treating Thorpe long enough to uncover most of the dysfunction in his personality?

She tilted her head to one side, challenging. "If they arrested every guy who indulged in rape fantasies, there wouldn't be a man left on the street."

He lifted one eyebrow, and his smile deepened. "Touché." His expression changed, softening. "How are you doing, Alex, really?"

She frowned and straightened to a standing position. "You gave up the right to ask me that question thirteen years ago." She sighed. "If you have no more professional questions . . ."

She didn't add, hit the road, but she might as well

have. He looked at her with an expression she didn't understand. "Just a warning. They're going to be releasing Thorpe's name and description to the media this afternoon, only as someone they want to talk to. Make sure you get those files to me by the close of business today." He turned and walked out of the room, leaving the door open behind him.

For a moment, she stared after him. He could take her abrasiveness any way he wanted as long as he left her alone. That was a precaution for both their benefits. She closed her office door, crossed to her seat, and flopped down on it. Only then did she contemplate the last bit of information he'd given her. They were releasing Thorpe's name. Good God! Now it would begin for sure.

Seven

Zach's sister-in-law opened the door to him when he arrived at his brother's house that night to collect his niece. He'd left Alex's office in a foul mood and his disposition hadn't improved since then. He'd attended the press conference held at 1 Police Plaza where Commissioner Burke announced the formation of the Alpha Task Force, assembled to track down the so-called Amazon Killer and to name Captain Victor Craig as the new head thereof.

Zach could almost feel the steam coming off McKay as the news was announced. He hadn't even lasted the day. Zach couldn't find fault with whoever had made that decision, or whatever calmer head had decided to keep Thorpe's connection to the case quiet until they'd run down whatever leads they already had on him.

The bad news was that McKay had already ordered records for Alex's work, home, and cell phone numbers, hoping to find some evidence of communication between the two of them. Tapping her phone might not be far behind, if they could convince some judge to sign off on it.

Why McKay insisted on bringing Alex into this, Zack didn't know. It smacked of a vindictiveness that had nothing to do with job advancement as he'd suspected, but of something more personal in nature. Alex would probably call it a fixation; he'd call it trouble waiting to happen.

"We were beginning to think you weren't going to show up," Barbara said, ushering him inside the door.

To Zach's eye, her smile looked brittle. Too bad. He liked Barbara. Whatever difficulty she was having with Stevie or his brother, he hoped it was resolved soon. The whole family had more than its share of grief at the moment. Besides, who other than Barbara would ever put up with Adam?

"Long day," Zach said. "Is Stevie ready?"

Barbara gave an exasperated sigh. "Does Martha Stewart wear white after Labor Day?"

Zach chuckled. "I guess I should have known." If he had to hang around he might as well see what his brother was up to. "Is Adam around?"

"The usual spot."

Which meant he was off in his study, probably brooding like the last time. Except now there was a hint of a smile on Barbara's face. "Thanks, I think."

Barbara patted his shoulder as he turned to make his way to the study. "Have fun."

He knew the reason for Barbara's smile even before he reached his destination. Adam wasn't alone. He heard Jonathan's voice as well as Adam's as he approached the open door.

"Well, if it isn't the Brothers Grimm," Zach said, taking a position by the door. "Plotting more tales to frighten the bejesus out of unsuspecting children?"

"It's about time you showed," Adam said. "We were beginning to think you weren't coming."

"So I heard." Zach crossed to the bar Adam kept in the corner to pour himself a scotch. Something told him he was going to need it. "So what were you two up to when I came in?"

"Joanna." That came from Jon. "*We're* worried about her."

Zach recognized that tone and what it implied—that Zach wasn't, which wasn't true. Ever since Ray's death, she'd done nothing but stay at home and look after her kids, which wasn't like her. She hadn't even returned to work two months ago, as she was supposed to.

Her house was sparkling, but every time Zach saw her he sensed the emptiness inside her, the loss. But since he didn't know what to do about that, he'd let her be. He didn't know what his brothers expected him to do about it now.

"She needs to see someone, get past this." Adam cast a glance at Jon. "Dana's tried talking to her, but she's not getting through."

That didn't surprise Zach. If they shared one family trait in common it was that no one could get them to do something they didn't want to do. "What do you want me to do? Hog-tie her and leave her on a shrink's doorstep?"

Adam sighed. "It's a thought, but no. We were just expressing our frustration, really." He sipped from his own glass. "How are things going with you? I hear you got pulled in on this Amazon Killer thing."

Zach slid into the seat next to Jon. "Yeah."

"It's not going to be a problem having Stevie stay with you?"

"Not as long as all parties realize I'm probably not going to be in much. But Stevie's a responsible girl."

Adam made a face suggesting that wasn't entirely true. Zach grinned. "Don't worry. I'll lay down the law. Or if you're so worried about her staying with me, why doesn't she stay with this one over here?" He gestured toward his younger brother with his drink. Jon had a spare bedroom, just as he did.

"That one moved in with Dana two months ago."

Zach cast a surprised look at Jon. *Two months ago?* It surprised him less that his brother had made the move than the fact that no one had told him about it.

Zach winked at Adam, letting him know he intended to have a little fun with their younger brother. "Poor girl. Is this a short-term deal or are you planning to make an honest woman of her sometime soon?"

Jon's expression didn't betray the barest trace of humor. In fact, his jaw tightened and his eyes narrowed. "I'm not the one who has trouble finding the right bed."

Zach exhaled, letting his breath flow out over clenched teeth. He should have known better than to expect a different reaction. Neither of his brothers possessed much of a sense of humor, especially not where their women were concerned. He'd always been the odd man out in that regard. Hell, in any regard. Adam and Jon got along together in a way that he did not with either of them.

Both of them blamed him for the destruction of his own marriage. Nearly six years after the fact, Jon in particular still couldn't let it go. He'd considered Sherry a sister, much like Zach felt toward Barbara. Neither of them had forgiven him for what they saw as his betrayal of her.

He couldn't blame either of his brothers for thinking poorly of him for cheating on her. That's what they'd assumed and he hadn't told them any different. What difference did it make if they castigated him for imagined sins when he went unpunished for the ones he had? It seemed like a fair exchange, though it hurt sometimes to think his brothers could so easily think the worst of him.

Zach downed the remains in his glass, deposited it on the side table next to his chair and stood. "Well, it's time for me to get what I came for and go. Any chance Stevie's ready yet?"

As if on cue, Stevie burst into the room and launched herself at him. She threw her arms around his neck. "Uncle Zach, I'm so glad you're finally here."

Zach hugged her back, looking over her shoulder to where her mother stood framed in the doorway. He wasn't sure what to make of the expression on her face—concern, sadness, disappointment, or a combination of the three. Again, he wished someone would confide in him what was going on between mother and daughter. But if no one found it necessary to divulge such simple things as his brother's living arrangements, the chances of being informed of a more complex situation were nil.

He released his niece. "Are you ready to go?"

"My bags are by the front door."

Bags? Adam had given him the impression her stay would last only a few days. Then again, he was dealing with a teenage girl. He had no clue what all she might find essential to bring on a stay away from home.

"Let's go, then." He gestured toward the doorway. Just to be perverse, he added, "It's getting late."

Stevie went around to give her father a hug, but no similar gesture was given to her mother. Still Barbara followed them to the front door.

"Behave yourself for your uncle Zach," Barbara said.

Stevie just rolled her eyes and picked up the smallest of the three bags. "I'll be out in the car." She slung open the front door and marched out.

Zach turned to Barbara and embraced her. "Don't worry, I'll take care of her."

She hit him on the shoulder. "I know you will." She took a step back from him. "You better."

For a minute, Zach contemplated asking her to confide in him. Barbara was the only one who knew the truth about his marriage, having weaseled it out of him at a low moment. She'd kept his confidence all this time. He wished she trusted him enough to share hers.

The sound of the horn blaring outside cost him the opportunity. Barbara gestured toward the door. "Her Highness awaits."

With a sigh Zach picked up the remaining two bags and headed outside. He put them in the trunk before sliding into the driver's seat. Stevie had already switched from his radio station to one that blared rap noises at a high decibel. He switched it back and lowered the volume. She looked at him as if he'd just killed her pet hamster. "I have a few things to say before we get home."

"Go ahead. I figured as much," she said in a voice that sounded both bored and impatient.

He pulled out of the driveway onto the quiet suburban street. "I'm glad to have you stay with me if that's what you want." Even if Jon hadn't moved in with Dana, Stevie would have picked his place as her spot of refuge instead of his younger brother's. Zach was the cool uncle, the one she thought she could cajole into giving her more freedom and keeping a less watchful eye. She wasn't wrong, but he didn't intend to let her steamroller over him, either.

"I know, Uncle Zach, and if I didn't say thank you before, I mean it."

"But there are a few rules you'll have to follow."

She sighed, resting her elbow on the window frame. "Now you sound like my dad."

Since that was his intent, he didn't argue with her. "No cutting school, no 'forgetting' to do your homework."

Her mouth dropped open. "I go to Fieldston. They'd kick me out if I did that."

"No running up a huge phone bill talking all night."

"I have my cell phone."

Zach slid a glance at her. That addressed the expense of her phone habit but not the hours of it. He could live with that. "I don't suppose I have to get into drinking or drugs."

"Please. My dad told me he'd take me in himself if he ever caught me doing drugs."

Zach smiled. It was the same thing his father had said when they were young. "No boys unless I'm in the house."

"You're not serious, right? That's so unfair."

Zach noticed that was the only condition of his she objected to, leading him to believe that might be the issue she and her mother clashed over. "We can always turn around."

Her hand shot out to cover his on the steering wheel. "All right, all right. But can I have someone over if you're home?"

"We'll see."

She relaxed against her seat, folding her hands in her lap. She was staring out the opposite window, pensive.

"Any chance you want to tell me what's going on between you and your mother?"

She shook her head.

Well, that made it unanimous, at least. Zach pulled off the New England Thruway at Connor Street, the same exit Ingrid Beltran had used the night she was killed. He traveled the same length of service road where her body had been found, only now there was a patrol car stationed there.

"This is where that girl got killed, isn't it?"

That was close enough to the truth for him to agree. "Yes."

"She was only a year older than me."

Zach hadn't thought about it in those terms before, or in relation to Stevie. Adam and Barbara worked hard to afford a nice house outside the city, the best schools, but given the coverage the story had garnered in the media already, she could hardly have missed it. From all accounts so far, Beltran had lived a life nearly sheltered as Stevie's. Which led him to the question that bothered him that no one yet had answered: How had this man gotten this girl to get in his car?

The prostitutes were easy to figure out. That's what hookers did. They got in the car to earn their money and, as often happened, they got something they hadn't bargained for. Even Stevie knew not to get in a stranger's car. Why hadn't this other girl figured that out? He couldn't say. It was an unfortunate truth that often when you shielded your children from the ugliness of life you deprived them of the ability to cope with it when it was shoved in their faces.

"Are they going to catch him, Uncle Zach?"

He smiled in a way that he hoped reassured her. If he had anything to say about it they would.

Alex sat in her living room, nursing a glass of wine while she waited for the eleven o'clock news to start. She didn't usually drink alcohol of any kind, but today she'd needed something to take the edge off. She'd dug up her personal files on Walter Thorpe and had Alice xerox a copy for Zach. She'd made sure they got there by five o'clock, preferring to take him at his word that he'd be back if she didn't comply. However, most of her records were still with the hospital, as they were work produced from that job. If he wanted them, he'd have to look there for them.

She'd brought the original files home. For the first time, she regretted taking such detailed notes, since there was a lot to go through. But if Thorpe had revealed to her his propensity for such violence, it would be here, which meant she'd missed it. She intended to be more thorough this time around.

The first papers in the file were Thorpe's intake sheet

that held personal information. Thorpe had refused to give her any of the information pertaining to his family, not even his mother's name. That in itself wasn't un-usual. Many clients had difficulty revealing personal in-formation at the start. There were plenty who had given her fake addresses and phone numbers so that they were untraceable should they decide not to come back. She couldn't remember how it had gone with Walter in par-ticular, especially since his referral had come from the state.

She scanned through the notes she'd written on Thorpe's childhood. Or at least his childhood as he'd re-ported it to her. That was part of the trouble with psychi-atry: You didn't know any fact; you only knew what the client told you. But Thorpe reported only the last of the triumvirate of predictive behaviors evident in the histo-ries of serial killers: animal cruelty, fire starting, and enuresis—bedwetting—until he was twelve years old.

But that didn't mean Thorpe's life had been problem-free. He reported having been abused by an older boy in grade school and his mother died when he was ten. Thorpe and his sister had been scheduled to go to the same foster home, but the sister ran away before the placement was made.

He didn't hear from her again until he was in his twenties. She was still living upstate while he was here in New York. The two started up a long-distance relation-ship. Alex didn't know if that relationship continued, but his sister had divorced herself from his crimes, refus-ing to attend his trial. Alex had never met her and got the impression she didn't approve of his therapy despite the fact that it had been court-ordered.

At first glance, nothing jumped out at her suggesting that Thorpe could turn out to be the kind of monster who could kill and mutilate so many young women. She intended to be more thorough in her examination of her notes, but tonight the wine was making her sleepy. After the news she'd head up to bed. Tomorrow was another day, one she would hopefully greet more well rested than she had the present one.

Alex closed her folder and tossed it onto the coffee table in front of her as she heard the music signaling the news was about to begin. She yawned, trying to banish her sleepiness long enough to make it through the first couple of stories. She figured this story had to be one of the first items if not the lead. Despite what Zach had told her about the police releasing Thorpe's name, that part of the story hadn't made it into the afternoon newscasts.

After the anchor team of a black man and an Asian woman introduced themselves, the camera narrowed in on the woman. "This just in on the case of the Amazon Killer that claimed the life of young Ingrid Beltran." A picture of the young woman in what looked to be a cheerleading outfit appeared in the top left corner of the screen. "A source close to the police investigation has revealed that investigators are focusing on this man, Walter Thorpe, as the Amazon Killer." Thorpe's mug shot replaced Beltran's picture on the screen. "Thorpe, also known as the Gentleman Rapist, was convicted of attacking several Upper East Side women in 1999, and has apparently turned toward the macabre. Thorpe is believed to be armed. Anyone spotting him should immediately call police."

Alex watched the broadcast, her mouth opened, her surprise increasing with every word the woman spoke. Given the fact that Thorpe was missing, it didn't entirely surprise her that the police might release Thorpe's name as someone who they wanted to interview in connection with the crimes. This was different; they'd practically announced that they believed Thorpe to be the killer. That she didn't understand. Serial killers often fed off their own publicity. It was like handing a terrorist an

Uzi. More than that, it gave every crackpot in the city incentive to phone in false tips or claim to be the killer themselves, deflecting police resources from legitimate leads. Damn.

But the Asian woman wasn't finished yet. "Police have already questioned this woman, Dr. Alexandra Waters, Thorpe's former psychiatrist, in connection with the case." Alex didn't hear any more after that. Her attention was taken up by the photo of her that came onto the screen, a four-color version one that had appeared on the front cover of the *News*.

She'd forgotten how unflattering that picture was. She looked like an idiot and she felt like one every time she saw it. If she hadn't gone to see McKay, that part of the story, inaccurate as it was, would never have made it onto the screen.

Oh God. She'd thought it would have been bad enough when anyone digging into Thorpe's story might have stumbled on her name. Now no one had to go digging. There she was, live and in color. Zach had definitely not mentioned that.

Part of her was certain that Zach would have told her about it had he known. If he'd told her about the planned release of Thorpe's name, why wouldn't he have told her about the release of her own? Still, doubt niggled in the back of her mind. She'd once thought the young man she knew would never betray her, but he'd proven her wrong about that, too.

The sound of her phone ringing startled her. Her first thought was that it might be Zach. She didn't want to speak to him now. She let the phone ring until whoever was on the other end of the line gave up.

Eight

Zach stood at the doorway to his spare bedroom that had been decorated in early IKEA, facing his niece. He'd left her alone for fifteen minutes to take a call. In that short span of time, she'd spread her things through the small room in a way that suggested she'd been living there for years. Again he wondered how long she intended to stay, but since he didn't plan on bringing that up again, he let it slide. He'd just wish her good night and go to bed himself.

"What's up, Uncle Zach?" Stevie asked from her spot on the bed. She was brushing the fur of a stuffed dog with the same care you would lavish on a real pet.

"I came to ask you if you needed anything, but I can see you've made yourself at home. If that veterinarian thing you want to do doesn't work out, you should give decorating a try."

She laughed. "Thanks."

"Do you need me to drop you at school in the morning?"

"No, my dad already called the school. The bus will pick me up here tomorrow."

For the exorbitant price Adam paid for the service, they'd better. "Good night, then. Go to sleep. It's getting late."

"Yes, Dad," she teased.

He winked at her, backed out the door, and closed it behind him. But as he turned to walk away, he heard Stevie's cell phone ring.

Shaking his head he made his way down the hall toward the stairs. Good Lord, what had he gotten himself into? He didn't know a damn thing about handling teenage girls. Aside from the one's he'd known during his own adolescence the only teenage girl he'd had any experience with was Alex. But Alex had never been a girl in the same way that Stevie was.

He couldn't say even now why it had been so important to him to win Alex over. It went beyond wanting to get along with his partner's family, though that was there, too. Sammy was the first parental influence he'd known since his father died so many years before. Although he was way too old to really need one, he appreciated it. With Alex it was something different.

If he wanted to be truthful with himself, he knew that part of it was the wound to his male vanity. He'd met few women, young or old, black or white, rich or poor, or whatever, who didn't have some positive reaction to him. His mother had labeled him the charmer of the family long before he was old enough to know what that meant. Alex, when she chose to look at him at all, pondered him as if he were some medical curiosity science had yet to figure out.

He had also sensed a sadness in her and a wariness unexplained by anything he knew of except the loss of her mother. He identified with that, even though he'd had longer than she to deal with his own loss. But at least she'd still had her father, overbearing and overprotective as Sammy was. Zach had once remarked to Sammy that he'd never seen Alex go out, that she didn't seem to have any friends.

Sammy had cast him a scoffing look. "She's got me. What does she need with friends?"

This from a man who could have dined at a different house every night of the year if he chose, a man Alex seemed to regard as suspect as she did him.

No, Alex was all alone. He identified with that, too. Even though he had siblings, none of them understood him; none of them tried to. He'd learned to cope with that, but in the end it was probably what drove him to befriend her—that maybe he could show her that someone understood, at least a little.

He hadn't given up, and eventually he'd come to realize she had sort of a crush on him. He'd been careful not to encourage that, but in the end what did it matter? He'd cost her both her father and her innocence. In retrospect, she would have been better off without him.

He settled on the sofa in the living room sofa, intending to watch the tail end of the news on one of the cable channels servicing the Bronx. Almost immediately the male of the anchor duo affected a somber expression.

"Recapping our top story, Walter Thorpe, the so-called Gentleman Rapist, is being sought by police in connection with the Amazon Killer case. Police have already spoken with this woman, forensic psychologist Alexandra Waters . . ."

Zach tuned out the minute an unflattering picture of Alex replaced Thorpe's mug shot on the screen. Damn. Who the hell had leaked that information to the press? His first thought was McKay, who hadn't bothered to hide his disgruntlement, both at being replaced and that Thorpe's name hadn't gone public already.

Had he taken it on himself to disseminate the information and impugn Alex in the process? From the tenor of the report it sounded as if Alex was either collaborating with the police or hiding something from them, neither of which was true. Or had Craig changed his mind? Zach doubted it. They'd spent the day tracking down leads on Thorpe without any success. But as Zach saw it, desperation had yet to set in. But he suspected whoever let out the information was on the force. No one on the outside could have known about Alex's involvement. One thing he knew for certain, Alex hadn't spilled the beans herself.

Someone's head was going to roll tomorrow when he found out who it was, even if it was the new boss. There had been no reason to give Alex's name to the press except to embarrass her or perhaps coerce further cooperation. Neither motive was acceptable to him.

Damn whoever it was. He could imagine how Alex must feel seeing herself on the eleven o'clock news. She had to figure that he'd known about the story beforehand and neglected to warn her about it. He had enough to make up for without adding more shit to the pile.

For now, he'd have to live with that. She'd made it clear that she didn't want anything to do with him except as it pertained to his case. She wasn't thrilled about that either, but she'd put up with him on those terms. She wouldn't appreciate him doing what it was in his mind to do—go see her and explain. She probably wouldn't even open the door to him. There was nothing more he could do tonight. He might as well go to bed.

As he passed Stevie's room on the way to his own, he thought he heard a girlish giggle. He couldn't see any light coming from underneath the door, but that didn't mean anything. He knocked on the door. "Go to sleep."

Silence.

That didn't fool him either. He waited a moment, listening, then heard Stevie say in a hushed voice, "It's okay. I think he's gone," presumably to whoever was on the other end of her cell phone line.

"Is this somebody's idea of a sick fucking joke?" Captain Craig strode into the office space at the corner of the second floor that had been allotted to detectives working the case. They'd been accorded a small open area and a few desks, phones, computers, plus a small office and an interrogation room cum conference room.

Zach looked up from his own paper and focused on Craig. Rumor had it that the captain's ruddy complexion was owed to a bad case of rosacia or too many martini breakfasts depending on who you spoke to. Today the cause of the redness in his complexion was clear: anger.

Craig slapped the newspaper down on the nearest desk, scanning the faces in the room. "If there's anything anyone needs to tell me, I'll be in the office. Oh, and somebody find me Walter Thorpe."

As the captain stalked away, several heads, including Zach's, turned in McKay's direction. He stared back with an expression that spoke more of indignation than of guilt. Despite McKay's disgruntlement, Zach didn't think he was responsible. He was too much of a company player, too ambitious to risk being censured for something like this. Beside that, the guy just didn't have the balls.

But too much of the information was accurate and known only to the police to have been anything but an inside job. But if not McKay, then who?

Regardless of what McKay thought, Craig pulled the plug for a variety of reasons, all of which made sense to Zach: The foremost of which was that no one had yet determined what reaction seeing his name in the press would have on Thorpe. Would he revel in it or would it force him farther underground? Some of these guys craved publicity and would go to outrageous lengths to perpetuate it—including killing again.

Smitty and one of the other guys trained by the FBI had come up with a profile. It contained the usual white male between thirty and forty, yadda, yadda, but any profile was flawed in that it could tell you who but not why. It could tell you, as this one did, that the subject was highly organized and rigidly ritualistic, but not what prompted the ritual. Nor could it explain the killer's absence from the scene. From late June to the middle of November, there had been a killing roughly every twenty-eight days, then two months with nothing. Now he'd picked up again on a date consistent with his original timeline.

Nor could it get inside this guy's head. The profile was a tool more of the criminalist than the psychologist, and certainly not the province of psychic faith healers or whatever like you saw on TV. It was a tool, but Zach wondered if they would ever catch this guy if they didn't know what made him tick.

Zach looked over at Smitty, who was seated at the desk beside his.

Smitty hung up from a call and grinned. "That was one Jack Meoff, who called to inform me that Thorpe was at that moment getting a blow job from my imaginary sister." Smitty shook his head. "Damn kids."

"Want to get out of here?"

"You got something?"

Zach shrugged, hoping Smitty would get his message.

Smitty grinned again. "I think I'm beginning to like you."

Zach chuckled as both he and Smitty rose and put on their jackets. Outside, Zach breathed in the cool morning air. Overnight the temperature had risen substantially, promising spring wouldn't be too far off. Neither he nor Smitty had been assigned a car, so they took his own.

"So, where are we heading?" Smitty asked as Zach pulled away from the curb. "Sammy's daughter's office isn't far from here."

Zach slid a glance toward Smitty. "I knew there was a reason I liked you, too."

"Is this a professional visit or is something else going on between you two?"

"No." That wasn't a complete answer, but it seemed to mollify Smitty. Or at least he didn't say anything for a few moments. True, he did want to see Alex. He wanted to make sure she was all right. But he had another reason as well. Despite what flimsy evidence they had to the contrary, he was beginning to believe her that Thorpe wasn't involved.

He'd spent the small hours of the morning when he couldn't sleep checking her out online. She'd worked on some pretty high-profile cases, almost always for the prosecution. He'd even heard of some of the cases, but the change in last names had thrown him. He'd assumed the Dr. Alex Waters in question was a man.

She'd once been on the staff of Bellevue Hospital, an assistant professor of psychiatry specializing in forensic psychology. He wondered whether she'd given up that position or been forced to after the debacle with Thorpe. Either way, she had the chops to help him get inside this killer's mind, whether it proved to be Thorpe or not.

"She's grown up to be a fine-looking woman," Smitty said.

Zach darted another glance at Smitty. His face bore a benign expression, as if he were just making conversation. Zach wasn't that stupid. But he couldn't argue with Smitty. Part of the reason he could dismiss her so easily as a former conquest when he saw her in the conference room was that he could have imagined himself with her. He could still imagine it, and had over the last couple of days. But at the moment, his libido didn't enter the picture, not when he could barely get her to speak to him. Part of the reason he'd brought Smitty along was so that she would see this visit as an official one and not throw him out before he got a chance to speak with her.

To Smitty he said, "What's your point? You looking for a date?" That came out with a little more of an edge than Zach intended, but what the hell?

"Not me. I leave those sweet young things alone. I've got a sweet old thing at home that would kill me dead."

Zach chuckled. "I'm just trying to do what McKay should have done in the first place. Figure out why she doesn't think Thorpe is the guy."

"You believe her?"

"Maybe."

Zach turned onto Tremont Avenue at the corner where Alex's building sat. There was a crowd outside looking bored that he immediately recognized as reporters: three television news vans and at least twenty people. Damn. He could imagine how much Alex liked this. He drove past the vans to the entrance to the parking lot on the other side of the building and pulled into a spot near the entrance.

In the short time it took him to park, the reporters had galvanized themselves and surrounded the car. Though they were in an unmarked car and neither his face nor Smitty's had made the news, those savvy enough recognized the police when they saw them and peppered them with questions, mostly regarding what information Alex might be hiding from them. Zach ignored all of them, but his mood soured, knowing Alex must have gone through the same gauntlet herself that morning.

The first time he'd come here, the office had been quiet but the small waiting room had been full. Now it was just quiet. The receptionist stood as they approached. She recognized the police when she saw them, too and apparently she wasn't happy about it.

He stepped up to the desk. "Is Dr. Waters in?"

"She's in, but I doubt she wants to see you."

He doubted that, too, not that that would stop him. He was about to ask her to let Alex know he was here when she walked into the reception area. She was looking down at a folder. She stopped abruptly when she looked up and saw him.

A frown turned her lips down and her eyes narrowed. Her gaze went from him to Smitty beside him and back. "Unless you're here to clear that pack of vultures off my front door, I have nothing to say."

He could understand her anger, but that didn't change anything. "Has it been that bad all morning?"

"No. Some of them gave up and went home." She sighed and he could feel the exasperation in her. "Let's make this quick."

She turned back toward her office. At the same time Smitty gestured toward the bathroom in the corner with his chin and rubbed his hands. Zach nodded. He hadn't noticed Smitty had a cleanliness fetish before and doubted that was his motive now. He was deliberately giving him time alone with Alex. He didn't know whether to appreciate the gesture or not.

When they reached her office she turned to face him and motioned for him to enter first. "Where's your friend?"

He stepped inside her office but didn't go far. "Bathroom."

She shrugged, walking around her to lean her backside against her desk with her arms folded. "What's on the agenda today? Shredding my reputation or driving off my patients?"

"Neither. I need your help with something."

"I already told you that there's nothing I can tell you about Thorpe."

"Not him. Not exactly. I want your opinion on the profile we've developed. This is one sick bastard. I want to get inside his head."

"Then you believe me that it wasn't Thorpe?"

"I didn't say that."

She gave him a hard assessing look. After a moment she extended her hand toward the folder he carried. "What did you bring me?"

He gave her the folder. It contained the profile, photos from each crime scene, a couple of the autopsy reports, and assorted notes. She took the file, sat on the edge of the sofa, and spread out the information on the low glass coffee table in front of her. "Does McKay know you're showing this to me?" she asked without looking at him.

"McKay isn't in charge anymore." He hadn't cleared it with the new boss either, but since she didn't ask he didn't tell.

"You're right. This is one sick puppy. He abducts these girls, beats them, cuts off their breast, rapes them, and then strangles them. Is that the order of things?"

"It appears to be. Then he dumps them along the same stretch on the service road to the New England Thruway."

She nodded abstractedly, her attention still on the file. "There's a legal pad on my desk. Would you hand it to me."

He found it and gave it to her, then came around the other side of the sofa to sit next to her. Automatically she moved over a little, either to make room for him or to avoid him. Either way, the subtle scent of a floral perfume reached him.

Since she wasn't paying him any attention, he leaned back, resting an arm along the back of the sofa, watching her. She leaned forward to write something he couldn't see on the pad. In that position, her skirt had hiked up, displaying her long legs to midthigh. She'd always had an abundance of jet-black hair, even in her ponytail days. She brushed the mass of it back over her shoulder as if it were a bother. In that instant, he would have liked nothing more than to tame it for her with his own hands.

To distract himself, he asked, "Do you mind if I ask you a personal question?"

She glanced back at him over her shoulder, one hand holding down her hair so that she could see him. She said nothing, but her expression suggested he had to be out of his mind to attempt it.

"Where did the Waters come from?"

Her brow furrowed. "What waters?"

"Your last name."

"Oh." She turned back to what she was doing. "My married name."

Since he could see from there that she didn't wear a ring, he asked, "What happened?"

"The usual nonsense. I wanted a child; he was one."

That sounded like a pat answer, the one she reserved for nosy people butting in. He didn't believe her, but he couldn't get into that now, as Smitty chose that moment to make an appearance.

He sat in one of the seats opposite the sofa. "Any progress?"

Alex sat back and looked at Smitty. "I don't know about progress, but I do have several questions."

"Fire away," Smitty said.

She picked up her pad and surveyed it. "First, was it definitively established that these girls were prostitutes from the area?"

"I don't know," Zach answered honestly. He knew a couple of the girls were spotted in the area by witnesses. And when you found a woman with both PID, an inflammation of the cervix caused by multiple sex partners, as well as track marks or drugs in her system, the first thought was pro. "Does that make a difference?"

She shrugged. "I find it interesting that two of his victims were white. That strikes me as interesting, considering that the neighborhood is predominantly black. Even the hookers I've seen over there have all been black. So where did the white girls come from?"

He didn't have an answer for that. The assumption that the girls had been local prostitutes predated his involvement in the case. He'd simply taken it as a given. "What else?"

"Assuming for a moment the facts are right, you've got one bold killer on your hands. He hunts the same place he dumps. Even if the local police are only halfway competent they've got to figure they'll increase patrols in the area, making it harder to both troll and to dump. That's part of his game. He probably thinks he's very clever to outwit you."

"Why do you say that?"

"Think about it. You find a middle fingerprint under the seat. From what I've read, you didn't find a single print in any of the cars except those belonging to the owners. He didn't wipe the cars down, so that meant he must have been wearing gloves. What are the odds he took them off to adjust the seat? He was sending the police a giant fuck you."

He hadn't thought of that. He glanced at Smitty, who gazed back at him with a look that said *Didn't I tell you she was something?* He didn't need Smitty to remind him of that.

She brushed her hair over her shoulder. "This last murder is different in other ways, as well. If you look at the other girls' body type, they're all well endowed. This last girl is much thinner. Has her autopsy been done yet?"

"This afternoon. Why?"

"I'm betting the killer knew she wasn't a pro."

"Why?"

She dug through the stack of photos until she found the one she wanted, a picture of the girl's car. She passed it to Smitty "Was this her father's car?"

"Her mother's."

"How many hookers do you know who drive around with MD plates?"

Smitty handed him the photo. He'd noticed the plates before, but since it had been assumed the killer had mistaken her for a hooker, the car hadn't come into it. But if Thorpe or whoever had followed her from the gas station, he would have known. As he understood it, the gas station attendant that night, an eighteen-year-old boy, hadn't identified Thorpe as being in the station that night. Zach didn't know if he'd been asked about seeing the station wagon.

One thing he did know was that there'd been far more assumption than police work so far in this investigation.

Zack asked the next logical question. "So if she knew she wasn't a hooker, why did he pick her up?"

"This guy's a joker. What fun is there playing a game if you're the only one who knows you're playing? The police weren't paying him any attention so he decided to up the ante. Even if she was merely a doctor's daughter, her death was sure to draw more attention than a hooker's."

Zach sighed. Well, he had the answer to his question of whether the killer would shun the limelight or enjoy it. If Alex was right, he'd sought it out. That brought Alex to another question: Now that the killer had their attention, what did he plan to do with it?

Nine

Alex watched Zach as he digested the information she'd given him. He looked tired, as if he wasn't getting any more sleep than she. That would be understandable if it were true. It wasn't his case, but he worked it. If he was as conscientious now as he was when she had known him, that must weigh on him.

But it wasn't her job to soothe him. Surely there was a woman somewhere whose place she'd be usurping if she did. He didn't wear a ring, but that didn't mean there wasn't a woman in his life, or perhaps women. Her father used to call him Casanova in a way that was both censorious and approving. She didn't expect that he'd changed much in that regard.

She shook her head, as if clearing it. She didn't want to think about Zach, his women, or even her own relationship with him. There had been a time when if he'd asked her a question, she wouldn't have lied.

Alex stood and crossed to her desk to retrieve a file she'd left there. "There's something else." Better to focus on the case than the way her mind had been going. "I did a little checking on the Internet about Amazons. I haven't read through all of it yet."

She handed a stapled sheaf of papers to Smitty. "They

were purportedly a race of women living in Asia Minor in the Third Century B.C. They pinched off or cut off the right breast for ease in hunting but kept the left in order to suckle their girl children, which they kept. The male children were given to the neighboring tribe of men, the Gargarians, with whom the Amazons coupled. They raised the girl children themselves. By killing these women he may see himself avenging himself against some powerful woman who abandoned him, probably his mother."

Smitty passed the papers to Zach. "Talk about your twisted Oedipal complexes."

That wasn't quite accurate, but she wasn't going to argue about it. "That is, if mythology plays a part in this at all. He may have some other motivation. The press named him the Amazon Killer because of what he did. Only he can tell us definitively why, and only if he wants to."

Even then, who knew how much of what a psychopath said could be believed? Berkowitz had claimed some dog had told him to kill, part of his "crazy act" that he hoped would lead to commitment to a mental hospital rather than incarceration. It was only later that he'd revealed that claim had been a sham. Currently he was pretending to be a born-again Christian. Only God knew whether that was another scam.

Zach's cell phone rang. He excused himself and rose from the sofa to stand off to the side to take the call. Though he spoke too softly for her to make out his words, his posture and the timbre of his voice suggested he was talking to a woman.

Whether he was or not wasn't her business. She turned her gaze away from him, back to Smitty, who'd stood. Again, she was struck by the familiarity of his face.

As if to answer her unspoken question, he said, "I knew your father, years ago. A good man. A bit of a hard-ass."

It didn't surprise her that this man knew her father.

Everyone knew him. She couldn't count the times some cop or other person related to law enforcement had found out she was the Bull's daughter and insisted on relaying some story of her father's exploits, particularly back when she had her maiden name. Part of the reason she'd kept Devon's name was to discourage the association. But saying her father was a bit of a hard-ass was like saying Mussolini had been a bit of a dictator.

Her gaze drifted to Zach, still on the phone, then back. "So are you two going steady?" she asked, referring to them partnering on this case.

He winked at her. "Only until I find someone with better legs."

She smiled. She liked Smitty, especially since he'd been her only champion in that disastrous conference room meeting. Without her meaning to, her gaze slid back to Zach, who seemed to be wrapping up his conversation.

"Not to worry," Smitty said, drawing her attention. "I've got my eye on that one."

For a moment she wondered what he'd read in her face to prompt that comment. Usually she wasn't that transparent. But Zach abruptly closed his phone and turned back to them.

He looked from her to Smitty, then back. "So where does that leave us?"

She wondered if he was referring to the case or her conversation with Smitty. She chose to believe the former. He'd been all business since he walked in the door, aside from that one "personal" question he'd asked, which anyone who knew her as a girl might have asked out of simple curiosity. Even when they were alone, he'd never mention their past or whatever it was that had driven him to seek her out that first night. She wondered, with a touch of bitterness, if the woman on the phone had anything to do with his willingness to take no as an answer from her.

Alex shrugged, returning her mind to the man they all sought. Up until now, this guy had operated like clockwork. Even when he didn't make a kill he stuck to his schedule as if he had. But he had deviated from his pattern, picking a woman who didn't fit his usual victim profile. He was upping the ante, making sure the police and the media paid attention to him. She wished she knew what had caused him to skip those two months— maybe illness or unavailability to his hunting ground. Barring that knowledge, she made the best guess she could.

"Considering he's off his pattern, what he does next is anyone's guess. At the most you've got twenty-four days before he strikes again."

"Who was on the phone?" Smitty asked once they were back in the car and out of the reach of the reporters.

From the tone of Smith's voice, Zach figured he didn't think it was an official call. He was fishing. Since Zach had nothing to hide, he said, "My sister-in-law. My niece is staying with me a few days. She wanted to make sure she got to school all right."

"Jon got married?"

Zach had forgotten Smitty and his younger brother must know each other since both worked homicide in the same precinct. "My older brother Adam's wife."

Smitty shrugged and settled back in his seat, as if it made no difference either way, which it didn't. "Where to next?"

"I'm thinking of going to see the girls' parents. Alex got me wondering if there's some connection between the girls that no one has explored yet." It had bothered him from the beginning that no witness could be found who had seen either Thorpe or the cars he'd stolen driving around. The spot where he'd left the car was deserted save for a few businesses on the block east and a series of private houses one block south.

How did he know the girls would be there? There wasn't even anywhere from which to observe the area, unless maybe the overpass that served pedestrians crossing over the highway into Co-Op City. But then, he would have to be on foot. Then again, he could have stashed his car in one of the motel lots and waited for his prey to show up. But wouldn't it have been easier to lure someone there, maybe to one of those motels than to lie in wait? Otherwise, there was no guarantee of keeping his schedule.

The bodies of the first two girls had been claimed by families out of state. The third girl's body had never been claimed. Her identity remained a mystery, since no one responded to the missing person's bulletin and her prints yielded no hits. The fourth girl lived on the west side of the Bronx, off Orloff Avenue. They headed there first.

Like the apartments in Co-op City, the building they went to was part of the Mitchell-Lama housing initiative that provided affordable co-ops to Bronx residents. The buildings were well cared for and the apartments were spacious.

Veronica Hassler's mother answered the door to their knock. "Yes."

Looking at Magda Hassler, Zach could imagine from whom the daughter had gotten her figure. She was tall and what his father would kindly have referred to as big-boned, not obese. He'd put her in her midsixties, a bit on the late side for having a fourteen-year-old daughter. There was a hardness in the woman's green eyes Zach didn't expect considering they'd already announced they were the police, the ones ostensibly working to find out who'd killed their daughter.

He showed the woman his badge, in the event that

would help. "I'm Detective Stone. This is Detective Smith. We'd like to talk to you about your daughter."

"We've already spoken to the other detective."

The way she spoke the word "detective" clued him in to the problem. Damn McKay, was there anything about this investigation he hadn't screwed up yet? "We're here to follow up," Zach said in a tone that suggested they were there to clean up his mess rather than exacerbate it.

The woman hesitated a moment. "All right."

She led them to a large living room just off the front hall. It was decorated in shades of cream, pastel green, and gold. She gestured toward the brocade sofa. "Please, sit down."

They did as she suggested. The plastic slipcovers crinkled as he and Smitty settled down.

"Thank you, Mrs. Hassler," Zach started. "First let me say we're sorry for your loss. We don't want to take up too much of your time."

"It's all right. Just so you understand, my daughter was no prostitute like they're saying in the papers. She was a good girl. She didn't even have a boyfriend."

Zach said nothing to that. He'd seen the autopsy report. Her daughter had been found with cocaine in her system. From the condition of her nasal cavity it wasn't a new activity. He was no Pollyanna, but if the girl was doing drugs, he'd bet she was into other things as well. He'd also bet mom and dad had no clue about any of them.

"Do you know what Veronica was doing in that neighborhood?"

As he expected, he shook her head. "As far as I know, she didn't even know anyone in that area."

"Had you noticed a change in her recently? New routines? New friends?"

"She'd started staying out, late, you know?"

Zach nodded.

"It was those girls. She'd started a new school. Things were different. We bought her a computer for her birthday. When she was home she was on that thing."

Zach swallowed. If the killer had contacted her on the Internet, it wouldn't be the first time some naive girl had been drawn into a situation with a person she didn't expect. "Can I see her room?"

An uncertain expression came over Mrs. Hassler's face, as if the request surprised her, but she stood. "All right."

Zach followed her down a narrow hall, irritation rising in him, wondering if McKay had gotten this far or if he'd stopped at making the notification.

Mrs. Hassler stopped at the third door down the hall. "This is Ronnie's room."

She opened the door, turned on the overhead light, then stepped back for him to enter.

He crossed the threshold, examining the room. A four-poster bed covered with a pink comforter and pillows in matching shams rested along one wall. A dresser with a circular mirror took up the wall perpendicular to the door. A rolltop desk sat at the opposite end of the room. An Apple laptop sat on its surface.

The maple furniture smelled of lemon polish and the curtains had been opened, letting in warm late morning sunshine. The girl had been dead since October, but the entire space looked as fresh as if its owner were expected home later in the day after school.

"Ronnie always keeps her things neat."

This *is* Ronnie's room. Ronnie *keeps* her things neat. Her mother spoke about her as if she were still alive. He felt sorry for the woman, not only because her only child was gone, but because she hadn't dealt with it in any meaningful way. He'd seen it a million times— parents who couldn't deal when death or harm came to their children. He couldn't fathom the depth of their grief and didn't pretend to. All he could provide them with were answers, and he did his best to find them.

He was grateful though that she hadn't been observant enough to notice that Smitty hadn't followed them, leaving the other man time to scope out what he could of the rest of the apartment without being intrusive. Zach intended to keep her here until Smitty surfaced, then give her something to do to get her to leave them alone.

"Did Veronica have an address book that you know of? Did she keep a diary of any kind?"

"She had one of those Palm things, you know, an organizer. She probably had it with her when . . ." Mrs. Hassler's eyes brimmed and she lowered her head. "I'm sorry." She sniffled. "I didn't find a diary."

Smitty chose that moment to make his appearance. "Do you think one of her friends might know if she kept one? It might be helpful."

Mrs. Hassler turned in Smitty's direction. If she found anything strange about his rejoining them, she didn't show it. "Eleny might know. They were friends since they were girls. She lives two floors down."

"Can you write down her name and apartment number? And any of her other friends you know of?"

Mrs. Hassler nodded. "I'll be right back."

As Smitty came into the room Zach walked to the window. He brushed aside the sheer white curtain to look out. There was a tree outside the window, but not close enough for someone to get into her window or for her to sneak out. To Smitty, he said, "Did you notice anything?"

"Only that this place feels like I've slipped into a time warp. When was the last time you saw plastic slipcovers? I think my grandmother got rid of hers in '73."

Maybe that was the problem here. Too many generations separated mother and daughter. He couldn't imagine the woman he'd seen knowing how to manage an out-of-control teenager. Hell, he was the cool uncle, and he couldn't get Stevie to go to sleep.

They spent a few moments checking the room, finding nothing of note, before Mrs. Hassler came back holding a sheaf of paper in her hand. She extended it toward Zach. "These are all the names I can think of. Will that help?"

"Thank you." He gestured toward the desk. "We'd like to take a look at what's on her computer, if you don't mind."

"No, take it. Neither my husband nor I know how to use it."

Smitty, who was closer to the desk, picked it up. "We'll get this back to you as soon as we can."

They left after that, with a promise to Mrs. Hassler to keep her and her husband informed of their progress. Once they were back in the car, Zach said, "Where to next?" in imitation of Smitty's earlier words.

"What say we drop the computer off and head over to Lilly's? There ought to be enough time for a quick bite before we need to go to the autopsy."

"A meal and a show," Zach said, though he wasn't looking forward to either.

Ten

About five o'clock Alex decided to call it a day. Usually she kept Wednesdays light, not accepting any appointments after four o'clock. She used the rest of the day to transcribe notes, fill out paperwork, and take care of other drudgeries. She could just as easily do these things from home on her laptop.

Only a few stalwart reporters were waiting for her when she left the building. Apparently not every media outlet in the city had the wherewithal to keep a crew all day on a story that wasn't producing results. She got into her car with a minimum of fuss and went home.

Dressed in a short apricot nightgown and robe and eating a dinner of reheated Chinese food from two nights ago, Alex quickly finished the work she'd brought home from her office. But as she turned her attention to the printout she hadn't finished reading, restlessness set in. She knew it wasn't the case or even Zach's reappearance in her life, though both weighed on her mind. It was this house.

It had been a mistake to move back in here after her marriage dissolved. There were too many memories, both good and bad, clinging like ghosts to this place. She'd known that almost from the beginning, but she'd held on. This house was the only place on earth that for her held the memory of her mother.

But before, those memories had been mostly dormant, an underlay to her conscious mind. Zach's reappearance in her life breathed new life into them, making them stronger and more potent. She didn't want to remember, but apparently she had no choice. Even her dreams were swamped with images she thought she'd forgotten.

Brushing her papers aside, she stood and walked to the piano. Maybe part of her malaise was her own fault. The same photos still stood on its surface as a visual reminder of what was. She picked up a photo of herself and her father taken at her high school graduation. Zach had held the camera.

The picture itself was an oddity, one of the few in which she'd been smiling. She'd known then that freedom was only a few months away. She'd be going to Adelphi in the fall, much as her father hated that. She'd learned from the master. When the time came she'd blackmailed him into letting her go. Her grades ensured her a full scholarship; he only had to pay for room, board, and books.

She'd loved being at school. For the first time in her life she had friends and freedom, and she flourished. She hadn't worried about how her father was faring in her absence until the last night she was home during Easter break.

For no reason she'd woken in the middle of the night. The sound of the TV playing low drew her to the living room. Her father was sitting on the sofa wearing his robe loosely tied over a wife beater T-shirt and a pair of boxer shorts. His feet, encased in a pair of leather slippers, rested on the coffee table. He looked disheveled, exhausted, and, beyond that, ill.

"What are you doing up, little girl? Don't you have to go back to school tomorrow?"

"The TV woke me." It was a lie. The skeptical look he cast her told her he knew it, too. But she wasn't the only one telling untruths lately. In the last week her father had taken to having a "lie down" after dinner almost every night, and particularly those nights when Zach was here. That wasn't like him, and as domineering as he'd always been it surprised her that he'd leave her alone in the same room with any man for that long, regardless of the fact that he was in the house and the man in question was his partner.

She'd never asked him about it directly, but she did now. "What's up with you? Why do you keep leaving me alone with Zach?"

That question hadn't come out as she had hoped. It sounded as if she were complaining, which she wasn't. She'd harbored a secret crush on Zach since almost the first day he walked in the door. At least she hoped it was secret. If either her father or Zach had noticed, neither had said anything to her about it.

"You could do worse, little girl." He paused, adjusting his robe, for so long that it made her wonder what he meant by that, until he continued. "As far as company goes, I mean."

She agreed with him, but that wasn't the point. She studied his face. Dark circles discolored the area beneath his eyes, though the rest of his complexion seemed pale. She hated knowing that she cared about the health of this man she both loved and hated, but she did. "Are you sick, Daddy?"

His eyebrows shot up at her use of the word "daddy." She never called him that except when other people were around. "What's the matter with you, girl? Can't a man get a little tired every once in a while without folks thinking he's going to die? I've worked this job more than twenty-five years. Whose business is it if I want to lie down every once in a while?"

She didn't believe him. It was too much bluster even for him. "If you're sick, I have a right to know."

"Don't you worry about me, little miss. Ain't nothing going to kill me except the job, and even that's a long way off." He turned his attention to the TV screen, ignoring her.

She went back to her room after that. For the next week back at school she considered calling Zack to ask if he knew anything about her father's condition. In the end she decided against it. If her father had confided in Zach and asked him to keep the secret, Zach likely would. She didn't want to put him in the position of lying to her, nor did she want to hear him lie to her. Besides, it wasn't his responsibility to tell her, it was her father's.

In the end it didn't matter. Two weeks later her father's prediction came true. He was shot to death while on duty. He'd bled to death in Zach's arms waiting for an ambulance to arrive. And it had been Zach who'd taken her to see her father's body when she'd insisted. He'd been the one to stand beside her as they put him in the ground. And later, when everyone else had gone home . . .

She shook her head, not wanting to dwell on that time. She'd known Zach was vulnerable, that he blamed himself for her father's death, that he'd needed comforting as much as she'd needed something else. She couldn't blame him for walking out on her the next day. He'd considered himself an honorable man, one of the good guys, and that being with her would have tarnished that self-image.

It hadn't done her much good, either. She'd gone back to school to finish the semester, but she'd been changed, both by her father's death and that night. She'd held it together all those years after her mother died, yet when she was finally free, she lost it, drowning herself in the one thing every man in her life had seemed to value her for.

It wasn't until she'd found herself standing at the campus precipice known less for its beauty than the number of suicides who leaped from it each year that she got herself together, sought help, and tried to rebuild her life. She never wanted to go back there again, either literally or any other way. Watching stones crumble at your feet to fall into the watery ravine below, wondering if the unstable land would hold you or set you free, was no way to live a life.

The sound of the doorbell ringing pulled her from her reverie. She put the photo back where it belonged, then tightened the sash on her robe. She could imagine only one person showing up at her house at this hour. He still needed something from her, though she wasn't exactly sure what.

If it was absolution, he hadn't asked for her forgiveness. If it was her renewed friendship, he'd allowed her to rebuff him easily. But she did notice the way he looked at her. He wasn't exactly broadcasting his attraction to her, nor was he hiding it, either. It simply existed between them. She recognized it because she felt it, too. On some level she wondered if that one night between them had been a fluke or if things between them could really be that good.

Whatever he wanted, she couldn't give it to him. She had used his vulnerability against him once and she would do it again if she had to to preserve herself. She only hoped it didn't come to that.

When she opened the door to him, she saw he wore the same clothes he'd had on earlier. Didn't this man ever go home?

She noticed the way his gaze strayed from her face, down her body and back again. His perusal of her wasn't obvious, but noticeable enough for her to detect it. His

Adam's apple bobbed, but he made no reference to her appearance. "Can I come in, Alex?"

Since whatever conversation they were about to have was best accomplished away from her doorstep she stepped back and let him enter. He proceeded to about the same spot he had two nights ago.

Unlike the other night, she didn't bother to claim a seat on the sofa. She drew to a stop a couple of feet away from him and folded her arms in a silent challenge. "Well?"

For a long moment, he said nothing, leaving her again to wonder what he wanted. He'd told her before that if he wanted to talk to her about the case he'd see her in her office. So, did that make this a personal visit of some sort? She doubted it, since the strongest emotion she read off him was not supplication or even desire, but agitation.

She sighed. "What is it, Zach? It's late and I was about to go to bed."

It wasn't a total lie. Once she'd started strolling down memory lane, she'd known she no longer had a head for much of anything else that night. Already, a dull pulse beat at her temple signaling another migraine.

His eyes scanned her face. It wasn't a sexual gaze, yet in some ways she felt laid bare in ways that had nothing to do with her lack of clothing. Did he know how much these nocturnal visits of his were killing her, and if he did, why didn't he stay home?

"I just wanted to tell you, you were right. Thorpe found the girls on the Internet. The Hassler girl's best friend told us she'd snuck out of the house to meet some guy. Three of them had Web pages at Yourplacedotcom. It's a site kids frequent. They all had pictures up, where they went to school, everything but their goddamn home addresses. More information than you'd give to a stranger on the street."

True, but a stranger on the Internet seemed much

more harmless. "Kids assume their information is only going to be viewed by other kids."

"Obviously, they got that wrong. There are a hell of a lot of sick folks out there waiting to prey on the naive."

She couldn't argue with that. But it wasn't necessarily naivete that got the kids in trouble. The adolescent personal myth that they were invincible was more likely to blame. Bad things happened to other people, not them, except when they didn't. She doubted he needed a lecture on the subject, anyway.

"What are you going to do about that?"

"We've got a couple of detectives working a sting already. We put this guy on their radar. Though we don't know what screen name he goes by. We're looking for a correlation between users all three girls corresponded with. The chat room for the site doesn't keep a log, and as far as we can tell, none of the girls saved instant messages from him."

Alex nodded, not knowing what else to add. Computer stalking wasn't an area of her expertise, though she knew it occurred with greater and greater frequency with more and more people online and the increasing deviousness of some of its users.

She regarded Zach, who'd stopped talking, shoving his hands in his trouser pockets. Although they'd exhausted their topic, there was something more, something he left unsaid. It was impossible to read what that might be from his expression, but she thought she knew anyway.

"Is that it, or are we going to get to the real reason why you're here?"

His gaze narrowed as he surveyed her face. "Which would be?"

She tilted her head to one side, considering him. "Let's face it, Zach. There's nothing you told me right now that couldn't have waited until morning, which begs the question, why did you bother to drive over here in the first place?"

He let out a heavy breath. "Look, Alex, I—"

"You don't need to put a nice face on it, Zach. Don't you think I noticed the way you looked at me? Not just now, but in my office? In that damn conference room when you didn't even know who I was?"

"That's not why I came here."

"Sure it is." She lifted her chin in a way that suggested she was sniffing the air. "I can practically smell it on you. You're thinking about that night. We'd just put my father in the ground, and there we were, just you and me. Do you remember that night, Zach? I know I do. "

If he hadn't been thinking about what happened between them before, she knew he was now. His gaze darkened and his nostrils flared. His voice when he spoke was huskier and deep. "What's your point?"

She paused a moment, gathering strength to say the words she planned. "How much money have you got this time? I'm not as cheap a date as I used to be."

His expression was half confused, half incredulous. "What the hell are you talking about? I never tried to buy you, Alex."

"No, but you sure as hell paid for me, didn't you?" For a moment, she stared up at him, angry, defiant. Until that moment, she had no idea how close to the surface her own emotions ran. She'd thought she'd been looking at the situation from a veil of distance, but all the old hurt and shame washed over her, making her more a victim of her words than he.

She started to move away from him, but he pulled her back with a hand on her arm. She didn't want to look up at him, but she felt drawn to do so nonetheless. Her gaze locked with his. His expression was no more readable than before. His hand rose to stroke his knuckles across her cheek. "It wasn't like that, Alex, and you know it."

She inhaled, willing her emotions to settle. It took all her willpower not to show him how much that simple caress affected her. Why did he have to be the only man to ever touch her like that, as if she were something precious deserving of his protection?

Unable to hold his gaze, she looked away. "Go home, Zach. Don't come back."

"Alex." He tilted her face up with a finger under her chin.

Reluctantly she looked up at him. His gaze searched hers. She knew what he wanted, but she couldn't give it to him. "Go."

His expression darkened as if a shadow had fallen over him. What she saw there was not anger, but pain, more pain than she'd intended to inflict. She shut her eyes as he released her, knowing what he'd do. A few moments later she heard her front door slam. A moment after that, his car roared to life and screeched away from the curb.

She opened her eyes and went to the front door to lock it. That accomplished she leaned her back against the surface, exhaling heavily. All she'd wanted was to ensure that he left the past alone, but she'd hurt him badly, certainly more than she'd intended. She'd have to live with that.

She pushed off the door. She'd never get to sleep now. She might as well get back to work.

Zach sat in one corner of the black leather sofa in his study with the lights out and a tumbler of scotch in his hand. He couldn't remember drinking any of it, but his stomach felt warm and rumbly in a way usually only achieved by the use of alcohol. He couldn't remember driving home from Alex's either, but he must have done so, considering he was here. He never should have gone to see her in the first place.

She'd been right about him; he had harbored an ulterior motive for seeing her, though not the one she suspected. Maybe if he'd been straight with her, she wouldn't have jumped to her own conclusions.

He sipped from the glass now. He might not have gone to Alex's place with any seduction plans in mind, but she was right about him remembering that night. Sense memories washed through him, heating him more than the alcohol did. It was the best and worst night of his life. She was a week shy of her eighteenth birthday. He had just turned twenty-two. He was too old for her, a fact that he remembered during saner times.

He remembered waking the next morning with her by his side, the shame that washed over him, knowing what he'd done. He didn't even have the excuse that he'd been drunk or so grief-filled that he hadn't known what he was doing. The only thing he had going in his favor was that he didn't made the first move.

He'd needed to get out of there, since he had no idea what to say to her when she woke. He'd put on his clothes and pulled whatever bills he had from his pocket and left them for her, not knowing if she had any money she could get her hands on. He'd left her a note, too, saying he'd call, but he didn't. Not at first. What could he say to her? The truth? That it had been a mistake?

It hadn't felt like a mistake. That was the problem. It had felt like the first right thing he'd done in a long time. But he couldn't allow what they shared to continue. He needed some distance to get himself together. By the time he finally returned her calls she wouldn't take his. A few days later she went back to college and that was that.

He'd never imagined she'd viewed the money as some kind of payoff. He should have, though. She'd never allowed him to give her anything without some kind of quid pro quo. He shook his head, remembering their last conversation. She'd tried to brush him off, saying they were even, so not to worry about her. He hadn't understood what she meant until now.

She'd told him that she didn't hate him, and he hadn't believed her. He saw now that she hadn't lied, but his thoughtlessness hurt her badly. To his mind, that was worse; it meant that after all this time the wound was still raw. Damn.

Not knowing what he was going to do about that, he downed the rest of the liquid in his glass and deposited it on the table in front of him. Maybe it was too late to do anything, but his prospects had to seem better after a night of sleep, not that he really expected one awaited him.

He climbed the stairs, pausing briefly at Stevie's door. Thankfully, she'd already been in her room when he got home. He hadn't done right by her either. He'd allowed her to stay in his home, in part because she needed to and in part because he wanted to find out what was going on with her. But for the most part, he'd ended up ignoring her in favor of Alex and the case he was working.

At least she hadn't used his home for a trysting spot as he'd first suspected she would. Good thing. He'd probably kill some boy who'd done with Steve half the things he'd done with Alex so many years ago. So what did that make him? Not only a cad but a hypocrite.

He sighed. He'd make it up to her this weekend when he had some time off. If he had some time off. He'd make time. He only wished he could solve his problems with Alex as easily.

Officer Joe Morgan approached the black Ford Escort station wagon reported stolen two days ago with a sense of trepidation. It wasn't that the gruesome scene he expected to find would unsettle him, but because of what it would mean: He wouldn't be getting to his girlfriend Rhonda's house any time soon.

Damn. This spot hadn't been worth a damn since the former mayor Giuliani had decided the new sheriff needed to clean up the town. He'd turned Times Square into a haven even Disney could love, and even here in the hinterlands of the Bronx hadn't been immune. Morgan supposed that was for the best, but he missed the days when he could roll by for a quick hand job as quid pro quo for leaving the ladies to their business. Now only the occasional down-on-her-luck hoochie ventured over to ply her trade in the cab of an eighteen-wheeler pulled off the highway or with a patron of two motels on the strip.

Back in the day there had only been weeds and woods out here to tell the tale, but in the last couple of years a string of new houses and almost houses had replaced the wilderness. The Escort was parked next to a set of doorless, windowless houses. The large and low-slung full moon lent the structures a mournful look, like wailing, openmouthed faces.

A shiver went up Morgan's spine and he shook himself to dilute its effects. He'd been doing this job for ten long years, seen more shit before nine o'clock than most people did all day. But from the minute they'd received the job to check out an abandoned car matching the day's hot sheet, he knew what they'd find.

He lifted his flashlight and almost laughed, since the first thing he noticed was a baby's car seat on the backseat. Real terrifying stuff. He took another step forward, adjusting the flashlight to survey the front seat. The light shone on a girl's face, bruised, cut, her hair wild and matted. He tilted the beam lower down on the woman's nude body and swallowed. Just like all the others.

He focused the beam of his flashlight on the face

again. Even with the bruising, he could tell she was young, maybe fifteen, with long black hair. For some reason he thought of his kid sister, a sophomore in nearby Cardinal Spellman High School. If anyone had done to her what some bastard had done to this girl . . . Even in his own mind he couldn't complete the thought. Unconsciously he crossed himself.

"You got anything?"

Morgan gritted his teeth. Why his chickenshit partner, Jenkins, had to rouse himself out of the car just in time to startle the crap out of him he didn't know. Annoyed, he said, "Call it in. It looks like we've got another one."

Jenkins trotted back toward the car without looking in the window.

"Putz," Morgan muttered as he rounded the front of the car to the passenger's side. He doubted any woman could survive what this bastard had done to this one. Besides, whoever had attacked her seemed to like his women dead when he was through with them. But he opened the unlocked door and felt for a pulse at the base of her throat.

He straightened away from the car, calling Jenkins.

"What's up?" Jenkins called back.

"Better tell them to send a bus," Morgan said. "This one's still alive."

Eleven

Zack parked his car where the uniformed officer stationed at the outer perimeter of the crime scene was directing and got out. A series of news vans had already set up camp a little bit behind him. Several other uniforms kept them from charging the scene. Good. After finally falling asleep somewhere around three in the morning, he'd been awakened less than a half hour later and told to come here. Despite what happened in her apartment earlier, he'd called Alex to see if she wanted to get a look at the scene, knowing she'd have a hard time getting in without a police escort. Either she'd slept through his call or she wasn't there. It was the latter possibility that soured his mood, though where she went and what she did, now more than ever, was really no concern of his.

He ducked under the yellow barrier tape that was tied to a chain-link fence, stretching to a street sign at the curb, then stretching lengthwise seemingly to infinity. His goal was the inner perimeter, the small delineated section of the street where a black station wagon, nearly identical to the one Ingrid Beltran had been found in, sat. The stretch of sidewalk between the two perimeters was lousy with uniforms, techs—all the usual suspects at a crime scene, plus a few brass, probably looking for an opportunity to press flesh with the media or whoever else might be around to gladhand.

McKay was standing on the inside of the inner perimeter, his back to Zach. Zach hadn't spoken much to the other man since their morning meeting a couple of days ago. Smitty had been happy to fill the higher-ups in on the turn their end of the investigation had taken, and Zach had been happy to let him do so. The less he said to McKay, the better, considering Zach disliked this guy for so many reasons that had nothing to do with his treatment of Alex.

To Zach's mind, McKay was hiding something—chiefly his reason for having such a hard-on for Thorpe. Every cop had the ability to develop tunnel vision when he thought he had the right suspect in his sights. But with McKay it seemed to be something different. From the beginning he'd focused on nothing else, not even something as rudimentary as discovering if any of the victims were linked. While Zach didn't quite buy that Thorpe wasn't involved, he was willing to keep his options open. Unfortunately, he wasn't the one running the case.

McKay turned around as Zach approached. McKay's usual dour expression deepened. "Where's your friend?"

He didn't doubt McKay referred to Alex, but he seemed to be implying Zach would have Alex with him since they were together to start with. Either he was fishing for information or he was looking for a punch in the mouth. Zach wouldn't dignify his question by giving him either. "What have we got?"

McKay shrugged, perhaps signaling he'd given up on that line of thought. "A break for a change. This one's alive, though just barely."

As they spoke, McKay led the way around to the passenger side of the car. "And for a change," McKay continued, "given the amount of blood the car seems to have been the crime scene as well."

A series of lights had been set up around the vehicle illuminating the interior of the car enough for blood to be visible on the passenger seats, the floor mats, even the dashboard. Now, that surprised him. Why would Thorpe or whoever resort to using a stolen vehicle to commit this type of crime unless his usual spot had become unavailable to him? Or maybe he was becoming more desperate or disturbed? A killing now was certainly off his usual pattern. With these types it usually took something to set them off, both initially and later on.

In the beginning, a personal blow like a wife of girlfriend leaving, the loss of a job, or some other wrong might start a killer on his path. But no kill was ever as perfect or thrilling as imagined. The high of stalking and finding a victim often led to depression after the kill was made. That only started the cycle all over again.

This killer, whoever he was, had gone off his pattern, both in the location of the killing and the duration between them. But the killer finally had the media's attention, something he hadn't aroused before. And there was another difference, too. This victim had been left alive. Had that been intentional or had the killer slipped up? With any luck she'd survive long enough to give them some of the answers they sought.

"What hospital was she taken to?"

"Jacobi. Trauma center."

That's where Zach would head when he left here.

"Detective Stone?" he heard someone shout.

Zach turned in the direction of the voice. "Yes."

"There's a woman here who says she needs to see you. Alex Waters."

So she finally roused herself from wherever she was and decided to show up. "Let her through."

He followed the officer's departure until he reached

where Alex stood waiting. The officer held the tape for her to duck under, then pointed in his direction. She walked toward him with confident, unhurried strides, but even when she reached him she didn't look directly at him.

"I got your call," she said by way of a greeting. "What have you got?"

"Same as before, it looks like. The victim had already been transported to the hospital before I got here, but from the information we have, she was done the same way—blows to the face, strangulation, and her right breast removed. But this time the vehicle appears to be the primary crime scene."

As he spoke, they walked around to the passenger side of the car. Alex nodded, pulling a pair of surgical gloves from her pocket and putting them on. "Can I borrow your flashlight?" she asked.

He'd forgotten he still carried it until that moment. He offered it to her. She took it from him and turned it on, shining the beam on the passenger's seat, starting at the headrest and moving downward.

He wondered what she was thinking as she shifted the beam to examine other parts of the interior. For one thing, she didn't seem the least disturbed by the amount of blood saturating the upholstery. He'd done some checking of his own and discovered she wasn't a psychiatrist, an MD, but she held a PhD in forensic psychology from Adelphi University. Her consultation work on several grisly crimes explained the lack of squeamishness, he supposed. If anything, she seemed intent and curious.

A moment later she took a step back and looked up at him. "Something isn't right here."

Something about this scene bothered him, too, but he'd rather she give her take on what she saw before offering his. "What do you mean?"

"For one thing, the mirrors are intact. The rearview is

smashed, but that could have happened during a struggle. Was that detail ever reported in the papers?"

Honestly, he didn't know. The smashed mirrors were what lead McKay to single out Thorpe in the first place—the similarity in crime scenes. But now he knew where she was going with this. "What else?"

"The headrest."

She shone the flashlight on it. The rest was made of some porous material that had once been tan but was now soaked through with blood. "What about it?"

"I'm just wondering how badly the girl was beaten. That's an awful lot of blood and if it came from a face wound it would probably flow down the body, not back toward the headrest, unless maybe the seat was back. Otherwise I would think that would be more consistent with a wound to the back of the head."

He could see her point. "So maybe this one didn't come as willingly as the others."

"Even so. A few of the girls had burn marks on their arms consistent with having a stun gun used on them. If that's true, why would he need to resort to whacking one of his victims on the head?"

That was another question for which he had no answer. "You don't think the same guy who killed the other girls did this?"

"Either that or something drastic has happened in this situation, something to push him further over the edge. Aside from being off his schedule, this scene is a mess. Sloppy. If nothing else, this killer has been meticulous so far. Your guys didn't find so much as a fiber to link back to him. I'm sure crime scene will have a field day with this."

With any luck, Thorpe had gotten sloppy and there would be some evidence here that would lead them to wherever he was hiding out. At worst, they had a copycat on their hands, one who might be as dangerous as Thorpe himself.

"After you left, I did a little reading. I finished the printout on the Amazons."

That was the first mention she'd made of how they'd left things. "What did you find out?"

"I was wondering what happened to them," she continued. "Apparently their decline started when Heracles I killed Hippolyte, the queen of the Amazons. One of his labors was to retrieve her belt that had been a gift from Ares, the god of War. When she wouldn't give it up, he ran her through with a sword and took it. Things went downhill for the Amazons from there."

Zach thought about it for a minute, wondering how that information might fit in with what they knew. "Wouldn't it make more sense for him to have stabbed the women, then, if he imagines himself to be this Heracles?"

"Maybe. What were they strangled with?"

"Inconclusive, so far. Probably some sort of leather strap."

"Or a belt?"

Zach shrugged. "Maybe."

"There's something else. Heracles took the belt as one of the twelve labors that, if completed, would make him one of the gods, an immortal. How do humans become immortal these days?"

"He wants his fifteen minutes of fame."

"More than that, I'm sure. How do you think he'll feel if this isn't his handiwork?"

Zach didn't want to contemplate that prospect too much. They already had a dangerous crazy on their hands. What that madman might do if shown up by someone of lesser talent he couldn't begin to guess. With any luck, the girl, if she awoke, might be able to give some information that would help them one way or the other.

"Where did they take the girl?" she asked.

At least their thoughts on the case seemed to be flowing the same way. "Jacobi. I'm heading there in a few minutes."

"I'd like to go with you, if you don't mind."

He didn't. What he did mind was that she still hadn't really looked at him. He didn't really blame her for that, but it bothered him nonetheless. "Give me a minute, and then we'll go."

He walked over to where McKay and the captain stood to relay what he and Alex had discussed. It didn't surprise him to find that McKay was unconvinced that anyone besides Thorpe could have done this. The captain seemed a bit more open-minded.

"You'll be at the hospital when she wakes up?" the captain asked.

He noticed the captain said "when," not "if." Zach wasn't holding out that much hope, not after seeing the amount of blood in the car. If Alex was right about the head wound, that would be another thing to contend with. "I'm going there now."

"Is she going with you?" That came from McKay, who gestured toward Alex with his chin.

Zach couldn't tell if the captain had missed the venom in McKay's voice, but Zach hadn't. He plastered a fake smile to his face and said, "Yeah, I might need someone who knows what they're doing once I get there." Without another word he walked back to where Alex waited for him.

The only indication that he noticed the two of them walking away was the slight smile he allowed to stretch across his face. Otherwise, he stood at the post he'd been assigned, his body rigid, simulating vigilance. Half the cops in the Bronx had turned up, some in uniform and some without, at the prospect of another hit by the Amazon Killer. Half the neighborhood had turned out, too. He'd been snagged for crowd control.

He smiled remembering how he'd acquired the uniform. He hadn't intended to kill its owner. That was The Mirror's fault. He'd strangled him from behind, not wanting to soil the uniform, which he'd thought might come in handy one day. He'd been right again. No one had questioned the authenticity of the badge he had pinned to his chest or his right to be there.

Even she'd walked right by him without noticing. Even now he imagined he still smelled her perfume—the delicate musk of arousal mixed with a good dose of fear. The arousal wasn't his doing, not yet. That belonged to the other, but the fear was his. He inhaled, imagining her scent flowing into his nostrils, invading his lungs, circulating through his body until there wasn't a pore, or vein or capillary, that wasn't taken over by her. His body hardened as he thought about it.

Maybe he should pay her a visit. He let the pleasure of that prospect wash through him for a moment before he tamped it down. There would be time for that, but later. She would come to him and then he'd know the time was right.

The crowd shifted, reminded him of his supposed duty. A police tow truck had arrived to transport the vehicle to the police lab where it would be photographed again and every fiber, blood spatter, and hair would be analyzed. He wondered how long it would take them to figure it out or if she had already. He hadn't seen it in her face or caught the whiff of it in whispered conversations, but soon he'd know. They'd lead him to the answer and then he'd strike.

But for now it was over. He relaxed his rigid posture, then shook himself like a mongrel. He slipped through the shifting crowd until he emerged on the other side.

A heavy voice called out from behind him. "Hey, kid, where do you think you're going?"

He glanced back over his shoulder to see the heavyset uniformed sergeant looking back at him. "Gotta water the plants," he called back.

The sergeant nodded and turned away, obviously disgusted with any officer who couldn't hold his bladder better but unwilling to stop him.

He turned away, heading left at the corner. All the noise, the flashing lights, the activity seemed to be swallowed up by the surrounding buildings so that none of it touched him here. He liked that. The car he'd boosted was less than a block away. He smiled to himself as he walked the rest of the way through the still, black night.

Twelve

"How are you doing over there?"

At the sound of Zach's voice, Alex turned her head in his direction. She'd spent the last five minutes of the ten-minute ride to Jacobi Hospital pretending to be fascinated by the view outside her window. In truth, she hadn't known what to say to him, so she'd remained silent. While they were surrounded by others it had been easy, though she was sure he'd noticed she'd avoided eye contact with him. Now that they were alone, she needed to deal with how they'd left things. She'd been putting it off, part of the reason she'd declined a lift to the scene from him. That wasn't like her. She'd learned the art of confrontation from a master.

For a moment, she studied his profile. His posture and facial expression appeared relaxed, but she knew better. Underneath he was as driven and intense as he used to complain about his brother's being; he was only able to camouflage it better. She knew he was worried about this case and that that girl neither of them knew would wake up to tell them something they could use.

They were alike in that way. Devon had accused her of being able to hide behind a clinician's detached pose, her own brand of mask. He hadn't been wrong. That bit of emotional armor had served her well when everything fell apart. Yet, she'd lost it earlier that evening and shown him a vulnerability she hadn't intended. Then she'd taken it out on him when he'd noticed. He deserved an explanation from her, even though she dreaded giving one.

She exhaled slowly, turning her gaze to the road in front of her. "I shouldn't have come down so hard on you before. I know why you did what you did. I've always known. I shouldn't have said what I did."

"Then why did you?"

"You kept pushing. I pushed back. I know that for you, seeing each other is like some stroll down memory lane. I know how much you loved my father. But for me, it was one of the worst times of my life—a time I'd rather forget."

It was in her mind to add that his presence in her life had been the only thing that made it bearable, but that would defeat her purpose. She wanted distance from him. She wanted her safe life back, the one she'd had before she walked into McKay's conference room. She wanted the sleeping dog of the past to remain dormant, and it never would if she allowed him to keep poking at it.

For good measure she added, "We knew each other once, briefly. It doesn't have anything to do with what we are trying to do here or who we are today."

He said nothing for a long while, but she noticed his jaw tightened and his grip on the steering wheel clenched. Damn. She'd hurt him again, but hopefully it would be the last time. Maybe he'd back off for good.

He turned onto Pelham Parkway. She could see the hospital from there. They'd need to head up to Williamsbridge Road to make a U-turn and double back on the other side of the road. The parking lot was tiny and under construction. They parked on the street at a broken meter.

Once they were on the path leading to the emergency room, he said, "Do you mind if I ask you a question?"

Alex swallowed. Was this what she'd reduced him to—feeling the need to check with her before speaking? "Go ahead."

"What were you looking for when I left you alone at the car?"

She hadn't expected that, but she'd take it. "I think I was getting paranoid for a moment there. I had the feeling someone was watching me. I looked around, but I didn't see anyone."

"You thought it might be Thorpe?"

"I don't know. As I said, I was just being paranoid. I'm sure your officers were briefed on Thorpe. His picture was all over the news. If he'd been there, I'm sure someone would have spotted him."

Zach shrugged, but she knew better than to interpret his nonchalance as not caring.

Once inside, they were informed that the girl was still in surgery, that she had suffered a wound to the back of her head that had caused a blood clot and swelling. Being right about the girl's condition didn't offer Alex any solace. The doctor suggested they wait in the small doctors' lounge across from the elevators on the surgical floor, though he left them little hope she'd be waking up any time soon.

Zach lounged in one of the wood and fabric hospital chairs, his feet stretched out and crossed at the ankles, his arms folded, his eyes closed except for a thin slit through which he watched Alex watch a small television set hung from the ceiling by a long metal arm. He adopted the posture mainly because most people left him alone long enough for him to think. Alex was no exception.

He doubted she noticed he watched her or cared if he

did. Her entire concern was for the fate of the girl. He wished his focus was as singular, but it wasn't. His mind kept drifting back to what she'd said in the car. He'd known back then that Alex was having a tough time of it. Sammy hadn't been blind to Alex's wishes; he simply dismissed them as being unimportant compared to his own. Though Zach had loved Sammy, he had been aware of his faults. He hadn't wanted to be like Sammy or even the same kind of cop Sammy was. Sammy hadn't been a crooked cop, but he hadn't been quite clean either. He survived by having more dirt on others than they had on him.

If she thought his sole purpose in coming around was to be with Sammy she was mistaken. Until she'd spoken, he imagined she remembered him as a friend, someone she'd looked up to until the night he'd gone and ruined that. He hadn't considered she regarded him as one big reminder of a time she'd rather forget.

We knew each other once. It doesn't have anything to do with . . . who we are today. Did she really mean that or was that something to say to back him off? He couldn't speak for her, but the night they'd spent together had changed him. It had stripped him of even the pretense of being an honorable man, made him question himself and wonder if his brothers hadn't been right about him from the get go. He'd lost himself for a while—until he met Sherry, the first woman in a long time to interest him in more than a temporary way. He'd married her because it seemed to be the next step in the logical course of events, but in his heart he knew he'd screw that up, too. It hadn't taken him long to prove himself right.

And now here they were again. She was wrong about him, though. He didn't view seeing her again as a stroll down memory lane, rather a chance to redeem himself a little in her eyes. But he'd give her what she wanted.

He'd back off. The last thing he wanted was to cause her any more distress than he already had.

The television was tuned to a cable station flashing local news stories. An Asian woman with big hair spoke while a helicopter's eye view of the scene showed a CSU tow truck removing the car. The sound was too low for him to hear what was said, but there was McKay being interviewed by another woman. He was really beginning to hate that bastard.

He refocused his gaze on Alex, wondering what she was thinking. She seemed utterly calm, the slight movement of her left foot the only clue to any distress. She shifted, recrossing her legs. "I would really love to know what that man has against me."

Zach wanted to know the same thing. He knew McKay believed she'd been in contact with Thorpe or rather that he'd tried to contact her. A dump of her phone records confirmed that he'd called, but not that she'd spoken to him or that Thorpe had even identified himself. For all anyone knew Thorpe had breathed heavy a few times and hung up. The calls were too brief for much more than that.

Aside from that, he suspected McKay had some personal stake in the outcome of this case, though Zach would be damned if he knew what it was. From what he understood, McKay pretty much kept to himself, having few friends on the force in whom he might confide. Truthfully, though, Zach didn't really care what McKay's problem was as long as he kept it to himself. Alex didn't need or deserve any shit from him right now. And with the crime scene wrapping, the others would start showing up soon. No one would want to be left out of the loop. Zach only hoped he made it through the night without having to go at it with McKay.

Smitty was the first to show up, bearing a tray from Dunkin' Donuts. "So what did I miss?"

Zach stood as did Alex. "Where the hell have you been?"

"Enjoying that visit with the in-laws in Connecticut I told you about. Real shame to cut it short," he said with a roll of his eyes that said it was anything but. To Alex he said, "Help yourself. They're all light and sweet."

Alex took one of the cups. "Thank you." She returned to the seat she'd occupied and crossed her legs.

Zach turned back to Smitty. He'd forgotten about Smitty's trip and the day off he planned to take tomorrow. Zach took a cup from the tray. "Thanks."

Smitty took the remaining cup from the tray and tossed the tray in the garbage pail by the door. "You got a minute?" He nodded toward the doorway.

"Sure." Alex glanced at him as he walked toward the door, but said nothing. A pair of uniformed officers stood in the hall. Each of them cast a look at him and Smitty before returning to their conversation.

Zach leaned his shoulder against the wall, facing Smitty. "What's up?"

"I heard on the way over here. They ran the girl's prints. No hits."

So they still didn't know her identity. "What about missing persons?"

"They're checking. So far nothing. Nothing in the car either."

"Shame," Zach said. The girl deserved to have whatever family she possessed here pulling for her. But so far, Smitty hadn't told him anything he couldn't have said in front of Alex, nothing he wouldn't tell her himself in another minute. "Anything else?"

"How's she holding up?"

Zach almost laughed. Smitty was worried about Alex? What was it about her that seemed to bring out the protective instincts of every man who met her, with the exception of McKay and her own father? Especially since she'd never appreciated any attempts at coddling her. "Careful, Smitty, your paternalism is showing."

"I can't help it if she reminds me of my own kid. I wouldn't want her involved in this mess either."

Zach said nothing to that. Smitty's daughter taught high school English in a school in Hunts Point. She was probably a lot tougher than her old man gave her credit for.

The double doors leading to the surgical suites opened, drawing Zach's attention. A single grim-faced doctor in green scrubs came through, the man he'd spoken to before but whose name he didn't remember without consulting what he'd written down.

Zach straightened, expecting to hear bad news. That might be his cynicism showing, but that's what he'd expected from the beginning.

"What is it, Doctor?"

The doctor brushed his hand over his head removing his cap to reveal a shock of salt-and-pepper hair. "I wish I had better news for you. We got the young lady stabilized, but she hasn't regained consciousness. We're hoping once the swelling in her brain comes down."

"Where is she now?"

"They'll be transferring her to the ICU in a minute. The SARS nurse is finishing up. I'm sorry, but we couldn't get to it before now."

Zach nodded. The SARS nurse was trained in evidence and information collection following a rape. Sooner was better than later when it came to evidence collection, but saving the girl's life was the priority. They'd have to live with any contamination or loss of evidence.

"Is there any family?"

"We're still trying to figure out who she is."

"She'll be admitted as a JD, then."

Zach extended his hand toward the doctor. "Thank you."

Sighing, the doctor shook his hand. "As I said, I wish I had better news."

The doctor turned to walk away.

"Can we see her?"

That came from Alex. Once he'd found out the girl's condition, Zach had planned to take Alex home. Smitty could handle getting any other information that was needed and he was feeling a bit protective of Alex himself at the moment. But he could tell by the steel in her expression and the fact that she didn't look at him that she wouldn't back down.

"If you wait until they bring her down to the ICU."

It took nearly an hour before a pair of orderlies flanked by a pair of uniforms brought her downstairs. If it weren't for the coffee Smitty had brought, Zach was sure he'd be snoring in a chair by now. But Alex seemed filled with a sort of nervous energy unattributable to the effects of caffeine. He wished he could pull her into his arms and soothe her, but she'd made it plain she didn't want that from him. So he simply stood beside her watching through the broad windows as the staff worked to hook the girl up to several monitors as well as a breathing machine, the hiss of which he could hear even through the room's closed door.

Alex rocked back on her heels, her arms crossed in front of her. "Good God, Zach, she's such a baby."

Unlike the other victims, this girl's face had been left mostly intact, allowing them to see the youthfulness of her features. "I know, baby." The words were out of his mouth before he had time to consider the endearment at the end of them.

Alex seemed not to notice. "What are you going to do next?"

In a couple of hours he'd see about hooking up with his friend who worked computer stings on pedophiles. Then in the afternoon he'd go to the autopsy on the last girl. He didn't tell Alex that. "Right now, I'm taking you home." In case she planned to protest, he showed her a little steel of his own in the gaze he sent her way.

"All right, as long as you let me know how she's doing."

"Of course." He only hoped that when the time came he'd have something good to tell her.

Dawn had started to spread across the horizon as he pulled up in front of Alex's house fifteen minutes later. She hadn't said one word to him during the trip, sitting with her legs crossed, her arms folded, and her eyes closed, and he'd let her be. But even when he pulled to a stop and cut the engine she didn't stir. She'd probably fallen asleep. "Alex?"

She inhaled and her lower lip quivered. That surprised him. He'd never seen Alex cry, except the one time he was responsible. Even at her father's funeral she remained dry-eyed and stoic. "Are you all right?"

She swiped at her eyes. "I'm fine. Just overtired, I guess."

He knew she meant that as an explanation for her tears, but none was necessary. He understood what she felt—sorrow for the girl combined with a profound frustration that they hadn't been able to stop this guy before he got to her. He felt it, too. Given the choice of her honest reaction and a facade, he'd take the former. The trouble was she hadn't offered him that choice.

"You don't have to put a brave face on it, Alex. I get enough of that from the folks at home." Without thinking, he lifted his hand to wipe away with his thumb a drop of moisture she'd missed.

She looked away from him, lowering her head so that he couldn't see her face. "Zach," she started.

He cut her off, since he knew what she was about to

say. "I know. I shouldn't have done that." He dropped both hands to his lap. "I don't want to hurt you, Alex. I never have."

"I know that."

Did she? Not as far as he could tell. "But you still don't trust me."

Her head came up and she regarded him with an expression he didn't understand. "Trust has nothing to do with it, at least not as far as you are concerned."

What the hell did that mean? That she trusted him or that her lack of trust in him didn't factor into her feelings at the moment or something else?

Before he got a chance to question her on that, she unclipped her seat belt. "I'd better go. I have to be in my office in less than an hour." She opened the car door and slid out. "Thanks for the lift, both times."

She slammed the car door closed and hurried up her walk. If he'd thought it would help the situation he would have gone after her. As it was, he was tired and disheartened and every time he clashed with her he came out the loser. He didn't want to clash any more with her right now.

He waited until she'd made it inside her door before he started the engine. He'd head home himself, change clothes, and get back to the precinct and start in. As long as the wicked weren't sleeping the weary wouldn't get any rest either.

He slipped in bed beside her hoping she wouldn't waken. He only planned to sleep for a couple of hours before getting back to the job. He could have done the same at the station house, but then he wouldn't have gotten to lie next to her, to check on her to make sure she was all right.

He'd barely made it beneath the covers when her

head popped up and she whispered a weak, frightened "John?"

"It's me, baby. Come here," he whispered back.

She turned into him and he wrapped his arms around her. She was shaking and her breath fanned across his chest in shallow, rapid puffs. He smoothed his hand through her hair and down her back, whispering words of comfort to soothe her.

Damn. They'd been to the point where what Thorpe had done to her was merely a distant memory. They'd been through the night terrors and the cold sweats, the trembling, with fear, not desire, every time he touched her. She still wouldn't let her kids in the house until she, baseball bat in hand, made sure it was clear and sneaking up behind her was likely to get you a blow to the head thanks to a self-defense course she'd taken. But the worst of it had been behind them. Then Thorpe had resurfaced.

He couldn't blame her for being terrified that this newer, more vicious Thorpe might come back for a repeat visit. He feared that, too, though in an odd way he owed his being with her to the man. She'd been in the courthouse to testify against Thorpe while he'd been there on some other case, he couldn't remember which one now. She'd been standing against a wall, her eyes closed, obviously trying to compose herself. He'd recognized her immediately since he'd spent four years at Columbus High School lusting alternately for her or one of her friends, the cool girls who paid no attention to his geeky self.

She confessed to him later that the only reason she'd accepted his offer to go for a cup of coffee was that she'd remembered him, too, though she'd pretended not to at the time. She'd felt safe with the grown-up nerd boy John McKay, who was also a cop. She hadn't explained either what she'd been doing in the building, and he hadn't pressed her for anything except her phone number. It didn't take him long to figure out she'd given him a fake one, nor much longer than that to ferret out the real number or the real reason she'd been there.

He'd wanted to kill Thorpe from that moment. That desire deepened as he discovered how deeply Thorpe's attack had wounded her. She'd been turned from a strong, confident girl to a woman who panicked every time someone touched her. Thorpe wasn't even convicted for what he'd done to her since his semen wasn't found in her body. But there was no doubt in her mind or his that Thorpe had been the one to attack her. Thorpe had gotten six lousy years, not nearly enough for all the lives he'd destroyed.

But Thorpe wouldn't get away this time. He didn't care what anybody said, he wasn't going to turn Thorpe loose unless he had ironclad proof he wasn't involved. He didn't intend to let Dr. Alex Waters **off** the hook either. If she'd done her job the first time, Melissa wouldn't have been in any danger in the first place. Thorpe would have been locked up some place where he couldn't harm anyone.

"John?"

He blinked, coming back to himself. "What is it?

"They found another girl tonight, didn't they?" A wracking shiver accompanied her words.

"Yeah, they did." He wasn't used to lying to her so he didn't bother. "She's still holding on, but it's anybody's guess if she'll make it."

"Oh." She sniffled and a moment later he felt a line of moisture from her tears on his chest.

He hugged her to him, wishing the pain she felt were his, not hers. "Shh, baby," he whispered.

"You have to catch him, John."

"I will." That was a promise he didn't mind making to her since it was one he intended to keep. He'd find some way to draw Thorpe out of his hidey-hole and that would be it. Thorpe would pay for what he'd done to Melissa and more. And then he'd see to it that Dr. Waters got what she deserved as well.

Thirteen

Zach walked in his front door a little after seven, calling Stevie's name. He'd called her from the road to let her know he was on his way home and gotten no answer. He got no answer now as he walked through the first floor, noting the living room, kitchen, and dining room lights were on though there was no sign of his niece. He found her at the top of the stairs in the small bedroom he used as an office on occasion. She was sitting at his desk, her eyes on the computer screen in front of her, a set of earphones hanging from her ears.

He leaned his shoulder against the doorjamb, feeling a combination of relief and annoyance. He flashed the lights to draw her attention. She drew in a startled breath and swiveled around to face him. "Uncle Zach. I didn't know you were home."

"Do the words 'my name is not Con Edison' mean anything to you?"

"What?" She pulled the earphones from her ears.

"Never mind. Don't you have school today?"

"I was just killing time before the bus got here. I hope you don't mind me using your computer."

"Not at all." He'd never set any ground rules for

computer use, though he probably should have. "As long as you behave yourself."

She cast him a droll look, as if his suggestion were too little too late. "Now you sound like my mom." She turned back to the computer. Even from where he stood he could tell she was shutting it down as a means of preventing him from seeing what she'd been up to.

He thought of Ronnie Hassler, the girl met Thorpe on the Internet. "Do you have one of those Yourplace accounts?"

"Yeah. Most of the kids I know do. Why?"

"You don't give out any personal information, do you? A phone number or an address? What school you go to?"

She spun around in the chair to face him, a patient expression on her face. "Have you noticed that my dad is a cop? Uncle Jon is a cop? My best friend Heather's dad is a cop? What do you think they all have in common?"

He knew where she was going, but to be perverse he said, "They're cops?"

"Aside from that. They've all warned me about all the creepos and pervs on the Internet. I know how to handle myself. I thought *you* might give me a little credit."

"I do."

She rolled her eyes, disbelieving. The sound of a bus horn honking forestalled any further discussion of the topic. Stevie grabbed the handle of her backpack and slung it over her shoulder as she stood. "There's my ride."

For the first time, he noticed what she was wearing—a crop top that didn't completely meet the waistband of her skirt and a pair of thigh-high stockings that didn't quite meet her hem. "Are you sure your mother would let you out of the house dressed like that?"

"Bye, Uncle Zach." She hurried up to him, smacked a kiss on his cheek, and was out the door.

He supposed he had his answer, to that question at

least. He still hadn't gotten any further in finding out
what was going on between her and her mother. Barbara
called him every day to check on Stevie, and he sensed
Barbara held something back from him that she'd rather
spill. Something kept her from doing so; maybe she
feared he'd tell Adam whatever she said. But she had to
know him better than that. She'd kept his secrets; he'd
do the same for her.

Oh well, he didn't really have time to worry about it
now. He needed to get changed and get back on the job.
They needed to find the girl's identity and if she was the
latest victim of the Amazon Killer or some other foul play.
He shut down the computer and went back to his room.
The king-sized bed that dominated the room called to
him, though most of his dreams of late centered on Alex,
either her present incarnation or the one he'd known in
the past. Maybe if she were here in the flesh rather than
merely tormenting his psyche, he wouldn't have had the
same degree of resolve. That was something else he
couldn't dwell on—the prospect of Alex's soft body under
his. That was a long-ago event never to be repeated except
in his own imagination. He showered, changed, and
headed back out the door.

"We have to stop now."

Alex watched the frown spread across Damaris Free-
man's face. It was the same every week. Damaris might be
a narcissistic complainer, but she had no pressing need
for therapy, or rather none she made use of. Damaris
wasn't interested in self-examination or change. She
simply wanted a sounding board for her petty whinings
and complaints. But since Alex was in no position to turn
patients away she put up with her. Besides, every time she

tried to end their sessions, Damaris would phone her ceaselessly until Alex relented and took her back.

"Are you sure that was the whole fifty minutes?"

"Quite sure."

Damaris pouted. "I never even got to tell you about the dream I had two nights ago."

Alex said nothing, merely waited with her hands folded. Eventually Damaris picked up her teeny pocketbook from where she'd left it on the floor and slung it over her shoulder. "I guess it will have to wait until next time," she said in a voice designed to guilt Alex for making her leave.

"Next time," Alex echoed, wishing there would be no next time, both for her sake and for Damaris's. What Damaris needed was to cultivate some interests outside her own shallow problems—something Alex had been unable to help her accomplish. Then again, Alex had never envisioned herself in this sort of practice. Maybe it was her father's influence, but the criminal mind fascinated her, it always had. They honestly didn't think like other people. She'd devoted her training and her practice to making sense of those others found unfathomable. She hadn't intended to spend her life coddling young women with juvenile complaints.

Alex sighed. That wasn't a fair assessment of her practice. Many of her clients were helped by her and went on to live fuller, happier, more productive lives. Nor was she being fair to Damaris. But seeing the other woman provoked in Alex a sense of impotence in her and invariably annoyed and depressed her. That's why Alex always scheduled her early in the day and made room for a break after she left.

When Alex considered that there was a young girl in a nearby hospital fighting for her life, who would be scarred both mentally and physically forever if she survived, Damaris's melodrama over minor complaints grated more than usual.

With her fingertips, Alex rubbed her temples where a dull throb beat. These headaches of hers were getting worse. She knew it was the stress of dealing with this case—one more reason she hoped it would be over soon. But as her mother used to say, if wishes were horses beggars would ride. She needed to do something proactive to feel like she was accomplishing something. But what?

Her phone rang, startling her. It was her private line, not the one that went through Alice. Very few people had that number, but since it was one number off from the main one, people often dialed it by mistake. "Dr. Waters, how can I help you?"

"Dr. Waters, this is Ginnie Thorpe."

Alex sat up in her seat. Walter's sister was calling her? "What can I do for you, Ms. Thorpe?"

"You can't believe the things they're saying about my brother, can you? My brother is no killer."

Alex didn't know how any human could state that so unequivocally about another human. No one could know completely the depths of another's psyche. But given the nature of these crimes, she could see how Ginnie Thorpe's mind would rebel at the possibility that her brother could be responsible.

"Do you know where Walter is?" Alex asked.

"He hasn't tried to contact me, if that's what you mean. I don't think he would now considering his name is all over the papers. He wouldn't want to get me involved."

Alex didn't know if she bought that. Walter had looked to his big sister for protection and had railed about her running away and not providing it.

"What is it you really want to tell me?" she aked Ginnie.

"I'm not trying to say we had an ideal childhood. My mother had no use for Walter, but not because he was a boy. He was born sickly and problematic. She couldn't be bothered. But let's face it Doctor, my brother was not the brightest bulb in the box, if you know what I mean. I doubt he'd know a Greek god from a can of tuna fish. But if he did, they'd have to better than the flesh-and-blood men my mother brought home."

"What do you mean?"

"My mother made her living on her back. She brought men home. Most of them slapped her around before or after, you know what I mean? I hated it, but Walter used to watch. If the door was cracked a little, you could see them in the broken mirror over her dresser without them noticing you."

Well, that might explain Thorpe's predilection for shattered mirrors and the linkage between violence and sex. "You didn't watch?"

"No. I figured I might be next."

"Were you?"

There was a long pause before the sister answered. "Sometimes."

Alex exhaled. Such a warped family, but nothing she hadn't seen a hundred times before. What did surprise her was Ginnie Thorpe's candidness, especially since the purpose of the call was ostensibly to prove her brother's innocence. Nothing she'd said so far had been all that helpful in that regard.

"Someone must be framing him, Ginnie continued, "someone who hates him. I don't know. Our mother might have been a whore, but she died when we were ten years old. Walter was never fixated on that junk."

It wasn't unheard of for one criminal to mimic another's pattern in order to deflect suspicion from themselves. Whoever was committing the murders might have co-opted Thorpe's m.o. and added his own sickness to it. But could she believe that happened here? She honestly didn't know.

The line went dead and Alex hung up the phone, wondering what Ginnie Thorpe's true motive had been for making the call. Could someone be framing Walter? Or could someone be using Walter's psychosis as the basis for a killing spree? Even if either implausible scenario was true, who could it be?

Alex leaned back in her chair. There always the possibility that Walter's sister was as nuts as he was. No one survived such a childhood unscathed. They didn't all become serial killers or criminals of any kind, but a good dose of therapy wouldn't hurt. She rested her elbows on the table and put her forehead in her hands.

A knock sounded at her door. "Anybody home?"

Alex looked up to see Roberta peeking in her door.

Roberta slumped into one of the visitor chairs. "You look like hell anyway. Late night?"

Roberta sounded far too hopeful for Alex's liking. "You could put it that way."

"That wouldn't have anything to do with that hunky police detective who keeps showing up here, would it?"

Alex sighed again. She wasn't the type of woman to run to her girlfriends with every bit of dirt from her own life. She didn't mind being a shoulder for others, but her secret thoughts she kept, well, secret. If Sammy had taught her anything it was to guard closely what she held dear, and that included her emotions.

Still, it would be nice to have the opinion of someone who wouldn't judge her, berate her, or cause her name to be mentioned in the *Daily News*.

"What are you so worried about spilling? I already know he's your father's ex-partner."

"How did you find that out?"

Roberta offered her a wicked smile. "A certain lawyer and I are following the case. We shared."

Alex cast Roberta a disgusted look. Leave it to a lawyer to ferret out things that were none of their business in the first place. "So what if he is?"

"That means you two have some sort of history, no?"

"We knew each other. If you must know, I had a monster crush on him." That wasn't an accurate description of what she'd felt, but it was one Roberta would understand. In truth, she'd cared for him as if they were equals, though in fact they hadn't been.

"So what's the problem? I caught a glimpse of him looking at you. He's interested. Worse things could happen to a girl than to have her girlhood crush panting after her."

"Here's the problem, as you put it, in a nutshell. Zach idolized my father. He was young and my father took him under his wing. I'm sure you can imagine that the things that make one an ideal cop and mentor are not the same things your average girl is looking for in a father."

"I guess not."

"If someone has to disabuse Zach of his notions about my father, I don't want to have to be the one to do it."

The minute the words were out of her mouth Alex knew she lied. That's what she'd been telling herself, but Zach was a big boy. He could handle the truth about her father. It was Zach's opinion of her she worried would change. Even after all this time she still cared what he thought of her.

Roberta shook her head in a way that suggested she didn't believe Alex either. "I'm no shrink," she said. "But it sounds to me like you still have feelings for this guy."

That was the problem; she had too many feelings, all of them jumbled on top of one another not making any sense. She didn't tell Roberta that, though. Alex didn't bare her soul to anyone, not even the shrink she'd been required to see as part of her training. She'd already done more sharing with Roberta than she usually did. "What's your point?"

Roberta shrugged. "I have to have a point? I was just making an observation. But tell me this—has he said or done anything to make you think he wants to start something on a more than platonic level?"

Alex sighed. She'd accused him of that, but honestly he hadn't done anything, unless looking counted. For all she knew she'd projected onto him her own desires, since despite everything going on and everything that stood between them, she still wondered if there would have been any future for them if things hadn't turned out the way they did.

But enough was enough. She'd said all on the subject she intended to. "I thought you wanted to hear about the case."

Roberta affected a child's pout. "Fine, spoilsport. Go ahead."

"On one condition. You've got to tell me what you think from your professional perspective."

Roberta scrutinized her for a long moment, perhaps picking up that for the first time in a long while Alex questioned her own judgment.

Roberta sat up and crossed her legs. "Deal. What's going on?"

Alex capsulized the events of the last twenty-four hours, leaving in the call from Thorpe's sister, but leaving out her own feelings about the girl. She ended with the supposition that at least some of the girls might have been contacted online.

"As for the sister," Roberta said, "I can't help you with that. She's probably one fry short of a Happy Meal herself."

"No kidding. But at least I know why he became so agitated when I pressed him for information about his childhood. Who would want to reveal that?"

"As far as that online thing goes," Roberta continued, "I've got a friend who does work with that. They track and 'out' child predators on this Web site he runs."

Being that Alex was a cop's daughter, Alex's first question was, "Is that legal?"

"I'm not sure. I know they used to threaten to arrest him every other week until he started cooperating with the local PDs, giving them information they used to catch these guys. And his heart is in the right place. His sister was abducted by some scumbag she met online. They got her back, but she wasn't the same after that."

Alex could imagine she wouldn't be. "How do you think he could help? I doubt whoever killed these girls announced his intentions online."

"He monitors the chat rooms kids go to. Maybe a particular wacko will stand out to him. And think about it, he's got to be local or someone who travels to the city monthly. If he's targeting girls here, he might stick to chats based in New York or this region. Honestly, I don't know enough about it to be much help either. But if you want to talk to him, I think I can arrange it."

Well, she'd wondered about something she could do to feel proactive. This might come to nothing, but she didn't see how it could hurt. "Sure. See what you can set up."

Roberta checked her watch. "I'll call as soon as my next session is over. Which reminds me, I better go."

Alex hid a yawn behind her hand. She hoped Roberta set something up early since Alex doubted she'd make it through the day without a nap.

* * *

"Is that it?"

Zach shifted in his uncomfortable chair, hoping that the early morning meeting was drawing to a close. Each of the detectives had been asked to report the results of what they were working on. A preliminary report had come back from the techs examining the car. A fingerprint not matching Thorpe's, the victim's, or the car's owners had been found in the blood on the dashboard guaranteeing that the killer had been a copycat, not the real deal. Damn. As if they needed more complications in this case. The fingerprint wasn't on file either, which also didn't help. When that news came out, Smitty had whispered to him, "It was probably the boyfriend." Zach couldn't argue with that, but it disturbed him to think that someone this girl had known had done this to her.

A couple of the guys had been searching abandoned, incomplete, or in-progress houses in the area as a possible primary crime scene, without success. Even that chickenshit McKay claimed to have a new lead on Thorpe's whereabouts, though he hadn't elaborated on where that was or how he'd come by such a lead.

Honestly Zach didn't care, since McKay having something to do meant he'd be staying away from Zach. The girl in the hospital hadn't woken either. The doctors were keeping her in a coma hoping her brain would have a chance to rest and heal. More bothersome was the fact that no one had come forward to claim her. Given that they knew the identity of neither the victim nor her assailant, someone coming forward to identify her might be their only shot of finding out either.

That wasn't quite true either. Alex had been right about the crime scene. It was sloppy, full of evidence, including DNA that could be linked back to the doer when they came up with a suspect. Right now, the neighborhood from which the car was stolen was being canvassed to see if anyone had seen who stole the car.

A knock sounded at the door. One of the civilian aides poked her head in the door. "I hate to interrupt, but there's a Mr. Parks here. He thinks he might be Jane Doe's father."

If Zach had been given a moment for a prediction, he'd have guessed all eyes had turned to him. This was his area of specialization, talking to the grieved or bereaved after one of their own was a victim of sexual assault. He was an expert in asking the ubiquitous litany of questions: Was there penetration? With a penis or other object? And on and on. You got used to asking them, even if the victim was a ten-year-old girl or a seventy-five-year-old granny, but they were never comfortable. Nor was it a picnic dealing with the relatives or the crazies that showed up looking for five minutes of attention, but that was the job. He stood before any one of the people staring back at him had a chance to ask if he'd handle it.

Avery Parks was a beefy man of Polish or maybe Slovakian heritage, but short on stature. He wore a windbreaker over the blue uniform of a Transit Authority worker. He held a cap in his hands that he'd twisted into an unnatural shape. He turned in Zach's direction as he approached.

Zach immediately felt sorry for this man. He wasn't one of the crazies; he was the genuine article, at least if his demeanor and the sheen of banked tears in his eyes could be believed. Even if his daughter were not the girl in question, some situation had brought him here that in all likelihood would not turn out well. Zach extended his hand toward Parks. "Mr. Parks, I'm Detective Stone. Let's go somewhere that we can talk."

Parks nodded as he shook his hand. Zach led him to the small interrogation room. It was quiet, there was a tape recorder to capture their conversation, and if anyone else was interested in listening in they could do so without Parks's knowledge.

After getting Parks's permission to record his statement, Zach took the seat opposite the other man. "What do you want to tell me, Mr. Parks?"

"The TA they put me on nights. I told them I had a daughter to raise. Her mother died four years ago. It's just us. But they don't listen. They don't care. I didn't know anything about this girl in the hospital. Nothing, until I came home and turned on the news. I think my daughter is in school, but I see this girl has dark hair like my Nancy and I worry. I call her school and they say she's not there. I go to her room and she's not there. I'm afraid this man got her, this Amazon Killer. I went to the hospital, but the men there won't let anyone near her room. So I come here. I need to know if this is my little girl."

Zack scrutinized Parks's face. The man was on the verge of melting down. Whatever information he wanted, he'd better get now, because whether this girl was his daughter or not, Zach doubted he'd be in any shape to talk later.

"I understand that, Mr. Parks. I have a few questions for you first. Is that all right?"

Parks nodded. "I understand."

"How old is your daughter?"

"She'll be sixteen in August."

"She was home alone last night?"

He nodded. "I didn't like it, but I had to work."

"Did she have a boyfriend?"

Parks shook his head. "Some boy from around the neighborhood came sniffing around, but she didn't want him."

Famous last words. He passed the paper and pen he'd been making notes on to Parks. "Can you write down his name and address?"

Parks seemed surprised. "You think he had something to do with this? I heard on the news that it was that killer."

Since he wasn't ready to part with any information regarding their suspicions, he said, "If he was coming around your daughter, he might know something."

That seemed to mollify Parks, who wrote a name and a Morissania address on the pad. Zach knew the area somewhat. A couple of blocks of private houses sandwiched in between bombed-out buildings and run-down tenements—Eden in the middle of chaos.

He had Parks write down his address and other contact information while he had the pad in front of him. Parks laid down the pen. "Can we go now?"

"In a minute." Zach stood. "I'll be right back, and then I'll take you to the hospital."

Parks nodded, keeping his head downcast.

Zach went to the adjoining room where he found the captain, McKay, and Smitty in a huddle. Zach held the pad up showing the information Parks had written. Just in case they hadn't been paying attention, he said, "We need to pick this guy up."

Smitty copied the information onto his own pad. "I've got this one."

The captain nodded as Smitty rose to leave. "Both of you report back whatever you get ASAP."

"Poor bastard," Smitty said, referring to Parks, once he and Zach were alone in the hall together.

Zach grunted his agreement with Smitty's assessment. At least he didn't gloat with any I-told-you-so's about the boyfriend angle.

Zach went back to Mr. Parks, who was in much the same position he'd been in when Zach left. "Mr. Parks?"

Parks looked up, seeming closer to tears than before. "What do I do if it's her?"

Since Zach had no answer for him, he didn't bother to formulate one. Instead, he helped the man to his feet and escorted him out of the station house into the bright spring morning.

Zach had seen many loved ones' reactions to learning that one of their own had fallen at the hands of some predator. Some responded with sorrow and tears, others with angry accusations and threats. Still others resorted to hysteria or appeared totally bloodless and cold, in shock. Some just affected a kind of calm resolve that was probably what was truly needed.

Zach hadn't figured Parks would fit into the last group. Standing just outside the girl's room, Parks dried his eyes and tucked his cap into the pocket of his wind-breaker. "Did she have a ring on when she came in? A Claddaugh ring. Her mother was Irish."

There wasn't a ring, but there was an untanned portion of her right ring finger that suggested there had been one. "Is that your daughter, Mr. Parks?"

Parks nodded. "Can I be with her?"

"That's up to the doctors." At this point there was no official reason why he shouldn't be. While they'd been en route, Park's story had been checked out. His whereabouts could be verified for the entirety of the previous night. The captain had called Zach with that news as they'd pulled up to the hospital.

Parks nodded, then turned doleful eyes to him. "You catch that bastard who did this to my Nancy and the other girls."

It wasn't so much a question but an exhortation; a demand that he make sure justice was done.

Zach focused on the girl, for the first time really looking at her. Her father said she was fifteen, but she appeared much younger, fragile, pale in the garish fluorescence of the room's lighting. He supposed he saw now what Alex had seen when she looked at her. Waste. A young life nearly snuffed out for no earthly reason other than the perversion of another.

Damn. Zach swallowed down the bile that rose in his throat. All this time he'd thought he was doing the work he was supposed to do. But there was the job he did that was assigned by his superiors and the obligation he had to the victims, plural in this case. He'd been doing the first but falling down on the second. Even his reaction to McKay had been skewed. He'd been angry with the man for being a sloppy cop, but not so much for his shirking his obligation to the victims.

He'd acknowledged a sense of cynicism and ennui creeping up in him for some time now. But how long had it been since he'd really looked at any victim as anything more than another case to close? He honestly didn't know.

But Parks wasn't really looking for an answer, so Zach didn't bother to try to give him one. He left him in the capable hands of the hospital staff, went back to his car, and drove back.

Fourteen

"What's his problem?"

Zach nodded toward the kid on the other side of the two-way glass in the interrogation room. There was something hard in Freddy Morales's face, despite its youthfulness. Something else was off, too. Despite being dressed only in a T-shirt and jeans and the air-conditioning blasting full bore, Morales was sweating and his skin was pasty-looking and pale. And neither the captain nor McKay had said boo so far. Maybe he simply knew he was got, but Zach didn't think so.

The man beside him, one of the precinct detectives named Kraft, shrugged. "Probably on something, though we didn't find anything at the house. Nothing illegal anyway. When we got to his place he was sitting on the sofa in his underwear drinking beer and watching the tube like he was waiting for us."

That might explain why Morales hadn't asked for a lawyer or protested his statement being taped. The kid had been read his rights already, which meant they had no intention of letting him go unless Mother Teresa appeared from the heavens to say he didn't do it. Smitty had already reported back that they'd found traces of blood on a baseball trophy hidden in the kid's closet and a sweater from St. Catherine's Academy was found in the trash. It was the same school outside of which Thorpe had been accused of exposing himself. Zach, however, wasn't in the mood to appreciate the irony.

The captain set a can of Coke in front of Morales. "Can we get you anything else, Freddy?" Obviously he was trying to play it nice. Or get the kid's prints on the can so they could take them without officially putting him in the system. With McKay's perennially sour expression, who could tell what he was playing?

Morales ignored the soda. Instead he started scratching a spot on his upper arm through the armhole of his shirt. "I don't want any damn soda. Let's get to it." He glanced up at McKay. Surprisingly there were tears in the kid's eyes. "We all know what I did to Nancy."

"Nancy Parks?" the captain asked.

"No, fucking Nancy Reagan." The kid wiped his arm across his face. "I killed Nancy." His voice had risen in volume and pitch, but he toned it down to a low monotone. "Or I thought I had."

The captain sat in the chair opposite Morales. "Tell me what happened."

Morales sniffled and brushed his hair back from his face. "I convinced her to come over to my place, you know. I told her a friend of mine's dog had puppies and I wanted to show them to her. She was crazy about dogs and her old man wouldn't let her have one."

"So she came over to see the puppies?"

Freddy shook his head as if disgusted by the captain's stupidity. "There wasn't no damn dog, man. I just told her that so she'd come over. She was a tease, man, always walking around in that little Catholic girl skirt. She told me she liked me, but she wouldn't give me any, you know? I got tired of that shit. You know what I'm saying?"

"What happened after she got to your home?"

"I told her to come to my bedroom 'cause that's where

the dog was. When she saw there were no puppies she started tripping. But I wasn't having that. I hit her a couple of times and threw her on the bed and did it anyway."

"You raped her?"

"Nah, man." Morales opened and closed his mouth a few times as if he was searching for the right words with which to express himself. He ended up hanging his head, as if defeated. "Yeah, I guess I did."

Then he started to cry with sobs that wracked his shoulders but produced little sound. Trails of mucus ran from his nostrils unchecked. "I was high, man. I neva woulda hurt her if I was all right. She just made me so mad. She got up screaming how she was going to tell her pops on me. How she was going to call the cops. I hit her just to get her to stop, to listen to me. But she fell and there was so much blood and she wasn't breathing."

"Son of a bitch," Zach heard Kraft beside him mutter. Zach had a few choice words himself, but he kept them to himself. He felt nothing but contempt for Morales, despite his pathetic display of emotion. Especially since Morales didn't consider he'd hurt the girl until he'd delivered the blow that had rendered her unconscious. The rape had been his right. Then, rather than seek medical attention for her he'd brutalized her further so that he could deflect the blame from himself. Morales hadn't said that, but that's what had to come next.

Zach had heard enough, but something about Morales's demeanor bothered him. As he'd spoken, he'd seemed to wind down like a child's toy, slurring his words by the time he finished talking. He sat now, slumped back in his chair, his head down, his arms hanging limply at his sides.

McKay, who'd stood by quietly while Morales spoke, stepped up to the kid and tugged his head back by his hair. "Sit up, you sick piece of shit. What else did you do to her?"

The captain stood to wave back McKay, blocking the view. Something was going on, but Zach couldn't tell what. A second later, there was a crashing sound and both men jumped back. Morales was on the floor, his body seizing with convulsions.

"Holy shit," Kraft said, racing fro the room.

Zach stayed where he was. He'd leave the lifesaving techniques to those better versed in them. In another moment Morales quieted anyway. Kraft felt for a pulse on the kid's throat. He obviously didn't find one, since he shook his head.

Damn. Zach felt the breath whoosh out of him. As much as he hated what this kid had done, he didn't want to see him dead on the station house floor. More waste. There was a ringing in Zach's ears that he slowly recognized as the sound of his phone.

Without looking at the display he opened the phone and barked, "Stone," into the phone.

It was Smitty reminding him that they had the autopsy in less than an hour. Zach didn't need the reminder.

The offices of Juvenile Justice were housed in a small office building on Pelham Parkway, a ten-minute drive from the office Alex and Roberta shared. The door was unmarked save for a sign that instructed callers to ring the bell.

"You're sure you want to do this?" Roberta asked.

"Absolutely." But Alex wondered about Roberta's hesitancy. Was she having second thoughts about involving her friend? If that was true it didn't make sense, since according to Roberta, this was what he did. Or maybe he preferred to work directly with the police, not civilians.

"Just checking," Roberta said, then pressed the button.

"Coming," called a male voice from the other side. The door pulled open, revealing a dark-haired man with gray eyes that widened in surprise when he saw Roberta. "Hey, sis." With a broad grin he enveloped Roberta. "You didn't tell me you were coming by."

"You didn't listen to your messages again." Roberta stepped back from his embrace. "Alex, this is my big brother, Eric. Eric, this is Alex Waters. We sort of work together."

"Good to meet you, Alex," Eric said, shaking her hand. "Roberta's told me a lot about you."

"Good to meet you, too," Alex echoed, but her eyes were on Roberta. Until that moment Alex hadn't known she had a brother. Their friendship had been based mostly on professional matters. Roberta had never said much about her upbringing, and since Alex didn't want to talk about hers either she hadn't pressed. But her mind went back to that morning when Roberta had told her that this organization had been founded after the owner's sister had been abducted.

Roberta must have been reading her thoughts, since she whispered, "Our younger sister."

Still, that event must have affected her profoundly and could explain, at least in part, some of the cynicism in Roberta's nature.

"Come on in." Eric beckoned them forward with a wave of his hand. "The guys are just starting to come in now. No point in being here when the kids are in school." He led them through a large room full of computers and telephone equipment to a small office in the corner. "We can talk in here."

None of the furnishings Alex had seen in the outer office were brand-new, and those in the inner office seemed a bit more worn. The desk that dominated the room was old, scarred, and cluttered with papers. The black Dell laptop that sat at one corner of the desk threatened to topple over until Eric righted it as he moved around the desk.

Once everyone was seated, Eric said, "I take it this isn't a social call."

"Not exactly," Roberta said. "Have you heard of the Amazon Killer?"

"Who hasn't? Didn't he dump another girl last night?"

"Something like that." Alex didn't want to cloud the issue with suppositions that hadn't yet been proved.

"What about him?"

"Although it's been reported in the papers otherwise, not all of his victims were prostitutes. He might have approached some of these girls online and persuaded them to meet him."

Eric muttered something under his breath that Alex didn't catch but doubted was for public consumption anyway. "How many girls?"

"Four or five. The police are still checking into it."

Eric looked from her to Roberta, then back. "How are you two involved with this?"

She assumed he already knew her occupation, so she didn't bother to repeat it. "The man doing this may be a former patient of mine."

"And you don't like how the police are handling it?"

"I felt the need to do something."

He gave a short, self-deprecating laugh. "I know how you feel. That's how this place was born." He leaned back in his chair gesturing in a way that seemed to encompass the whole office. "When our kid sister, Georgie, went missing, I couldn't stand by and do nothing. This was right after our dad died. The police tried to convince us she'd run away, but she'd left things behind she would have taken if she hadn't intended to come back."

Eric sighed. "Turns out she'd gone off for the weekend with some guy she met at the store where she worked after school. She'd thought it was love, but he'd had other plans. He'd had her for a week before I found them. He probably would have killed her when he got tired of her. I'm just grateful to have found her before that happened."

Alex said nothing for a moment, considering both brother and sister. There was a sheen to both their eyes that bespoke unshed tears. Neither of them had gotten past this, but then violence was often just as difficult for loved ones as it was for the victim. And then the victim was expected to be coddled and looked after, to be given counseling and support, while those around the victim were supposed to be strong and nurturing despite having their own needs going unmet. They also often felt guilty for not protecting the victim from harm in the first place or selfish for needing support themselves. No wonder so many marriages or relationships ended once tragedy struck. Alex wondered how old Georgie was when this happened, but didn't ask.

"Is that what you do here?" Alex asked. "Look for runaways?"

Eric inhaled and shifted in his seat. "That's how we started, but we didn't really have the manpower for that. Everyone here volunteers and we still need to eat. We figured it made more sense to go after the predators, since a single one could create hundreds of victims, especially nowadays with the Internet. We enter chat rooms pretending to be young boys or girls and see who bites. A girl can get as many as twenty IMs, instant messages, the moment she enters a chat room. For boys it's slower. Many of these folks are just being friendly, but a lot are trolling for young people to molest."

Remembering what Zach said about the girls having similar online accounts, she asked, "Have you heard of Yourplacedotcom?"

"Yeah. It's one of the newer sites kids frequent. They're popping up all the time. Kids fill out detailed profiles including pictures, mostly so the site's advertisers can target them, but the profiles can be viewed by anyone. Kids don't realize how much information they're giving up to belong. That's how these scumbags fixate in on who they want. If a kid is vulnerable in some way they pick up on it and exploit it, like Georgie with her daddy issues."

"So not all of these guys pretend to be kids?"

"Not always, but you don't need to pretend to be a dad to make a kid feel special and appreciated, which is what most needy kids want, regardless of their particular issue."

That was true enough. Zach had done that for her when he was barely older than she. "Once you make contact, then what?"

"We chat them up for a while and wait for them to offer to meet in real life."

"Why?"

"We don't want to be accused of entrapment. These days we take everything we get to the police. It's hard to prosecute these guys if proper procedure isn't followed. In the beginning, all we were interested in doing was outing the bastards, putting their names and addresses out there so that parents and kids could watch out for them. As you can imagine, the cops weren't too thrilled with us."

"They threatened to close you down or kick your ass every other week."

Those were the first words Roberta had spoken since Eric talked about their sister. The smile on her face was still a bit watery, but she seemed to be getting herself together.

Eric laughed. "Yeah, well, we've gotten a lot more vigilant than vigilante lately. In fact we've been trying to get special victims interested in doing a sting on this site but haven't worked it out yet. Thanks to our inauspicious beginnings we always encounter a little resistance at first.

Maybe now they'll be more amenable." Eric turned toward the computer, his fingers poised over the keys. "What's your guy's screen name? If he's got an account we can check him out."

Alex shrugged. "I have no idea. As far as we know, he doesn't own a computer."

Eric tilted his head to one side considering that. "That might make things more difficult. What's his real name?"

"Walter Thorpe."

Eric typed the name into the computer, pressed the ENTER key, and waited. "Nothing. It was a long shot anyway."

"Why is that?"

"If you were going online to seduce underage girls, would you give your real name?"

"I guess not." And guessing what screen name he might have used was tantamount to guessing how many grains of sand there were on Orchard Beach. Then she remembered the printout on the Amazons she'd given to Zach. Choosing the Greek rather than the Roman version of the name, she suggested, "Try Hercules."

As they reached the parking lot on Crosby Avenue adjacent to the Bronx coroner's office, Zach turned to Smitty. "That was a colossal waste of time." The autopsy hadn't shown them anything except what they'd expected. The girl's tox screen had come back clean, her body showed no signs of drug use or the type of wear you'd expect to see with a prostitute. Her murder had occurred in the same way as the others. The only thing they'd accomplished was to ask the coroner to try to identify more closely what sort of ligature had been used to strangle the victims. That could have been done on the phone.

Smitty shot him a droll look. "Someone's missing their nap time."

Zach did feel beat. He'd had only two hours of fitful sleep the night before and his ass, as well as the rest of him, was dragging. "I think I'm going to head home for a couple hours."

"Same here." Smitty checked his watch. Zach would guess it was around three thirty. "Want to meet back around seven? We still have those computers to go through."

Zach nodded. For a change he'd get to see his niece for more than five minutes. While he'd vowed to make time for her this weekend, that didn't look like it was going to happen. Since he and Smitty had arrived in separate vehicles, Zach went to his car and drove home.

Pulling up in front, Zach noticed not a light was on that he could see. Then again, it was the middle of the afternoon. Brilliant sunshine was the only illumination needed. At least, that's what he thought. He was glad to see Stevie was behaving herself. That is, if she was home, as she was supposed to be.

Once he got closer to the house, he knew Stevie was home. Rap music blared loud enough for him to hear it through the closed door. He unlocked the door and entered, tossing his keys on the occasional table in the front hall. "Stevie," he called, but wasn't surprised when he didn't get an answer. Who could hear him over that racket?

He unbuttoned his jacket as he walked farther into the house to stand under the archway that opened onto the living room. The first thing he needed to do was turn off that noise emanating from the stereo in the corner. He took a step forward, then noticed movement coming from the couch in front of him. But it wasn't Stevie he saw.

Zach closed the distance to the couch, grabbed the kid by the back of his clothes, and hauled him off the sofa, off Stevie. Zach pushed him away. The kid flailed, trying to right himself. Zach didn't care if he fell on his ass. His concern was with his niece. "Stevie," he shouted, over the sound of the music.

She sat up, clutching her school sweater together with one hand. In the other she held the remote for the stereo that she used to turn it off. Her hair was a wild mess and her eyes were bright. She blinked as if she couldn't quite fathom what was going on. "Uncle Zach?" What are you doing here?"

Zach inhaled, trying to calm his temper. It wouldn't do him any good to throttle his own brother's oldest child or beat the crap out of some mother's son, but at the moment that's what he wanted to do. "I would ask what's going on here if it weren't so damn obvious."

Stevie opened her mouth, but it was the boy who spoke. "It was my fault, sir. Stephanie told me not to come in, but I wanted to make sure she was all right."

Slowly Zach turned his head in the boy's direction. The kid looked scared but resolute. Zach had to admit the kid earned points for taking responsibility for his actions, but Zach couldn't deal with that now.

In the most controlled voice he could muster, he said, "Go home, while you still have everything you came in with."

The boy didn't exactly bolt, but he didn't waste any time getting to the front door. As he left, he called to Stevie, "See you tomorrow."

After the boy left, slamming the front door behind him, Zach sat in the opposite corner of the sofa from his niece, leaned his head against the back of the sofa, and closed his eyes, wishing he knew what to say to her. He'd never try to lecture her on the exercise of her own sexuality. He had no moral high ground to stand on in that regard. But he'd promised her parents to keep her out of trouble and she'd promised him she wouldn't entertain boys in his house. Neither one of them had really kept their word.

"You didn't have to throw Rashad out," Stevie said in a quiet voice. "He'd only been here for ten minutes."

Zach turned his head to face his niece and popped one eye open. "What would have been going on after twenty minutes?" He turned away from her and sat up. So he wasn't as lecture-free as he'd thought.

"Nothing. He was about to leave when you came in. Come on, Uncle Zach, he called you 'sir' and he calls me 'Stephanie.' He says Stevie sounds like a boy's name."

The way she said that did make him sound like a bit of a straight arrow. If Zach hadn't walked in on them, he might have believed that. "What did you say to that?"

"I said, yeah, like a boy that gets beat up after school every day."

Despite himself, Zach laughed. He draped his arm around his niece's shoulders and pulled her closer for a hug. "Do you remember telling me you weren't going to be any trouble?"

"Yeah, and you believed it."

He supposed he had that coming. "Look, kiddo, what's really going on between you and your mom?"

Stevie pushed away from him to sit up. "You'd have to ask her. That's her thing. She was just acting so mopey, you know. Every time I asked her about it she'd say nothing."

Knowing how relentless Stevie was, that could mean every fifteen minutes. "You didn't believe her?"

Stevie shook her head. "The next thing I knew I got sent here."

That wasn't how Adam laid it out. He'd made it sound as if Stevie wanted to get away rather than the other way around. Of the two of them, Zach believed Stevie since she seemed genuinely distressed, while Adam had seemed merely preoccupied. Whichever way the truth lay, he needed to talk with Adam. Thanks to this case, he couldn't give Stevie the time or attention she needed.

He unwound his arm from around Stevie's shoulders. "I'm going to lie down for a couple of minutes and then I have to head back out. Can I trust you to behave yourself?"

Stevie nodded. "I've got a ton of homework."

Not completely mollified, Zach went up to his bedroom, stripped off his suit, and lay down on his bed. He didn't really expect to get any sleep, but a little rest would suit him fine. He closed his eyes, but his mind was too active to even accomplish that. Despite everything else he had going on, his thoughts turned to Alex. He'd called her earlier, figuring she'd want to know about Freddy Morales's being their copycat. His call had gone directly to her voice mail. He hadn't bothered to leave a message. He'd tried her office next, but had been told she'd gone home. She hadn't called him back yet, which didn't worry him, but he'd prefer she got the word from him rather than from the nightly news. Maybe he should stop by her place on his way back in to tell her.

Zach sighed. Who the hell was he kidding? He wanted to see her. The fact that she didn't want to see him didn't change that. She'd told him before that she didn't hate him. She'd told him last night that she knew he didn't want to hurt her. Yet she still kept up a wall between them. Didn't she want anything from him? Not even a better explanation of his behavior than the one he'd given her. Maybe that's what bothered him most: She seemed content to put the past behind her while it still haunted him.

But what did he really want from her? Despite the attraction, he didn't expect her to fall in his arms. For one thing, Alex was too sensible for that; for another, he'd killed any tender feelings she might have had for him. Maybe he just wanted closure, a definitive end where there had been none before.

He hated that word: closure. Who had even heard of it ten years ago? But now everyone seemed to need it for every event, large or minor, in their lives. He hated most of all needing it for himself.

Regardless, lying there was a waste of time. He got up, pulled on a T-shirt and a pair of jeans, and went back to work. His own needs would have to wait.

Everything he told her was a lie. From his profession to his age to his name to where he was born. All of it. The biggest lie he'd told her was that he was harmless, since right now half the cops in the city were looking for him. For the moment, at least, she had nothing to worry about from him. But later . . .

Lying had never been a problem for him. He'd been spoon-fed them as most children ate cornflakes. Almost from the moment of his birth his whole life had been one lie or another. *She* had seen to that. Even now, he couldn't think of her by her given name, not even in his own head. She had given him life, and it had been the only positive thing she'd ever done for him. The rest of it was full of untruths and beatings and other horrors most people couldn't imagine much less survive. That knowledge fueled his sense of pride and superiority. He'd survived with his intelligence, his drive, his sense of self intact, while The Mirror, well, cracked.

He almost laughed at his own humor. He held back knowing that he might wake her. He wanted to go on watching her sleep—vulnerable, unprotected. She was strong, independent, sure of herself. He liked that, especially since he knew he could, little by little, break her of that strength until all she thought about was him and how to please him. One day, he would, but not now.

Part of him wished that day would never come. She was beginning to love him. He could see it in the way she

looked at him, the way she touched him. He was the first
one in a long time. He knew because he'd hurt her the
first time he'd taken her. Not much, just enough so he
noticed. Then he'd found a novel role to play, the gentle
lover. He hadn't thought he had any tenderness left in
him, but she brought it out in him. Part of him wished
he could forget the rest and enjoy what he had never
known, a woman who genuinely cared for him.

But every time his thoughts wandered in that direction, he heard *her* voice in his head. *Men ain't nothing but
trouble. Sooner or later every woman realizes that. Too bad we
can't live like those Amazons—hide off by ourselves and only
use men for the only thing they're good for.* This from a woman
who'd gotten knocked up turning tricks in strangers'
cars in the middle of nowhere. When he was through
with her he'd hidden her all right. As far as he knew no
one had ever found her.

She stirred, turning toward him. Her dark, dark eyes
settled on him. Then her brow furrowed. "Blake?"

He schooled his features into a benign expression,
wondering how much of the previous one she'd noticed.
She called his name again, or rather the name he'd
chosen since to him it sounded cultured. "What is it,
sweetheart?"

"You were looking at me funny." She brushed her
long, black hair over her shoulder. "How long have you
been awake and what were you thinking about?"

He stroked the side of her face. "Nothing important.
Just some trial I've got coming up."

She smiled. "But since I am awake . . . ?"

Her smile broadened as her words trailed off. He
forced an answering smile to his face. "What did you
have in mind?"

She glanced toward the lamp that stood on the table
next to his side of the bed. "Turn off the light and I'll
show you."

He did as she asked, then returned to her. Her soft hands wandered over him and her pliant body melded to his. Once again, the urge to forget everything else to be with her washed over him.

Unfortunately, he had a schedule to keep.

Fifteen

The next morning, Alex dragged herself into work at eight o'clock. Saturdays were usually early and short, worked for the sole purpose of accommodating patients that couldn't make it in during the week. She'd slept fitfully the night before, when she'd slept at all, the case and its implications, both professional and personal, weighing on her.

She'd heard on the news about the senseless killing of Nancy Parks and the even more senseless way her young killer had tried to cover his crime. Now Morales was dead. No one would ever know if his overdose was intentional or not.

Alex supposed she should feel grateful that the boy felt any remorse at all. But the only thing he seemed to regret was mutilating the girl when he didn't know she was alive. That was the part of the night's events that seemed brutal and out of place for him. It only proved that people could rationalize any behavior as necessary as long as they wanted to badly enough.

She guessed that's what Zach had called her about yesterday. She'd turned off her cell phone before the meeting with Roberta's brother and hadn't turned it back on until she got home. She'd seen he'd called then and listened to the message from Alice telling her that he'd called the office. It had been nearly six o'clock then. She hadn't bothered to call back, since it was almost time for Zach's nightly visit. That is, if he kept to his schedule.

Or maybe she hadn't called back, figuring he'd come if he couldn't reach her. She'd wanted to see him, and not only because she wanted to share with him the information she'd gotten from Roberta's brother. She'd been trying to deny to herself and him that there was still anything between them. She'd been punishing him for the fact that there was. His abandonment had hurt her as nothing else in her life had. She'd been walking around with that ever since, allowing it to color every relationship she'd had since, including her marriage.

She knew she'd never get past any of that if she didn't face it. Isn't that what she told her patients all the time—they had to own their own pasts, to look the events of their own lives in the face and put them in the proper perspective? So far, she'd done a lousy job of taking her own advice.

Sitting at her desk, she picked up the phone to call Zach. Her first patient wasn't due for another fifteen minutes. That should give her enough time to arrange a meeting between them.

Before she could finish dialing the number, there was a knock on her door. "Anybody home?" Roberta peeked her head in the door. "When did you get in?"

"About five minutes ago. What's up?"

Roberta pushed the door open and stepped in. She carried a long white box, the type florists used for long-stemmed flowers. "Believe it or not, these just came for you. Alice asked me to bring them back."

Yeah, right. Roberta just wanted to snoop. "Who are they from?"

"Doesn't say. There's no card. Could someone have a secret admirer?"

Alex stood to take the box Roberta extended toward her. Aside from the pink ribbon around the box, there was no marking on it of any kind, not even an address tag from the florist. Undoubtedly, Roberta referred to Zach, but flowers weren't his style. He'd simply show up on your doorstep and melt you with that smile of his. If he wanted something from her, he'd have been there last night. "Don't start that again."

Roberta held up her hands as if to surrender. "All I'm saying is that maybe whoever sent them expected you to know who they were from."

That wouldn't be a bad idea, except no one she knew would be sending her flowers out of the blue. Maybe they came from some reporter hoping to butter her up for an interview. Although the press was no longer swarming around her office, a few stalwarts were still calling.

The intercom on Alex's desk buzzed. "Tommy Barnes is here for you."

Alex pressed the appropriate button to be heard by the receptionist. "Thanks, Alice. Can you send him back?"

"No problem."

To Roberta, Alex said, "Duty calls."

"Yeah, well, I'm expecting an update as soon as you open them."

"We'll see," Alex teased, though she admitted to herself that she was curious, too. But whatever lay inside that box, she didn't want it distracting her while she attended to her patients. She stowed the box behind her desk where it couldn't be seen, then went to the door to greet Tommy.

Zach sat across the table from his brother in the Royal Coach Diner on Boston Road. Over breakfast they'd discussed the usual topics, sports, recent cases, their sister, Joanna. Adam had asked how Stevie was doing, but hadn't mentioned Barbara. Now, as they lingered over coffee, Zach remained silent, hoping to give his brother an in to talk about his marriage if he wanted to.

But it didn't look like Adam was going to take the bait. He set down his coffee cup with an air of finality. "I should be going."

Zach should have known better. Usually, you had to hold a figurative gun to Adam's head to get him to tell you anything. Zach wasn't opposed to holding a literal gun either, if that's what it took. "Not yet. How are things going with Barbara?"

Sighing Adam sat back. "Is that what you really asked me here to talk about?"

"Partly. Mostly. What's going on with you two?"

Adam fingered the napkin at his place setting, an action that struck Zach as a nervous gesture. Adam letting his emotions get the best of him was a novel concept, but there was a first time for everything.

"I didn't want to discuss this with you for reasons that will become obvious. I didn't think you'd understand."

Adam paused just long enough for Zach to wonder whether there was a particular reason for Adam's statement, or if it was the same old one: his brothers' belief that since he didn't share their temperament he couldn't understand them.

"We've never had any secrets between us before, but suddenly she's going places and not telling me where she's gone. She's distant and when I ask her what's wrong she says 'nothing.'"

Zach inhaled and let his breath out slowly. What Adam meant was that *Barbara* had never kept secrets from him before. *She* had always let him know about her whereabouts and explained her moods. Zach knew his brother didn't have it in him to be that forthcoming with anyone. But he thought he knew where Adam was going with this and he didn't like it. "What do you think it is?"

Adam lifted one shoulder in a shrug. "She's having an affair."

Zach shook his head. He didn't believe that. For one thing, most people having affairs went out of their way to appear normal, unless they didn't care or unless they wanted their spouse to know. They made up plausible excuses for where they were so their spouses wouldn't question them, or at least tried to. Stevie described her mother as having been mopey, and even Adam noticed something was off. That didn't sound like an affair to him.

Besides, Barbara was more straightforward than that. If she ever tired of his brother, she'd give him ample time to pack his shit, then throw him out and go on with her life from there. Still, whatever was going on sounded serious enough to concern Zach.

"How's your sex life?"

For the first time since they'd started on this topic Adam looked him squarely in the face, his expression thunderous. "Do you have to reduce everything to its basest element?"

"No, not always. But I remember reading somewhere that people who were having affairs were often more affectionate, either to cover their tracks or their guilt."

The waitress came by, depositing their check on the table. Adam snatched it up before he had a chance to. Adam edged his way out of the booth.

"Thanks for listening."

As Adam strode away, Zach muttered under his breath, "Not a problem." It occurred to him to go after his brother and tell him that if he really wanted to know what was going on with his wife he should sit her down and have a decent talk with her, but he doubted Adam had listened to one word he'd said.

* * *

"Well?"

Alex almost laughed at the look of expectation on Roberta's face as she reappeared in her doorway. Alex was sure it was only the demands of Roberta's clients that had kept her at bay for the last couple of hours. "I haven't even opened them yet."

Roberta flopped into the same chair she'd occupied before. "Now, don't keep a girl in suspense. What did he send you?"

"Let's not get ahead of ourselves. We don't even know if they're from *him*, as you put it." Though Alex admitted to herself that some small part of her wished they were.

She picked up the box from where she'd left it and set it on her desk. The elasticized bow slid off more easily than she'd anticipated. She tossed it aside, then worked on getting the box open. It was taped shut on either side. Using a fingernail she sliced through the tape on one side and managed to get the box open. Inside were two dozen white roses in perfect condition.

"Damn," Roberta said standing. "Someone *really* likes you."

"Mmm," Alex agreed. Someone who'd left the card inside the box instead of out. She picked up the envelope that bore her name. It wasn't written out but cut from what she recognized as one of the business cards she'd had a lifetime ago when she worked at the hospital and taped onto the envelope.

That in itself was odd, but the card inside held another surprise. For a long moment she simply stared at the letters pasted together to form words. Her mind struggled to wrap itself around their import, aside from the obvious Bogie reference.

"Son of a bitch."

"What?" Roberta rose to her feet again. "What does it say?"

Alex didn't answer. She'd already picked up the phone to call Zach.

Zach drove to Alex's office, with what his nephew would have called the quickness. He arrived even before the two squad cars he'd asked to sit on the place until he got there. Before he'd hung up with her, he'd told Alex to lock her doors and not to allow anyone in or out until he got there. He was glad to see she'd taken him seriously, since the downstairs guard wouldn't let him in until he showed his badge.

"Are you new?" Zach asked him, since there'd been no one on guard the last time he'd been there.

"Started yesterday."

Zach looked the kid over. His height topped Zach's and Zach would be surprised if he couldn't bench-press twice his own weight. Considering the NYPD was practically knocking kids like this over the head and dragging them off to the academy, Zach wondered what this guy was doing in a low-paying security job—unless for some reason he couldn't make the grade. That might make him someone Zach didn't want in Alex's domain. They had enough crazies running around already.

To test the waters, he asked. "You take the test?" Anyone who had would know what he meant.

There was pride, not guile, on the kid's face as he answered. "Waiting to hear back."

Zach nodded. "I've got a crime scene team on the way here," he said before moving off toward the stairs.

Alex was waiting for him in the reception area, sitting in one of the chairs that lined the wall. She was wearing a simple blouse and a slim black skirt that rode up to bare her knees and long shapely calves. His gaze snagged for a moment on her legs, encased in sheer white stockings to match the color of her blouse.

Damn. He'd had a thing for white stockings ever since he could remember. They reminded him of his sister back in the day when she was a nursing student, and her friends, particularly the one who, when he was fifteen and untried, let him take them off her.

He blinked, as if to banish the image from his mind, and focused on Alex's face. There was a time for fantasies, both those involving Alex and those that didn't. This wasn't it. But at least the memories and the sight of her calmed him a little. She seemed relaxed, but there was something brittle in the smile she sent his way. She stood, and only then did he pay attention to the dark-haired woman sitting beside her. She had a Mediterranean look to her, either Greek or Italian, very pretty. He knew Alex had two partners in this office. He hadn't met this one before.

"Zach, this is Roberta Rosetti, our resident social worker," Alex said by way of introduction. "Roberta, this is Zachary Stone."

"Zach," he corrected, shaking Roberta's hand.

"Well, *Zach*," Roberta said, "if any of my father's partners had looked like you, I might have let him fix me up with one of them."

She wasn't flirting with him. He knew that because her gaze wasn't on him, but on Alex.

Alex gave her partner an arch look before shifting her gaze to him. "Maybe you'd like to have a look at that package now?"

Her tone held no jealousy or even annoyance, only impatience. It also held none of the contentiousness she'd exhibited every other time he'd seen her. That surprised him most of all, but all he said was, "Sure."

She gestured for him to precede her to her office, which he did. She unlocked the door for him and he went inside. The box was sitting on top of her desk, still open. One thing he could say for this bastard: He had great taste in flowers. "When did these come?"

"Early this morning, around eight thirty. I just got around to opening them right before I called you."

Zach pulled a pair of examination gloves from his pocket and put them on. He probably needn't have bothered. Alex's fingerprints must be all over the box anyway, possibly smudging any prints left by the sender. Besides, if Thorpe was the one who sent her the flowers, there probably wouldn't be any prints anyway. So far he'd been careful not to leave a print, a hair, a fiber, any evidence at all that could be traced back to him. That was the problem with all those CSI shows. It was like Crime School 101—how to cover your tracks without really trying.

He picked up the lid and examined it for any markings. "Why the delay?"

"I had a patient waiting, and I'd figured they'd come from some reporter trying to butter me up for an interview. Even though they're not camped out on my doorstep anymore, they still call. And, well, I wanted to annoy Roberta a little."

"Why?"

"She was under the impression that they'd come from some man. Possibly you."

Why hadn't he thought of that? "Would that have been such a bad thing?" When she didn't immediately answer, he glanced over his shoulder at her. She was still standing in the doorway, her shoulder resting against the doorjamb. He'd swear he detected a hint of amusement in her expression. "Would it?"

"It's not your style and I'm not partial to roses. Any man who knew me well enough to send me flowers would know that."

He wondered if that was a dig aimed at reminding

him that he didn't really know her anymore, but decided to let it pass. "That's the only reason?"

She lifted one shoulder. "Until a few days ago I didn't know Roberta had a romantic bone in her body. Now she's gotten herself involved with some lawyer, of all things, and the world is a sunny place."

"What's so wrong with that?"

"You know the old saying, scratch a pessimist and you get a disappointed optimist. I'd say the reverse is true also: Scratch an optimist and you find a pessimist who thinks he's found the way. I hope she's not setting herself up for disappointment."

"Which one are you?" he asked. He already knew the answer, but he'd prefer to keep the conversation going. Answering his questions precluded her from asking any of her own, or so he hoped. Undoubtedly she wanted his take on why the killer contacted her and what he meant by this little gift. As of yet, he didn't have one.

The problem with this guy was, he couldn't seem to rape you or kill you or stalk you without investing it is some sort of psychological meaning. But what sentiment was he trying to express here? As ominous portents went, a couple dozen roses with the heads still attached wasn't high on the list. Maybe he wasn't trying to threaten her, at least not yet. Maybe he simply wanted her to notice him.

He thought back to the phone calls she'd received before Thorpe started this madness. Any rube watching TV these days had to know about phone dumps and that finding Alex's number among his contacts would lead the police to her. Is that what he'd counted on all along? Now he wanted to make sure she was paying attention? It was a possibility, one he didn't like, since it suggested she fit in his scheme somehow.

To Alex he said, "Well?"

"I'm optimistic things will turn out poorly."

That was some comedian's joke, which made it a

nonanswer. He decided to let that slide, too, but he wondered about her sudden ability to joke with him. "The card was inside or outside the box?"

"Inside. I wouldn't have opened it if I knew who they were from."

He picked up the card and read it. *Here's looking at you, kid.* He remembered Alex telling him she'd had the feeling of being watched. If Thorpe had been there, where had he hidden himself? Officers had taken down the names and addresses of everyone in the crowd and the license plates of all the cars in the vicinity. They'd tried checking IDs, as well, but since most people had come out in their pajamas they had nothing on them.

Even so, wouldn't blond, blue-eyed Thorpe have stuck out in a sea of black and Latino faces? Thorpe's presence would have been more expected if he'd actually been the doer. Many perps, especially arsonists, liked to hang around the scene to see the reactions to their handiwork. Then again, reports of the discovery had made it to the radio news stations before he'd even gotten to the scene. The only hopeful note in this bit of speculation was that Thorpe must have been relatively close by in order to make it to the scene in order to see Alex there. Maybe those guys beating the bushes for Thorpe locally weren't wasting their time.

"How were they delivered?"

"Alice said some kid brought them up."

The receptionist hadn't been at the front desk when he'd come in, but had heard the phones ringing and being answered. "Can you get her for me?"

"Sure."

Alex disappeared and a few moments later a tall, dark-skinned woman with shoulder-length locks took her place at the door. By her demeanor, he'd place her in her midforties, though she possessed the kind of ageless face that made such assessments difficult.

"I'm Alice Blanchard," she said, entering the room. "I'll help in any way I can."

He shook the hand she extended. "You can start by telling me about the flowers."

"As I told Alex, some kid, maybe thirteen or fourteen, brought them up. He came up to the desk and said, 'Dr. Alex Waters?' as if he was asking me if that was my name. I said something like, 'No, but this is her office.' He plunked the box on my desk and started to walk out. I called him back to offer him a tip. I figured he might be the deliveryman's son or something helping his dad out. He waved me away, saying it had already been taken care of."

In other words, someone had already paid him to bring the flowers up. Zach wondered if the same person had paid him to spend as little time in the office as possible, therefore making it more difficult to identify him. "What did he look like?"

"Typical kid. Dark-skinned, skinny, baggy clothes like the kids wear. I didn't get too good a look at his face. He had this white baseball cap for a team I've never heard of, the Rockford Reds, pulled down low. The hat looked brand-new, though. And he was wearing elbow pads, like skateboarders do, but no deck." She shrugged. "I have a nephew."

So did Zach, and he doubted any boarder would leave his deck outside somewhere for someone to steal it. Maybe the guard had made him leave it downstairs. That would be a break, since the guard might be able to flesh out Alice's description a little. "What time were they delivered?"

"About eight thirty. I should have known something was wrong then. Who can get a florist to deliver that early?"

Zach placed a reassuring hand on her shoulder. It wasn't unusual for people to feel guilty for not being more observant in such situations. "You couldn't have known."

Alice shrugged and tilted her head from side to side as if she were weighing whether or not to accept what he said as true. "She's in danger, isn't she?" Alice asked, her concern evident in both her voice and her dark eyes.

Zach didn't mince words. "Yes, I think she is." For all he knew, Thorpe might be as fixated on Alex as he was on the young girls he killed. The only thing he knew for sure was that he needed to keep her safe. He only hoped she trusted him enough to let him do his job.

Sixteen

Later, after the reception desk had been dusted for fingerprints, the offending box had been removed, and the office shut down for the day, Alex sat in the corner of her sofa waiting for Zach to return. He was downstairs talking to the new guard, a man whose name she hadn't learned yet.

She sipped from the glass Roberta had pressed into her hand. The brandy, which the other woman claimed she only kept in her office for medicinal purposes, slid down her throat heating her insides. She rarely drank strong liquor, but at the moment she'd settle for any warmth she could get. She'd been chilled ever since she opened that envelope to find the killer's handiwork on the card inside.

Here's looking at you, kid. She wasn't up on her *Casablanca*, but weren't those the last words Bogie spoke to Ingrid before putting her on a plane to be with another man, her husband? Did he select those words because of what they meant in the movie or was it a taunt because he'd been close enough for her to feel his eyes on her and she hadn't detected him? Or was it a promise that he was watching her? Whichever, his choice of quote held a note of familiarity to it, suggesting it came from someone she knew.

Walter Thorpe. It seemed more likely now that he was responsible for all this mayhem, though she still couldn't wrap her mind around the idea. There was something, weak, ineffectual at the core of Walter Thorpe that made her mind rebel against the notion he could have pulled off an elaborate set of murders, not to mention her doubt that he possessed the intellectual capacity to conceive of it in the first place.

But if not Walter, who? Surely someone she knew. Perhaps one of her former patients who wanted to let her know they were out and off the wagon. Or maybe it was just some kook in the crowd or a disgruntled member of one of Thorpe's victims' families who'd wanted to let her know they'd be watching her for slipups this time.

Who knew? The only thing she did know was what Zach would say to her once he came upstairs. Whatever the source, he'd want her to treat that note as a credible threat. He'd want her to do what the police always wanted people in her situation to do: to lie low, disappear for a while until the threat was past. She couldn't do that. Not only did she have patients that depended on her, but altering her plans in that struck her as turning tail and running. But she was still Sammy the Bull's daughter. She couldn't do that. Whether that made her brave or foolhardy she didn't know, but she wouldn't change her mind.

She heard him now, talking to the officer stationed outside her office door. She downed the contents of her glass and set it down on the table. There was no point in giving Zach more ammunition by letting him know she'd already resorted to drink. Although the liquid warmed her insides, the rest of her remained as chilled as before.

He came into the room a moment later and sat in one of the chairs facing her. Lines of fatigue stretched around his eyes and mouth. She knew he hadn't gotten any more sleep than she had and she felt ready to drop. But she knew she'd go home eventually and sleep well that night. Would he?

He stretched out his legs in front of him. "Alex, we need to talk."

She knew that. She counted on that. But still she wasn't sure she wanted to hear all he had to say. "Did the guard get a better look at the delivery boy?"

"Only slightly. The two of them have agreed to work with a composite artist to see if they can come up with something. And, yes, the kid left his skateboard downstairs. Alice was right about that."

"In other words, this killer was close enough to the office today for a kid on a skateboard to ride up and make the delivery."

"Or he could have been right outside. There's a florist a block from here, but she hasn't fill any orders for white roses in the past week."

"You're trying to trace the box?"

"It's about all we have to go on, until the fingerprints come back."

Alex rubbed her fingertips together. She hadn't done a great job of removing the ink from when they took her prints to make a comparison. "I take it no one else saw anything," she said, referring to the canvass of the neighborhood she knew had been conducted.

Zach shook his head. "Aside from this building, the florist, and the grocery store, this is a residential neighborhood. Most folks were probably asleep or minding their own business that hour of the morning. There weren't many people out on the streets."

He didn't seem to hold out much hope of anyone having seen either the kid or the killer, and truthfully, neither did she. "So where does that leave us?"

"When you leave here, a car will follow you home and sit outside your place. You should take some time off."

She smiled without mirth. "How did I know you were going to say that?"

"You're a cop's daughter and not too slow on the uptake?"

"I can't do it, Zach. I have patients who rely on me. Not on the strength of one crackpot letter whose source we don't even know. If your guys want to follow me around, that's fine."

He shot her an impatient look. "I admire your bravado, but it's misplaced. We're talking about a guy who's already killed several women. We know who he is but not where. For all we know he slipped into the crowd last night unnoticed. If you're thinking you're safe because he contacted you here, how hard do you think it will be for him to find where you live? I checked the phone book. You're listed."

She couldn't argue with any of his statements, but one. "You're sure it's Thorpe now?"

"I never stopped thinking it was Thorpe. I wasn't as content to rush to judgment, as were some of my colleagues. Did he ever make any threats against you?"

"None I took seriously."

"What does that mean?"

"Threats from patients aren't all that uncommon. Neither are love letters for that matter. It's called transference. The patient projects onto the therapist the emotions he feels for someone significant in his life. Which one you get depends on the emotions churned up by therapy."

"How did Thorpe threaten you?"

"Nothing specific. Something of the 'make me sorry I was ever born' variety. I was trying to press him for more information about his childhood that he refused to give me. All I knew about him was that his mother died when he was ten years old and that he and his sister were sent to separate foster homes. There was no other family, or none that would take them in."

"That was a sore point?"

"Everything was a sore point. You have to remember, he was here because of a court order, not because he wanted help. A lot of these guys would rather put out their own eyes than tell you anything. They'll show up because they have to, but they'll spend the whole time reading the paper or listening to music with headphones on. The court can only mandate their appearance, not that they are actually benefited by the therapy provided. But you have to keep trying."

"Was Thorpe coming around?"

She nodded. "He'd started to. He was talking to me, anyway. Mostly, I think he wanted to convince me he was innocent, that he hadn't been trying to hurt those girls. He never told me outright but my gut says he was abused himself, which is probably why he didn't want to discuss his childhood."

Alex inhaled. She was tired of discussing Thorpe herself. She stood and crossed to her desk. "I didn't get a chance to tell you before, but Roberta and I might have found out something."

"You and Roberta?"

Alex pulled the file she wanted from her bottom drawer, stood, and met Zach's gaze. She wondered if the incredulousness she heard in his voice came from the fact that they were two women, that they weren't cops, or that he hadn't been aware she'd been looking into the case herself.

"Yes, me and Roberta. Have you ever heard of an organization called Juvenile Justice?"

"Yeah. From what I understand they're a bunch of crazy vigilantes out to stamp out kiddie porn and pedophilia."

"And you're against that."

"Not their mission but their methods. They've managed to screw up quite a few investigations by tampering with evidence of online crimes. Aside from that, you've got to wonder about some of the people who get involved in that sort of group. Even though they say they are against child sexual exploitation, how do you catch someone involved without having to view the material yourself? How do you lure a pedophile without listening to the list of things he wants to do to you? Maybe that's what really gets their rocks off. In your neck of the woods isn't that called sublimation?"

Since she couldn't argue with his assessment, she didn't bother. Some of the volunteers might have found a socially acceptable way to view material they claimed to abhor. That thought had occurred to her, too. What bothered her was the scorn with which he spoke. He didn't sound like the man she knew. "That's awfully cynical."

He shrugged. "That's the place I'm in right now. How did you and Roberta get involved with these people?"

"Her brother is head of the organization. Their sister was held hostage and raped by some man she thought she was in love with."

"Is she all right?"

"From what I understand, mostly." She walked back to the sofa and sat. "Do you want to know what we found out?"

"Of course." He held out his hand for the file.

She handed it over and sat back, folding her feet underneath her. "We were looking for men who had Yourplace accounts going by the screen name Hercules. There were fourteen of them." Inside the folder were printouts of the profiles the men had registered with the company. "I don't know if any of them is your killer, but I thought it was worth checking out."

He closed the folder. "It is. Thank you."

Sensing in him an urge to get going, she stood. "Let me know what you find out."

He rose to his feet. "I will." He closed the gap between them. She could feel in him the urge to touch her, but he held back. "Be careful, Alex." That smile she loved formed on his face. "And lay off the hard stuff." He winked at her and he left.

She wrapped her arms around herself, watching his departure. If he'd given her the opportunity, she would have told him she'd welcome his embrace. She wasn't foolish enough not to be scared. She wasn't immune enough from him not to want to be held by him. It had been such a long time since she had even the promise of comfort that she craved it.

Who knew he'd pick now, when she was softening, to follow her wishes? Between leaving her undisturbed last night and untouched today, he was giving her what she said she wanted, damn him. But he hadn't tried to convince her again that she should disappear for a while. She thought she knew why. At least, she hoped so.

"So we finally meet."

Zach shook the hand of Darryl Ferguson, the detective from online crime that he'd been trying to meet with the past couple of days, but either Darryl's schedule or his hadn't permitted it. Although Darryl was off today he agreed to meet as long as Zach was willing to do it on his turf. Both men settled into lawn chairs at the back of Ferguson's house while the family barbecue sizzled on the grill. "What's going on?"

"You tell me." Ferguson pulled a Corona from the cooler beside him. "Want one?"

Zach accepted the beer and twisted off the top. The liquid felt cool and refreshing going down. Just what he needed. "You know I'm working on that Amazon thing."

Darryl nodded before taking a swig. He wiped his mouth with the back of his hand. "That's some nasty business."

"And getting nastier. It turns out some of his victims

weren't pros as originally thought. He might have met some of the girls on the Internet. All of them had pages on this site called Your place."

Darryl nodded again. "I've heard of that site. Popular with the teenyboppers. We're just starting to look into that one. A couple of months ago, a mom catches her daughter sneaking out her bedroom window to meet some pervert she met online. The only information the girl will give us is that she met the guy in one of this site's chat rooms. But there's nothing on her computer—no saved chat logs, no IMs. The kid had 102 names on her buddy list, but she told us we were wasting our time since his name wasn't there. Apparently the perp told her to delete anything of his she'd saved so if her parents disapproved of them seeing each other, they couldn't find out who he was and stop them."

Obviously the girl had fallen for that explanation, since she'd done what he asked. Had Thorpe done the same thing with his victims? Or could Thorpe and the man Darryl was after be the same man? Two months ago had been the first time the killer hadn't left a victim. Had this mother's attentiveness kept her daughter from meeting the same fate as the others?

"What night was this?"

"January twenty-fifth, exactly one month after Christmas."

"What did she look like?"

"Like every other kid these days: thirteen going on thirty-five. Too much hair, too much boobs, too much makeup."

Just the way Thorpe liked them. "A Catholic school girl?"

"Yeah. Why?"

"We like a guy named Walter Thorpe for the killer. Seems to be his type. A kill on January twenty-fifth would fit his pattern, but there wasn't one that month."

Darryl took a long pull from his bottle. "Then this kid

might be luckier than she knows. Last I heard, she was mad at her mother for taking the computer away."

That seemed a reasonable reaction for a thirteen-year-old, if his Stevie was anyone to go by. "Assuming for a moment that your guy and my guy are the same guy, what can we do? Without getting into too much detail, we believe he's probably going under the screen name Hercules or some variant. So far we've found fourteen guys." Zach had rested the file containing the profiles on his lap. He picked it up and handed it to Darryl. "We're running down the profiles. So far, nothing yet."

Darryl opened the file and scanned the profiles. "I don't think I've seen any of these guys yet. We can add a page with a girl more to this guy's taste and see if he bites."

"I appreciate it." Zach stood. "I'll let you get back to your family."

"No problem." Darryl stood and shook his hand. "I'll let you know if he pops up on the radar. "What do you want me to do with him if we hook him?"

Zach winked. "Make him fall in love."

She'd expected him to show up and he didn't disappoint. He came to her house a little after nine. She'd already changed into her nightgown and bathrobe and enjoyed a catnap on the sofa that was thankfully dream-free. She opened the door to him and the first words that sprang into her mind tumbled out of her mouth. "You look like hell."

He gave a snort of laughter. "And to think I thought I missed that bluntness of yours."

She ushered him inside the door and closed it behind him. "Have you eaten?"

His answer took a moment to come, as if he had to consider it. "Actually no."

"Unfortunately, I haven't cooked in days, but I can offer you a sandwich."

"I'll take it."

She led the way back toward the open space that housed both the kitchen and the dining area. She paused briefly at the table. "Have a seat, I'll have it ready in a minute." She continued on to the refrigerator, taking out the fixings for his meal, and brought the items to the counter. Zach was still standing pretty much where she'd left him, looking around the space in that way he had that seemed to drink in his surroundings while giving away nothing of what he felt about them. Was he seeing the room the way it had been thirteen years ago, how it was now, or was one superimposed on the other?

Then his gaze focused on her. "It seems you have done some redecorating."

She shrugged. At one time the cabinets had been a dark wood, the stove and refrigerator had been two avocado relics from the seventies, and the only dishwasher in the place had been her. Now the cabinets were a lighter wood and the appliances were white, which gave the room an airier feel. "Those pesky people from Sears kept coming around. They made me an offer I couldn't refuse."

He smiled. "Looks good."

"Thanks." That's all the conversation she could muster at the moment. She supposed he'd fill her in on his progress, which she wanted to hear once she was seated with a glass of merlot in her hand. She also knew he'd try to convince her to stay somewhere other than her own home tonight. She'd rather hear that under the same conditions, as well.

Luckily, she'd finished the sandwich. She brought it and a bottle of beer to the table. "I hope you don't mind roast beef."

He slid into the seat that had traditionally been his as she set the food down in front of him. "Thank you."

She went back to the counter to claim the wine she'd poured for herself. By the time she got back to her seat he'd already devoured half the sandwich. She remembered Zach as a more deliberate eater. He really must have been busy if he hadn't taken the time for a meal. "Did you find out anything new?"

Zach put down the sandwich and wiped his mouth on a napkin. "Our latest tip on where to find Thorpe turned out to be a bust."

"Why is it so hard to find him?"

"For one thing, we've got every crazy and his mother calling in tips, and each has to be checked out. Besides, Thorpe was a loner. He's got one ex–cell mate and one living relative, both of whom claim not to have seen him. He doesn't have a bank account or a credit card that we know of that we could have used to track him. If it weren't for his gift to you, we couldn't even be sure he was still in the area."

"Glad to know it served some purpose other than scaring my office half to death."

"I met with one of the detectives that works with online crime. They've already started working on the Yourplace site. It seems some other girl was approached by a similar type of guy."

"You don't think it's the same man?"

"Probably not. When you think about the number of wackos and perverts out there, especially in New York, it would be too much of a coincidence. But a lot of these guys operate in the same way. This guy was probably just looking for some supposedly consensual underage sex, which is bad enough. Not all of them are as sick as Thorpe."

He took a last swig of his beer and set the bottle on the table. His gaze settled on her, assessing her with the same intensity with which he'd surveyed the room. What did he see when he looked at her like that? Not really wanting to know, she stood and picked up the empty bottle. "I'll get you another."

Before she could move, he grasped her arm to prevent her from going. "What's going on with you, Alex?"

"What do you mean?"

He gazed up at her, a sardonic expression on his face. "For one thing, why are you being so nice to me?"

She sighed. He was too observant not to have noticed a change in her. He'd probably noticed this afternoon. But how could she explain to him what she felt? That Roberta was right, she did have lingering feelings for him and not all of them were bad. Most of them were quite good, which was the scary part. Mostly, it took too much out of her to still be angry with him.

She felt him take the bottle from her fingers. "Tell me."

She took a step backward to slide back into her chair, dislodging his hold on her. "I realized I was punishing you for things that weren't really your fault. I thought it was time to let you off the hook. You've been very good to me. You've kept me in the loop, and I know you're the one who got McKay off my back. You've even taken my ideas seriously, which I know is hard for a cop to do."

"Is that the only reason?"

She shook her head. "It's odd, but at one time you were the only person with whom I could be myself. But I don't know how to act around you anymore. I think that's part of the reason why I was angry with you, too. Being angry provided me with a definitive role, the injured party. But we hurt each other, didn't we?"

He didn't answer that, which didn't surprise her since she hadn't really expected him to. He looked away from her for a moment, seeming to be debating with himself what to say next. When he looked at her again, he gestured toward her attire. "I take it you haven't packed anything yet."

"No."

"You know you can't stay here, Alex."

She did. She didn't want to stay, either. She'd found sleep only because she was exhausted, but since waking every creak and groan of the old house had put her on edge. She'd answered the door when Zach arrived before he'd had to knock. She'd heard him when he pulled up. Unfortunately, she had nowhere else to go. She'd given up her apartment in the city when her marriage dissolved. She couldn't bring risk to anyone else she knew by staying with them. In truth, she'd planned on staying at a hotel for a few days, but she feared she'd be as alone there as she was at home, which was part of the reason she'd put off doing anything about finding a place to stay.

More than she feared anything this killer might do, she didn't want to feel so isolated any longer. At least in her home, things were familiar. Even if the memories haunted her, they were hers.

Obviously he took her silence as protest. "This man is dangerous, Alex. If he's set his sights on you, there's no telling to what lengths he'll go to in order to get to you."

She heard the concern in his voice and wondered if it was the cop in him that engendered it or the man who had once meant a great deal to her. "I know," she said, even though she believed his message was sent not to threaten her but to prove how clever he was. What else would he do to prove his cleverness? "But don't waste your time trying to scare me. I'm already scared."

"Then maybe I can persuade you to get ready to leave. It's getting late."

True, it was. She needed to stop stalling. "Do you suppose I can just show up at the Sheraton or should I call for a reservation?"

He shook his head as if he couldn't believe she'd made that comment. "Alex, you're staying with me."

Her eyebrows lifted. As laissez-faire as Zach was known to be, he also possessed an authoritarian streak that had often annoyed her. "I am? How convenient for you."

He grinned in a way that said he hadn't missed her implication. "Don't worry. I don't have any ulterior motives in mind. Besides, we'll have a sixteen-year-old chaperone. My niece is staying with me."

Even if that were true, it didn't change the inappropriateness of her staying with him. "Won't your superiors have something to say about that?"

"Why should they care? You're not a suspect. Although Thorpe contacted you, it's not a crime to send flowers, so you're not a victim. The car outside is a courtesy and, if you're right, a vain attempt at hoping to spot Thorpe. I don't see a problem."

She wet her lips with the tip of her tongue, wishing she had some other argument to present.

"Don't try to outstubborn me on this, Alex. I promise you, you'll lose. Besides, you'll be doing me a favor."

"How's that?"

"It's my turn to host the family dinner tomorrow night. My sister's husband was killed a year ago. Ever since then things have been strained and I don't know what to do about that. On top of that, my brother and his wife seem to be having problems."

"Her name is Barbara, right? I thought they practically came out of the womb married."

"They did."

"What do you need me for? As a cook or to organize a family shrink-a-thon?"

"Neither, but I would appreciate a little advice."

She scanned his face. His expression was somber, concerned. She thought she understood him now. In every family, but especially in those that were abusive or formed by trauma, familial roles tended to be strictly pre-scribed. From what he'd told her, his older brother and sister had become mama and papa. His younger brother the baby to be protected. He, on the other hand, was viewed as more of the black sheep, the outsider—or in his own terms, the family fuck-up who couldn't get with the program.

She'd known thirteen years ago that being cast in that position had hurt and alienated him. But now that wound must go deeper, especially considering that the outside world didn't view him the same way. He had the respect of his colleagues and peers but none from the people who mattered most to him.

He wanted now what he'd always wanted—to be the hero for a change, not the villain. He wanted to be the one with the answers, and if she could do that for him, she would.

"All right, Stone," she said. "You win. This time. I won't be long." She rose and headed up to her room to pack.

After Alex left, Zach went to back to the table, cleared his place, and rinsed his dish in the sink. That done, he leaned his back against the counter, crossing his arms.

Alex had surprised him tonight, both in her easy acqui-escence to leaving her home and her change in attitude toward him. He'd seen a glimpse of it this afternoon, but not full-blown like tonight. If anyone asked him, he'd prefer it if she were still mad at him. At least then if she changed her mind about him, he'd deserve it. This way, he hadn't earned the redemption he'd sought; she'd simply let him off the hook.

But could she really do that? Set aside her emotions simply because she chose to? Maybe, if all that stood be-tween them was the way things ended. But he remem-bered that day, a beautiful spring afternoon. They'd been out patrolling the area around Fordham Road and the Grand Concourse. It had rained the previous two weekends, but this day the population was out in droves: young mothers out in the stores, pushing strollers and trailing a line of older kids. Gray-haired *abuelitas* sitting on the stoop or in folding chairs drinking coquito talking about their grandkids. Young punks in wife beaters and jeans prowling for chicks; clutches of young girls gathered together, giggling, pretending not to notice the boys. And all the noise: the bell of the *coco helado* or icey man, raised voices and shouting, Latin music vying with hip-hop, blaring from storefronts and car windows.

It was barely past one o'clock and the streets were already littered with store advertisements taken and discarded, spent wrappings from meals sold by restaurants or street vendors, and whatever other waste could be discarded by passersby. A typical Saturday afternoon.

So it seemed incongruous that an hour later Sammy would be lying in the hallway in some run-down tenement, his lifeblood seeping out of his body from a gunshot wound to his belly. They'd been chasing a pair of teenage purse snatchers who'd pushed down one of the grandmothers and stolen her bag.

Sammy had taken off after the pair, and Zach had no choice but to follow. They headed into the building on Webster Avenue and up the stairs that smelled of urine and other bodily secretions. When one of them veered off onto the third floor Sammy followed him, motioning for Zach to keep pursuing the other.

Even then, Zach had known it was a mistake. Everybody knew Sammy's days of charging in were over except Sammy. He'd probably give himself a heart attack if nothing else. Or he'd be too winded by the time he cornered the kid to actually cuff him. But Zach had continued up the stairs, knowing Sammy would never let him hear the end of it if he didn't follow orders.

He'd kept running up and up, until he heard the gunshot. One single report that sounded loud enough to shake the building. That wasn't Sammy's gun. Zach abandoned his chase and sped down the stairs. He found Sammy on his back, in the hallway, bleeding badly.

Oddly enough, Sammy was smiling. "I know that punk was carrying."

Sammy was delirious. That was the only explanation for it. Zach used his radio to call in while he tried to stop the flow of blood. His eyes burned and his chest constricted in a tight knot, making breathing difficult. This man had been the closest thing to a father he'd had in the past two years and he didn't know if he could stand to lose another. "Hold on, Sammy," he said, but he'd never seen so much blood. The bullet must have nicked an artery. He'd probably bleed out before anyone arrived to help.

Sammy shook his head. In a weak voice he said, "You tell Alex I love her." Sammy's bloodstained hand gripped his arm. "You take care of my little girl. She's your—"

Sammy never got to finish. His hand slumped to his side and his eyes rolled shut. Sammy hadn't finished, but Zach filled in the words for him. *She's your responsibility now.* Though Sammy had charged him with that task, he hadn't been man enough to handle it. He'd failed them both. He didn't see how Alex could forgive him for either.

But they'd forged some sort of truce tonight. For now, that would have to be enough.

Seventeen

Alex looked up at the two-story brick house Zach pulled to a stop in front of. It was a solid house, sturdy, the type of house young couples trying for kids bought hoping the house had the stamina to withstand the onslaught. That surprised her, as she'd thought the home he'd been referring to was really some bachelor pad in a more hip part of town.

Zach cut the engine and got out, going to the trunk to retrieve her bags. She opened her door and got out. The living room light was on, which suggested Zach's niece was still awake. She hadn't given much thought to the girl on the way over. She and Zach had engaged in a stilted and awkward attempt at making small talk, something neither of them proved good at. But now she wondered what kind of welcome she'd receive from the girl.

When Zach opened the door for her to enter first, Alex's attention was immediately drawn to the stairs to the right. A young girl came bounding down. She was dressed in a pair of shorts and a T-shirt, probably what she planned to wear to bed. Alex's first thought was that the girl was beautiful in a way that highlighted the blood-tie between her and Zach. They had the same eyes, the same coloring. Only secondarily did Alex notice that the girl was speaking.

"Uncle Zach, I've been waiting up to apologize for this aftern—" The girl stopped both her speech and her advance. "Oh?" Her gaze traveled from Alex to Zach and back. "Who are you?"

There was no animosity in the girl's face, only curiosity, which suited Alex fine. "I'm Alex Waters."

"Way to be rude," Zach added. "Alex is going to be staying with us a few days."

The girl's eyebrows lifted. "I see."

"No, you don't," Zach countered. "Now scoot. You can apologize to me later."

"We'll see." The girl turned and huffed up the stairs.

"In case you're wondering," Zach said, setting down her bags. "I caught her on the couch with a boy this afternoon."

"I take it that's against house rules."

"That and she's worried I'll tell her dad."

"Would you?"

"Are you kidding? He'd probably assume it was my influence rubbing off on her. Besides, I'm not exactly credible playing the sex police."

She supposed not, considering her presence there. Obviously the girl assumed she was there for some reason other than her personal protection. "Well, I'm ready to turn in if you point me in the right direction. Then you can deal with your niece."

"Thanks."

There were three bedrooms on the second floor: the master bedroom, the one Stevie occupied, and a smaller one barely big enough to accommodate a bed and dresser.

Zach set her bags inside the room. "I put clean sheets on the bed this afternoon. The bathroom is down the hall. If you need anything, just holler."

"Thanks, but I don't think I'll be needing anything."

"Good night, then." He paused, his eyes skimming her face. "It's going to be all right, Alex." He trailed a finger down her cheek.

She blinked, surprised. It was the first time he'd touched her in any way and she wasn't prepared for it.

The smile eased away from his face. "Well, anyway, good night." He turned and left, closing the door behind him.

Alex let out a heavy sigh. Obviously he'd taken her surprise for revulsion, which was far from the case. Feeling tired and disheartened she stripped out of her clothes and got into bed. The mattress was soft and the room was cool. She drifted to sleep within seconds.

After he left Alex, Zach went to Stevie's room and knocked on the door. She answered almost immediately, crossed her arms, and shot him an impatient look. "What?"

He chose to ignore her belligerence. "I'd like to talk."

She stepped aside to let him enter. He sat on one corner of her bed, which was still made up. "Say what you have to say, Stevie."

She seemed to consider that a moment. "Seriously?"

"Sure."

She shook her head, as if in disbelief. "Well, you got on my case about having a guy here. Then you move your girlfriend in. Not too much of a double standard."

He'd expected as much. "First off, you didn't just have a guy over, he was all over you. If anything, you should be thanking me for letting him get out of here with all his body parts intact. But I don't blame him; I blame you. You agreed to the rules before you came here."

"I know."

"Then is there something you want to say to me?"

"I'm sorry for this afternoon. I said that already."

"That's not it."

"I won't do it again."

He wondered if her crossed-arm, head-down stance was for effect or if she actually did regret what she'd done. Either way, he felt too much like a stern father, too much like his brother, for his own comfort. He patted the bed beside him as an invitation for her to sit. She did and leaned her cheek against his shoulder.

"And just so you know, Alex isn't my girlfriend. She's a friend who needs a place to stay. If you weren't so busy moping in here"—he tugged on the set of earphones around her neck that still emitted a tinny whine of music—"you might have noticed she's in the room next to yours, not in mine."

"Oh."

"So are we cool now?"

She gave a shudder. "Don't say cool, okay? Adults just shouldn't try to sound like kids."

He resisted the urge to tell her cool was cool long before she was born. "Have we an accord, then?"

She made a groaning noise. "Yeah, we're cool."

He patted her leg. "I'm going to bed. Don't stay up too late."

"I won't."

Yeah, and he was Joan of Arc, too. "See you in the morning."

He went to his bedroom, stripped off his clothes, and got into bed. It had been a long, mostly unproductive day. Sleep didn't come easily and his mind refused to settle down, turning the investigation over and over until nothing made sense.

Then there was Alex only two doors away. Was she asleep already or was she as tormented as he?

* * *

Alex woke to the scent of waffles and bacon cooking. In her sleepy state she contemplated what distinguished the scent of waffles from ordinary pancakes and couldn't put her finger on it. She only knew she knew the difference.

Her second thought was a bit of wonderment that waffles were being cooked at all. In order to cook waffles one had to be domesticated enough to own a waffle iron. She hadn't expected Zach would be.

She stretched and threw off her covers. Regardless of what was cooking or who was cooking it, she realized she was hungry. She put on her robe, grabbed a pair of jeans, a T-shirt, and underwear and headed to the bathroom. A brief shower later, she was dressed and heading down the stairs toward the kitchen. She doubted Zach was the one plying his culinary skills, since his door was still closed and his niece's was open.

"I hope you're hungry," the girl said as Alex walked into the kitchen.

Alex had to stop thinking of her as "the girl." "What's your name?"

"Stevie. It's really Stephanie, but everybody calls me Stevie."

"My real name is Alexandra, but everybody calls me Alex."

Stevie smiled, gesturing toward the table in a way that indicated she should have a seat. "Hi, Alex. You want some waffles? I only burned them a little."

"Sure." Alex sat at the table where milk, sugar, butter, and syrup were already laid out on a little tray. Alex wondered at that, since it was obviously a breakfast table. Did she plan on serving Zach, also?

"I made some coffee, too." She placed a mug of it in front of Alex before removing the items from the tray and putting them on the table.

So it was she, not Zach, whom Stevie had planned to butter up with a breakfast tray. Interesting. What exactly did this girl want from her? Alex added milk and sugar to her cup, deciding to let the girl play her own hand. "Can I help with anything?"

"No, I got it covered." Stevie came over to deposit a plate with three whopping waffles and several rashers of bacon in front of Alex.

Maybe the girl was trying to fatten her up, as well, Alex thought, amused.

Stevie slid into the seat across from her, one leg curled beneath her and one elbow on the table. She propped her chin on her fist. "So how do you know my uncle?"

That didn't take long. Alex took her time pouring syrup on her waffles. "Aren't you going to have some?"

"I don't eat carbs and fat."

Alex almost laughed, since Stevie didn't mind practically shoving the same down her throat. Alex cut a piece of waffle off with her fork and brought it to her mouth and chewed. "They're really good. You should try some."

Stevie made an impatient noise. Silently Alex chided herself. As a psychologist she should be above playing head games with a sixteen-year-old. "My father was your uncle's first partner. I was a little bit younger than you are when I met him."

"Oh." The girl eased into a regular sitting position. "Your dad was a cop? That bites, doesn't it?"

"Yean, pretty much," Alex had to agree, though she hoped Stevie's motivation for thinking so was different from her own.

"I mean, he thinks he knows everything and every guy I know is terrified of him."

"I know what you mean."

She shrugged. "Uncle Zach is all right, though, most of the time."

Alex supposed that most of the time didn't include when he'd walked in on her. Alex studied the girl's face a moment. Despite the turn of the conversation, she suspected Stevie was well loved and cared for. Her malaise was probably situational, predicated on whatever problem had led her to staying with her uncle instead of at home. And if Alex read her right, protective feelings for her uncle had led her to question Alex, not pure nosiness. But since Alex was a cop's kid, Stevie apparently figured she was okay.

Alex swallowed another bite of waffle. "How long have you been staying with your uncle?"

"Just a few days. But he's never here. He's working on some case."

And providing her none of the attention she needed to get from somewhere. "You knew he was on his way home yesterday, didn't you?"

Stevie's eyes widened. "Yeah. I called the station house and they said he was on his way. How did you know?"

Alex shrugged. "You don't seem that stupid to me."

Stevie laughed. "Are you trying to get something going with my uncle?"

That veered into none-of-your-business territory, but Alex was curious as to whether Stevie thought that was a good idea or not. "I don't know. Should I?"

Stevie tilted her head to one side and bit her lower lip, contemplating her answer. She leaned forward and whispered conspiratorially, "I think my dad thinks he cheated on his ex-wife."

Zach had been married? She didn't know why that information surprised her. Few decent men in their late thirties survived without being snared by some woman. "But you don't think so?"

Stevie shook her head. "I don't know. I thought he really loved her, and she was, well . . ."

"What?"

"Did you ever go to the zoo and see the baby monkeys clinging to their mothers' neck? That's what she reminded me of."

Alex couldn't resist a chuckle. "Too needy?"

"Way too. Not that it's any of my business."

True, but Alex wondered at the reversal in the girl's attitude. She had her answer a moment later when she felt Zach's hand at the back of her chair.

"What are you two talking about down here?"

She looked up at him. There was a smile on his face, but whatever sleep he'd gotten hadn't completely erased the look of fatigue from his face. Or maybe he was still half asleep. He still looked damn good, but he was waiting for an answer.

She glanced at Stevie. The girl had obviously shifted gears knowing Zach approached and wanted to make it appear that Alex had been the one asking questions in case Zach heard them. Smart girl. Alex wouldn't give her away—this time. "Just girl talk."

From the look on Zach's face, Alex knew he didn't believe her, but he didn't challenge what she said either.

"Do you want some breakfast, Uncle Zach?" Stevie vacated her seat. "I can make you some waffles."

"Sure." Zach went over to the coffeemaker and poured himself a cup. "Try not to burn mine."

Stevie laughed. "I can't make any guarantees."

Alex watched Zach, who added a bit of milk to his coffee but no sugar. When he looked up he winked at her. Alex tilted her head to the side considering him. She'd known last night would serve as some sort of turning point between them. She'd wanted to end the hostility between them, or rather her hostility toward him. But considering their stilted attempts at conversation last night, she hadn't expected either of them to be at ease with each other so quickly, either.

Then it occurred to her what that wink meant: He'd been listening the whole time. How else could he have known about her waffles being burned? Stevie had placed them on her plate briquette-side down. He must have come down right behind her, but he hadn't made a sound. He'd probably only made his presence known out of fear that Stevie would divulge even more personal information.

Once Stevie had finished preparing her uncle's meal, she claimed to need to get dressed and left. Alex pushed her plate away and sat back. "Is everyone in your family as devious as the two of you?"

"Actually, no. By the way, if you ever do try to start something up with me, let me know. I'll help you out."

He was teasing her, which seemed to be a means of distracting her from what Stevie'd said. Of course, that only made her more curious. "Is what she said true? About your marriage, I mean?"

"Yes. Her father believes I cheated on my wife. So does most of the rest of my family."

He'd misunderstood her. She'd been referring to the apparent unhappiness of it. No one could be content while another human kept a stranglehold on them. She'd learned that firsthand. But she noticed he hadn't told her what was true, only what was believed. He left her to think what she wanted. She should have obeyed her first instinct and left the subject alone.

"I shouldn't have asked that."

He put his fork down and sat back. "It's all right. I don't mean to make this a bigger deal than it was. We were together for a couple of years, separated for more than twice that. She finally got around to divorcing me last year so she could marry someone else."

He spoke as if what he said should answer all questions on the topic. It didn't, but she was willing to let it go. "So what's on the menu for tonight?"

"I have no idea. I hadn't really thought about it."

There was a man for you. "If you don't mind, I'll take care of it. I'd rather not get indigestion from your cooking or burnt offerings from your niece."

She'd been teasing him this time, but he didn't take the bait. "Be my guest. If you need anything I'll get it for you." He rose from the table and put his plate in the sink. "I'd better get dressed. I'll be down to do the dishes in a minute."

She looked after him as he walked out the kitchen. "Way to go, Alex," she said aloud. Whatever little bit of camaraderie they'd shared for a moment she'd destroyed with her curiosity. She should have known she had to be the last person he'd want to discuss his failures with, but her nature was to probe the layers to see what lay beneath the surface. It's what made her a good psychologist. But she should have kept it to herself that time.

She got up from the table and did the dishes Zach had promised to do.

The doorbell rang for the first time at five o'clock. Zach wasn't surprised to find that Adam and Barbara were the first to arrive. They always were, regardless of the occasion. Barbara greeted him with a kiss to the cheek. "How's my baby?"

"She's fine. She's in the kitchen."

Barbara excused herself and went to find her daughter, pulling her son reluctantly behind her.

When she'd gone, Zach turned to his brother. Something about Adam's demeanor with his wife suggested things between them had changed. "How are things going with Barbara?"

"Better, in a manner of speaking. Stevie told me you brought some woman home last night."

Zach ground his teeth together. He hoped the night ended before he had to throttle his niece. "She's not some woman. Her name is Alex Waters. She's Sammy the Bull's daughter."

Adam's response was a low whistle. "She's involved with this whole Amazon thing with you, isn't she?"

Zach nodded. "It was kept out of the papers, but Thorpe contacted her yesterday. I didn't think she should be at her place alone."

"I agree with you." Adam patted him on the shoulder, which was as close to an apology as he was going to get. "How's she doing?"

"Alex? She's Sammy's daughter. She made lasagna."

Adam snorted. "I think I like her. How long have you been sleeping with her?"

The doorbell rang again. Zach excused himself from his brother without bothering to give an answer and doubled back toward the door. It was going to be a long night.

No day was sacrosanct on the calendar of a detective, no birthday, no holiday, no anniversary celebration. Despite it being a perfectly good Sunday night, McKay found himself picking through the detritus of an abandoned one-story house by the train tracks running behind Co-op City.

The place was little more than a shack now, with a tumbledown appearance from the outside and filth and decay on the inside. When they'd opened the front door, the smell had hit them, driving a few of the younger officers back. It was the smell of fetidness and rank dampness coming off the surrounding waters. It wouldn't surprise him to find Thorpe in here dead, since there was the smell of that, too, here.

McKay stepped over the threshold into a sea of garbage. Old, broken, and rotted furniture, moldy clothing, spent condoms, chips of peeled paint, and other articles he couldn't identify littered the floor. Something scurried at his feet, probably mice or rats, but in this area it could be raccoons or possums as well.

Even before he'd come in, a perimeter of lights had been set up outside the house. A search team had done a quick sweep looking for anything live and human and found nothing. A series of lights had been set up on the inside as well, but anything could be hiding in this mess, anyone. Or no one.

That was McKay's fear—that Thorpe was playing games again, making them waste their time on a fool's errand, digging through dirt and slime to come back empty-handed. He'd been skeptical since the call first came in through the switchboard. The caller had asked for him personally, which was the only reason he'd picked it up.

"I know where that guy you're looking for is at," the caller had said without preamble.

"Which guy?" McKay had asked, even though he'd already been told what the call was about.

"Thorpe. Walter Thorpe. I was with him today."

Despite himself, adrenaline started to flow at the mention of Thorpe's name. He knew better. How many calls had they logged in that provided information that went nowhere? "Where were you with him, Mr. . . . ?" McKay prompted.

"I don't have to give no name, do I?"

That dampened his enthusiasm a little. People willing to give their names were more credible than those who weren't. "No. Where were you?"

"I don't know the address." But he went on to describe the little house out in the middle of nowhere. That got him going again. They'd all assumed Thorpe was hiding out somewhere remote. The information fit in with what they knew.

"How do you know Walter Thorpe?" he'd asked next,

but the line had gone dead. Regardless, a mixture of anticipation and hope had begun to stir in his belly.

Now, standing in this filth, he didn't know what to expect. An excited voice called from the other room, "Detective, you gotta see this."

He stepped over the debris to find the voice. Several of the officers were standing grouped together staring at something farther inside the room. He made his way inside, and found what they were looking at. A nude body lay among the debris, its skin looking more mummified than decayed. It was impossible to tell how long the person had been dead, though he suspected the body had been dumped here not too long ago. Otherwise the four-legged friends would have picked it clean by now.

Three things struck him as he looked down at the body: The mouth had been sewn shut. The genitals were missing. So was the middle finger of the right hand.

Eighteen

After the meal, Zach sat in his first-floor office facing his older brother. This tête-à-tête had been Adam's idea, but so far he hadn't said a word. Adam had said things at home had improved, and Zach had noticed how solicitous he had been toward his wife during dinner, so he was partially mollified on that account. But since Zach didn't want to leave Alex alone with the rest of his family too long, he figured he'd get the conversation rolling. "You and Barbara are getting along better."

"She wasn't having an affair."

Zach let out a relieved sigh, not that he ever thought she had been. He was just glad his brother realized that. "Then what's the problem?"

"She was seeing someone. A doctor. She's got cancer."

Zach hadn't expected that, but he didn't immediately think the worst. With early detection, the disease wasn't necessarily a death sentence. He wondered briefly what Alex would think of that bit of optimism on his part. "Where? Breast?" Seeing the ravaged look that came over his brother's face, Zach guessed his optimism was misplaced.

"Pancreas. Her mother died of the same thing."

Zach didn't know what to say to that. No platitudes

sprang to mind, not that Adam would have believed them coming from his mouth. "I'm sorry."

Adam nodded. "I noticed her losing weight, but I thought she was doing it to please some man."

"You can't beat yourself up about that. Barbara could have told you what was going on."

"Looking back, I think she did try to tell me a couple of times. I can be a bit of an ass sometimes."

"I've noticed." Zach leaned back in his chair. "What's her prognosis?"

"Not good. Five-year survival rates can be in the single digits."

Damn. Knowing his brother, Adam was probably focusing on the most negative statistics rather than the more positive ones. Still it didn't sound good.

"Do the kids know?"

Adam shook his head. "We're going to take Stevie home with us tonight. We're thinking of keeping them both home from school tomorrow so we can discuss it."

"If there's anything I can do."

"You already have. Stevie was the only one paying attention. She knew something was wrong with her mother and wouldn't let her be so that she could come to terms with it—or tell me."

Obviously Adam wasn't going to take his advice about not blaming himself. "You're there for her now."

Adam shrugged and stood. "I'm going to collect my family and go home."

"Can I do anything to help?"

Alex had noticed Joanna go upstairs with the baby, diaper bag slung over her arm, and followed. Joanna had taken the baby to Zach's room and laid her down on his bed. It was the first time Alex had seen his room. The king-sized bed didn't surprise her. The neatness and airiness of the room did.

Joanna glanced back at her over her shoulder. "Not unless you can make babies stop pooping."

Alex chuckled. Joanna moved with the smoothness and efficiency with which one might expect a nurse to change a diaper. Alex sat on the bed far enough away from the baby not to be in the way. "She's a beautiful girl."

Joanna paused a moment, staring down at her daughter. "She looks like her father." Joanna shifted her gaze to look at Alex. "I suppose Zach told you what happened."

"A little bit."

"Did *they* send you up here to talk to me?"

"Not exactly, but I do know Zach is concerned about you."

Joanna adjusted her daughter's stockings over the clean diaper. "Yeah, I know. Everyone's concerned. *I'm* concerned. I thought I would have gotten myself together by now."

"Depression can be a hard thing to cope with on your own."

"Who's depressed?" She gave a short, mirthless burst of laughter. "I'm angry. I'm angry at my stupid husband for not telling me he'd gotten involved in something as a kid that would get him killed as an adult. I'm angry at myself for letting this happen again. I raised my two boys mostly alone. I never wanted to go through that again. But here I am. If I'm quiet it's because I have nowhere to put that anger. I feel like if I open my mouth it will all come spilling out and no one wants to deal with a constantly screaming virago of a woman."

"You mean, like now?"

Joanna smiled, as Alex hoped she would. "You could say that."

"You can come scream at me in my office if you like. I won't be there next week, but after."

Joanna picked up her daughter, who was busy trying to crawl away. "I think I'd like that. Thank you."

"A girl's got to drum up business somehow."

Joanna eyed her shrewdly. "You don't let my brother get away with anything, do you?"

Unsure how to answer that, or if she wanted to answer that, she asked, "What do you mean?"

Joanna shot her a droll look. "We're both girls here. We know what kind of men my brothers are. They ride right over whatever they don't want to hear or see or face. Sometimes you get run over too if you're not paying attention. Zach is the least guilty of the three of them, but he's still a Stone."

Joanna adjusted her daughter on her shoulder. "I was opposed to Dana and Jonathan getting together at first. That seemed like the immovable force meeting the rolling object. But I think you can handle yourself." Joanna winked at her. "It's time I got my brood together and got home."

Fifteen minutes later, they had all had made their good-byes. Zach closed the door behind the last of them—Jonathan and Dana—then returned to the kitchen. Alex stood at the sink finishing the last of the dishes. He came up behind her and put his hands on her shoulders. This time she didn't flinch. "You don't have to do that."

"I know, but I've only got a couple of glasses to go."

Looking down at her, he felt the urge to lower his head and nuzzle her neck assailing him. Hell, he wanted more than that, but it would be a start. But since he had no idea how she would take that he backed away to lean his shoulder against the archway leading to the dining room. "Thanks for tonight." She'd been sandwiched between his two brothers during dinner. He'd spare even a mortal enemy that fate. "I hope they didn't bore you to death."

"Not at all. I like your brothers."

"Then you must have been taking your own happy pills."

She laughed. "No, I have not. I spoke to Joanna, too."

That surprised him. When he'd told her of his family's travails he hadn't dwelt too long on his sister. "When was this?"

"While you were with Adam."

"What did she tell you?"

"That's covered by doctor-patient privilege. She agreed to come in to the office when I go back." She put the last glass into the drainboard and turned off the water. She turned to face him. "If I'm not being too intrusive again, what did Adam tell you?"

She hadn't been intrusive before. He'd bristled at the thought of another family recounting of his supposed sins. He'd expected more of the same tonight for Alex's benefit, but everyone behaved themselves tonight.

"Barbara has pancreatic cancer. I'm not sure how advanced it is."

The look that came over Alex's face told him what she thought of Barbara's chances. "I'm so sorry, Zach."

His heated gaze met hers as she walked toward him and slid her arms around her neck. His arms closed around her, one at her waist, one tangling in her hair. He lowered his head to bury his nose against her neck. Damn, it felt good to hold this woman. Her soft body melded against his, her gentle hands moved over his back, soothing. Still, he felt a restlessness in her that was mirrored in his own body.

He lifted his head to look down at her. The last time he'd seen that look in her eyes, there'd been two sweaty naked people in the room. He chucked her under her chin. "Isn't this where we got ourselves in trouble last time? This comforting thing?"

A hint of a smile tipped up her lips. "I'm afraid so."

He trailed a finger down the side of her face. "What do you want from me, Alex? You're going to have to tell me, 'cause I damn sure don't know."

Before she could answer, his cell phone went off, startling them both. He didn't bother to look at the display. He simply answered as he always did. "Stone."

He listened to the voice on the other end of the line, knowing this was the end of whatever might have started between them, at least for now. He told the captain that he'd be coming in, but not that he planned to bring Alex with him. He disconnected the call and put his phone back in his pocket.

"We have to go," he said. "They just found Thorpe."

"Finally. Has he started to talk yet?"

"That would be kind of impossible. Walter Thorpe is dead."

Alex stared out the window as Zach drove to the precinct. From his house it was only a fifteen-minute ride. Walter Thorpe was dead? For how long? Either Zach hadn't been given that information or nobody knew. She'd never believed Thorpe was responsible, but she'd been too busy deflecting those who insisted he was to contemplate who else might be the culprit.

It was someone she knew. Of that she was certain. She'd already started going through whatever files she had at home and could find no one who made a better suspect than Thorpe.

She also knew whoever it was sought to blame Thorpe for the crimes, at least for a while. Zach told her that an anonymous tip had led them to find the body. She doubted some random individual would have called with that information. It had to be the killer himself who wanted everyone to know he was still out there and not who they thought he was.

She glanced at Zach's profile. His jaw was set and his expression was sober and intent. She much preferred the way he'd looked a few moments ago, desire dancing in his dark brown eyes. He'd asked her what she wanted. In a way his phone going off hadn't been a bad thing since she had no answer for him. At that moment, all she could think about was being held by him, wanting him. He had offered her a chance to save herself from making a mistake, but she wasn't sure she wanted it. They were both adults, presumably capable of handling a night of sex without falling apart.

The point was moot now, anyway. If Walter Thorpe wasn't the Amazon Killer, both their focus had to be on finding out who was.

The small conference room was packed with both detectives and uniformed officers by the time they made it into the precinct. Smitty was already there toward the back of the room. He stood to let Alex have his seat. The two men stood with others along the wall.

Both the captain and McKay stood at the front of the room, but the captain let McKay do all the talking. Such a laissez-faire management style could often prove useful, but not, to Zack's mind, when the subordinate was McKay. But McKay looked different today, and not just because he had on jeans and a T-shirt rather than a suit. He seemed deflated, his features sunken into his face. Zach wondered if it was finding out the man he'd believed to be the perpetrator all along was more than likely completely innocent.

Zack tuned in to what McKay was saying, droning on

in an emotionless monotone. "The m.e.'s preliminary assessment is that Thorpe has been dead at least a few months, possibly a year. The house was not the primary crime scene, but a dump site. A team is still at the house collecting evidence, but so far it doesn't look like this is his kill site either."

McKay paused looking into the crowd assembled. As he found who he was looking for, a sneer crossed his face. "I see Dr. Waters is here with us now. How does it feel to know you were right all along?"

Zach's hands fisted and he took a step forward. Then he felt Smitty's hand on his arm. "Just wait."

"Pretty damn shitty. Thanks for asking. But while we're on the subject, maybe you boys wouldn't be in this freaking mess if you'd listened to me in the first place."

Beside him Smitty shook his head and tsked. "When is that boy ever going to learn?"

Zach wouldn't mind pounding the lesson into McKay's head himself. But apparently McKay wasn't finished yet. "What do you suggest we do next, Doctor?" he asked in a tone that said he doubted Alex would come up with anything.

"Find out who owned the house last. It obviously means something to your killer."

"We're already on that," the captain said, in one sentence asserting his authority over the room. He went on to say that the only real clue was a tire print found at the scene. Assignments were discussed before the meeting broke. The captain motioned him over. "I'd like to speak to you, Smitty, and Dr. Waters in my office in five minutes."

"No problem." As the room cleared, Zach went back to where Smitty stood next to Alex.

Smitty nodded to where the captain and McKay stood. "It appears to me someone is getting dressed down."

Zach glanced over his shoulder. Whatever the two men were saying, he couldn't hear and didn't really want to, as long as McKay got his act together. "The captain wants to see us in his office."

"Do tell," Smitty said. "Wonder what we did now?"

Zach shrugged. They'd find out soon enough.

They'd only been in his office a couple of moments when Captain Craig came in. He sat behind his desk and folded his hands and leaned forward toward Alex. She assumed the smile on his face was for her benefit, but it looked forced and uncomfortable. "First let me thank you, Dr. Waters, for your cooperation so far."

Which sounded like he was going to ask for more. "It was my pleasure."

"What's your take on what happened tonight?"

"Your killer wants to take credit for what he's done. He coopted a bit of Walter's pattern to divert attention from himself. He could have known Walter or known enough about Walter to find him and kill him to keep him from either getting picked up or trying to claim he wasn't responsible. But if this man is after immortality, he can only gain that by eventually revealing who he is."

"You think he'll do that?"

She nodded. "But not yet. He's got something else planned. Something that will eclipse what he's done so far."

"And he wants you watching."

"Apparently, though I'm not sure why. My only certainty is that the man you're looking for is in some way connected to my old practice. Hence the business card on the envelope that came with the flowers. Mine were the only fingerprints found on that, correct?"

"Yes. And we're waiting until tomorrow to show the sketch of the kid around to some schools to see if anyone can identify him."

Alex nodded. She didn't hold out much hope that the boy would be able to tell them anything even if they

could find him. Anyone clever enough to pull off all this
had to be capable of putting on a disguise.

The captain sat back. "Thank you, Dr. Waters. If you
can think of anything else, let us know. If you'll excuse
us for a moment, I'd like to talk to the detectives."

"Sure." Alex stood. A trip to the ladies' room wouldn't
be out of order at the moment. She glanced at Zach,
who winked at her. But his arms were crossed and his jaw
was as grim-set as it had been on the drive over here.
What was that about?

She let herself out of the office, got directions to the
nearest bathroom from one of the officers, and went
inside.

After Alex left, the captain sat back in his seat and
wiped his hand across his face. "This is some shit."

Zach couldn't disagree with him, but he was waiting to
hear what Craig said next. He thought he knew where
this was going and he wasn't having it. The case had
shifted in more ways than one with the discovery of
Thorpe's body. This was no case of one sicko enacting his
fantasies through murder. Whoever they were hunting
was more gruesome, more calculating, and definitely a
lot scarier, particularly since they had no idea who he was.

He didn't know how Alex fit into this mess, but he
wasn't going to allow anyone to use her in any way to
lure this man out. That was Zach's first thought when he
first heard Craig's comment about her "cooperation."
Despite his obligation to the job, his first mission was to
protect Alex.

Craig cleared his throat. "I want someone with that
girl at all times. Where is she staying?"

"She's at my place."

He knew from the expression on the captain's face
that he wanted to say something, but didn't. "Then I

hope you don't mind being watched because I'm putting a car outside your place. I've already subpoenaed Dr. Waters's files from the hospital. I want her to look through them and see if she can find anyone with a connection to both her and Thorpe."

Zach relaxed a little, seeing that the captain was more interested in Alex's protection than her participation. "Anything else?"

"Check out the victims of Thorpe's trial. See if any of the male relatives are still holding a grudge."

Zach had already thought of that and dismissed it as a possibility. Why go through all this trouble doing to other young women what was done to their own loved ones and worse? Why not just hunt Thorpe down and kill him outright? Then again, if criminals made sense, ninety-nine percent of cops would be looking for another job.

Both he and Smitty turned to leave.

"By the way, Stone," Craig said. "McKay has been reassigned."

Zach nodded, instead of spoke, since the most likely words to come out of his mouth were "About fucking time." He didn't ask what McKay was transferred to since he couldn't care less. Not until he stepped outside the office and realized Alex wasn't outside waiting for him.

Alex surveyed her image in the mirror above the basin as she washed her hands. Most of her makeup had worn off and lines of fatigue showed around her eyes. What she wouldn't give for one long, uninterrupted night of sleep. Since that didn't appear to be coming any time soon, she splashed some water on her face hoping for a temporary improvement in her appearance, then shut the water off.

She patted her face dry and threw the towels in the

trash. She needed to get back upstairs. Zach and his captain must have finished their conversation by now. Undoubtedly, she was at least part of their topic of discussion, which necessitated her leaving the room. She wanted to know what was said and what more they planned to do to find the killer.

She pulled open the bathroom door, then took a step back in surprise. She hadn't heard anyone outside the door, but Detective McKay was standing on the other side. The expression on his face was both weary and troubled.

"Dr. Waters," he said. "Can I talk to you for a minute?"

Nineteen

Alex swallowed. McKay had startled her, but she wasn't afraid of him. She was in the middle of a police station on top of that. But all things considered, his sudden appearance was unnerving. Aside from that, she couldn't imagine what he wanted from her considering his behavior during the meeting. Perhaps his superior had suggested an apology was in order, but she didn't want one, even if it was his own idea. "What about?"

"I want to apologize for the way I've treated you, both now and before."

At least she'd had his motives down. "That's not necessary."

"I honestly thought it was him. If we hadn't found the body, I'd still think it was him."

She didn't doubt that. He went after Thorpe with a single-mindedness she'd rarely rarely exhibited by those who couldn't use her services. She'd always wondered why and it occurred to her this might be her only chance to find out. "Why?"

McKay ran his hand through his hair and sighed. "I have a woman waiting for me at home who was one of Thorpe's victims. That's the question she wants answered, too. Why? Why did he pick her? Why did he put her life and her children's lives in danger? I wanted to be there when they caught him and ask him that for her. What am I supposed to tell her now?"

He spoke the last words so quietly, as if they were more for himself, not to be shared with her. She couldn't believe she actually felt sorry for this man. But he was thinking like a man, not a cop. Half the time these predators didn't even have a motive or one they could recount to others. The truth of it was, his woman fit Thorpe's victim pattern and she was available. Beyond that, Alex hadn't a clue. "That you love her and that he can't ever hurt her again."

McKay looked at her for a long moment, then slunk away without saying another word. She let out a sigh as she watched his exit, thankful that for the moment, at least, she wouldn't have to contend with him again.

"What was that about?" Zach asked, coming up beside Alex.

She smiled up at him. "It's not important."

Maybe it wasn't, but he had the feeling she was covering for McKay, which surprised him. As long as the man hadn't done anything to hurt or upset Alex he didn't really care. She looked tired, which was understandable considering it was almost midnight. He lifted his hand to graze his knuckles along her cheek. "How are you doing?"

"If I yawned now, would that give you a clue?"

He chuckled. "Then let me get you home."

"Don't you have work to do?"

"I'll get to it."

He slung his arm around her shoulder. Either she didn't object or she was too tired to put up a protest. Considering the scene in his kitchen earlier, he chose to believe the former. What he still didn't know is what her answer would have been if his phone hadn't rung.

The car Craig had promised was already parked across the street from his house when they drove up. He was sure Alex noticed, but since she said nothing neither did he. Despite their presence, he went inside to check the house before he let her in. Now more than ever he couldn't afford any carelessness.

When he finally let her in, he asked her, "Do you want to switch to the bigger bedroom?"

"Right now, I'm too tired for anything but sleep."

He knew the feeling.

At her door, she turned to face him. A small smile tilted her lips. "I guess this is good night."

"Mmm," he agreed. "That it is." But he didn't move. He studied her face in the pale light from the hallway. Although he could see the fatigue in her, she looked as beautiful as he'd ever seen her. God, he wanted her, and not just sexually. He wanted to understand her, the woman she was now, to know what made her tick. To know how she could remain so calm and steady given all that had happened in the last few days. Surely she had to realize that their perp was gearing up for something, which probably included hurting her. Most of all he wanted to know why she'd walked away from him all those years ago.

"Tell me something before I go. Why did you give up on me, Alex?"

"Why did I give up? You were the one who disappeared. You were the one who wouldn't answer my calls."

"I was ashamed of myself, Alex. I'd fucked up. The last words your father spoke to me were to protect you. I don't think putting on a condom was what he had in mind."

She shook her head. "Oh, Zach. I know you have this built up in your mind that big bad you seduced poor little me out of her virginity and that's just not what happened. I wanted to be with you. I didn't want to be alone and I didn't want you to be alone. I wasn't even a virgin."

"But—" he started to protest, but thought better of it. He remembered asking her, but she hadn't said anything. She'd buried her face against his neck and he'd figured she was embarrassed by her own inexperience. But he also remembered her tears when he'd eased himself inside her. "Then why did you cry?"

She huffed out a breath and gestured in a way that showed her exasperation. "I guess I was a virgin in all the ways that counted. You were the first man to show me any tenderness or consideration or kindness. I cried because it didn't hurt, not because it did."

He didn't ask the question, but he knew the answer. He wanted to find whoever had hurt her and smash them and smash them until there was nothing left but pulp. He pulled her to him and buried his face in her hair. "I'm sorry," he whispered against her ear.

She let him hold her for a moment before she pushed away. "A woman answered your phone."

He had no idea what she was talking about. "When?"

"Thirteen years ago. I wasn't stupid, Zach. I knew there wasn't really a future for us in that way. I knew I wasn't a match for women your age. I wanted that one night, but I didn't expect it to cost me everything. That woman who answered the phone was laughing. I could hear you in the background laughing, too. It was like being slapped in the face with the fact that I was just wasting my time. I hung up and never called back."

For the life of him he couldn't remember any such call or any laughing woman in his apartment save for his sister-in-law Barbara, who, when he'd told her what had happened with Alex, told him to man up and make things right with her. But by then it had been too late.

"There was no other woman, Alex." In many ways

there hadn't ever been another woman, not one who gained more than a little piece of him, not even Sherry. Yes, she'd been needy, like Stevie said, but he'd done that to her, casting her in the position of constantly knocking on the door never to be let in. That's why he'd never really found it in his heart to fault her for what she'd done.

It occurred to him that when it came to Alex, both of them had let their insecurities waylay them. He'd believed she'd never forgive him and she'd believed that any interest in her on his part ended with her father's death. Then they'd each proved the other right, at least as appearances went. He could understand Alex's behavior, as she'd been little more than a child; he'd been a grown man who should have known better.

But did any of that really matter now? He stroked his thumb over her cheek. Her eyes were, huge, luminous, and trained on him. He had no idea what she was thinking, but when her tongue darted out to trace her bottom lip, his first impulse was to lower his head and claim it.

He stopped himself, knowing she'd never really answered his question about what she wanted. As much as he wanted her, he wanted more not to make another mistake with her. He started to pull away when she leaned up and pressed her open mouth to his.

Zach squeezed his eyes shut at the pleasure of the contact. His tongue plunged into her mouth and his arms closed around her, crushing her to him. Her arms wound around his back and her fingers went beneath the fabric of his shirt to touch his bare skin. She pushed the fabric upward, obviously seeking to divest him of it. He obliged her by pulling the shirt over his head and tossing it aside.

Then she was back in his arms, her mouth under his, her fingers gripping the flesh at his shoulders. This is what he remembered of her, the all-consuming heat of the passion she aroused in him. He was no more able to resist her now than he'd been then. He ran his hands down her body to grasp her buttocks in his palms. She moaned into his mouth, a guttural cry that inflamed him further.

He lifted her with his hands under her hips, carried her to the narrow bed, and laid her down on it. He straightened, long enough to set his gun on the small end table next to the bed and toe off his shoes. He gazed down at her. What a sensuous picture she presented with all that dark, dark hair spread around her and her eyes narrowed in passion. Maybe he should put an end to this madness now, since he knew in many ways there would be no turning back if he did what he wanted.

But she offered him a siren's smile and called his name. He couldn't walk away from that, not that he wanted to. He wanted her, whatever she would give him. He covered her with his own body, his lips finding hers, then the side of her throat, then the valley between her breasts over the cover of her clothing.

She pulled the shirt over her head, exposing a lacy black bra. Leaning up on one elbow, he undid the front clasp of her bra and ran his hand over one breast and then the other, squeezing, kneading the malleable flesh. His mouth sought one hardened peak and then the other. Her head tipped back and a soft sound of pleasure escaped her lips. She moved against him restlessly, one of her thighs insinuating itself between his legs. A groan rumbled up from his chest having any part of her rubbing against his erection.

She laughed, the only sound in the room aside from the rasp of their breathing. The only light in the room washed in from the hall, casting sensual shadows on her body. The only scent in the room was the aroma of their arousal mixed with the perspiration that had broken out on both their bodies. It was a heady mix of sensations that left him feeling reckless, out of control.

His hand strayed down her rib cage to her belly and his lips followed. He unbuttoned her jeans and pulled down her zipper, using his lips and tongue on the skin he uncovered. Her stomach contracted beneath him and her fingers gripped his shoulders. He slid the rest of her clothes from her body, then shed his own.

And then he was inside her. His entire body shuddered with the pleasure of it. His mouth found hers as he started to move inside her, slowly at first, but neither of them could handle that. She wrapped her legs around his waist, urging him to go faster. He buried his face against her throat and thrust into her, giving her what she wanted.

Her hips bucked against his, as her orgasm overtook her, serving as the catalyst of his own. His fingers locked with hers as he came in several bursts of the most intense pleasure he could remember.

For a moment, they lay together recovering, their bodies still tangled, their fingers laced. When he could breathe somewhat normally, he rolled over, pulling her on top of him. With her cheek resting on his chest, he couldn't see her face. She seemed contented, but he didn't know what he'd do if he looked in her eyes and saw regret.

He scrubbed his hands up and down her back. "How are you doing?"

Only when she lifted her head and smiled down at him did he relax. "Do you really have to ask?"

What they'd shared had been spontaneous, hot, unadorned sex that had almost literally left him breathless. "Yeah, I do."

Somehow she managed to stretch her whole body without toppling off him. The way she moved against him almost brought him to life again. "If I weren't so damn tired, I'd feel great." She laid her cheek on his chest again.

Contented, sated, exhausted, he tightened his hold on her. He had one more question for her before he'd let her sleep. "Just how crazy was your husband?"

She lifted her head. "What do you mean?"

He brushed her hair away from her face. "How'd he walk away from you?"

She rolled her eyes and a mocking smile came over her lips. "It was more of a gallop than a walk. Although Devon worked, his family had been wealthy for a couple of generations. Still nouveau riche by some standards. I think he enjoyed my work as a novelty and the source of occasional funny stories at dinner parties, but he never took it seriously. When my name started appearing in the papers and not in a good way, he took off. His family couldn't tolerate any scandal that didn't in some way make them richer."

Rat bastard. "Did you love him?"

She shrugged. "I don't know if that's what I was looking for when I met my husband. I wanted someone stable, even tempered. Someone I might have children with one day. I think I mistook stodginess for dependability. See, even headshrinkers make mistakes."

She snuggled against him. Whether this was an attempt to stifle this avenue of conversation or simply a sign of her fatigue he wasn't certain, but he was willing to let the topic go. He secured the covers more tightly around them. "Good night, sweetheart," he whispered against her ear.

He held her until he was certain she slept; then he carried her to his room where they would both be more comfortable. After arranging her under the covers, he went to the bathroom to wash up. When he returned to the smaller bedroom to retrieve his weapon, a thought occurred to him. How had Alex known that there were condoms in the nightstand drawer? Even he'd forgotten they were there. He wondered if there were more of them in there should the need arise. He hadn't had much reason to take a condom inventory of late.

He picked up his gun from the nightstand with one hand and slid open the drawer with the other. Amid a smattering of condoms lay a little .22 revolver that he knew didn't belong to him.

Alex woke again while it was still dark. She didn't immediately recognize where she was but she knew the man lying beside her. His nose was buried against her neck and his arm draped over her belly. She inhaled and stretched without dislodging his contact with her body.

She let her breath out in a long slow sigh. If it weren't for the fact that they were both here and both nude, she could have imagined that last night had been a dream. She'd spent years wondering what it would be like if the two of them even got in the same bed again, but the reality outstripped what she'd imagined: sexy, hot, sweaty sex that rocked her down to her toes. It wasn't pretty but it was what she'd wanted. Other women might long for romantic interludes and pretty words. She preferred the honesty of what they'd shared.

She shifted on her side to face him more fully. His hand went to her hip, stilling her. "Quit wiggling around," he said in a rough, sleepy voice. "I have to get up in an hour."

She hadn't realized he was awake. The smile on his face told her he was teasing her, but he still hadn't opened his eyes. "I'm not wiggling. I'm getting comfortable."

"Then come here." He turned onto his back and pulled her into his arms. "Now hush."

She laid her head on his shoulder and let her hand wander where it wanted to, over his chest, his belly, and lower. She liked his body, though it wasn't as tight as it had been in his twenties. He possessed a man's physique, not a boy's, now. She liked it especially that he groaned and his body jerked as her fingers closed around his shaft. She leaned up and whispered, "And I thought you said you wouldn't be up for another hour."

He opened his eyes then and looked down at her incredulously. He shook his head. The Alex he'd known would never have made such a comment. Maybe he should understand right off that she wasn't the same girl anymore.

He flopped back against the pillows and closed his eyes. "Are all of you shrinks such perverts?"

She answered honestly, "Pretty much."

He chuckled, but the next time he spoke his voice was more serious. "What are we doing here, Alex?"

She answered him truthfully again. "I don't know." She only knew she didn't want to kill it through analysis. She didn't want any promises from him and she had none to give. She'd managed to do the impossible: let him in a little without giving away all her secrets. She never would if she could help it.

Last night he'd held her, he'd comforted her, and he'd loved her. That was enough for now.

She leaned over him and pressed her mouth to his. He responded by pulling her on top of him to straddle his body. And in a moment, nothing else mattered.

Joe Morgan wanted no part of the Amazon Killer. Not since the night he'd discovered the man's handiwork in an abandoned car. But he'd been pulled from his regular assignment to help the CSU and the detectives sort through, sift, and bag up any of the crap in this old abandoned house where they'd found Walter Thorpe's body. They'd been at this for hours.

Well, mostly he was there to guard the perimeter from

the prying eyes of the curious, be they civilians or cops. It was a need-to-know basis and most of the people here didn't need to know jack.

The real pain-in-the-ass part was that a case like this brought out the brass. Like he was really going to tell the chief of detectives or the deputy commissioner their presence wasn't wanted inside. Let one of the brilliant geniuses from the dick squad handle that.

The very worst part was he had to take a wicked leak, and a smoke wouldn't do him any harm either. One of the home owners about a half mile back had opened her house to them, offering them coffee and the use of her john. When it came his turn, he took a shortcut some-one had found through the brush. It wasn't much of a path and it was mostly overgrown. He didn't have any problem finding the house, but on the way back he no-ticed something peculiar. At one point the path seemed to fork, one way leading back the way he'd come, that seemed to lead off away from the house.

He followed the second path, more out of curiosity than anything else. Maybe this was a shorter shortcut than the first. He could see the house, maybe a hundred feet in the distance.

What drew his attention next was the sound of the tall grass rustling. Up ahead he saw movement in the foliage and figured it was maybe rabbits or raccoons or skunks. God only knew what lived out here only five minutes from civilization. He shone his flashlight on the area, but found nothing.

Laughing at himself he shook a cigarette free from his pack. He was still far enough away for no one to notice him in the moonlight. He paused for a minute to light his smoke, when the ground beneath him shifted. He found himself tumbling down a set of stone steps trying as best he could to protect himself and his weapon from the fall.

When he reached bottom, he lay there for a moment,

trying to assess the damage before he got up. His left shoulder ached and his right ankle throbbed, but other than that he seemed okay. He stood and turned on his flashlight. He was in a large square room with a low ceiling. The walls were made of stones piled one on top of the other. The smell of damp musty earth pervaded his nostrils.

Everything in the room was made of metal, save for the mattress on the neatly made single bed in the corner of the room. A large metal table sat in the center of the room. Metal shelving ran the length of two of the walls. Careful not to touch anything, Joe moved closer to take a better look at what they contained. Wicked-looking knives were laid out on one shelf on top of a blue cloth as if they were a surgeon's instruments. Several strops in various widths lay coiled on another shelf.

Everything about this place was obsessively neat; even the line of jars that sat on one shelf were spaced equidistant from one another. He shone the flashlight on the first of them. Something floated in cloudy liquid inside. He counted eight full jars and then and empty one. The last contained the unmistakable shape of a pair of balls.

Joe turned and vomited onto the earth floor. He retched until there was nothing left to bring up. He knew what he'd found and it terrified him to be there alone and injured. Forgetting the stairs behind him, he pushed forward to a passageway cut out of the far wall. He found himself in a narrow tunnel that was pitch-black and spanned as far as he could see.

It wasn't as bad as he thought since the tunnel curved upward and he could hear the sound of familiar voices once he'd gone a couple of feet. After he'd gone about as far as he could go, he felt along the wall with his fingertips. A thin panel of wood was loosely nailed to a wooden frame. He pulled back the panel that turned out to serve as the back of the only closet in the house where Thorpe's body had been found.

Twenty

Zach stood beside the bed watching Alex sleep. She looked so peaceful he was tempted not to wake her to tell her he was going. Considering how well it went over the last time he'd tried that, he decided against it. He sat on the bed, braced a hand on either side of her, and leaned down to kiss her shoulder. "Baby, wake up. We've got to go."

She turned onto her back, dislodging the covers around her. He tried to concentrate on her face rather than her bare breasts, but wasn't entirely successful.

She smiled a knowing, sleepy smile. "Did you just call me baby?"

He chuckled. He'd surprised himself when that word slipped out of his mouth instead of her name. "What? Too much?"

She lifted her shoulders in a way that suggested she was considering it. "I don't know. I don't think anyone aside from my mother has ever called me by any sort of endearment. The closest my father got was 'little girl' and that was a put-down, a reminder that I amounted to less than big bad him."

Zach smiled, remembering that he'd once tried to give her a nickname a long time ago—squirt or munchkin or something. She'd stared at him with a look of such unconcealed disgust that he'd given it up.

But what about her ex-husband? No sweeties or honeys or sweethearts from him, either. He guessed that wasn't too surprising either since she'd practically confessed to him that her marriage had been loveless, or tenderness-free, maybe. God, he hoped he never had the displeasure to meet that man.

In regard to the topic at hand, he said, "I'll try it out a few more times. You tell me what you think."

She reached out and touched her fingertips to his cheek, the first time she'd touched him of her own volition in a nonsexual way. "What's going on?"

He'd intended from the start to go back to the precinct to continue working on all the loose ends he'd dropped every time a new piece of evidence presented itself. He hadn't finished reinterviewing the girls' families or tracked down the perverts on the list Alex had given him. With McKay off the case, the rest of them would have to take up the slack.

Smitty had called a few minutes ago to tell him they'd found the prime crime scene. One of the uniforms had literally stumbled onto his work area. Zach wanted to see it for himself. "They found the primary crime scene."

She sat up. "When? Where? Why didn't you say so?"

"I just did. Now hurry up and get ready."

He started to rise but she pulled him back with a hand on his arm. "Why do I get the feeling that you're not all that enthused about going?"

She misread him. He wasn't all that enthused about her going. He wanted her somewhere safe with someone who would protect her in his stead. But he knew how she would feel about being left behind. They'd invited her to this dance and she'd want to stay till the last song played. He knew he would, too. That's why he'd contemplated leaving without waking her for a second and a half. Considering how well that had worked the first time he'd tried it, he decided to skip it.

She gritted her teeth and huffed out a breath. "Don't tell me it's some kind of macho crap. I let you sleep with me, and now you want to treat me like a girl. I am not some helpless female."

"I know that. By the way, where'd you get the gat?"

She laughed at his use of slang, as he knew she would. He didn't want her angry with him over feelings that were, to his mind, natural. What kind of man didn't want to protect a woman he cared for?

"It was a present from my father when I was fourteen."

Something about the way she said that made him want to question her on that. Sammy had never mentioned giving Alex a gun or any other weapon.

"Don't worry. It's registered. I have a carry permit and, though I haven't been to a range in a while, I know how to use it."

He'd already assumed the first two and was glad for the third, even though he hoped she'd never have to test her prowess. Still, they needed to go. "I'll be waiting for you downstairs."

Alex stood in the middle of the room surveying her surroundings. The area had been photographed and the scent of black powder and other chemicals used for lifting prints reached her nostrils, but the room had been left basically intact until she and Zach got there.

Her gaze traveled from the tidily kept bed to the rows of shelving to the huge vat-sized tub over which hung a pair of inside-out industrial-type gloves pinned to a bit of clothesline. There was a small refrigerator and a hot plate that sat on top of a small table in the corner of the room. The presence of these items and the generator found in an alcove to the side suggested the killer had spent part of his time living here as well. Or did he only eat and sleep here when there working on one of his victims?

She wrapped her arms around herself as she contemplated the large metal table that was the focus of the room. Each of its corners was outfitted with a leather restraint. That was consistent with the m.e.'s reports that she had seen, as there were ligature marks on the girls' wrists and ankles. This is probably where he did it all— from the mutilations to the rapes to the strangulations. He could do it all here with no threat of discovery, no one to hear the girls scream, no one to help them.

She shivered, not from cold, but from the unnamed, unseen presence in the room. She wouldn't call it evil since she didn't conceptualize evil in that way. But there was sickness, depravity; probably generations old judging by the age of nearly everything in the room, save for the shelving. That was new.

She wouldn't call it evil, because killers didn't spring from the womb; they were made by other humans, formed by abuse and violence or merely neglected into existence. Innate tendencies might explain why some victims of abuse turned violent while others did not, but it couldn't explain it all. She wondered what had been done to this man, probably in this very room, to give birth to such cruelty.

"Shades of OCD, huh, Doc?"

Alex focused on Smitty, who had come up beside her. She nodded. The highly ritualized killings, the degree of orderliness exhibited here spoke of the kind of obsessiveness characterized by the disorder, which often manifested as a means to make sense and order out of a chaotic environment, a means of asserting control.

"So why'd he let us find this place?" Smitty asked.

That was the question Alex had been pondering since she'd found out that the place where Thorpe had been discovered was directly above his kill site. Although they'd stumbled on the place from what she understood, the killer had to figure they might have found the entrance down here by searching the house.

An optimistic assessment might be that he was giving up. He'd dumped Thorpe and exposed this place because he didn't need them anymore. But then there was the empty jar on his shelf, the one waiting to be filled. He had one more kill to go, and she didn't have to reach too far to imagine who his next target might be. That's why he'd sent her the flowers. The empty jar was a message, too.

To Smitty, she said, "He doesn't need it anymore. He's got something else planned." What that might be, she had no idea, which made the prospect more terrifying.

Zach came over to them then. He'd been talking with one of the CSU guys. "Had enough?" he asked.

"They didn't find any fingerprints, did they?"

"No."

"Any traces of blood or fluids?"

"Absolutely nothing so far, but then they haven't really gotten started yet."

In other words, the lab guys had been waiting for them to look their fill before removing what they could and examining what they couldn't here. She didn't really need to see the techs do their thing. Besides, anything they found would be reported to them whether or not they were in the room. She'd seen enough. It was time to go.

"You're awfully quiet over there," Zach said after they'd been driving for about ten minutes. Alex had spent that time staring out the window, pensive.

She turned her head to look at him. "You may think this is crazy, but I was feeling sorry for Walter at the hands of that madman. Sure, he was a scumbag rapist and there would probably be a line of women willing to castrate him, but still. Have they done his autopsy yet?"

"Not as far as I know."

"I wouldn't be surprised if they found he'd been tortured first, or dismembered while alive. This guy gets off on pain, inflicting it, watching its effects on others. Does anybody deserve to die like that?"

He could think of a few folks he'd like to put in this killer's path, but he knew what she meant. He recognized her sentiments as evidence of an innate compassion and a loyalty to her patients despite their own illness. She'd done a better job of hiding her tender feelings as a girl, masking them behind an aloof manner and a sharp tongue. As a woman, she didn't seem so averse to showing them, at least not in front of him.

"Has anyone notified Thorpe's sister that he's dead?"

He didn't know. "I can find out."

"I'd like to talk with her."

He thought he knew her reasoning, but asked anyway. "Why? She claimed not to know anything about what her brother was up to."

"That was while he was alive. She may have thought she'd implicate Walter in some way by speaking. But obviously Walter knew who we were looking for, otherwise why silence him both literally and figuratively? Once she knows Walter is dead she may be more willing to talk."

Now to the real question. "Why you?"

"You may not have noticed this, but not everyone in society is enamored of the police. You guys helped put her brother away. I on the other hand ended up being his advocate, if not completely by design, then by practice. She might tell me things she wouldn't tell you."

He couldn't argue with that logic. His mind went to the case his brother had been on last year, the one that brought Jon and Dana together and ultimately cost

Joanna's husband his life. A lot of strife could have been avoided if one old man who hated cops had been willing to come forward sooner. But he suspected Alex knew something she hadn't told him. "Why else?"

"She called me."

"A few days ago. She wanted me to let you know that her brother couldn't have committed the murders."

There was sisterly devotion for you. "Anything else?"

"That they had a pretty messed-up childhood, which I already suspected, and that as far as she knew Walter wasn't obsessed with mythology, which was neither here nor there. She seemed to believe someone was framing her brother, which now seems to be the case."

"And now you think she knows more than she's telling?"

Alex shrugged. "I don't know, but it would be a good place to start."

He agreed. Thorpe's sister might know more than she'd been telling. Getting a trip up to her home near Ithaca okayed probably wouldn't be too much of a problem. Getting it cleared for Alex to tag along might be another story.

Then again, it might make more sense to get Alex out of the city. Thorpe's sister wasn't a suspect in any regard and not considered dangerous in any way. From what he understood, she was for the most part a recluse in the small town where she lived. Alex had told him that the sister had divorced herself from her brother's activities, declining to come to his trial. He didn't see any inherent danger in the trip, but still the idea didn't sit well with him. "I'll see what I can do." But first he wanted to see if he could find the man they were looking for without involving Alex at all.

Smitty was already at his desk by the time Zach got back to the house. "If it isn't Zach himself," Smitty said, by way of greeting. "I would have thought you'd spend a little more time enjoying the benefits of the doctor's couch."

"Don't start," Zach warned. He knew Smitty meant well and that his comment was intended to signal his approval of the arrangement, but Zach wasn't in the mood. "The sooner I find this perp the sooner I'm sure she's safe."

The smile eased away from Smitty's face to be replaced with a more sober expression. "Can't argue with that. Where do you want to start?"

"Let's see if we can find this kid and get a description. I've got someone working on the list of screen names Alex came up with."

Smitty stood and slung his jacket over his shoulder. "Let's go."

They found Will Jenkins in the third school they tried. When he realized they wanted to talk to him about the delivery made to Alex's office, he gestured in an exasperated way. "Man, I should have known that was bogus."

He seemed to think his participation put him in some kind of trouble, which Zach wanted to assure him wasn't true. "We just want to know what happened."

"Man, I was just rolling down on Waring. It got this sweet set of bumps good for tricking out, you know. I see this white dude by a white delivery truck. It didn't have any kind of name on it, though. He was fiddling with the engine. Then he gets inside trying to start it and nothing. He calls me over, but I don't go, you know. Don't talk to strangers," he said, making quote marks in the air.

"What did he look like?"

"A white dude." Zach cast him a droll look and the kid continued. "I don't know, dark hair, kinda long, glasses. He was on the short side, skinny."

"What did he want?"

"He asked me if I knew where that address was, you know, the doctor's office. I said sure. We were like two blocks away. So he said he had one delivery left but the van wouldn't start and his boss was going to fire him if he didn't get it there and he couldn't leave the van."

"I thought you weren't speaking to strangers."

The kid shrugged. "The guy offered me a fifty if I would take the box over there for him. Who's gonna turn down a free fifty?"

That's what this perp counted on. "What were you doing out that morning?"

"I deliver the papers, the *News.* Then I hang out. That is, if my mom doesn't call me and make me come home."

In other words the kid had a pattern that might be observed. "Is there anything else you can tell us?"

"I told the dude I liked his cap and he put it on me, said I could have it. I felt bad after. I mean, I didn't mean for the guy to give me his cap, especially after he gave me the fifty up front. I went back to give it back to him but he was gone."

He'd probably hightailed it out of there the moment the kid rolled off. "Do you still have the hat?"

"It's in my locker."

They went with the boy to retrieve it. It was as Alice described it, white with a Rockford Reds logo on it. He'd already checked to find that the Rockford Reds were a girls' softball league that played for a high school about 150 miles upstate. As far as he could tell, there was nothing remarkable about either the team or the location, but then he'd been too sidetracked to do too much digging.

After securing the permission of the boy's principal and his mother, they brought him back to the station house to work on a sketch. When it was complete Zach surveyed the sketch. He looked like . . . a white dude. Dark hair, dark eyes, and nothing remarkable about his features, complexion, or expression. No distinguishing marks, aside from a bushy mustache, like scars or tattoos. He looked like every other thirty-something white guy out there. Maybe someone out there in the public would see something special in him when the sketch hit the news.

Twenty-one

By noon, Alex had finished calling all of her patients to let them know she wouldn't be in the office this week. She hoped it didn't take any longer than that to find out who was committing the murders, but her hopes had been higher before they'd discovered it couldn't possibly be Walter Thorpe.

Next she'd tackle the files Captain Craig had sent over—so many cases, boxes of them. She didn't think she'd been at the hospital all that long to have acquired so many. She wasn't looking forward to it, mostly because she held out little hope she'd find something there. She'd always seen Walter alone, never in a group. If he'd struck up any sort of waiting room friendships with one of the other men, this would be the first she'd heard of it. She'd never noticed any of her other patients fixating on Walter's crimes in a way that suggested they'd want to emulate him.

Then again, Thorpe's crimes were part of the public record. Anyone reading the newspapers could have copied him. But then there would have been no need to get rid of him or to sew his mouth shut—another example of overkill. Or did that action serve some other purpose?

If there was one, Alex couldn't think of it. After a

while, she put aside her papers and called Roberta. "How are things in I-Love-a-Lawyerland?" she asked when Roberta picked up the phone.

"No too shabby. Believe it or not, he wants me to meet his mother." Roberta sighed dramatically.

"When?"

"Tonight. I broke out in hives ten minutes after he asked me."

Laughing, Alex said, "I'd be happy to go with you as a buffer of sorts, only the cops outside my door might have something to say about that."

"Don't you mean Zach's door? How's that going, by the way?"

Alex sighed. For once she felt like sharing, but didn't know how. She blurted out, "We slept together last night. Twice."

Roberta whooped. "So I was right about you still having feelings for him."

"Yeah, I told you that already."

"So," Roberta prompted. "What was it like?"

If Alex had answered she would have said hot, sweaty, and sexy the first time. But the second time was different, slower, more sensual, more connected in some indefinable way. Afterward, she'd fallen asleep in his arms far more contented than she'd felt in a long time. In other words, she was in way over her head, just what she'd feared. "Let's just say the man knows what he's doing."

"Do you?"

Ever the social worker, that Roberta. "Nope. I haven't a clue. If I wanted to be honest with myself I'd probably say that sleeping with him was a mistake when we have so much history between us and I don't know what either of us is looking for. There's absolutely nothing settled between us. All I know is that I wanted to be with him, so I was."

"Well then, welcome to the human race, kiddo. You forget I met Devon a few times, that walking stick. He didn't deserve you and what he did to you in the end was unconscionable. If Zach makes you happy, you should go for it."

Happy. She didn't know if that word applied to how she felt. Right now, there was so much going on that it seemed absurd to describe anything in positive terms. Especially when she knew the time would come eventually when Zach would seek answers she didn't want to give him. But she also knew she couldn't go back. One way or another she had to free herself from the emotionally barren life she'd exiled herself to.

"We'll see," she told Roberta. But for the first time in a long while an alien feeling built inside her: hope.

"What have you got for me?" Zach asked Darryl Ferguson after settling into a chair beside his desk. He'd been surprised to hear from Darryl so soon. He and Smitty had been on their way back to the precinct when Zach's cell phone rang. Zach had dropped Smitty off and continued here.

"After you left last night, my youngest, a girl, comes and sits in my lap and looks up at me with those big brown eyes. I'm thinking if someone hurt her one day I'd want to know as soon as possible who the son of a bitch was. So I came back in and started working on it. My wife was ready to kill me. Needless to say, you are not welcome in the Ferguson house again."

Zach chuckled, but he thought of all the times he'd left Sherry under similar circumstances or those even less pressing. It was easy to imagine that when you were out making the world safe for other people the ones who loved you should always understand. It made a great excuse

anyway for doing exactly what he wanted. He hoped
Darryl wasn't on the way to making the same mistake.

While they spoke, Darryl had picked up a file from his
desk and opened it. "I subpoenaed the subscriber information from your guy's Internet service providers, the
ones I knew about. Three of them were from one company. That came in. Here's your problem, though. Four
of these guys had free accounts that don't bother to
check subscriber information. You could put down you
were Count Dracula from Transylvania and they'd be
none the wiser. I did track the IPs back to their originat-
ing computers. Two are private homes in New Jersey.
One is a library in Westchester."

Darryl leaned toward him and turned over the top
page. "Here's something interesting, though. Either this
is new or your guy missed it. Hercules 912 has a home
page and a picture."

Darryl turned one more page and Zach's entire body
went on alert. Staring back at him was the flesh-and-
blood version of the sketch the kid had worked on that
afternoon.

Virgil Williams had no criminal record, had lived in
the same apartment building on Paulding Avenue for
the last ten years, and according to his driving record
had never received so much as a parking ticket. That
didn't mean anything. Lots of bad guys were good at not
getting caught at anything minor. According to the fi-
nancial records from his credit card company, Williams
had bought a Dell laptop over a year ago.

Darkness had already fallen by the time Zach sat in his
car outside the apartment with Smitty beside him. Soon
the ESU team would go in first, the detectives after, to
bring in Williams and any evidence they could secure
to help nail this guy. According to the super, Williams

was home, but seemed perplexed why all these cops were interested in him. They were just waiting for Captain Craig to give the go-ahead.

"This could be it," Smitty said.

Zach grunted an agreement, but the adrenaline rush that had seized him at first seeing Williams's picture had fled. Something about this seemed too easy or maybe directed. Why the sudden appearance of the photo right after they'd come up with their own sketch? Something told him they wouldn't find what they expected on the other side of Williams's door.

Craig gave the command, and ESU swarmed inside. They'd secured a no-knock warrant for Williams's arrest, which meant they'd just ram his door down and go in. They wanted him contained in the apartment without a chance to hit the fire escape before they got to him. It only took a few minutes for them to get the all-clear sign. Had they taken Williams by surprise or had he gone down without a fight? Zach wouldn't know until he got up there to see for himself.

Williams's apartment was on the third floor in the corner directly across from the stairs. The door was open, hanging on its hinges. Several members of the ESU team were standing about. The only other person in the room seemed to be an old man in a wheelchair, breathing heavily as if a heart attack were imminent.

"Where the hell is Williams?" Zach heard Craig say behind him.

"I'm Virgil Williams," the old man said. "You can check my wallet." He extended it toward Craig with shaky hands. "What do you officers want?"

Craig took the wallet and surveyed its contents before passing it to Zack. "Do you have a son, Mr. Williams?"

"He's in Iraq. Has been for the past year and a half."

Zack surveyed the contents of the wallet. Not a single credit card, only a few bucks and a driver's license that expired in 1972, long before pictures were required. Zach passed the wallet to Smitty, who surveyed it quickly and snapped it shut.

Craig pulled out a copy of the sketch and handed it to Williams. "Do you recognize this man?"

Williams pulled a pair of glasses from his pocket and looked down at the photograph. "He's the one on the TV." Williams glanced up at Craig, new lines of worry creasing his forehead. "You thought *I* was *him?*"

An expression of displeased annoyance came over the captain's face. "We're sorry to have troubled you, Mr. Williams. We can see we've made a mistake."

Williams harrumphed. "Where were you a year ago when my apartment was broken into? Nobody ever showed up to take the complaint."

"Was anything taken?"

"Just the TV, but they left the place a mess."

"I apologize for that, too," Craig said. He turned and nodded to Zach and the detectives for them to follow.

Once they were outside, Zach leaned his back against one of the patrol cars waiting for whatever Craig had to say. But it was Smitty who spoke first. "How long do you think it will take for him to file a lawsuit against the city?"

Craig's frown deepened. "We'll keep a car on this place in case the fake Williams shows up. We'll check on the son. That guy isn't going anywhere."

Zach had noticed too that the man's legs were shriveled inside his pants legs. He couldn't have killed anybody if he wanted to.

"Anyone else have any brilliant suggestions?"

Zach had only one, which meant he and Alex would have to leave early the next morning.

Zach got out of his car in front of his house, relieved to find the two officers in the unmarked car still outside his house. That meant she was all right. He hadn't spoken to her much that day, except to tell her he would be home late. She hadn't asked what he was working on and he hadn't volunteered it, not wanting to get her hopes up about catching Williams. Now he was glad he hadn't since the whole thing had been a bust.

She opened the door to him as he headed up the walk. Had she been waiting for him? He hoped so, and for a better reason than she wanted to hear what he'd been up to on the case. He'd missed her and hoped she'd felt a tinge of that emotion herself. Though with Alex it was difficult to tell what she was feeling unless she told him.

He opened the screen door and pulled her into his arms, unheedful of the two cops parked across the street. He doubted either of them would believe he hadn't touched her until last night anyway. He buried his nose against her neck as her arms closed around his neck. With his hands at her waist he lifted her and carried her inside, kicking the door closed behind them.

He brought them to the sofa, sat, and pulled her onto his lap. She leaned back to survey his face. Her fingers, cool and gentle, brushed his forehead and cheek. "I guess I don't have to ask you how your day went."

No, she didn't have to ask. He was sure it was there on his face, but he wanted to tell her anyway. "We thought we had him tonight. Turns out he used an old man's Social Security number to get a driver's license and credit cards."

"How is that possible? Wouldn't the old man keep getting the bills?"

"Not necessarily. Once the first one showed up, he could have switched the mailing address to a PO box, which he did. Williams didn't remember seeing this guy, but a couple of the other neighbors remember him hanging around the lobby a while ago. All he'd have to do is pry open the one mailbox or wait for the mailman to deliver and claim he was from that apartment. We'll check with the post office tomorrow."

"Where does that leave you?"

He stroked his hand over her hair. "It looks like you get your wish. I want to leave at six for Thorpe's sister's house."

She nodded. "I saved you some dinner."

He smiled, pleased that she'd thought of him, but he wasn't hungry, not for food anyway. He wanted her, but he needed to move slow. In his bed, she'd given him everything, held nothing back. Outside it, he knew she withheld part of herself from him. Not that he didn't expect that. Only two days ago they were barely speaking. But, perhaps selfishly, he wanted all of her, and not just for the present. He never should have walked out on her in the first place and never would again, if he could help it.

Despite the cautions ringing in his ears, he pulled her closer and brought her mouth down to his. God, she tasted sweet, but the kiss they shared was nothing but wicked. Her hands went to his tie, loosening it so that she could undo the buttons on his shirt. Then her fingertips touched down on his bare flesh. Her thumbs strummed his nipples and her tongue mated with his. He felt as he always did with her: as if he were being consumed by fire. His heartbeat picked up and his breathing shallowed.

He leaned over and laid her down on the sofa, wanting to rid himself of his clothing. He stood to do so, his eyes riveted to her as she rasped down the zipper on her shorts. She pushed them down her body to reveal she wore nothing underneath. His breath came out on a ragged groan.

Next came her T-shirt. She pulled it over her head and tossed it to the carpet. Her hands captured her own breasts, squeezing them in a way that she seemed to be offering them to him. They skimmed lower, over her rib cage, down her belly, to between her parted thighs.

All the while he fumbled with his clothing, his fingers not seeming to work properly. He trembled with the need to be inside her, a part of her. Then finally he was free. He got the condom from his wallet and rolled it on. He knelt on the floor and pushed her legs wider apart and lowered his head. Rather than push her hands away, he used his tongue to delve between her fingers, to delve inside her, lapping at the sweet juices that flowed between her thighs.

He could feel the tension mounting in her. Her legs trembled and her breathing became shallow. She wrapped her legs around his shoulders and her hips rocked against him. She called his name as her body contracted with the force of her climax.

She called his name again. Something in that one word made him look up at her. Her hands reached for him and he didn't hesitate. He covered her with his own body and thrust into her. His body shivered and a grunt of pure pleasure tightened his jaw.

He lifted himself up on his elbows to look down at her. The rapturous expression on her face enflamed him. He leaned down to claim her mouth for a wild kiss as he thrust into her. She wrapped her legs around his waist, taking him deeper, deeper.

He was sinking into a fiery abyss. Perspiration coated his skin and it was an effort to drag in the slightest bit of air. She broke the kiss and pulled him down to her with her arms around his neck. She whispered in his ear, "Come for me, Zach."

It was too much. He lost it then, his body shuddering with the force of his orgasm. He pumped into her, his control forgotten, his mind and body consumed with the wash of pure pleasure that flooded through him.

After a moment he rolled onto his back, pulling her on top of him, wishing he had something with which to cover them. He stroked his hands over her back to warm her as their bodies cooled. He could have stayed like that forever with her snuggled up to him, her body still restless with the aftermath of sex, but she started to shiver. He found her T-shirt and helped her put it on. She settled back against him with a sigh.

Again, he was tempted to question her as to what they were doing together. She'd brushed his concern aside before, but it hadn't gone away. Was sex all she really wanted from him? If so, it wouldn't be the first time, nor would it be the first time that's all he wanted from a woman.

He couldn't believe that, though. She'd greeted him at the door with genuine concern in her eyes. She'd stroked his face with a tenderness he hadn't experienced in a long time, if ever. No, she felt something for him, maybe not what she once had, but still something. He hadn't killed every gentler feeling she had toward him. He had to be thankful for that.

The first rule was that you didn't tell. No matter what she did, you didn't tell, not even the old lady, though the old lady already knew. The Mirror knew that, but he had been ready to break the rule. He had been about to tell, and that couldn't be allowed.

Even though she was dead, she still whispered to him sometimes. She reminded him of how useless The Mirror had been. If it had been olden times they could have left him on a mountain to rot, but as things were they had to keep him.

After all they'd been through, The Mirror had been ready to tell every sordid little secret. He regretted killing him, not because he was dead, but because the connection was gone. Even all those years they'd been separated, he'd still felt the bond, frail and tenuous, but there. Once he'd killed The Mirror, he was alone, all alone for the first time in his life, and he hated it. He couldn't live like this, so totally unconnected.

He'd known what he was going to do almost immediately. He was almost at the end of it now. He was going to tell now, himself, but it didn't matter. She wouldn't live long enough to pass it on. But she'd been good to him and deserved to know why she was about to die.

He looked at her and smiled—all that dark delicious hair and a slender body, not sloppy, neat. She surveyed the photos on the wall, all of them pictures from his youth. He and his brother, tumbling around the backyard like two puppies. There were others, but these seemed to fascinate her.

She pointed to the girl in one photograph. "Is that your sister?"

He smiled, his lips drawn back, feral. "No."

She looked puzzled, what he expected.

"Mother always wanted a girl. Walter couldn't do it. He was too weak. He nearly died. No use to anyone. There was only me."

She took a step back from him, incredulity and indignation on her face. "You're telling me your mother used to dress you like a girl?"

"It wasn't so bad really. Except for the men. She'd give me to them sometimes. Sometimes it didn't matter, but sometimes when they found out I wasn't what they thought I was they'd kick both our asses."

He saw it in her eyes now—revulsion, disgust, and a burgeoning sense of fear. "Why are you telling me this?"

"So that you understand. Life tricked her. All she asked for was that the baby she carried would be a girl. God gave her two boys instead. Me and The Mirror." That's how he'd come to think of them. She used to say they were a reflection of each other: The Mirror weak and him strong, The Mirror useless and him mommy's little helper. They were the same, yet different. Opposites. Although she'd trained him otherwise, he'd started in the world left-handed, *sinestre*. Sinister.

To her he said, "She couldn't stand for that."

He'd thought he would be able to tell her all of it, but he'd miscalculated. She wouldn't be able to accept it. He wanted to tell her how powerful he was, what he'd done. But all that was left was to show her. Such a waste, but it couldn't be helped. If he hadn't gotten her away before the news hit she would have known. She would have told. And that might have ruined everything. He was in the process of telling himself, in the biggest way he knew how. Then it would be over. But not yet.

He reached for her, wanting it over quick, but she fought him, striking him, using her feet and elbows to wound him. She was strong and her blows hurt, but he was beyond that now. He managed to knock her to the floor, and then he was on her, unfurling the cord he'd kept in his pocket for this purpose. She wouldn't die like the others. If she cooperated, it would be quick. He owed her that. She fought him as the cord tightened around her neck, choking her. Six minutes, that's all it would take for her brain to shut down and die. He had a special place picked out for her, in the center of the orchard outside, waiting. He would put her there and go back to the city in the morning. He still had work to do.

Her body went slack, but he kept the cord tight, mentally counting off the minutes until it was done. He let her body slide bonelessly to the floor and stood.

Twenty-two

The three-hour drive up to Granville, New York, proved uneventful, mostly because Alex spent most of that time drifting in and out of sleep. They'd left the highway a bit ago, traveling a backwoods route. He had to admit this was beautiful country, though the trees hadn't yet started to bud and grass still showed winter pallor. It was the sort of place families came for apple and pumpkin picking in the fall.

Alex stirred beside him. She wore her hair in a single braid down her back, but several wisps had escaped to frame her face. She brushed them back as she sat up. "Are we there yet?"

He chuckled. "We should make town in a couple of minutes. I'll need directions out to Thorpe's sister's place."

He'd stop by the sheriff's office in town, partly as a professional courtesy since he had no jurisdiction here and partly to find out what he knew about the sister. The sheriff's office was in the center of town, a one-story office building that looked freshly painted.

Zach parked in front of the building. It was barely nine thirty, but the street was busy in a small-town sort of way. Very peaceful. Living here would drive him stir-crazy in a week. He collected Alex from the other side of the car and went inside.

Sheriff Harrold Bates was standing at the front desk when they walked in. Agewise, Zach would put him in his midforties. He had a full head of dark hair that had started to go white at the temples and a belly that had started to strain against the dark blue fabric of his uniform. But his blue eyes assessed them with a shrewdness Zach wouldn't have expected in a small-town cop. "What can I help you people with?"

Zach introduced himself and Alex, but he had the feeling such introductions were unnecessary. "We were heading out to Ginnie Thorpe's place and needed directions."

"I'll take you people, if you don't mind. Ms. Thorpe appreciates her privacy."

In other words, he didn't mind them going out there but wanted to be along in case the big city people started some trouble. "That's not a problem."

"Linda, I'm going out for a while," Bates called. A pretty blonde came to take over his spot at the desk. Bates gestured for them to precede him out the door. "The regular girl's on maternity leave, so we're all taking turns," he said.

Outside they climbed into the sheriff's car, Zach in front with Bates, Alex in back. As they drove he looked back at her. She'd been uncharacteristically silent since they got to the sheriff's office. True, there hadn't been much for her to say, but she seemed pensive in a way that bothered him. He wondered what he was thinking, but Bates spoke, claiming his attention.

"What do you folks want with Ginnie Thorpe, anyway? I was just out there yesterday afternoon to let her know about her brother."

Zach focused on Bates. Wasn't that a question better asked before he'd agreed to bring them out here? "How did she react when you told her?"

"She wasn't there. That's not unusual. She doesn't stay up here too much, except in the winter."

So now Zach understood. Bates would give the city slickers the chance to do the dirty work. "Where is she the rest of the time?"

Bates shrugged. "Don't know. She's not the friendliest girl, if you know what I mean. Likes to be by herself. She comes into town every so often wearing one of those smocks. She's a painter, you know."

Zach nodded for want of a better reaction. "But you think she's there now?"

"One of the deputies noticed her car in the drive this morning. Here's the road to her place."

The sheriff made a left turn onto a dirt road. Soon two buildings came into view, a large clapboard house and another building that was either a garage or a storage shed. What struck Zach was how isolated these two buildings looked, how drab, without even a garden to brighten up the gray of the house. Then again, it was a bit early for any flowers to have bloomed, but there didn't seem to be any beds in which said flowers might grow. Wouldn't an artist appreciate color?

Bates pulled to a stop in front of the house behind what Zach presumed was Ginnie's car, a black Ford Taurus, and got out. He walked up to the house, leaving Zach to let Alex out of the car. He did, noticing how Bates approached the house, calling Ginnie Thorpe's name.

Zach and Alex reached the front door just as Bates began to rap on the door. "Ms. Thorpe," he called. "You've got visitors."

The door slid open a way with the force of Bates's knock. "Ms. Thorpe," he called again. "You in here?" Bates pushed the door open farther. "Ms. Thorpe?"

Bates glanced back at him. "Folks around here don't have much use for locks, but they don't leave their doors open." Bates said that almost to himself, as if it were an excuse for what he was about to do. He eased inside the house, looking around. The expression in his eyes showed more curiosity about this woman who lived on the outskirts of town and had no use for the people in it, than concern for her welfare. For all they knew, the woman was out back and couldn't hear them. Bates turned into a room on the right. "Well, I'll be."

There was more wonderment than alarm in Bates's voice. Zach pulled Alex behind him. "Stay close to me," he said, though he doubted such a warning was necessary. He eased in behind Bates, who stood at the center of the room, craning his neck around.

The only way Zach could describe what he found was a shrine. Photo after photo, all elaborately framed, hung from the walls, sat on every surface in the room. There must have been hundreds of them. Each one featured the same pair of children, a boy and a girl, depicting their passage from infancy to eight or nine. Thorpe and his sister, no doubt. Zach's first thought was, who could have taken so many pictures? His second thought was to wonder why anyone would keep so many of them preserved in this way.

He gazed at Alex for her take on this. She was staring at one picture in particular. "Oh my God," she whispered.

She turned to look at him, but before she could say a word a crash sounded at the back of the property. Zach looked at Bates, who didn't appear to be in any hurry to find out the source of the noise. "Stay put," Zach said to Alex. He went to the back of the house and looked outside the kitchen window to the building out back. The door was open when it hadn't been when they drove out. He eased his weapon from its holster and let himself out the back door.

* * *

How could she not have seen it before? Now that the answer was crystal clear in her mind she wondered why it hadn't come to her before. She remembered the conversation with Thorpe's "sister." She'd told her to look elsewhere for who killed the girls, to someone who hated him. That hadn't been an attempt to clear Walter's name, but a clue. She'd known it the moment she saw a picture of that girl standing behind her brother, a rock in her hand, poised to throw it at the back of her brother's head. Alex wondered what had stopped her—perhaps the act of someone catching it on film. It was the kind of thing a little girl might explain away saying she hadn't really intended to do it, but there was a blackness in that child's eyes that couldn't be explained that easily.

And there was something else. If Ginnie Thorpe were older, that difference must be able to be measured in minutes. These children were the same age. Ginnie had said it herself. *My mother died when we were ten years old.* They were twins who shared every feature. Identical. Which meant Ginnie Thorpe couldn't be a woman at all.

She was so engrossed in the pictures that when she heard a sound behind her, she jumped. She caught a glimpse of Sheriff Bates sliding to the floor before a pair of hands closed around her, one around her waist, trapping her arms against her body, the other hand clamped painfully around her mouth. She could feel his face next to hers, his breath, smelling of whiskey, fanning her skin. "Hello, Alex," he whispered against her ear.

She knew that voice. It wasn't the breathy voice of Ginnie Thorpe but one identical to Walter's. Panic rose in her, making her heartbeat treble and her stomach cramp into a tight knot. If he was here, where was Zach? She hadn't heard a gunshot or any sounds of struggle to indicate he'd met up with Zach at all, but she feared for him anyway. She struggled against his hold, but the fingers at her waist dug into the flesh at her side.

"Keep still," he warned. "I don't have much time. I see you figured it out. Finally. I thought you were smarter than that, Doctor."

She managed to jab her elbow into his solar plexus, but not with enough force to do much damage.

His hold on her tightened painfully. "Quiet, Doctor. I have a little secret to share with you. You know all those naughty rapes my brother was convicted of? That was me, too. I just thought about what the little bastard would do if he ever got up the nerve to stick his dick into a woman. The semen in the last victim was a nice touch, don't you think? Nobody knew about me so they went after him."

"Why?" She managed to get that one word out.

"He was going to tell you everything. Even when he got out of prison he called you. He just couldn't get up the nerve to talk to you. I had to shut him up. But none of that matters anymore. See you around, Doctor."

He pushed her forward toward the wall with such force that she cracked her head on one of the pictures. She fell to the floor, dazed, landing on her purse. She grabbed it, searching inside for the .22. She found it, slid onto her stomach, and turned to aim, but Thorpe was already gone.

Outside, a car engine roared to life. Thorpe planned on getting away. "Zach," she screamed. She scrambled to her feet. If she made it to the doorway, she'd at least be able to tell in the direction he'd left. He pulled out the opposite way they'd come, traveling toward a grove of bare trees in the distance.

"Alex."

She jumped before she realized the soft voice calling to her belonged to Zach. She turned and buried her face against his chest. She couldn't seem to stop trembling. If he'd wanted her dead she would have been gone by now. Or he would have taken her with him if he could.

"It's all right, baby," Zach said against her ear. He eased the gun from her fingers and tucked it in his waistband.

She lifted her head. "We should go after him."

Zach shook his head. "Look at the tires."

She looked over her shoulder at the police car. Both tires on the passenger side had been slashed.

When she turned back, Zach tilted her head up with a hand under her chin. "What happened there?"

She touched her fingertips to the spot at her temple. "He pushed me and I cracked my head on one of the pictures. What about the sheriff?"

Keeping an arm around her waist he led her back into the room. Bates was just coming to. He lifted himself into a sitting position and shook his head, then groaned. "What the hell happened?"

"That's what I'd like to know," Zach said. "He was in here. Weren't you watching her?"

Alex could feel the anger radiating off Zach. If she guessed correctly, he was more angry with himself for leaving her alone than with anything the sheriff had done. She tightened her grasp on him. The last thing they needed was for these two men to go at each other.

"How's your head?" she asked.

Bates touched his head to the back of his neck and his fingertips came back bloody. He shook his head again and rose to his feet with Zach's help. "I better get my people out here, plus somebody to take a look at that. How are you doing, young lady?"

"I'm fine."

Bates nodded. He used the radio at his belt to call into his office.

"In the meantime," Zach said, "you should see what's out back."

The smaller building was an art studio. One side was dedicated to the sort of landscapes that sold well to casual art buyers, which was probably how Thorpe's twin supported himself. It was the type of occupation that afforded great mobility and didn't tie him down to one place of business.

But along one wall was another type of painting, comprising deep purples, blacks, and stark crimsons, depictions of death and dismemberment so graphically painted bile rose in her throat. There was one painting left on an easel, the acrylic used so fresh that its scent filled the air. In it, a young woman with long dark hair rested underground with her arms crossed over her chest. Aboveground was a headstone with the words REST IN PEACE spelled out. Beside the grave was the figure of a blond man whose grotesque features mocked the handsomeness the Thorpe twins had shared.

This is how he saw himself, as some sort of monster. Whoever this girl was, he regretted killing her in his own fashion. It hadn't stopped him though. She wondered if he'd felt the same thing when he'd killed his brother. The paintings might tell her that, but she wouldn't get a chance to look for that now. In the distance, the sound of sirens rose. She only hoped someone on Bates's force was a little quicker on the uptake than he appeared to be.

Once Bates's men arrived, Zach took Alex aside. "How are you doing, really?"

"I'm fine." She touched her fingers to the cut at her temple. "Believe me, I've gotten worse scrapes."

That wasn't what he meant, and she had to know that. He remembered how fiercely she'd trembled in his arms. Considering how little emotion she showed on a regular basis, her fear had to be extraordinary. "What did he want?"

"Primarily, I think he wanted to gloat about how clever he was. He had everybody fooled. He created this life as a woman, which left him free to do whatever he wanted as a man. He also told me that Walter hadn't committed those rapes, he had."

Although their fingerprints would be different, their DNA would be the same. He'd seen criminals get off before after they gleefully reported they had a twin, thereby introducing reasonable doubt without having to give another piece of evidence. In this case, it worked in reverse, since everyone assumed Thorpe had a sister. There was no one to blame but him. Damn.

He wondered how that made Alex feel, knowing that she had been right all along. Thorpe had been innocent, at least the Thorpe they'd convicted had been. But that didn't seem to be on her mind.

"I want to go back to the house," she said.

"Why?"

"Between the studio and the room inside, it seems to be a testament to the twins' lives. The answers have to be inside."

He would have asked her what answers she sought, but he thought he knew. Who were these people, really? How had Walter's twin assumed a female identity? He couldn't conceive that any hospital would have falsified birth records that needed to be sent on to the state, even in a backwater town like this. But he had to admit, whatever had been done had been accomplished a long time ago for the ruse to work, long before computerization had taken over the record keeping of the world.

He led her back to the house with an arm around her waist. He pulled a pair of gloves from his pocket and handed them to her. He didn't want to disturb any physical evidence, but he wanted to see what she'd find.

Once inside, she circled the room, not focusing on the pictures but seeming to look for something else. She

settled on a photo album that rested on a plastic book
holder. The cover had a quilted green and yellow pattern covered in plastic. There was nothing on the first
page, but the first spread showed two old-style sepia birth
certificates that like negatives had white writing. One was
for Homer Williams, the other for Virgil. The birthday
didn't match Thorpe's. This would make him a year
younger than they believed. The birthplace listed was
Rockford, New York.

Good God. When he'd looked into that town, he'd
been trying to find a Thorpe family that had lived there.
No wonder he'd come back empty. He'd been looking
for the wrong name.

Alex turned the page and found copies of two more
birth certificates, the ones for Walter and Virginia
Thorpe. These were more modern certificates garnered
from a town in Louisiana. The birthday they had for
Thorpe was on there. Virginia was listed as a year older.
He'd bet anything the original owners of the birth certificates had died a long time ago and Thorpe's mother had
used their identities to fashion new ones for her children.

He'd already called Craig to let him know what was
going on. He and some of the others were on their way
up. Now that she'd found what they needed, he wanted
to get her out of there, first to have her head looked at
and then somewhere quiet where he could really assess
the toll seeing one of the Williams brothers had taken
on her.

Even though it was the middle of the day, all she
wanted was a shower and a bed, in that order. Zach had
brought her to the one hotel the town boasted, which
was little more than a bed-and-breakfast. She didn't care.
Without a word to him, she slipped into the bathroom,
shed her clothes, and stepped into the shower. The first

blast of water was icy cold, but she didn't care about that either. She adjusted the temperature and, leaning her forehead against the cool tile, waited for the water to warm.

Her head throbbed, not from the bruise, which didn't require anything more than a Band-Aid. A migraine was building behind her eyes, in her sinuses, and it was going to be a doozy.

She heard the bathroom door open and a second later Zach stepped into the shower behind her. She hadn't anticipated that he would follow her. She hadn't thought of anything other than washing that man's touch from her body. Intellectually, she knew that couldn't really be accomplished, but emotionally she needed the illusion.

Zach pulled her against him, wrapping his arms around her waist. He kissed her temple, her cheek, the side of her throat. "Are you okay, baby?"

She turned in his arms, buried her face against his neck, and shook her head. She wouldn't be okay until Williams, whichever one he was, was caught. Only then could she be sure he wouldn't hurt anyone else. "He blames me," she whispered against his neck. "He blames me for getting Walter to talk. He did call me after he got out of prison. His brother found out about it and killed him. I think that was the catalyst for everything else he's done. As much as he hated Walter, he probably loved him as well."

"Shh." Zach stroked her hair from her face. "You can tell me all this later." He tilted her face up to his. "I'm sorry I left you alone. You're not alone. I won't let that happen again."

She shook her head. She didn't blame him. He'd only done what Bates should have. Whatever sound they'd heard was probably engineered by Williams to draw at least one of the men from the house, leaving her less protected. Bates had gotten more than what he deserved for his inaction—a slight concussion that required an overnight in the hospital.

But she knew Zach meant more than that by his words. He was making her a promise that had little to do with physical togetherness. He'd always told her that he was there for her, and for a long time he was. He wanted to be there again. He wanted more from her than whatever this thing was between them. So did she. She'd never really stopped loving him; that emotion had just gotten tangled in with so many others. Losing him once nearly killed her. The only question remaining was, could she chance that?

Since she didn't have an answer, she leaned up and pressed her mouth to his. He crushed her to him as his tongue slid into her mouth, probing, tasting. But she whimpered, not from the pleasure she felt but the gathering pain in her forehead.

He pulled away and looked down at her, his hand cradling the side of her face. "What's the matter, baby?"

"Migraine. A big one."

He pulled her to him and turned off the water. He used one of the towels to blot her hair, and wrapped her in another. He slung a third around his waist and lifted her from the shower.

At least the bed was soft and clean smelling when Zach laid her on it. She closed her eyes, but she could tell what he was doing as he moved around the room. He drew the curtains and shut off every source of light. Then he came back to her, settled them both under the covers, and pulled her to him.

"Is that better?" he asked.

She nodded and pain sliced through her.

"Relax," he whispered against her ear. He massaged the juncture between her right thumb and index finger, a pressure point that was supposed to alleviate headaches.

She melted against him as he spoke to her in a sooth-ing, monotone voice. His voice was so low that she had no idea what he was talking about. It didn't matter. She felt herself growing drowsy and the pain of the migraine receding. She snuggled against him and let sleep over-take her. She'd worry about the rest of it later.

Even after Alex had fallen asleep, Zach continued to hold her. He pressed his lips to her temple. He hadn't al-lowed himself to dwell on it before now, but he could have lost her today. If Williams had been more inter-ested in killing than proving his own worth, she might be gone now. His whole body trembled with the repercus-sions of that thought. He couldn't lose her again, not in that way, not in any way. He'd tried to tell her that today. Heaven only knew if she'd gotten that message, but he'd tell her in every way he could think of until it sank in.

A knock sounded at the door. He quickly disentangled himself from her, hoping to get to the door before who-ever was on the other side woke her. He checked the peephole to see Smitty on the other side. The boys from New York must have driven like madmen to get here so soon.

"Just a minute," he told Smitty, went back to the bath-room, and pulled on his jeans. When he opened the door, Smitty gave him a once-over that left no doubt what he thought Zach had been up to.

To Smitty's unasked question, he said, "She's sleeping. What's going on?"

"For one thing, we found the girl depicted in the painting in a shallow grave a few feet back on the prop-erty. She was still warm."

Damn. If he and Alex had come up last night, they probably would have walked in on her murder. But the smile on Smitty's face told Zach he wasn't finished. "What else?"

"Way in the back in the corner in the dark of that shed there's an old freezer. We think we know what happened to Mama."

Twenty-three

It was nearly midnight when Alex started to stir. In the intervening hours, he'd gotten Smitty to buy them some clothes and other toiletries since he didn't plan to take Alex back to the city until she was better. Bates's deputies were guarding the entrances to this place, and since Williams would have to go through him to get to Alex, he wasn't worried.

About seven o'clock, Smitty had brought them some dinner. Zach had eaten his sitting at the desk, the only furniture in the room besides the bed and dresser. He'd consumed three-quarters of the bottle of wine that came with the meal, too. The alcohol had taken a little of the edge off him—a little bit, but not much. He wanted her to wake so that he could see that she was all right, but he didn't want to push her to wakefulness before she was ready.

Finally she sat up, gathering the covers around her. Her hair had dried wild around her face. That and the warm light from the single lamp he'd turned on presented a sultry picture. He tamped down on his libido, since this wasn't the time. Or maybe it was, but not yet.

She brushed a strand of hair from her face and smiled at him. "What are you doing all the way over there?"

He wasn't that far away, but he got up and lay down on the bed next to her, leaning up on one elbow. "Feeling better?"

"Much." She leaned down and kissed him, but withdrew almost immediately. "You've been drinking?" she asked.

She sounded so indignant it surprised him. He hiccupped in a way he thought she'd find funny and let his eyes go half-mast. "Only a teensy bit." He held up his thumb and forefinger with a wide space between them. He grasped her elbow to pull her toward him. "Come here and give Daddy some sugar."

He was teasing her, but the look of horror that came over her face told him he'd missed the mark. "Not when you're drunk." She actually fled from him, yanking the cover from beneath him to wrap herself in. She stopped at the entrance to the bathroom, leaning against it as if to protect herself from attack from behind.

He'd never seen her like this before, genuinely terrified, not even after Williams had gotten to her. "What's going on here, Alex?"

"Nothing." She lowered her head so that he couldn't see her face. "Nothing. I just don't like to be with a man who's drunk."

He wasn't. Maybe if she hadn't just been recovering she might have noticed that. But what got to him was that she said "a man," not him. He knew without her telling him that she'd been assaulted. Was that how it started? "Tell me what happened, Alex. Who hurt you?"

Her head snapped up. "Why?" She brushed her hair from her face with an impatient gesture. "So you can run out and kill him for me? Nothing you do can make him deader than he is already."

She thought he asked out of some macho territoriality bullshit? He couldn't care less. He only cared about her. "Tell me."

"Why? It happened a long time ago. It doesn't mean anything anymore. I've already worked through it. It doesn't matter."

If she could see herself she wouldn't try to foist that lie on him. "Then why are you trembling?"

"Can't you just let it be? You can't change anything."

No, he knew that very well. The past remained immutable beyond his capacity to change it. But if anything she said could help him understand her in the present, he wanted to hear it. "Don't you think I'm capable of understanding what happened to you?"

"No," she said in a voice so quiet he barely heard her. "You wouldn't understand this."

"Try me."

Her eyes squeezed shut and he could see that she was fighting tears. Her hands were fisted against her chest. "Let it be, Zach."

Didn't she realize he couldn't do that? He wanted to shake her and make her tell him, but by force of will he stayed where he was. "Damn it, Alex. I'm not going to let this drop."

She sniffled and her throat worked. She looked away from him, obviously struggling with whether to confide in him or not. She shook her head, but when she looked at him again, he saw the anger and resignation in her eyes. "It was Sammy, all right?" She spat the words at him, her voice raised. "It was Sammy. He raped me when I was fourteen. Is that what you wanted to hear?"

He squeezed his eyes shut, feeling as if he'd just taken a blow to the gut. His eyes burned and he couldn't seem to take in air properly. Sammy? He'd never expected that. Not as overprotective as Sammy was. Or that's the label Zach had given it at the time. But in another light Sammy's attempts to keep Alex to himself could appear to be a sick sort of possessiveness.

Nausea roiled in his belly along with a white-hot rage

against the man he had once considered his father. Another example of his impotence, for as Alex said, nothing he could do would make that man any deader.

He opened his eyes and looked at Alex. She'd sunk down along the wall until she sat on the floor with her face in her hands. Her shoulders shook and he could hear her sobbing. He inhaled, willing his anger to recede. It was futile at this point and she didn't need that besides.

He went to her and sat on the floor in front of her. He pulled her to him so that her upturned knees fit between his parted ones. She didn't acknowledge him in any way, but he held her, rocking them both gently until her tears subsided.

"It was a little more than a year after my mother died. I still missed her so much. Sometimes when my dad was working nights, I'd lie in their bed and pretend she was still there. That's what we'd do sometimes when he was working—lie in bed and watch old movies and talk. Half the time I'd fall asleep and she'd wake me in the morning to go to school. I missed her so much, I cried until I fell asleep."

She brushed a tear from her cheek. "When I woke up, there was something hot and heavy on me, inside me, hurting me. I could smell the liquor on his breath before I could make out that it was him, Sammy. I started to fight him, to try to get him off me, but he was so damn drunk, I don't think he even felt it. He said one word, my mother's name, then rolled over and went to sleep.

"I lay there for a long time, hurt, stunned. I tried to tell myself that he was so out of it that in his stupor he must have thought I was my mother. That would have been bad enough, but manageable somehow. It would have meant he hadn't intended what he did.

"He never said a word to me about it. I would have thought he didn't remember what happened, except I saw the guilt on his face. Sammy rarely accepted culpability for anything, but when he did, he wore it on his sleeve. Besides, if he hadn't remembered, wouldn't he have wanted some explanation for the blood on his sheets? When I came home from school the next day, he'd changed the bed himself so he must have noticed. I was so ashamed."

She laid her head against his shoulder and cried. He didn't know what to say to her. Of all the victims he'd comforted with pat words of encouragement, he couldn't bring himself to say any of them now. None of those other women had meant to him what Alex did. All he could do was hold her until her tears subsided.

"Do you blame yourself for what happened?"

"I put myself there where he could hurt me. It wasn't like I hadn't known what he wanted from me. I'd noticed the way he started looking at me, and it was not a father's look. Just like all those other narcissistic assholes out there that demand service from their families, if not their wife, then whatever female they can get their hands on. But he was such a coward he had to get drunk to do it. That was the man everyone idolized, a drunk and a man who would molest his own child."

"Why didn't you tell anyone, Alex?" He had to believe that if anyone knew, it would have cost Sammy his job and sent him to jail. They would have taken Alex from him.

"Tell who? You think any of his cop buddies were going to come there to arrest him? Even if they did, what then? There was no one else to take me in. I'd be put in some foster home. No way. I'd heard stories, knew kids who'd gotten placed with families worse than their own. Sammy was the devil I knew, and I knew how to handle him."

She brushed a tear from her cheek with an annoyed swipe of her hand. "I knew he kept a spare gun in a lockbox in the basement. I slept with it hidden inside my pillowcase every night, even though he basically left me alone for a while. I knew he'd be back, though. When he came to my room, I pulled out the gun and told him I'd shoot him dead if he ever tried to touch me again. I think it was the first thing I ever said to him that he actually took seriously."

Zach hugged her to him. What she said explained so many things—not the least of which was what she'd meant by the gun being a "gift" from her father. She could see herself as a young girl contemplating that she had no options save the one she took. But after a while, she did have another. "You could have told me."

She leaned back to look up at him. "Right. I was supposed to tell you, his protégé, that this man you idolized had raped his own daughter?"

She held his gaze for a moment before looking away, but he saw it in her eyes. She'd thought he might not have believed her either. That hurt him more than anything had in his whole life. He cradled her face in his hands, forcing her to look at him. "I loved you, Alex. I would have believed you." If he'd thought she could handle it, he would have added that he still loved her, but now wasn't the time for that.

"I know you would have. Do you think I would have wanted to see you go to prison for avenging me against my father? But once you came along, I was safe from him, anyway."

What the hell did that mean? "What are you talking about, Alex?"

She scrutinized his face. "You really didn't know?" She shrugged. "I guess Sammy wouldn't have bothered to tell you for fear that you'd bolt. I didn't realize it myself at first, but I came to realize it after a while. That manipulative bastard had picked you out for me."

He sputtered, not knowing what to say to that.

She laughed, but not with humor. "Don't look so shocked. I know Sammy. He figured if he couldn't have me he'd control who would. I should have known right away. He never brought his partners home or encouraged them to visit the way he did you. Didn't you find it odd that as domineering as he was, he'd leave us alone together, only to put up a token protest that you shouldn't be hanging around his daughter so much? Especially at the end, he'd leave us together for whole evenings at a time."

If she'd known, why hadn't she said anything? "Why didn't you ever tell me? Why didn't you put a stop to it?"

She shook her head. "Because I didn't object." She laughed again in the same way. "I was in love with you."

He noticed she said was, not am. That seemed logical since they were talking about the past, but it still stung. "Then what was it that killed that feeling? Was it when I left you?" He couldn't believe this would be true anymore, but he asked anyway. "Was it when your father died?" He couldn't bring himself to say "when I got him killed." No matter how he felt about Sammy now, that fact still remained.

"Zach, my father was dying. He didn't tell me, so I know he didn't tell you. I didn't know it until after he was gone, but he had cancer. By the time he went to the doctor it had metastasized throughout his body. It was too late. Sammy told me that nothing but the job was going to kill him and he made sure of that. You've heard of suicide by cop? His was suicide by perp. He knew what he was doing."

Zach thought of Sammy lying on the floor, his blood seeping out of his body, his pride in being able to claim he knew the perp was armed. That pride hadn't been about his prowess as a cop but his ability to predict the means of his own demise. Damn Sammy. All these years he'd been blaming himself when Sammy had gotten exactly what he wanted.

"Let me ask you," she continued. "What were his last words to you?"

"To take care of you, that you were my responsibility."

"Is that really what he said or are you embellishing it?"

"He said, 'She's your—' He didn't finish."

"He wasn't asking you to look after me, he was giving me to you."

Zach stared back at her, his brain reeling from all she'd told him. He'd been blind to all of it, all except Alex's feelings for him. As the difference in their ages seemed to mean less and less, he'd begun to feel the same things, too. He'd wanted her, and when she'd offered herself to him, he hadn't put up much of a fight. He hadn't understood that it was part of Sammy's master plan. But now he couldn't help but wonder if she would have given herself to him if she hadn't been programmed to do it. She might have hated her father, but she'd done what he wanted anyway.

It was too much information for his mind to process with any insight. He was bone-weary in more than a physical way. He stood, pulling her up along with him. "Let's go to bed," he said.

She nodded and let him lead her back to the bed. Once they were settled, he kissed her forehead. "Good night, Alex," he whispered, but he didn't touch her that night, except to hold her until she fell asleep. He stayed awake a long time after, his brain too busy to sleep.

Alex woke early, still in the haven of Zach's arms. She lifted her head and looked down at him. He looked peaceful now in slumber, but last night she'd seen the way he looked at her, as if she were somehow culpable in all Sammy's dealings. He'd hated her last night for keeping all that from him. She'd known that's the way he would feel, which is why she'd never wanted to tell him. If she hadn't freaked out over a couple of glasses of wine, she might have succeeded in that.

But more than wanting to preserve her own place with him, she'd wanted to be honest with him. Once the floodgates opened she'd wanted to let it all spill out. He deserved that, even if she lost him in the process. She should have told him long ago, the moment she realized he blamed himself for Sammy's death.

She kissed him again and got out of bed. They would have to go back to the city today. That would be more easily accomplished if she was ready to go. She noticed that someone had purchased clothes for her in roughly her size, bought shampoo and a much-needed brush and blow-drier. It had probably been Smitty. She'd have to thank him when she saw him.

She got in the shower, washed and dried her hair, and fashioned it into the same braid she'd worn the day before. The clothes were a bit loose, but they'd do. Barefoot, she opened the bathroom door. Zach was already sitting up in bed, watching her with an expression she couldn't read. She plastered a smile on her face, not even understanding her own rationale for that. All she knew was that after last night she couldn't handle another confrontation. "I hope I didn't wake you?"

"I knew the minute you got up."

He said that with so little emotion, she wondered why he bothered. "I'll call downstairs for some coffee."

"I already did. If they come while I'm in the shower tell them to leave it outside." He got out of the bed, still nude. She watched him walk toward her, her gaze traveling over his body, hungry, since they hadn't been together last night.

He paused when he got to her, tipped her chin up, and kissed her mouth, a brief unsatisfying caress, before going inside the bathroom and closing the door.

Alex shut her eyes. He'd withdrawn from her, the one thing she knew would happen and the last thing she wanted. She wasn't really sorry she'd told him. He'd deserved to know for a long time. She'd have to wait and see what the delay had cost her.

Zach was just coming out of the bathroom when a knock sounded at the door. She remained sitting on the bed while he went to answer the door. She'd already tidied the room so as not to be too obvious about the fact that they'd shared a bed last night, even if that's all they'd shared.

Smitty walked in carrying a tray laden with a coffee carafe, cups, and muffins. "Your continental breakfast has arrived." He looked from her to Zach and back. "How are you feeling this morning?"

"Better." At least physically she did, if she didn't count the expanding hollow in the pit of her stomach. "Why don't you join us?"

Smitty grinned. "I had every intention." He sat in the chair by the desk leaving Zach to sit beside her.

But he didn't. He fixed his coffee and stood leaning his back on the door. "What's going on?"

"The local boys released Mama's body to us. We got an ID on the dead girl. One of her neighbors called in to say that she'd seen her with Thorpe, Williams, whatever the hell we're going to call him. Apparently he'd been holing up in her apartment as needed. He only strangled her and buried her, poor thing."

Alex set her muffin on the bed beside her. She didn't have much of an appetite either, not for food or the conversation. She was sure she'd hear it all on the trip back with Zach, anyway.

She stood taking her coffee cup with her. "If you'll excuse me, I'm going to finish getting ready." "She took her pocketbook into the bathroom with her and shut the door.

* * *

As soon as Alex was out of sight Smitty turned to Zach. "Okay, what did you do? No woman gets a look on her face like that without some man having done something."

Zach ground his teeth together. He should have expected Smitty's reaction, but frankly he had other things on his mind. "Look," he said, "I appreciate your protectiveness of Alex, I really do, but stay out of it."

But Smitty wouldn't be put off that easily. "What happened? Did you two have a fight?"

Zach shook his head. He didn't know what explanation he could give Smitty anyway if he deigned to give one. His mental state had been a mess since Alex walked back in his life. Now his emotions were just as bad. The only thing he did know for sure he told Smitty. "We'll work it out."

"See that you do."

Zach laughed. Smitty never could miss that parting shot. "Getting back to business, what else is going on?"

"We found the last owner of the house. She still owns it though it's abandoned. Her name is Vernita Williams. Think there's any relation?"

"Grandma?"

"Thanks to the photo vault, we found pictures of her. They're dated, but who knows if someone will recognize her? We're releasing the photos here, in the city, and in Rockford. That's where the boys were born. Maybe someone there will remember something about them, maybe some childhood friend Williams might turn to."

They could always hope. "I want to take Alex back to the city. She's had a rough time of it here. Any word on where Williams might be?"

"No one's seen him, and we've already put it out on the news that he's wanted. If anyone's putting him up we don't know about it." Smitty stood. "I'll tell Craig you're going. I don't know what he has in mind for the rest of us, but I can't see him objecting."

"Thanks." He clapped Smitty's shoulder. "Take care."

"Always do." Smitty opened the door and headed out.

Almost immediately Alex emerged from the bathroom. He'd wondered what she was doing in there. He knew the minute he saw her. She'd been putting on makeup. Usually her touch was light, subtle, but today she'd used a heavier hand. She probably figured she needed to camouflage her tears last night.

Zach sighed. In some ways he wished he could go back and undo what she'd told him. He was glad to know, but if it was going to cause this chasm to open between them, he'd rather do without the knowledge. Besides, he knew it was his reaction that bothered her. He couldn't help that. But he knew he had to get himself together because he was hurting her now without intending to.

Smitty had also brought them a small satchel in which to store their things. She put the rest of hers in and zipped it.

"Ready to go?" he asked.

"Sure." She slipped on her shoes and headed for the door.

He wished he knew what to say to her at that moment, but he couldn't seem to formulate a coherent sentence in his head. Maybe they just needed to get back to the familiar. Maybe, but he wasn't holding out much hope of that at all.

Twenty-four

The first thing Alex did when she got back to New York was to turn on the TV, eager for some New York news—or anything that would take her mind off her stay north and how what happened there would change things. Neither of them had said much during the long trip back. Once they'd walked in the door, she'd headed for the living room while Zach had gone upstairs. Even though they'd only barely gotten together, it seemed like more separated them than a single flight of stairs.

She turned to the station that catered to Bronx events. One story about an accidental shooting was winding up to be replaced by an update of the Amazon Killer case. She reached for the remote to change the station. She'd had enough in-your-face updates to satisfy her. It was the picture that flashed on the screen above the anchorman's head that stopped her. Alex had seen that picture before, taken the day she'd gotten her master's degree in social work. She remembered looking at Williams's painting and having an image of Roberta flash in her mind. She'd pushed the idea away, not even allowing it to grow to a full thought. Alex wasn't a superstitious woman, but any comparison between the woman in the painting and her friend seemed like borrowing trouble.

". . . had apparently been hiding out with this woman, Roberta Rosetti, a social worker who in an odd twist worked with Dr. Alex Waters."

It made sense then—how Williams seemed to know what they were going to do before they did it. Roberta had been telling him everything she knew. Comparing notes, she called it. How could Roberta not have seen Thorpe in the man she was falling in love with? The simple answer was, he hadn't wanted her to. He'd gained weight, dyed his blond hair black, and adopted a pair of glasses. Besides, anyone looking for Thorpe was expecting to find some down-on-his-luck drifter, not a man with the means to impersonate a lawyer. Then there was that love thing that was known to cloud the judgment if not the vision as well. Roberta had paid for that blindness with her life.

Tears gathered in Alex's eyes and spilled down her cheeks. Her stomach seized and bile rose in her throat. While she'd been watching the report, she'd been numb, analytical. But with nothing cerebral to focus on, Alex's emotions took over, startling her with their depth. She wanted to scream and smash something, anything. But her rage was impotent as the one man she wanted to destroy was beyond her reach. She drew her knees up and wrapped her arms around them, bowed her head, and wept harder.

Although she'd never acknowledged it before, Roberta had been her best friend, her only friend, in the lonely life she'd created. She was alone again now. A wave of desolation swept through her, as pitiable as it was, to her mind, selfish. But she couldn't shake the feeling, not the sorrow, not the anger, not the feeling of isolation that claimed her—none of it.

After hanging up with Smitty, Zach loped down the stairs in search of Alex. Things between them had been strained since last night and he needed to make them right with her. He needed to explain why he'd reacted the way he did, something she obviously didn't understand and therefore held against him.

Unfortunately, he had one more task to accomplish before he could do that. He hoped she'd understand, since most of the heavy hitters in the investigation were still up at Williams's place, and not hold that against him, too.

Hearing a noise, he stopped his descent. He'd learned that sound in the past twenty-four hours. Alex was crying. He hurried down the rest of the stairs. She sat on the love seat facing the TV. She seemed to be curled in on herself, bowed, her shoulders hunched and shaking. Even last night, her grief hadn't been that profound.

He walked to the opening of the living room. "Alex?"

She didn't look up at him, but her hand swiped across her face in a poor attempt to dry her tears.

She wanted to hide her tears from him? Was he the cause of them this time, or had something else inspired them? He crossed to the love seat and pulled her into his arms. Or tried to. She fought him, hitting him in the chest with her fists. He didn't release her, since, if she'd really wanted to hurt him she could have. She seemed more frustrated than angry.

He pulled her closer, trapping her hands between their two bodies. "Baby, what's the matter?"

For the first time she looked at him and he saw such desolation in her eyes that it frightened him. "Why didn't you tell me Roberta was the woman Williams killed?"

He tensed. He'd had no idea. When Smitty told him they'd made identification, he hadn't bothered to ask who they'd identified. At the time it hadn't seemed very important. "I'm so sorry, baby," he whispered against her ear. "How did you find out?"

She relaxed against him a little. "It was on the news."

Zach ground his teeth together. He knew as of his hanging up with Smitty that no one on the NYPD had given any information on the girl in Garnerville to the press. He thought he knew who might have—the much incompetent Sheriff Bates. He was probably trying to find some way to look better in the eyes of his constituents. He wondered if Roberta's brother had learned of his sister's death in the same way. Damn.

At least Alex wasn't crying anymore, except for the faint occasional sniffle. He had to be thankful for that, but he also worried about her. Williams had obviously used Roberta to stay close to Alex and killed her when she wasn't useful anymore. That had to weigh on Alex. He stroked his hand over her hair. "Tell me what you're feeling, sweetheart," he urged.

Instead she pushed back from him. She swiped at her eyes again. "What did you come downstairs to tell me?"

He sighed. Maybe it had been foolish on his part to expect her to confide in him, especially after last night. Still, her dismissal of his concern stung. "It can wait."

A look of steel came in her eyes. "No. I don't want you to put off anything on my account. If you have to go, go."

He thought he understood how she felt a little. He'd hurt someone she loved. She wanted him caught now more than ever. "They found Williams's grandmother."

"Where is she?"

"Believe it or not she lives about ten blocks from here. Her lease is under another name." Which meant that Williams could have found her at any time if he'd known where to look. "I don't know how long I'll be. The officers in the car are still outside. I can have a policewoman come in if you like."

She shook her head. "I don't want to be in here with some stranger. I'll be fine. I need to call Eric."

Zach surveyed her face. If it weren't for the smudged

makeup he never would have known she'd been crying since she appeared completely dry-eyed now. He didn't know if it was a good thing or a bad one that she never seemed to dwell on her own emotions for long. She was already thinking about Roberta's brother.

He tucked a strand of hair behind her ear and leaned in close enough to ensure that she looked at him. "I'm going to catch this son of a bitch, Alex. I promise you that."

She didn't say anything to that, but the look in her eyes said *You'd better.*

Vernita Williams was a small, squat woman purportedly in her sixties but she hadn't aged well. Her face was a road map of creases. Her hair had gone completely white and had the texture of wet Brillo. She was dressed in a floral-printed smock over a white nightgown, neither of which looked terribly clean. The first thing she said when she opened the door to Zach and the other detective he'd brought along with him, Kraft, was, "Which one of those bitches ratted me out?" She gestured toward a group of women gathered together a couple of houses down, obviously gossiping about her.

Zach ignored her vitriol. "Can we speak to you a few minutes about your grandsons?"

She crossed her arms, shrugging her shoulders, but she obviously didn't intend to let them in. "So someone finally figured out what that daughter of mine done. I saw Homer's picture all over the news, but I knew he never done nothing. It was that other one. It was her own fault. Nothing good comes from putting a boy in a dress."

"Tell me about your daughter," Zach said.

"Ain't much to tell. Nessy was crazy. Everybody knew

that. She was pretty and young and all the boys were hot after her."

"Nessy?"

"Va-nes-sa. I named her after Vanessa Redgrave. That woman had class. But my daughter—from the time she was born she was nothing but Messy Nessy. That's what I used to call her. She'd lie down in the grass back by where we lived and spread her legs for anything with the right thing between them."

"Is that how the boys were conceived?"

"Who the hell knows how them boys came into being? When she got tired of doing it for free, she'd go down by where the highway is now. There wasn't nothing there but a dirt road and some trees. She made the men start paying for it." Vernita shrugged. "At least then she helped put some food on the table."

"What about the boys?"

Vernita shook her head gravely. "Nessy had followed some man upstate by the time the boys were born. But he left her, just like I told her he would. No man wants to raise another man's brats. When it came time for her to deliver, she called me. She was alone and I guess I was better than nothing.

"Virgil was always the stronger of the two. Even in the womb it seemed like he wanted to suck the life out of Homer. Virgil came out big and strong, but Homer had the cord wrapped around his neck. The doctors saved him, but he wasn't quite right. Nessy had no use for him, and ignored him, which was probably to his benefit."

"What do you mean?"

"Well, they say the favored child gets all the benefits, but what if that parent is nuts and sees in you a kindred spirit? That's got to warp a child, too. She used to sew them mother and daughter outfits and take them into town, though she never let those boys go to school. Every time someone seemed to wise up to her she'd move, always to some little hick town, always on the out-skirts where no one could see what she was doing. Like I said, Nessy was crazy."

Zach studied the old woman. If Nessy was crazy, he wondered what part the old woman had played in that madness. Harmless was not a word he'd used to describe this woman, especially considering the glee with which she recounted her family's misdeeds. She enjoyed know-ing they were out there committing mayhem, relishing it vicariously. He'd had enough of her.

"Where would Virgil go? Is there anyone he would turn to?"

"I haven't seen that boy in years and I could go to my grave happy never to see him again. Why do you think I'm here in this rat hole? I hope he never does find me. You make sure he stays away."

For the first time, he saw fear in her eyes. Did she expect Virgil would come seeking retribution? More than likely. Zach knew he'd get the captain to watch this place. But he took his own glee in telling her, "I'll see what I can do."

After trying him at his home and office numbers, Alex found Eric Rosetti at the number for his sister's apart-ment. When he picked up, she said, "Eric, this is Alex Waters. I'm so sorry about Roberta."

For a long moment there was no response, then the sound of a clearing throat. "Thank you. I'm glad you called." He gave a short, bitter laugh. "You won't believe what I was sitting here doing."

Eric struck her as the kind of man who, once he de-cided he liked you, held nothing back. So his familiarity with her didn't surprise her. "What?"

"I can't make any arrangements until I know when the

police are going to release her body, but I was trying to figure out what dress to bury her in."

She recognized that act as the desperate attempt of the grief-stricken to find something productive to do. It was a way of trying to trick themselves into believing they were actually moving on in the grieving process, when actually they were standing still. She couldn't imagine Eric's true emotions being anything but raw. But if that's what he needed to do to cope, she would oblige him.

"Try the cranberry pantsuit with the matching scarf."

"Yes. That will work, I guess. I'm no fashion consultant." There was another long pause. "It's not your fault, you know."

She knew that. She hadn't put the rope in Williams's hand, but he'd gone after Roberta because of the link between them. That was close enough for Alex. "She wouldn't have been in his path if it weren't for me."

"Maybe not, but you have to understand something about my sister. From the time she was little she brought home a string of wounded birds, homeless dogs, even a three-legged cat. She was the same way with people. Give her the kid everybody picked on or some child whose parents were getting a divorce and that was her best friend. She'd patch them up, too, like she did her animals. We had to draw the line at letting the neighborhood drunk live in our garage."

Eric snorted, a sound full of pride and remembrance. "I always knew she'd go into some form of public advocacy work. How else could she champion her underdogs? Unfortunately, she was the same way with men, too—always of the fixer-upper variety, even though she never saw it at first. If she seemed cynical sometimes it was because so many of them disappointed her when their true natures were revealed. Her relationship with you might have put her in this guy's path, but what made him attractive to her had to do with something innate in her character."

He sounded so philosophical, so detached that it worried her, until he added, "God, I miss her so much already."

She heard the tears in his voice and felt in herself an answering emptiness. Tears brewed in her eyes, but this time she fought them back. She listened for as long as Eric wanted to talk, sometimes offering advice or encouragement, sometimes just the um-hmm of verbal agreement. Like with most who grieved, the most important thing was to allow those who suffered a loss the opportunity to talk about the one they'd lost.

After a while, he became quiet. "Thanks for letting me bend your ear like that. Roberta was a very private person. The day you two came here, I don't think she intended to let you know I was her brother except I spoiled the whole thing by calling her 'sis.' But I know she wouldn't have minded me unloading on you. She spoke of you very highly."

So Eric had known about her while she'd known nothing about him. Hearing Eric talk she'd realized how little she'd known about her friend. It occurred to her that Alex could say the same thing about herself. Was there anyone on the planet who really knew her? Roberta had come the closest.

To Eric, she said, "I'm glad I could be there for you."

They talked for a few minutes more before hanging up, but as Alex disconnected the call she wondered if she weren't like Roberta in another way as well. Had she picked the significant men in her life because they needed fixing too? Devon's detachment had appealed to her. She knew he could never break her heart since he could never claim it either.

But what of Zach—a self-professed cynic, a man who allowed his family to think the worst of him, for what reason she couldn't fathom? Even as a young girl she'd recognized the loneliness in him. Did she want to fix him, too? And if she did, had she lost the opportunity by not confiding the truth to him before now?

Alex was already in bed by the time he got home. One thing had led to another and another until it was nearly nine o'clock when he walked in the door. He'd called her to check on her a couple of times. Each time she'd answered, tried to assure him that she was fine, but he didn't believe that. Still, it was early for her to be in bed already. He'd witnessed Joanna's depression after her husband's death. Remembering that made him worry more for Alex. Psychologist or no, everyone had their breaking point. Had Roberta's death pushed Alex to hers?

The one thing that heartened him was that she hadn't withdrawn from him into another room. She was there in his own bed waiting for him. Without turning on the light, he slipped out of his clothes and left them in the chair by the door. He slid into bed beside her and pulled her to him. She was warm and soft, but she wasn't asleep.

She laid her cheek against his chest while her fingers stroked his shoulder. "I left some dinner for you in the microwave."

He smiled and rubbed his hands up and down her back. Even after all she'd been through today, she still thought of him. "Maybe I'll get to it later."

"All right."

He heard the tentativeness in her voice and hated it. That wasn't the Alex he knew. He'd deal with that in a minute after he dealt with something more pressing. "I don't think it's safe for you to stay here any longer. I'm sure Williams knows who I am by now and it wouldn't take a genius to track you here."

"No, it wouldn't, but that's been true since I've been here."

"Before we weren't certain it was you he was after. I am now."

"What do you want me to do?"

"We'll move you somewhere neutral in the morning."

She nodded as if her own safety meant little to her. He supposed at the moment she had more on her mind than that. Although she allowed him to hold her, she shared nothing with him of her emotions, not in words or any other way. She seemed pulled up into herself, somewhere he couldn't reach. That didn't mean he wouldn't try.

He brushed her hair from her face. "Did you get to speak to Roberta's brother?"

She nodded. "He's pretty broken up. I don't know how her sister is faring."

He wasn't aware Roberta had a sister, but he doubted questioning Alex about her would do much good. "What about you? How are you holding up?"

She lifted one shoulder in a shrug. "I don't know."

While he appreciated her honesty, he wished she'd elaborated or that he could come up with some words to entice her to say more. One more reminder of how little he knew her. He hugged her to him, hoping the tenderness of his embrace communicated to her that he was there for her if she wanted him.

She had been here all along. There was a certain irony in that. Here within his grasp, and he hadn't known it. She had always been a crafty old bat, his grandmother. Like daughter, like mother, she'd found herself a new identity behind which to hide.

But nothing hidden could remain so forever, could it? The truth always sought the light, at least that's what he'd been told. And the truth was that Vernita Williams was as guilty as her daughter in helping create the grotesquerie that he was. And she would pay just as dearly.

She'd fled from him that day, the day he'd finally had enough. The day he realized Messy Nessy had stopped bringing home men for herself. The ones who came now were meant only for him. She took the money and they took him. In a rage he'd taken a knife to her while she slept. He'd been in such a rage that he hadn't noticed until the haze cleared from his eyes that he'd sliced off her breast, her right breast. He'd laughed then, because he'd given her her wish. Too bad she was too dead to enjoy it.

It wasn't hard convincing the hick cops that she'd run off with some man. She was already known as the town whore in every town they'd ever been to. All he had to do was hide the body, clean up, and get The Mirror to keep his mouth shut. He'd told him, "I'll sew up your mouth like she sews up those dresses." That had been all that was needed to gain his silence.

He'd wanted to kill her then. That's why he'd run away. He wanted to deal a death blow against everyone who'd made him what he was. That's what he required to start over. Even at ten years old he understood that. He had to kill what he was to become something new.

But he had her now. He'd seen not her but her house on the news. She had to know he would come. Would she be ready for him?

He walked down her block—trim attached houses with multicolored awnings. All except hers. Hers was the solitary eyesore, sans decoration of any kind, save for a falling-down fence and a screen door that hung off to the side. She'd never been able to keep anything worth a damn. Everything she owned she ruined, including her own family.

He continued down the block, past the police car parked in front, and rounded the corner. A drive ran the length of the length of the block by which home owners could pull into their own garages. There was no police car here, no one minding the store. It was a mistake.

He hopped the waist-high fence and climbed down into the yard at the corner. Nearby a dog barked, and he froze, but the mutt stopped yapping soon enough. From where he crouched now her house was the seventh from the corner. He inched along until he reached that yard, soundlessly slid over the rusty fence, and crept up to the house. He flattened himself against the back wall, momentarily looking up at the sky. The moon was low, full, and seemed to be winking at him. It seemed to whisper to him, "Go for it." What kind of warped lunar presence was that?

He'd come prepared tonight. He'd tucked a cord into his pocket, but he also carried a bowie knife disguised in the length of his pants. Choices again, but of the two of them he preferred the cord. Anyone could wield a knife, especially against an old lady. That took no skill and little strength. He enjoyed the challenge of the jerking body trying to free itself, knowing it was only his power and control that kept the ligature in place. He reveled in the slow lingering death, first the weakness, then the surrender, then nothing. Nothing was worth doing if you weren't willing to take your time about it.

He didn't expect the back door to withstand too much tampering. One butt with his shoulder and it eased open. Inside was pure darkness, but he shut the door behind him, softly, with as little click as possible. He pulled out his flashlight and turned it on, covering the muzzle so that it wouldn't shed too much light. He made it to the stairs through a maze of dilapidated boxes and other contraptions; all of it valueless and ill cared for.

The stairs curved at the base and also at the top, leading

to a flimsy wooden door that she hadn't bothered to lock. He eased the door open, but he wasn't worried about her spotting him yet. He knew where he'd find her, passed out or still drinking in a chair in the living room. Dull voices and a flickering light told him which way to go.

He edged along the wall until the archway that opened out into a front room. He peered around the corner to find her propped up in an old recliner, her feet up. A small lamp with a dim bulb and a bottle of whiskey rested on a small oval-shaped table beside her. Her hands were folded over her mound of a belly. Her eyes were closed and a strangled sort of snore emanated from her.

For a moment he contemplated killing her right then, before she knew what was on her. But that would kill his purpose as well. He wanted her to know it was him. He stepped more fully into the room, and she stirred, opening her eyes half-mast to peer at him.

"Walter?" she said, confusion written on her face. She'd always called them by the names they'd adopted when they were little older than babies. She shook her head, squeezing her eyes shut. But when she looked at him again, she knew. Her blue eyes bulged with realization, shock, but mostly fear.

He smiled, showing just an edge of his teeth. "Hello, Nana," he said.

Her eyes darted around the room, perhaps searching for some weapon to use against him. Finding nothing but her whiskey bottle, which she wouldn't part with unless she had to, she sat back, a look of steel in her eyes. Like a cornered rat, she turned on him. "What are you doing in here, boy? Don't you know those boys outside are looking for you?"

He understood her implication. All she'd have to do was scream and the cops outside would come in. But he knew she wouldn't do that. Nana was a Bronx girl; she'd fight her own battles.

"I came to see you, Nana." One last time. He'd needed to see her. He remembered her as a looming presence, but in reality she was a gnome of a woman. Nothing. Yet she'd been as terrifying to him as any ghoul unleashed from hell.

To think he owed his existence to her. First she'd pimped her daughter to whatever men would pay. Then she'd refused to pay for the abortion that would have killed them. For that alone she deserved to die.

"Well?" she demanded. "What do you want?"

She tried for bravado, but the fear was still in her eyes, fear he'd put there. He grasped the stiletto hidden in his sleeve and took a step toward her. "I just wanted to say good-bye."

Twenty-five

Zach woke in the early morning to the sound of his cell phone ringing. He retrieved it from where he'd left it, on the nightstand next to his gun, and connected the call without bothering to check the caller ID. Whatever had prompted the call was most likely urgent and not good besides. "Stone."

"Bad news," Smitty said without bothering to identify himself. "About an hour ago the boys outside Vernita Williams's house noticed the light was still on in her living room. Even an old lady's got to go to bed sometime. So one of the guys goes in to check on her. She was dead and Williams was nowhere to be found."

Zach ground his teeth together and muttered some words he was glad Alex wasn't awake to hear. He knew she could handle a little profanity, but he'd hoped to give her a little more time to adjust before the next wave of whatever Williams had planned rose to the surface. Anyone with half a brain could see that revenge was as much a part of Williams's plan as anything else. Even though he apparently killed his brother himself, Walter Thorpe's death had been the catalyst for the rest of it. McKay had brought Alex into it and Williams had made sure she stayed in it. By leaving Walter's body in his grandmother's former house, he'd initiated a police search for a woman he couldn't find.

When Williams had escaped leaving Alex mostly unharmed, Zach had been grateful, but that hadn't stopped him from wondering why Williams had done so. He knew the answer now. He planned to save Alex for last. Now that the grandmother was gone, hers was the only name on the list. That knowledge scared him shitless, considering how Williams had murdered Roberta, someone he ostensibly cared about. Or at least he'd been a good enough con to convince Roberta of that.

When he'd finally managed to get Alex talking last night, he'd remarked on that to her. She'd told him to look at Williams's paintings—not the sun-filled landscapes he made his living from, but the others—stark, horror-filled vignettes. To Williams, the world was full of horror. If he'd cared for Roberta in his own warped way, he probably thought he was doing her a favor.

"You still there, buddy?"

Zach wiped his hand down his face, trying to banish the remnants of sleep. "I'm here." His mind turned to focus on Vernita Williams. After he'd left her, Craig had tried to convince her to leave her home in the interest of her own safety. She'd refused, threatening to raise a stink about police brutality if they took her against her will. Zach hadn't agreed with the decision to leave her where she was under surveillance, but then no one had asked him, either. She'd seemed afraid of the possibility that Williams would find her, but if she'd put up much of a struggle before Williams got her the cops outside would have noticed.

"How did it happen?"

"Knife at the base of the head."

A nice clean kill. Hitting the cerebellum would stop all brain and bodily functions at once. There'd be no time to cry out, little blood, if any, hence the popularity of the execution-style kill—the .22 to the back of the head. The victim just fell over dead.

Zach rubbed his temples with his thumb and middle fingers. He'd say this for Williams, the guy was crafty, knowledgeable, and bold. Fearless, in a way only those with nothing left to lose can be. He suspected Williams did have one fear—being stopped before he finished.

"Any leads on where he might be now?"

"None. Ever since we got into his house we've been running down every contact in the place. There haven't been any hits on the credit card, but we weren't expecting any. He cleaned out one of his bank accounts a couple of days ago. For all we know, he's shacked up with some woman somewhere again."

Great, so he had enough cash and resourcefulness to disappear for a while, if that's what he wanted, though Zach didn't think he did. He'd struck within hours of his grandmother's location making it onto the news. He, like the rest of them, wanted this over.

Alex started to stir, stretching and making purring noises. For the first time that morning, he smiled. "I gotta go," he told Smitty. "I'll call you back in a little bit."

Smitty chuckled. "Try not to enjoy yourself too much."

Zach disconnected the call, but it wasn't pleasure of any kind he had on his mind. He needed to tell Alex about Williams's grandmother. He didn't know how she'd take that news, but it wouldn't please her, either. He needed to make arrangements to move her. For now, he'd take her to his brother Adam's house, which was at least one more step removed from the investigation. After that, he'd see.

Alex opened her eyes, a contented smile on her face. That smile eased away until a look of wariness replaced it. "What happened?"

Zach swallowed. How could she read him so well when half the time he had no idea what she was thinking?

"Williams paid a visit to his grandmother last night. She's dead now."

Alex sighed. "Damn. What now?"

He noticed she didn't ask any of her usual questions—how, where? Maybe it didn't matter anymore or maybe she was on overload, as he'd suspected last night. If she was, he knew he'd had a hand in getting her there. Forcing her to reveal what she had about her father coupled with his own response to her revelation undoubtedly contributed to her mental state. He wished now that he hadn't pushed her so hard, but he was glad for the information. It slid a large piece of the puzzle that was Alex Waters into place.

"I'm taking you to my brother Adam's house for now. We'll see after that."

She didn't object, though in the past she'd balked at going anywhere that might involve others. "I guess I'd better get dressed, then," she said.

She started to rise, but he pulled her back down. He stroked her hair from her face. "Sweetheart, understand something, I'm not going to let him get to you. We'll find him. It's not like when we were looking for Thorpe. It was like searching for a ghost since that's basically what he was. Live humans leave trails. And Williams's picture is out there, both as a man and a woman. Someone will spot him and turn him in."

Even to his own ears that sounded like an oversell job, but he couldn't seem to stop talking. "The best minds in the NYPD are on this."

She bit her lip, looking up at him with an expression he couldn't fathom. "I know. I'm just weary of all this, I guess. Weary and heartsick over Roberta. All this death, and for what? One man's perverted sense of justice. Whatever happened to him as a child may well have been horrific. I don't doubt that. As a psychologist, I can explain all of his actions. But as a human being it just sickens me. The fact that I'm his next target doesn't even factor into it that way. At this point, I'm too numb to be scared."

He hugged her to him. That was okay. He was scared enough for both of them. He didn't doubt his ability to protect her, but that didn't mean either of them would come out of an encounter with Williams unscathed, if not physically, then emotionally. Undoubtedly, Williams saw his brother's attempts to confide in Alex as the catalyst that got this ball rolling. It was their friendship that put Roberta in his path. Zach wondered if Alex took any of that blame on herself, but he was afraid to ask her that. He suspected she did, knowing how she'd blamed herself for her father's actions when she knew she shouldn't.

This he knew without a shrink having to tell him: Voicing something out loud made it real, made it something to reckon with. On the off chance she wasn't blaming herself, he wouldn't give her a new area of concern on which to focus. Still, however this played out, she'd be affected by the outcome. He wanted to minimize that as much as possible.

He smacked her bottom. "It's time to get up, woman," he said in a manner that suggested that the fact they were still in bed was her fault.

She smacked his shoulder. "Didn't I say that?"

Hearing the humor in her voice heartened him. "Come on." He swatted her butt. "Let's go."

Alex knew Zach hadn't bothered to inform his brother they were on the way the minute Barbara Stone answered the door.

"Zach, what are you doing here?" she asked. She ushered them in the door before closing it behind them.

"I was hoping to speak to your husband. Is he still here?"

"Barely. Another ten minutes and you would have missed him."

Stevie came bounding into the room and threw herself at Zach. "Uncle Zach, I missed you," she said as if she hadn't seen him in two years rather than a couple of days.

"Hey, munchkin," Zach said.

Alex braced herself as Stevie turned her attention her way. "Alex."

The embrace wasn't as fierce as Alex had expected, thankfully. "Hi, Stevie."

Barbara frowned. "Stevie, stop smushing people and let your father know his brother is here."

"I'm already aware of that."

Alex focused on Adam Stone coming down the stairs. Like Zach, he was a handsome man, though their coloring differed. Both Adam's eyes and hair were black. There was also a harshness to his features, lacking from both his brothers'. Or maybe it was the gravity of events in his life that was mirrored in his face.

Adam stopped beside his wife, placing an arm around her waist. "We're all on our way out the door."

In other words, whatever they wanted needed to be worth his time. Adam might be Zach's brother, but she had yet to decide whether she liked him or not. That kind of attitude wasn't helpful.

"It'll only take a minute."

Adam made a move that might have passed for a shrug. He led the way toward his study. Once they were all seated, Adam said, "What's going on?"

Alex would love to know that as well, since Zach hadn't been very forthcoming on the subject himself. She'd heard him speaking on the phone to someone while she was in the bathroom fixing her hair, but she couldn't make out what was said. When she asked him about it, he'd told her he'd tell her later. That had not been helpful, either.

Zach shifted in his seat. "I'm doing what I should have done in the first place. I'm getting Alex out of here. A friend of mine has a house out on Long Island that he'll let us use for a bit."

Zach glanced at her, she supposed to gauge her reaction. Why couldn't he have told her that? She had no objection to getting the hell out of Dodge, except for the fact that it didn't make tactical sense. If Williams wanted to find her, wouldn't he look for her elsewhere if she wasn't at Zach's?

Adam nodded his approval. "What do you need from me?"

"I want you to know where we are and the loan of a car. I spoke to Craig this morning. Two decoys will be picking up mine and going back to the house. If Williams acts with his usual urgency, he should make a move tonight."

"No problem. I can have Barbara drop me at work." He stood. "I'm sorry to have been so gruff before. I've got a lot on my mind."

Alex didn't doubt that. But she did notice the warmth with which Adam hugged her good-bye and wished them luck.

When Adam left to help get his brood out the door, Alex turned to Zach. "Why couldn't you tell me what your plans were?"

Zach turned to her. "It's not that I couldn't . . ."

But he hadn't wanted to. "You thought I'd object."

"There was the possibility."

And by getting her out of the house he eliminated the possibility that she'd turn stubborn and refuse to leave. In a way she couldn't blame him. They'd tried to get Vernita Williams to accept protective custody and now she was dead. Alex might be stubborn, but she wasn't crazy.

"You shouldn't have worried. What's the plan now?"

"Once the undercovers get here, they'll take my car back to my place. We'll head to the Island in Adam's car."

That sounded simple enough. They stayed out of the way while the others brought Williams down. It would have been simple if she didn't sense in Zach a desire to be the one to catch him himself. She didn't know if that was due to his cop's ego or to some macho protective thing, but she acknowledged either feeling as valid. Why shouldn't he want a hand in bringing Williams down? Half the cops in the city were champing at the bit for that opportunity.

Even so, she wouldn't mind some time alone with Zach, however long it lasted. She'd be deluding herself if she didn't acknowledge she'd fallen in love with him again, that is, if she'd ever really stopped. But she wasn't foolish enough to convince herself that a bit of passion and a few hasty promises constituted a future for them. Not a second time.

She had no doubt Zach wanted her physically and she didn't question his desire to protect her. But she'd seen the look in his eyes when she told him about her father. He'd tried to explain that away, but she wasn't sure she bought it. He'd been hurt to realize how Sammy had manipulated him, and worse, that she'd been a party to it. He said he wasn't angry with her, but she wasn't sure she could believe that, either. Or maybe the situation they found themselves in was so far from normal it was impossible to gauge what felt right. Maybe a couple of days alone would provide a little perspective.

As they drove from the Bronx to Long Island, that's what Alex hoped.

Zach's friend's house turned out to be little more than a cottage on the beach in a small fishing village toward the middle of the island. Living and dining rooms were

one large space on the first floor with a loft bedroom
overhanging part of the downstairs. It had an airy feel
with light-colored paneling, beige furniture, and lots of
windows.

Zach set the bags down beside her. "What do you
think?"

Early afternoon sunlight filtered in through the windows lending the space a homey glow. "I like it." Her
stomach rumbled. "I'd like it a lot better if we'd thought
about mundane things like food."

"Not to worry. My friend called a neighbor to do a
little shopping for us. What do you feel like eating?"

They eventually settled on a frozen pizza, put it in the
oven, and sat on the sofa to wait. Zach slung an arm
around her shoulders, pulling her closer. He kissed the
top of her head. "How are you holding up?"

Alex shifted so she could see his face. It occurred to
her that he'd asked her that question more times in the
last two days since she'd made her revelation than he
had the entire rest of the time they'd been together. Did
he see her as some sort of fragile thing now that he'd
seen her break down? She hoped not, but she suspected
he did.

She hit him on the arm. "I'm fine and I will continue
to be fine as long as you don't burn that pizza."

That was a lie; they both knew it was. But he seemed
willing to let it slide for the most part. "You just look
beat, that's all."

She did feel that way, beat up by life and recent events.
"So maybe a nap is in order after lunch."

"That sounds like a plan." He brought one of her
hands to his mouth, kissed her palm, and placed it on
his chest. "I could use some shut-eye myself."

For a long moment, they remained like that, neither
of them speaking. She remembered the awkwardness
of that long-ago car ride when neither of them could

find anything to say to each other. This was different. This felt right, comfortable, an embrace of affection rather than a sexual one. She snuggled closer to him, laying her cheek against his chest. Then the timer on the oven went off.

Zach disentangled himself from her and went to get the pizza. He came back with it balanced in one hand and a couple of beers in the other. He'd tucked a couple of plastic plates under one arm. He seemed to pause for a moment as he walked toward her, and she worried about his apparent hesitancy.

"What did you forget?" she asked as he set the tray with the pizza on it on the coffee table in front of her.

"Napkins. The beer is all right?"

She made an exasperated sound in her throat. So that's why he'd hesitated. At that moment he'd remembered her freaking out on him the other night. How could she explain to him that it wasn't really him or the wine? She didn't regard him in any way as she did her father. If her migraine had left her a little more lucid, she never would have reacted the way she did. Her conscious mind had already decided to keep its mouth shut; her subconscious hadn't agreed.

"It's fine," she said finally. She took the bottles from him and set them on the table, then did the same with the plates.

Once he retrieved a stack of napkins from the kitchen, Alex served each of them a slice. The pizza was good, flavorful and warm, but she barely tasted it after a couple of bites. Her attention centered on Zach. She didn't understand him. To her mind, he was one of the good guys, a dedicated, if slightly burned out, cop, a man who had always been kind to her. Even now, he'd let her cry when she wanted to and hadn't urged her to talk when she didn't want to. He'd held her so tenderly just a moment ago that it meant more to her than any other embrace they'd shared.

To the outside world he presented a confident, affable front, but underneath lurked a well of self-doubt, the depth of which she was only coming to understand. She also knew that some of that distrust she'd placed there herself. It hadn't occurred to her that he'd been as affected in his own way by what happened between them thirteen years ago. At the time she'd thought he'd already moved on.

But remembering the night of the family dinner and also the reception they'd received that morning from Zach's brother, she knew she wasn't the only guilty party. She'd wondered before why he allowed the family dynamic to remain intact, the one that cast him as the bad guy, which as far as she could tell was undeserved.

She set her plate on the table and tucked her feet underneath her. "Do you mind if I ask you something?"

"No," he said, but she could see the wariness in his eyes.

"Why do you let your family think the worst of you?"

He shifted to face her more fully. "You mean because of what happened with my ex-wife?"

That was only part of it, but she nodded.

"If you'd ever tried to unconvince either one of my brothers of something they're sure of, then you'd know what a waste of time that is."

"That sounds like a cop-out answer to me."

He took a swig from his bottle. "What else do you expect from a cop?"

Actually, she had expected resistance from him, but she answered, "I was hoping for a little honesty."

"You want honesty? Okay, let's start with you. Why do you care so much? Whatever happened, happened a long time ago."

There was no belligerence in his tone, only the

implication that she was curious for idle reasons or out
of a psychologist's need to analyze, nothing more.
"Maybe your marriage ended a long time ago, but it
seems to me your family is still making you pay for that,
or maybe it's for some other reason. All I know is that
when we walked into your brother's house this morning, he assumed it was for some frivolous reason, despite the case you're working on and the fact that you
had me with you."

"Adam's got a lot on his mind."

"I don't doubt that he does. So I wonder why he bothered to call me, ostensibly looking for you, mind you, at
a time when you were sure not to be at home, and try to
pepper me with all sorts of questions about our relationship. If I'm not mistaken, I think he was trying to scare
me off."

A thunderous look crossed Zach's face. "What did he
tell you?"

"Nothing I was interested in hearing. I hung up on
him."

Zach snorted. "He must have loved that."

Frankly, Alex couldn't have cared less what Adam
thought. As a family, the members' allegiance should
have been to one another, not some stranger they barely
knew. Or maybe in a strange way Adam's interference
had been for Zach's sake in that he hoped to save Zach
from the mistake of mistreating another "nice" girl,
which she was sure was how Adam viewed her.

But she hoped Zach realized she'd been honest with
him. "Your turn," she said.

"You want to know what happened? Here it is in a nutshell. It was the first family dinner that I showed up without Sherry. No one said anything until the Brothers
Grimm cornered me in Adam's study to ask what happened. I said we were getting a divorce. Of course they
asked why. Not wanting to go into the whole deal I said,

'Infidelity.' Of course, they assumed it was mine. I wasn't exactly the poster boy for commitment before I met Sherry, and neither of my brothers would have found it believable that she stepped out on me."

So he'd let them believe whatever they wanted. "What really happened?"

He took a long pull from his beer, but already she sensed in him the resignation to tell her. "I walked in on them. Her and some guy who had just transferred into the squad I was working. She was still in bed while he was putting on his clothes. He seemed as surprised to see me as I was to see him. Apparently she hadn't told him that she was married or to whom she was married."

Alex's breath hissed in through her teeth. She could imagine how Zach had felt walking in on that scene. "What did you do?"

"I walked out saying I didn't want to see either one of them there when I got back. I think if the guy had known about me, I might have blown his head off. But I knew Sherry had used both of us. I had a habit of calling her when I was on my way home. She knew I was coming and if she'd wanted to avoid a confrontation she would have rushed the guy out of there. She wanted me to find them together."

And she must have counted on Zach's having being more circumspect than to shoot first and ask questions later. A big chance in Alex's opinion. Her behavior was as juvenile as that of Alex's niece, seeking to gain Zach's attention by flagrantly breaking the rules.

"Was she gone when you got back?"

"No. She was sitting on the sofa drinking a glass of wine. The first words she said to me were, 'Now that I have your attention, can we talk?' At that point I didn't think there was much to say."

He took one last pull from his beer and set it on the table. "The truth is, I wasn't paying attention. If she was unhappy I didn't really know about it until that day. I knew she resented me working so much, but how many cops' wives don't? In retrospect, she probably did send up signals—her clinginess and growing dependency. But the truth is, we never should have gotten married in the first place."

"Why did you?"

"Her family was pressuring her to get married. I was old enough that the idea of having someone to come home to appealed to me. But in reality we had little in common beside what went on in the bedroom. That's not enough of a basis on which to build something that's supposed to be permanent."

She supposed not, though plenty of people had tried. "You didn't try to work things out?"

"What would have been the point? We didn't belong together. Besides, I knew she hadn't just been trying to get my attention. That I might have been able to forgive. Her picking someone I had to see every day was designed to hurt and humiliate me, since word of her infidelity was sure to make it around the station. The only saving grace was the other guy was so embarrassed that he never said a word to anyone and eventually transferred out."

She touched her hand to his shoulder. "I'm sorry." Both for the past and for making him relive it in the present.

"Don't be. I wasn't exactly blameless, myself. My response to all this was to lose myself in a half dozen women's beds, partly to convince Sherry I wasn't coming back, but mostly for selfish reasons. You know, a whole male ego thing."

He brought her hand to his mouth and kissed her palm. "Do you feel better knowing that about me?"

She bit her lip, surveying his face. He expected some kind of judgment from her, but she had none to give. So he had things in his life he regretted. What grown-up didn't? But she realized then why he let his brothers behave as they did. He saw it as fitting punishment, not for the sins they thought he committed but the ones for which he blamed himself.

Damn. Why was life so freaking complicated? She supposed she wouldn't have a job if human existence was something easily survived. But she was tired of talking. If he wanted to know what feelings his confession sparked in her, she'd show him. She leaned up, cradled his face in her palms, and brought her mouth down to his.

Twenty-six

Zach's arms closed around her, pulling her down to his lap as the kiss deepened. It was the first time they'd kissed like that since they'd been together in the hotel room, and he was ravenous for her and not just in a physical way. Her listening to his past without judgment touched something inside him that had nothing to do with sex, but managed to fuel his desire for her anyway.

Her tongue rubbed against his, tasting spicy from the pizza and cool from the beer. He captured it and sucked on it, causing her to moan into his mouth. God, he wanted her, but there was something they needed to settle first. Reluctantly, he pulled away from her. "Baby, there's something I need to say to you first."

She blinked and looked at him. Her hair was tousled and her eyes had already darkened with passion. "Can't it wait?"

He chuckled, glad to know she was as eager for him as he was for her. "No, it can't." While he was playing True Confessions, he wanted everything out, everything in the open so that nothing stood between them. "I want to apologize for acting like a horse's ass the other night when you told me about Sammy."

She shook her head. "I don't blame you for being angry with me."

That surprised him. He'd been enraged that night, but never had he suspected she believed it was aimed at her. "Baby, I wasn't angry with you. I was angry with myself and your father. No matter what you think, I know Sammy was no saint. I knew he was a great cop and a good partner, but he was a lousy father. The one thing I thought I knew in this world was that I had protected you from him as best I could. That was a lie."

"I did my best to hide that from you. I didn't want you to think less of me."

"How could I have done that? Sweetheart, you work with these people. You know it's never the kid's fault. The adult is always to blame." He supposed it was easy to know that intellectually, but when it happened to you it wasn't always easy to be so circumspect.

She rested her head against his shoulder. "Then why haven't you touched me since that night? I needed you."

It pleased him to hear her admit that. "Because, at first, I didn't want to touch you in anger, to take out on you what I could no longer take out on your father." He didn't elaborate on the previous night. He hadn't been sure what she'd wanted so he'd left her alone. If she'd given him any hint that she needed him in that way, he wouldn't have denied her. But then she'd thought he was angry with her for keeping things from him.

For a long moment, neither of them said anything. It wasn't a comfortable silence in that she started to stir against him and his hands, of their own accord, started to explore. Alex lifted her head and looked up at him. "Zach?" she whispered.

"What is it, baby?"

"Touch me now."

He didn't hesitate. They came together in a tangle of arms and legs, mouths and tongues, touching, caressing, wild. He couldn't get enough of her taste, her scent. And when she rolled a condom on him and guided him into her body, his whole body shivered. It was like being consumed by a fever. His body perspired more and his breathing became more shallow the deeper as she took him into her body.

He rolled over, pulling her on top of him. With one hand at her hips he helped her set their rhythm. He stroked his other hand over her breasts to capture one nipple and roll it between his fingers. She moaned and her back arched. He pulled her down to him then, close enough that he could take one nipple into his mouth and then the other. She bucked against him, driving him further toward the brink.

He opened his eyes half-mast and looked up at her. She was as far gone as he. He grasped her hips and thrust into her, over and over, as she gasped his name. Her nails dug into his shoulders as she came, her back arched, her head thrown back. He pulled her down to him, unable to hold back any longer. He groaned his release against her neck.

For a long time they lay together, each of them recovering. After a while he got rid of the condom, pulled the afghan from the sofa over them, checked his weapon and left it in on the coffee table beside them, and closed his eyes.

He could feel her smile against his chest. "By the way," she said. "When are you planning to give me back my gun?"

When Alex awoke it was dark and she was alone. How Zach had managed to get up without waking her she didn't know, but she didn't have far to look for him. He was in the kitchen at the stove. She could see steam rising from a pot or two and wondered what he was cooking.

She lifted herself on one elbow to watch him. He'd put his jeans back on but he was shirtless. For a moment she got caught up in watching the interplay of his muscles as he worked.

"Hungry?" he asked.

Either the man had the hearing of a bat or he was attuned to her in some way that she wasn't to him. "Very. What time is it?"

"Almost ten."

Alex rubbed her eyes, then shifted onto her back. She really must have been out of it to have slept so long. She stretched, feeling, for the moment, contented. Even though little was right with her world, she was here with Zach. They'd just cleared the proverbial air between them. She didn't know what the future held, but hopefully all the demons from the past were finally behind them or at least out in the open where they could be dealt with.

But for now their lives were on hold. Once Williams was captured they could figure out what came next. For the present, she'd try to relax and enjoy the time she had with the man she loved.

They ate dinner on the sofa, her tucked into one corner with the afghan still draped around her, him at the other. Alex sampled a bit of the grilled chicken, savoring its flavorfulness. "When did you learn how to cook?"

"One of the side benefits of living on your own. Either learn how to make something decent to eat or starve." He winked at her. "You spoiled me for the eating-out-every-night routine. I'm a home-cooked-meal sort of guy."

She poked him with her foot. "While you're being so industrious, why don't you see if you can get a fire started?" She pointed her foot in the direction of the stone fireplace set in the wall perpendicular to them.

"I'm a city boy. I don't know nothin' 'bout startin' no fires."

"If I'm not mistaken, those are Starter logs next to the fireplace. All you have to do is pull off the plastic thingie, put them in the fireplace, and set a match to them."

"I'll take your word for it." He got up, followed her instructions to the point of lighting the match. He found a box of long-handled ones on the mantelpiece, and in a few seconds the log started to burn.

He came back to the sofa, but rather than picking up his plate, he took her foot into his lap. "Better?"

She didn't know if he referred to the warmth of the fire spreading through the room or the gentle massage he was giving her foot, but her answer was the same, a purr of approval.

He laughed, a sound, she realized, she hadn't heard from him in a long, long time, at least not one unqualified by anything. She knew their talk before had been freeing for her. Had it been the same for him?

With mock indignation, she said, "Are you laughing at me?"

"No, baby, never. Not me." His hands moved upward to squeeze her calf in a way that made pleasure shiver through her. "I just enjoy making you happy." He took her other foot into his lap and rubbed the ball of her foot.

She didn't doubt his words, but she also knew he was probably trying to distract her as well. If Williams performed according to expectation, he should make some kind of move against her tonight. Since they'd been honest with each other about everything else, she saw no need to dissemble now. "You think Williams will strike tonight, don't you?"

His hand stilled. "You know I do. I'm hoping anyway. Then all this mess will be over."

What a succinct way to put it, but he was right. If they caught Williams tonight her life, the life of everyone involved could go back to normal. Everyone except Roberta.

She hadn't realized she'd looked away from him until he tilted her chin up.

"What's the matter, sweetheart?"

She shook her head. She didn't really want to go into it. If he was willing to distract her, she was willing to let him. "I was thinking it would be nicer closer to the fire."

The look of skepticism he sent her way told her he didn't believe her. That was all right, since he seemed willing to indulge her anyway. He stood, took the plate from her lap, and set it on the table. He scooped her up from the sofa, spinning her around in a way that made her shriek and cling to him. His mouth found hers and when his tongue plunged into her mouth she sucked on it, making him groan into her mouth.

He set her down beside the fire, unwrapped the blanket from around her, and lay down beside her. "Come here, baby," he whispered, pulling her on top him. His hands roved over her back and lower to grasp her buttocks in his palms. "Is this what you wanted?"

She tugged on one of the belt loops of his jeans. "Minus the pants, yes."

He rolled her onto her back and stood. She lay back watching him as he stripped out of the rest of his clothes, her eyes wandering down his body over a broad chest, a flat belly to his erection, full and heavy. She brought her knees up, squeezing them together, and shut her eyes, anticipating him joining her. She wanted him inside her, no fuss, no muss, no foreplay, just that ultimate connection.

And then he was beside her, pushing her legs wider to stroke the damp sensitive core between her thighs. His mouth claimed hers for one wild, brief kiss before he pulled away. "Look at me, baby," he said.

She did as he asked as best she could. Her eyes didn't want to open, much less focus. Already she was close to the edge and she wanted him inside her when she toppled. "Please," she whispered.

She bit her lip as he covered her and thrust into her. Her back arched and her legs wrapped around his waist, drawing him deeper.

He buried his face beside her throat, trailing moist kisses across her skin. He withdrew from her and thrust into her with the same exquisite slowness. Again and again, making her ache, making her writhe beneath him, seeking satisfaction.

He lifted his head and stroked the hair from her face. "Easy, baby. We'll get there."

She didn't doubt that, but she didn't know how much of this sweet torture she could stand. She was there on the brink, waiting, ready. All she needed was the slightest push from him. He gave it to her, thrusting deep and hard, and she lost it. She cried out his name and her fingertips dug into the flesh of his back. Her body trembled with the strength of her climax.

Still he was inside her, thrusting deeply until his own orgasm overtook him. He shuddered against her as he lowered himself onto his side pulling her flush with him. Leaning up on one elbow, he stroked her hair over her shoulder. "See, I told you we'd get there."

His breathing sounded as ragged as hers felt. She looked up at him, finding the smile she loved so much. She hit him on the shoulder. "Egotist."

He caught her hand and brought it to his mouth, kissing each of her fingers before he placed her hand on his chest. "Not at all. But I wouldn't be satisfied until I pleased you first."

She shut her tired eyes and smiled. "And here I'd thought considerate lovers had gone the way of the dodo bird."

"Not all of them." He stroked his hand over her breast, her waist, her hip, and back again. "Can I ask you something?"

She opened her eyes and scanned his face. That question sounded far too somber to suit her, and the unreadable expression on his face didn't help. "What is it?"

He lifted one shoulder. "This is in no way a complaint, but aside from the very first time, you've always been very free with sharing your body with me. After finding out what Sammy did to you, it surprises me."

She hadn't thought of that before, but it made sense. Most girls, after an experience like hers, went one of two routes, either shutting down sexually or becoming promiscuous. In her own way, she'd gone both: shutting down until that night with Zach and going wild afterward. Neither one had been satisfying.

"Believe it or not, that was the one thing my former husband was good for. He helped me see that I could either let the past control me or I could take control myself. It helped, too, that underneath his button-down suits Devon was a little bit of a freak himself, not the judgmental prude one would expect. That's why I could never completely condemn him. He'd helped me get back something invaluable in myself. I'll always be grateful for that."

She leaned over and pressed a single soft kiss against his chest. She didn't want to talk about Devon anymore or about anything. She wanted to enjoy being in this man's arms and nothing else. She smiled as his arms closed more tightly around her, giving her her wish.

He leaned down to whisper in her ear, "Remind me to send the guy a thank-you note in the morning."

The next time Zach woke, it was to the sound of a trilling noise he couldn't place. He had his gun in his hand in a second. He scanned the room and found nothing out of place. The noise trilled again. This time it penetrated that the sound came from a cell phone. Since he didn't have that ring tone, it must be Alex's, but the ringing stopped before he could get up to answer it.

He'd left his own phone in his pants pocket. He retrieved it now to check the time: a little after four in the morning. He had no messages from Smitty or anyone else, which probably meant the stakeout at his house was a bust. Damn. Had the police presence around his house scared Williams off or had he not planned to act at all? Either way, the question now was, what did he plan to do next? Zach hadn't a clue.

Alex's phone went off again. Whoever it was understood the word *persistent*. He knew Alex had given her cell number to many of her patients in case they needed to speak to her. On top of that she'd forwarded her private office line and home number to the phone as well. Anybody could be calling, and at this hour they probably considered getting in touch with her to be urgent.

Zach turned back to Alex and kissed her shoulder. "Sweetheart, your phone is ringing."

She opened her eyes and looked at him as if he were a Martian. "What?"

"Your phone is ringing. I thought it might be one of your patients."

The ringing stopped before she had the wherewithal to get up and answer it. But when she located it in her purse she opened the phone to look at the readout. "That's my next door neighbor's number. She's the only one I told I would be away for a couple of days."

He watched Alex as she pressed the button to call back and placed the phone next to her ear. She had her back to him, so he couldn't see her face as she spoke. "Gladys, what's wrong?" she said. "I'm sorry I didn't pick up when you called."

Alex was silent for a long moment. Then she said, "Oh my God, Gladys. Are you all right?"

Another silence, during which Zach grew more alarmed.

He'd wait until Alex finished her conversation to ask what was going on, but he wished she'd hurry up and get off the damn phone.

"Thank you for calling me. I'm sorry you had to go through that." Alex disconnected the call and tossed the phone onto the sofa. She turned to face him, a stunned expression on her face.

"Baby, what is it?"

"I have to go back. At this moment my house is burning to the ground."

Twenty-seven

Zach drove back to the Bronx with a feeling of unease tightening his belly. Why would Alex's house catch on fire with no one inside? And four in the morning besides? This had to be Williams's work. He must have seen through the ruse at Zach's house and looked for a way to draw Alex out in the open. He'd applaud the guy's ingenuity if Alex hadn't been dead set on going back. He couldn't blame her. Everything she owned was in that house.

They'd go back, but he'd already called the captain to let him know what happened. He'd also called his brother Adam to let him know to expect them some time that day. They'd need somewhere to rest a few hours before heading back. In the meantime, he didn't intend to let Alex out of his grasp, much less his sight.

The ruins of her house were still smoldering when they pulled up in front. He didn't need a fireman to tell him that everything was gone, nor that the fire had been deliberate. The air was heavy with the acrid smell of burned gasoline. He stopped the car as close to the house as he could, considering that there were still two fire trucks and a host of police vehicles, some marked, some not, in front of the house.

Alex got out of the car and so did he, quickly rounding the hood to stand beside her. She just shook her head. "I'd thought Gladys was exaggerating about the whole house burning down."

A middle-aged woman ran up to them. She had on a striped housecoat and a white scarf tied over the rollers in her hair. She threw herself into Alex's arms. "Look at your poor house. Everything's gone. I'm so sorry."

Alex patted Gladys's back. "There wasn't anything you could have done and you called me as soon as you could. I appreciate that."

Gladys took a step back. "I don't see how you can be so calm."

Zach wondered the same thing. This was a different kind of calm from her usual demeanor. This seemed, in an odd way, peaceful. He didn't know whether to be worried or not.

"I'm saving my breakdown until later," she told Gladys, "when I'm sure of how much damage has been done."

As they'd spoken both the captain and Smitty had made their way toward them. Craig extended his hand toward Zach in greeting. "Welcome back to the fray."

Zach shook his captain's hand. He didn't see any point in arguing the fact that he didn't plan to stay. Once he and Alex were ready, he planned to take Alex back to the Island. If Craig didn't agree with that Zach had plenty of vacation days stored up that he wouldn't mind using.

Craig turned to Alex and her neighbor. To Gladys, he said, "Would you excuse us?"

Gladys looked flustered but said a hasty good-bye to Alex before trotting off to her house.

To Alex, he said, "I'm sorry you had to come back to this, Dr. Waters. Please be assured we're doing everything possible to apprehend the person involved."

Craig hadn't said Williams's name, but they all knew

who he meant. Smitty grabbed Zach's elbow and nodded toward the other side of the car. Zach followed him, keeping his eyes on Alex.

"Relax, man," Smitty said. "This place is swarming with cops. No one's going to get to her."

Zach let out a pent-up breath. Maybe he did need to chill out a little, but he found that a little impossible to do at the moment. Someone had just burned down Alex's house, ostensibly to get her back to the Bronx. He wouldn't relax until they were somewhere safe.

But, he assumed, Smitty had something for him that he needed to hear. What's going on?"

"You know this was Williams, right?"

Zach nodded.

"Well, ever since we got into his place we've been checking him out. Seems he used to travel a lot painting those pictures of his. The guy kept meticulous records of where he'd been and when. A couple of those places have unresolved rape/murders for times he was there. We're looking into him for those as well."

"Damn." He glanced at Alex. She didn't need to know this, not now. "Anything else?"

"Not unless you count we don't know where he is as news. But it's definitely him. We already lifted a print off one of the gas cans."

So either he was either getting sloppy or he wanted them to know it was him. Somehow Zach thought it was the latter.

"There is one bright note," Smitty continued. "That girl came out of her coma."

"How is she?"

"All right, mostly. She doesn't remember what happened. The doctors think they can patch her up okay."

Since that was the best news he'd heard in a long time, he was glad Smitty passed it on. He chucked Smitty on the arm. "Thanks. I'm going to take Alex out of here."

"Sounds like a good idea. Keep me posted as to what you're up to."

"Will do."

Smitty walked to where Alex stood, said something to her he didn't catch, then walked away corralling the captain with him.

After they'd gone Alex turned to him. "What now?"

"We'll head to my brother's house, get something to eat, a couple of hours' rest, and get out of here. If there's anyone you need to call about the house we can do that before we go."

She nodded and got into the car. He did the same, sliding into the driver's seat and starting the ignition. He had to back out of the street, so he couldn't watch her, but when he turned at the corner he cast a look at her. She wore the same benign expression. "Not to sound repetitive, but how can you be so calm about this?"

She let out a heavy sigh. "I don't feel calm exactly. But in a way, our friendly neighborhood psycho did me a favor. I'd been living in that house, tormenting myself with the past, for six years. I knew I should sell it or at least get out of it, but I couldn't bring myself to do it. Now it's all gone, the good and the bad. If there's anything salvageable, I don't want it. I like the idea of having a fresh start."

She turned to him and smiled. A fresh start. Is that what they were having, too? Or could have once Williams was apprehended? That idea appealed to him, too.

Alex knew she liked Barbara Stone from the first moment she met her. She was the sort of warm yet stern mother Alex had enjoyed for the first thirteen years of her life. Alex had often wondered how her mother had ended up with a hard case like Sammy but had never gotten around to asking her. In a way, their relationship mirrored that of Barbara and Adam, except, though Adam might be a pain in the butt, he was no Sammy.

Barbara issued her kids out the door, then made breakfast for her and Zach, refusing Alex's offer of help. "You've been through enough without having to try to cope with my stove."

Alex could have said the same to Barbara. How she coped with such equanimity Alex had no idea. But her pancakes were delicious. When Alex asked what she put in them, Barbara whispered, "Bananas."

That was the ingredient Alex tasted but couldn't identify. She'd have to try that.

Once the plates were cleared, Zach went off with his brother into the study. When she was alone with Barbara, she volunteered, "How about you wash and I'll dry?"

"Obviously you have a compulsion to be helpful, but the dishwasher will do both for us. I'll take care of it later." Barbara sat at the table, her coffee cup cradled in both her hands. "I'm glad for the moment alone together."

Alex took a sip from her own cup waiting for Barbara to say what she wanted.

"I'm worried about my husband," she said finally.

That surprised Alex. If there was a man who exuded self-sufficiency and self-containment, it was Adam Stone. "Why?"

"I'm sure Zach told you about my condition. I have to go into the hospital for more tests next week, but it doesn't look good. If my disease follows the same progression as my mother's, there isn't much time."

"I'm sorry to hear that."

"Well, in a way it's my own fault. I haven't taken care of myself as I should. There are screening tests that I didn't keep up with. I just got so busy with the kids and work and Adam." She made a hopeless gesture.

"Why are you worried about him?"

For the first time Barbara met her gaze. "Because I know how he is. When bad things happen he doesn't wallow in self-pity, he looks around for someone to blame." She shook her head. "I know he blames me for not being as careful as I should be, but he blames himself more for not protecting me."

"That seems to be a Stone family trait."

Barbara lifted her coffee cup in salute. "Amen to that. I don't know what it is about them that makes them think they're responsible for the rest of the world. Part of it is a cop thing, I guess. You know, serve and protect. Sometimes it's enough to put your teeth on edge."

"I've noticed."

Barbara sighed, the humor leaving her. "How do I convince my husband to stop worrying about whose fault it is and enjoy the time we have left together?"

Alex placed her hand over Barbara's. "Tell him how you feel. Encourage him to share his feelings with you. There's a book I can recommend, if you like."

Barbara nodded. "You know, the worst part is knowing I'm never going to see my kids grow up. I'll never see them fall in love or get married or help them pick a career. Adam and I have had a lot of years together. I know he loves me and that there will always be a place in his heart for me. But the kids? They're so young."

"They'll remember you, Barbara. My mother died when I was thirteen and I can picture her in my mind like she was here yesterday. In fact, I was thinking before that you remind me of her."

Barbara brightened. "Somehow I think that's a great compliment."

"It is. Anyone who could put up with the man she married ought to be ready for sainthood."

Barbara stood and straightened her dress. "I'd better get a room ready for you and Zach. I know he said you two needed a few hours of sleep before you hit the road again."

"Thanks." In the meantime she pulled out her cell phone and her organizer. At the very least she needed to contact her insurance agent while she was still in the city. Heaven only knew what would happen with her house, her life when all this was over. But for the moment, she was more concerned with what Zach and his brother were talking about in the other room.

As it was too early in the morning for liquor, Zach had accepted a glass of orange juice from his brother. He didn't know why drinks were mandatory in this room, but he set his glass on the nearest coffee table and left it there.

Adam took his usual place behind the desk. "She seems to be holding up well," he said as his opening salvo.

Zach didn't know why his brother's words irritated him so much, but they did. "*She* has a name."

Adam's eyebrows lifted. "I know that. Alex seems to be holding up well."

"Yes, she does. But that doesn't mean I'm not worried about her."

Adam nodded. "You should get her out of here as soon as you can."

"I intend to."

Adam stared at him a moment. "What's with you today? I think this case is getting to you or maybe you got up on the wrong side of someone's bed."

"That's what it all boils down to for you, isn't it? Who I'm sleeping with. I don't remember you being a prude before you married Barbara, and frankly I never told you this, but I walked into the house once when you two were going at it. I could hear you down here. That's when I stopped letting myself in with my key. So what exactly is the problem you have with me? You think I was unfaithful once so I have to pay for that the rest of my life?"

For the first time in a long while Zach saw uncertainty in his brother's eyes. "Weren't you?"

"Not until I told her it was over and that I wasn't coming back. When I said 'infidelity' I meant hers."

"Then why did you let me go on thinking otherwise for so long?"

"I'd hoped you knew me better than that. In those days I had the same mistress I do now, my job, just like you, just like Jon. We have that in common, if nothing else. Besides, do you really think I wanted to talk about that?"

Adam tilted his head to one side. "No, I guess not. I got totally freaked just thinking Barbara was with another man. I don't know what I'd do if I knew it for certain."

Zach stood. "I need to see to Alex."

Adam nodded. "Go. If there's anything you need, let me know."

Alex had just settled under the covers in Adam and Barbara's guest room when Zach walked in the door. Her gaze wandered over to him. Although they'd only been apart a few minutes there seemed to be something different about him. "What have you been up to?"

Fully clothed, he lay down on the bed beside her and kicked off his shoes. "Nothing much. Just had it out with Big Brother. I told him the truth."

That didn't surprise her. "What did he say?"

"I think he was a little surprised, both that what he assumed wasn't true and that I'd never bothered to correct him. I probably should have done that years ago."

Probably, but she knew he'd been hurt by his brothers'

mistrust. It was easier for him to walk away or pretend that hurt didn't exist than to face it. At least it had been. She couldn't say that for certain anymore. The night she'd told him about her father, he'd withdrawn, but he'd come back almost right away. Still, he'd been there for her in every possible way when she needed him.

They weren't the same people they were thirteen years ago. For the first time that thought filled her with something other than dread. She didn't know what to call it, but it was something good, something to look forward to. He lay on his back and she leaned over and pressed her mouth to his.

He set her away from him, almost immediately. "Please, baby, don't start. I brought us over here to sleep, just sleep. I need my eyes sharp to keep you safe. I don't want to be falling asleep in the middle of the road."

She had meant the kiss as a simple sign of affection, but it didn't hurt her ego any to know he doubted his self-control around her. She lay back against the pillows. "All right, but you owe me one."

"I'll owe you as many as you like, just go to sleep."

"That could be dangerous," she teased.

"Don't I know it?"

She urged him to take off his clothes and join her under the covers. He did and after a while she fell asleep against his chest.

What woke her later was not the sound of the alarm Zach had set, but her cell phone. Considering the news the last time she'd picked it up, she wasn't looking forward to hearing who was on the other end. Zach didn't say anything as she rose from the bed to retrieve it from her purse, but she felt his eyes on her.

She connected the call. "Hello?"

"Hi, Dr. Waters?"

"Yes."

"My name is Winston. I work with Eric Rosetti."

"Yes?"

"Eric isn't in and I wasn't sure who to call. Your name and number were with the file."

"Yes?" She was beginning to sound like a broken record, but she wished this kid would get on with what he had to say.

"You were looking for some guy in connection with the Amazon Killer."

Alex ground her teeth together. "Yes?"

"Well, Hercules 912 just bit."

Twenty-eight

"What do you mean, he bit?" Alex asked, anticipation making her hand holding her phone tremble.

"We still had an operative pretending to be Jenna Thorne, the profile we put up for him. She was on last night and he contacted her. He wants to meet with her."

"When?"

"That's the problem. I don't know what to tell him."

Since she had no idea either, she turned to Zach, told him who was on the phone, and handed it to him.

While Zach spoke her mind raced. Why would Williams resurface on the Internet now? She doubted his compulsion for killing young girls was responsible, not when he'd picked the one girl designed to trap him. Had Roberta told him about the profile? She didn't know and Roberta was no longer with them to ask. Whatever he planned had to be some kind of setup, though what variety Alex couldn't fathom.

And what would happen now? They'd get some decoy to pretend to be this girl to meet with him? Even if that decoy were a policewoman and not one of Juvenile Justice's volunteers that would be one more life put in danger because of her. She already had Roberta's death on her conscience. She didn't think she could handle another.

Zach disconnected the call and handed her the phone. "Here we go again."

"Tell me."

"I've got to call in, but I'm sure we'll make some arrangement to meet with him. Or they will. I still plan to take you out of here."

She shook her head. "I'm not going anywhere. How can I run and hide while other people put their lives on the line for me? He burns down my house, but he could have taken down Gladys's as well. If he wants me, why don't we just let him come get me and stop him then?"

"Apparently, he doesn't want you this time, so that's a moot point."

She couldn't argue with that. Not that she really wanted to argue with him. She just wanted it to be over. She put her hands in her hair in a mockery of tearing it out. "This is so goddamn frustrating."

He grasped her wrists and pulled her down to him. "I know."

"If you want my professional opinion, it's some sort of setup. He has no more interest in this girl than he has in bicycling on the moon. For all we know, he wants to divert manpower away from watching me to make it easier for him."

"Don't you think I've thought of that? All the more reason you should be somewhere else while this goes down."

Maybe, but that didn't make it feel any less like cutting and running. "What if I stay here, under your brother Adam's protection?"

"And what will I be doing?"

"Hunting that bastard down. Your skills are wasted babysitting me. I want you to find him, and if it's possible put a few bullet holes in him for me."

"Alex, don't ask that of me. I sure as hell wouldn't

mind the bullet hole part, but don't ask me to leave you, not even on my brother's watch."

That's what he said, but she could tell that he was weakening. Then his cell phone rang. "I have to take this. Why don't you go downstairs and see if Barbara's got anything to eat?"

Yeah, anything to get her out of the room so that he could talk in peace. She slipped on her clothes and headed downstairs. They'd have to finish their conversation later.

Zach sat behind the wheel in the car next to Smitty, feeling uneasy. He'd let her talk him into joining this fool's errand, when he should be back with her now. He would have stayed, except he wanted to be there on the off chance they caught him, to be able to look into the man's face and know that Alex was out of danger. In that way, he was no different from McKay.

Zach scanned the area. There had to be a good fifteen pairs of cops hidden in plain sight around them—a couple of them "working" the all-night counter in the service station, a couple served as patrons in the Dunkin Donuts. Another couple of sets, like them, sat in darkened parked cars, waiting. Backup, in the form of several marked cars, waited back on a couple of side streets.

They'd set up an hour and a half ago, figuring they'd beat Williams to the area in case he decided to show up early. But if Williams had shown, Zach didn't see him. At least the decoy policewoman was only three stops away on the 30 bus. Whatever happened, it would be over soon and he could get back to Alex.

"Why don't you call her?" Smitty suggested.

Zach shook his head. Calling her now would only worry Alex when there was probably nothing for her to worry about. He was more concerned that he hadn't heard from Adam yet. While he and Alex had been sleeping, Adam had gone in to work. He was supposed to call when he got home, but so far nothing yet. How goddamn long did it take to drive across town? Then again, knowing Adam, if he thought Zach was overreacting he wouldn't bother to call.

He started to pull out his cell phone to dial Adam's number when Smitty elbowed him. "Here comes the bus."

It was the moment they'd all been waiting for. Zach trained his gaze on the approaching vehicle, breathing deeply, trying to control the burst of adrenaline that shot through his system. They couldn't mess this up. Not only was Alex's life in danger, but so too was that of the young officer who served as their decoy. The bus stopped at the corner of Boston Road and Connor Street to let off passengers. When it pulled away to turn on to Connor, several people got off. Most of them immediately dispersed. Only three remained: the decoy and a pair of cops posing as lovers waiting for the connecting 16 bus to show up.

But there was no sign of Williams. The decoy paced around, checking her watch as a young girl might when being kept waiting. She'd been outfitted with a microphone and a receiver. "Okay, guys," she whispered. "What do I do now?"

Before the words were fully out of her mouth a black SUV pulled into the Dunkin' Donuts end of the parking lot and drove toward her. The driver stopped beside one of the gas pumps but not close enough to actually fill his tank.

The driver's-side door opened and a man got out. He called to the decoy, "Hey, are you waiting for someone named Sam?"

Zach knew immediately that this man was not Williams. He was too tall and his build was too beefy. But he found himself running across the broad street, dodging traffic to get to the spot where the man had already been forced to the ground. One of the "lovers" was in the process of cuffing him when Zach got there.

The man was already blubbering and the strong smell of ammonia reached his nostrils. The asshole had peed on himself. Zach pushed through the others gathering around and hauled the man to his feet and pushed him back against his car. "Where's Williams?" he demanded.

"Who's Williams?"

The man seemed so genuinely terrified, Zach doubted he was trying to dissemble. "Who told you to be here?"

"Some guy I met online told me he had a girl meeting him here but he had another date. He asked me if I wanted to take his place since she didn't really know what he looked like."

Zach shoved the man away from him. If Williams wasn't here, he could think of only one other place he might be. He sought out Smitty in the crowd, nodded toward the car, and mouthed one word. "Alex."

Twenty-nine

Alex paced the floor in Barbara's living room, unable to keep still. It didn't bother her that Adam had yet to show up, though the strain of his absence showed on Barbara's face. There had been some sort of pileup on the Cross Bronx earlier that evening. A semi carrying toxic chemicals had jackknifed causing a several-car accident behind it. If Adam had gotten caught up in that, siren or no, who'd know when he'd get home?

Alex's concern was for Zach. She grew more anxious as the minutes ticked down toward the time Williams was supposed to meet them. Williams was one man against many, but if there was one man he'd tried to take down with him, it would be Zach. She knew he'd seen them together, if not the night of the copycat killing, then definitely on his own farm.

Alex glanced at the policewoman standing at the entrance to the room, the lone cop inside, while another pair guarded the front entrance in a car. She was tall with a beefy face and a hard expression. But when the shrill sound of the phone ringing invaded the silence of the room, she along with Alex and Barbara jumped.

Barbara reached for the cordless phone on the table

beside her. "Hello." Her face immediately brightened. "Where the hell are you?"

That had to be Adam. At least they knew where he was now, if nothing else.

Barbara spoke for a few more moments, then hung up. "As you must have guessed that was Adam. He was in that wreck on the highway. The damn air bag didn't deploy and he smacked his head on the steering wheel."

"How is he?"

"Fine now. But they're not letting him out of the hospital until someone can come and get him. He's got a mild concussion."

"Poor thing."

"Don't go worrying about him. If you'd seen the way my husband drives you'd wonder if he wasn't the cause of the accident. By the way, Adam contacted Jon. He's on his way over. He and Dana live five minutes away."

Alex nodded, but she wasn't really paying attention to anything past finding out if Adam was okay. She checked her watch. Nearly the appointed hour. She'd know soon one way or the other.

When the doorbell rang a couple of seconds later, Barbara rose to her feet. "That must be my brother-in-law."

The policewoman waved them back as she walked toward the door. "The car outside should have radioed if they were letting someone—"

The woman never got to finish her sentence. There was a crash and then a loud boom that Alex recognized as the report of a large-caliber gun firing. The officer slumped to the floor, a large circle of crimson spreading across her chest. She'd barely had time to get her gun out of her holster, let alone fire.

Alex had her own gun out a second later, trained on whoever might appear on the other side of the wall. She saw a wisp of blond hair before she saw anything else. It took her a moment for it to register that the woman's face that peeked around the corner at her belonged to Williams. By then she'd already squeezed off a round, just missing him, as he pulled back around the corner.

"That's not very friendly of you, Doctor," he said in a chilling high-pitched voice. "But I can kill your friend right now, and there's nothing you can do to stop me."

He was right about that. This was an old house built with cement and mortar, not drywall and plasterboard. A slug from her little .22 wouldn't make a good dent in one of the walls; much less reach him through one. And Barbara was out in the open, crouched low, but still accessible from where he stood.

"Put the gun down and come on out here, Doctor, and I'll let your friend live."

She really had no choice. She didn't intend to let him kill anyone else because of her, especially not Barbara, who as it was had so little time left to be with her family. Besides, Jon was supposed to be on his way here. If she could stall for a little while, she might have his help.

She dropped the gun to the coffee table as close to the edge nearest Barbara as possible. She ignored Barbara's quiet pleas not to go with him. If Alex saw any other way out of it, she'd have taken it. Besides, if all he had in mind was killing her, he'd have done that already.

She stepped out into the hallway. She saw all of him now and knew how he'd passed himself off as some sort of dowdy woman, as nondescript as a female as he was as a male—someone you could pass on the street and never be left with any lasting impression. "What do you want?"

Abruptly, he lunged toward her. At first she thought he intended to grab her. Instead, he touched something to her skin and electricity danced over every nerve ending in her body, sapping her of any control of her body. Her body jerked and she fell to the floor in a heavy mass, unable to move. Her head was turned toward the living room to where Barbara had risen to her feet and started to move toward her.

Alex wanted to yell at her to stay back, but her mouth didn't work. Nothing worked. She couldn't even react when a second deafening boom split the air and Barbara crumpled to the floor beside her.

Thirty

Zach dialed Adam's number again, hoping this time the phone would be answered before the machine picked it up. This time someone did on the fourth ring. "Hello?"

"Jon? What are you doing there?"

"Adam called me. He was in that mess on the Cross Bronx. What the hell is going on here? I just put Barbara in an ambulance. There's a dead cop in the hallway and two more outside."

"Where's Alex?"

"I don't know. She was gone when I got here. There was a car pulling away when I stopped. Out of habit I memorized the plates and called them in already."

Which might help track them down if they were still on the road. Where the hell would he have taken her? Every former haunt of his was currently either closed off to him or under police surveillance. He was so frightened for her that he could barely think. He disconnected the call, unheedful of whatever his brother was saying on the other end of the line. "Where the hell would he take her?" he said aloud to Smitty.

He got no response and didn't really expect one. When they got back to the car, Smitty had insisted on taking over the chore of driving. Zach knew where Smitty was heading, back to Adam's house to see if any of the neighbors had seen in which direction they'd driven. It was better than nothing, but it sure as hell wasn't much.

John McKay couldn't say why he'd started haunting the houses along the New England Thruway on nights he couldn't sleep. Maybe he expected to find the killer out there, or worse yet, one of his victims. Then again, he seemed to have moved on to tormenting Dr. Alex Waters instead. There was a time when McKay would have applauded the man's motives if not his actions, but no more. The investigation had vindicated her in every possible way and left him feeling lower than dirt. Maybe all he wanted was a chance to vindicate himself. But there was no chance of that, since he'd botched things so badly he'd been taken off the case.

He drove silently through the night. He knew about the sting they had planned for just a few blocks from here. If anyone asked him, Williams was too smart for that. But since no one asked he had no one to tell that to but himself. A light flickered from one of the empty buildings. Nothing bright, maybe some candles or a flashlight. Considering no one should be in here at all, he drew the car to a stop and picked up his cell phone.

He knew Zach Stone's number by heart and dialed it. He answered almost immediately. "Stone."

In a hushed voice he asked, "How'd the operation go over at the Dunkin' Donuts?"

"Who is this?"

"McKay. How'd it go?"

"South. He's got Alex. Why?"

"I'm over here on Baychester and Proust. I noticed a light in one of the vacant buildings. It could be him."

He didn't hear what Stone said on the other end of the line. His ears were trained to listen to any sound coming from the building. He heard a soft thud, like a body dropping a distance away. He knew Zach would be here, probably with reinforcements, but he couldn't wait. He eased his gun out of its holster and got out of his car.

Thirty-one

Alex lay on the unfinished floor of some half-done house curled into a fetal position. Sensation was coming back to her body in the form of a thousand tiny, excruciating pinpricks. She wanted to scream, but her mouth wouldn't work properly yet.

She heard the sound of something metallic scraping together, and then a table leg came into view. From above she heard his voice. "I really should have had this ready for you, but there were some kids hanging around before. I didn't want to draw attention to myself by frightening them off."

She heard other sounds, none of which made sense to her. But some of the strength seemed to be coming back to her limbs. She flexed one arm to test it.

"Lie there quietly, or I'll stun you again and this time I won't be so gentle."

She did as she was told, only because she knew she didn't have the strength to fight him. She might later, so she tried to conserve what strength she had for now.

He moved into her field of vision. He took off the blond wig and wiped his hand across his face, smearing what makeup he wore into a grotesque mask. "Ready for some fun?"

Again, the urge to scream claimed her, and this time sound made it past her throat into the still dark night.

"There's no one to hear you, darlin', or if they do, they'll just think it's some of those kids fooling around where they shouldn't be." He reached down and scooped her up, depositing her hard on the table.

She winced and her eyes squeezed shut as pain shot through her, mostly from her head hitting the table first. The throbbing had already started. She didn't need this now. She needed all her wits about her if she was going to survive this. For all she knew Zach had no idea where she was; no one did. She was on her own. And her only chance was to talk her way out of it since fighting was out of the question.

"Why do you want to do this to me, Ginnie?" She chose to use his feminine name since that's how he presented himself. "I tried to help Walter. I would have helped you if I'd known you needed it."

"You tried to help Walter?" he said in a scoffing voice. "You turned him against me. He was always there for me. Always. Until you got to him." He grabbed one of her wrists in a painful grip and brought it back over her head to fasten it to the table with a leather strap.

Good God, he really did intend to kill her just like the others, to rape her and mutilate her and leave her dead somewhere. She felt sick with both that knowledge and the impending migraine. She would have retched if a sound outside the room hadn't captivated her attention.

Immediately Williams crouched behind the table by her head. He had the .45 in his hand near her face. "Walter?" he asked.

"Walter's dead, you sick son of a bitch. Put down the weapon and kick it over to me."

That was McKay's voice. She couldn't see him, but she'd never been happier to know he was near her.

"Are you okay, Alex?"

That was the first time he'd used her given name. "For the moment."

Williams pressed the gun to her temple. "Stay away or she's dead."

"You won't shoot her," McKay said. "That isn't in the script, is it? If you want to do her like you like, you have to get rid of me first."

Perhaps crazed by being so close and being thwarted, Williams lunged toward McKay, his arm held high over his head. Alex saw this as her one opportunity to act. She swung her left leg in a crosswise arc, catching Williams in the belly. She heard the whoosh of his breath leaving his body and something metallic clatter to the floor. A single gunshot fired coming from McKay's direction. The acrid smell and the smoke of it invaded her eyes and nostrils.

Williams went down and McKay was on him. She couldn't see anything after that, but she heard one of the men grunt in pain. She hoped it wasn't McKay, but knew she'd hoped in vain when Williams came to loom over her. He cast her a look that was part defeat and part melancholy. For an instant she could only stare at him, bracing herself for what happened next. While the men had been fighting, she'd managed to almost free her hand. Another couple of seconds and she would have accomplished it. Then she would have been ready for him.

But the sound of sirens reached her. He must have heard them, too, because he froze. "Some other time, then, Doctor," he said before racing from the room.

That surprised her since he hadn't shown any particular fear of the police before. Maybe he didn't fear them now, but knew they would thwart him from carrying out his task—doing her like he liked as McKay had put it.

But there could be no other time. Tonight had to end it. She didn't think she could bear another round of Williams's type of madness. She freed her hand and slid

to the floor. McKay was already making an effort to
stand. She helped him to his feet, her hands noticing
something sticky and wet clinging to his clothing. "What
happened?"

"The son of a bitch stabbed me."

"We need to stop the bleeding."

"Once we get outside. I'm not dying in this hellhole."

She wouldn't argue with any man who sounded so
determined. Together they made it down the stairs and
out of the building. Out on the street there was no sign
of Williams. That didn't mean much since there were no
streetlights here, no moon, and any illumination came
from cars passing on the service road or the highway
beyond. The car in which he'd transported her was still
there, though, which meant he'd probably taken off on
foot.

She didn't have much time to ponder that. She had
McKay to deal with. She couldn't allow him to bleed to
death, but she had nothing with which to stanch the flow.
She wore a hooded jacked that zippered up the front
with a T-shirt beneath. The T-shirt was a better bet, since
it was softer and had no zipper to complicate things.

She looked down at McKay, who appeared pale and
listless. "If you tell anybody I did this, I will kill you
myself." She tugged off the hoodie, pulled her T-shirt
over her head, and replaced the hoodie.

A wan smile crossed McKay's face. "Stone is a lucky
man."

"Shut up," she told him. Neither humor nor a great
deal of talking was required now. She folded her shirt,
lifted his, and pressed the fabric to the knife wound in
his lower right belly. She knew they were coming. The
sirens that had once been faint were now almost deafening. But even before they arrived, she felt a pair of strong
hands at her shoulders. Smitty moved into her line of
view, taking over her ministrations with McKay.

Her mind filled with one thought. *Zach*. She turned and threw herself into his arms. He hugged her to him, his embrace lifting her from the ground. Alex couldn't help smiling. This big, strong man was trembling in her arms.

Thirty-two

Zach held her a long moment, trying to school his emotions into something manageable. He'd nearly lost her tonight. He didn't know what he'd do if that happened, and he didn't want to contemplate it too much, either. But she was still whole and still here, which meant they still had a chance to be together. He needed to focus on that, rather than the images of Alex dead, or worse, that had haunted him on the way here.

But first he needed to make sure she was really okay. He set her on the ground and cradled her face in his palms. "Baby, are you all right?"

"I'm fine, believe it or not, thanks to McKay. He saved my life."

So McKay was good for something after all. Zach looked at the man lying on the ground, whom Smitty still tended to. "And you have quite possibly saved his."

"I hope so. Williams has claimed enough lives. "Did you find Barbara?"

"Jon went to the hospital to be with her." He hadn't heard from Jon since. He didn't know if that was a good thing or a bad one, so he didn't elaborate. "Where's Williams?"

"I don't know. I think he took off on foot. It couldn't

have been more than five minutes ago. He's got to be hurting. McKay shot him once. I'm not sure if he's still armed."

Alex relayed the information as if it didn't make sense to her. It didn't make sense to him either. Why not get back in the car and get the hell out of Dodge before anyone had a chance to show up?

He took out his flashlight and scanned the ground. If Williams had been hit, he wasn't leaving any blood trail Zach could detect. Which meant Williams could be here anywhere or he could be long gone. Zach didn't know which, but he knew he needed to get Alex out of there, especially away from being out in the open. Then again, if Williams was somewhere with a good vantage point, he'd probably have tried to pick them off already. That is, if Williams was still armed with anything powerful enough to reach them from where he was, like the weapon he'd used on the policewoman. That had to be at least a .44. The fact that he hadn't fired on them lent credence to Alex's theory that he was unarmed.

As he turned, Zach's gaze snagged on the bridge that went over the highway into Co-op City. What seemed like a lifetime ago, they'd wondered from what vantage point Thorpe had been scouting for victims. That bridge had been one possibility.

He could imagine Williams watching from there now, watching the police scurry around vainly. That would appeal to his sense of holding power over them. He believed himself smarter than the cops and would probably enjoy watching from on high—godlike—while they scurried around looking for him. Even on a clear night, the domed fencing covering the bridge more deflected the moonlight than illuminated anything. On a night like tonight it would be next to impossible to spot a man up there unless you were really looking. But now Zach was.

"Son of a bitch," he said, detecting some sort of

movement among the fencing on the near side of the bridge. With a little effort he made out the frame of Williiams crouching. Even though the area was suddenly alive with cars and sirens, Zach didn't hesitate. He couldn't risk that Williams would get spooked by all the activity or decide it wasn't worth his time and run.

To Alex, he said, "Stay with Smitty."

Smitty, who'd just been relieved by an EMT, asked, "Where are you going?"

Zach nodded toward the bridge. "He's up there. See if you can get someone on the other side." That way they could fence Williams in. He wouldn't be going anywhere.

Zach moved off, hoping that the arriving cars proved enough of a distraction for Williams not to notice him approaching. It didn't hurt either that Zach was dressed all in black. Between the camouglaging effect of his clothing and the fact that the steps leading to the bridge ran perpendicular to it, he hoped to be almost on top of Williams by the time the other man noticed his presence.

Crouched low, Zach moved between two of the cars parked at the curb and made his way to the opposite side of the street. Hugging the fence that cordoned off the highway, he traveled quickly and silently. Even at this hour, traffic was pretty heavy, certainly dense enough to cover any sound he made, but he wasn't taking any chances.

The stairs were composed of several thick slabs of concrete that made for an awkward ascent, even if it were not a covert one. Zach had his weapon trained on Williams as soon as he got a clear view. He was almost on him—a step from the top—when Williams started and his head turned in Zach's direction. The bastard really hadn't seen him coming. Williams glanced over his shoulder, as if to check for someone behind him or to gauge his chances of escape.

"Don't even think about it," Zach said in a deadly

voice. "Lie on the ground and put your hands on top of your head."

Even in the dim light, Zach saw the feral smile that stretched across Williams's face. He had no intention of giving up. Too bad. Zach had no intention of letting him go. This needed to be over now, tonight, if for no one else's sake but Alex's.

Zach repeated his instruction, or started to. Without warning Williams drew back his arm and flung something at him. Zach ducked to the side, just as a knife whizzed past his head.

Williams used the opportunity to take off in the opposite direction. It wasn't much of a bridge, maybe fifty feet. Williams had made it halfway to the other side by the time Zach followed. But Williams skidded to a stop. Zach immediately saw why. Smitty and some uniforms were making their way up the stairs on the other side.

"Give it up, Williams," Zach said. You're not going anywhere." Zach's gun was trained on him and it occurred to him that he should just shoot him and get it over with. Put a few bullet holes in him as Alex urged, only half joking. There would be no trial, no chance of parole, no fear that he might get out one day and come after her again. It also occurred to him that he'd be exercising his own brand of justice, just as Williams had.

But Williams wasn't going to go down that easy. He was near enough to the other side, the part unprotected by the dome, to grasp the lamppost that stood next to the stairs and hoist himself on top of the fence.

Zach knew what he intended to do. It was a bit of a drop down to the northbound side of the New England Thruway, but there was also a fence he could grab on to to break his fall. He hoped to gain a few seconds' advantage, since no one in their right mind would follow his route. Williams himself teetered trying to get enough balance to jump.

Before Zach could say a word, a semi rumbled underneath the bridge blasting its horn. Williams lost his balance and fell backward.

Zach rushed forward, hoping to grab maybe a piece of the man if he could. But he was too late. Rather than landing on the shoulder of the road, Williams tumbled into traffic, landing on the hood of one car, rolled off, and was struck by the SUV behind it with such force that he flew in the air to land twenty feet away.

Zach pushed past Smitty and the others who had just gained the bridge, and hurried down the stairs. He scaled the chest-high fence and dropped down on the other side. Williams still lay facedown and motionless in the middle lane of the highway and traffic had come to a dead halt.

Zach checked for a pulse at Williams's throat. Finding none, he turned the man over. Williams's eyes were open and unfocused, his mouth slack and bloody. He was dead. He couldn't touch Alex anymore. That's all that mattered. For a moment, Zach closed his eyes and focused on drawing much-needed air into his lungs.

Then an equally winded Smitty came up beside him. He clasped Zach on the shoulder. "What lesson have we learned here today, boys and girls? Those who live by the car die by the car."

Laughter rumbled up in Zach's chest. "I thought you were supposed to be watching Alex."

"Actually, you told her to stay by me. I convinced her that wasn't such a good idea. She's with Craig."

Zach glanced across the highway to where Alex was.

Smitty nudged him again. "Go to her. The rest of us can handle the cleanup."

Zach didn't argue. He needed to be with her, to hold her and tell her it was all over. Then that fresh start they talked about could begin.

Thirty-three

It wasn't until a couple of hours later that Zach and Alex ended up at South Shore Hospital in Westchester where Barbara had been taken. Jon and Dana were the only ones in the waiting room on the floor. Jon sat with his legs stretched out in front of him, Dana had her head on Jon's shoulder and they were holding hands. Both of them looked asleep or on the verge of it.

Jon was the first to notice their approach. He sat up and pulled his legs under him. He turned to Dana and whispered something that made her rouse. By the time Zach and Alex reached them, Jon was on his feet. "What are you two doing here?" Jon asked. "I thought you'd be home sleeping it off by now."

"You heard what happened?" Zach asked.

"There were a couple of officers in here before. I asked them to let me know what they heard on the radio."

Dana stood and wrapped her arm around Jon's waist. "You must be glad it's over," she said to Alex.

"Very."

He had his arm around Alex's waist. He hugged her tighter to him, hearing a variety of emotions in that one softly spoken word. "How's Barbara?"

"She made it through the surgery fine. How that will affect her long-term prognosis no one knows yet." Dana, like Joanna, was a registered nurse.

"Can we see her?" That came from Alex. Dana told them what room to go to and gave them directions. As they walked, Alex added, "Did you see the size of the rock on Dana's finger?"

He had, and it hadn't been there the last time all of them were together. Jon must have finally decided to bite the bullet and not wait any longer despite whatever turmoil there might be in the family. The thought of it brought a smile to Zach's lips. "My baby brother must really be in love. I'm not trying to say Jon is cheap or anything, but he used to live in the South Bronx just to save on rent."

That wasn't exactly the truth of it, but he appreciated the benefit his white lie brought him—the sound of Alex's laughter.

When they reached the room, Alex took a peek through the glass panel in the door and took a step back. "Maybe we should wait until tomorrow to see her."

Wondering what caused her to say that, he took a look through the glass himself. Adam was sitting in a chair beside the bed holding Barbara's hand. Barbara was turned toward him. The body language of the moment spoke of an intimacy he didn't want to disturb either.

He glanced at Alex, who smiled back at him in a way he didn't understand. "What?"

"Barbara told me earlier that she wished Adam would stop worrying about who to blame and just appreciate the time they had left together. I think she got her wish."

Zach thought so, too. And something odd stirred in his chest, something he hadn't felt in a long time: hope. He looked down at Alex. "Let's go home."

* * *

Later, after a shower that was mostly rinsing the grime of the day from their bodies, they lay in bed together. After all that had happened, Zach figured he should be contented just having her there in his arms, whole, freshly clean, and relatively unscathed by Williams's actions, but he wasn't. Maybe it was seeing Adam with Barbara tonight that fueled in him the desire not to put anything off. But there was something he needed to know from her. He doubted, despite his exhaustion, if he'd get to sleep without it.

He rubbed one hand up and down her arm. "How are you holding up?" he asked.

She sighed and burrowed closer to him. "I was almost asleep, thank you very much." He chuckled at her disgruntlement and she smacked him on the arm. "Please don't tell me you want to rehash all this now."

No, he didn't want to rehash anything; he just needed an answer. "What if I wanted to tell you I love you?"

"I would have to tell you I knew that already and humbly request that you go to sleep before I do something terrible to you."

"You wouldn't have something you wanted to say to me?"

She leaned up using an elbow braced on his chest for leverage. "What do you think I'm doing here, Zach?" she said in a quiet voice. "Notwithstanding the fact that I have no home to go to, I'm not without resources. I wouldn't be here if I didn't want to be."

That's not what he was talking about, and she knew it. "For how long?"

"Damn it, Zach. What did you think I meant when I was talking about starting over? I meant *us*."

He knew that, but she still hadn't answered the question nagging at him. "Do you love me, Alex?"

"I've been *in love* with you since I was fifteen years old. And if you want to know how I know you love me, I could give you my standard shrink's answer that I'm trained to know such things. The truth is, you've shown me in every way but with words. I trusted you meant them, even if you didn't say them."

That was the crux of his problem right there. It had been a long time since he'd trusted in anything, and in an odd way, least of all himself. He thought back to what she'd said to him a long time ago about an optimist being nothing but a pessimist who thought he'd found *the way*. Had he found his?

All he had to do was look at her face to know the answer. If he hadn't made so damn many mistakes in his life—with her, with Sherry, with his family—there wouldn't be a question in his mind. But the truth of it was, no force existed in heaven or on earth that he would let stand between them again.

He cupped her face in his palms. "Come here, baby," he urged, wanting to draw her down for a kiss.

She resisted. "About this baby business. I never gave my official okay on that."

There was laughter in her eyes and a teasing smile on her lips.

He liked seeing her like that, carefree and playful. He wanted to see more of it, a lifetime's worth. He winked at her. "Give yourself a little more time to think about it. In the meantime . . ." He trailed off as he leaned up and took her mouth. She melted against him, as he hoped she would. In a short while, neither of them was thinking much of anything at all.

About the Author

Native New Yorker Deirdre Savoy spent her summers on the shores of Martha's Vineyard, soaking up the sun and scribbling in her many notebooks. It was there that she first started writing romance as a teenager. The island proved to be the perfect setting for her first novel, SPELLBOUND, published by BET/Arabesque books in 1999. SPELLBOUND received rave reviews and earned her the distinction of being *Romance in Color's* first Rising Star author and Best New Author of 1999. Deidre also won the first annual Emma award for Favorite New Author, presented at the 2001 Romance Slam Jam in Orlando, Florida.

Since then, Deidre has published 11 books and two novellas, all of which have garnered critical acclaim and honors. Deirdre has been featured in a variety of publications, including *Black Issues Book Review, Romantic Times, Affaire de Coeur,* and *Blackboard Bestsellers List.* Many of her titles have been issued in hardcover by Black Expressions.

Deidre is the president of Authors Supporting Authors Positively (ASAP) and the founder of the Writer's Co-op writer's group. She lectures on such topics as Getting Your Writing Career Started, Taking Your Writing to the Next Level, and other subjects related to the craft of writing. She is listed in the *American and International Authors* and *Writer's Who's Who,* as well as the *Dictionary* of *International Biography.*

Deirdre lives in Bronx, New York with her husband of ten-plus years and their two children. In her spare time she enjoys reading, dancing, calligraphy and "wicked" crossword puzzles.

Dear Readers,

When I started writing *Body of Lies*, I didn't intend to include any information on children being abducted by predators from the Internet. It was an element that grew out of the story, my own concern as a parent of teenage children, and a special I saw on TV about the subject. What shocked me was the number of predators that seemed to ooze out in response to the possibility of exploiting children.

As a parent, I monitor as best I can what sites my children visit and who they maintain contact with on the Web. I also make sure my children know that meeting anyone in real life that they've met on the internet is a dangerous prospect, one they might not survive intact. I also try to let them know they are valued so that they don't go seeking validation elsewhere. Most of all, I pray.

For the parents out there, I hope I've given you a little bit of insight as to how these predators operate or at least a reminder to be vigilant.

I'd love to hear from you. Please contact me at aboutdeesbooks@aol.com or write to me at:

P.O. Box 233
Baychester Station
Bronx, NY 10469

Also please join my list for readers: http://groups.yahoo.com/group/ladiesinred. This is the place for discussion of my books, giveaways and much more. Hope to see you there.

Wishing you all the best,

Deirdre Savoy